DESCENDANTS OF THE ALPHA

THE ALPHA KING'S BREEDER
BOOK SEVEN

BELLA MOONDRAGON

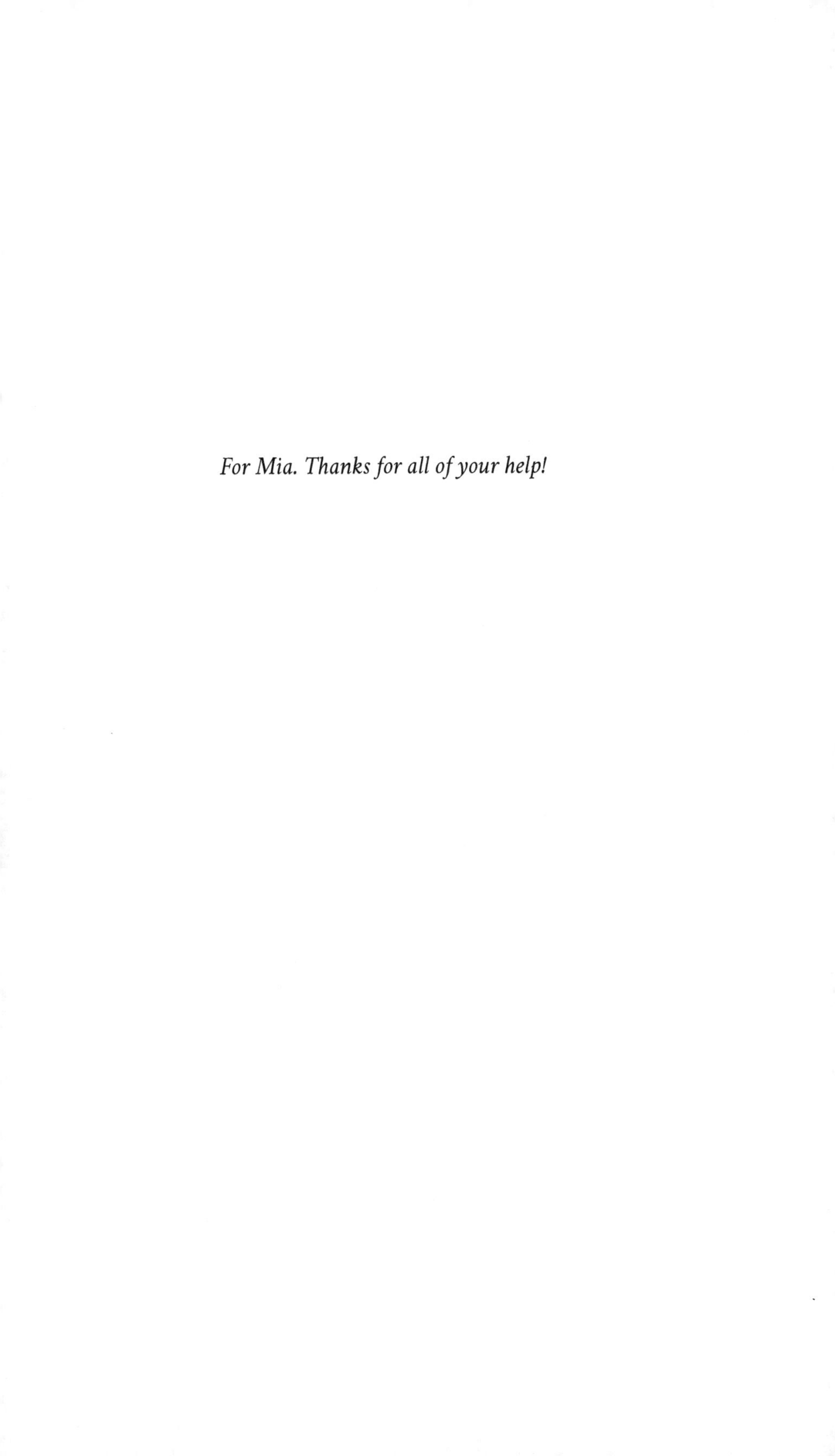

For Mia. Thanks for all of your help!

CONTENTS

HE'S ALIVE

Isla

"ELLA," I whisper. I'm in shock. My entire body hums with adrenaline as I try to step deeper into what remains of my living room. Everything is ash and embers. The ceiling is gone, revealing the glare of the midmorning sun.

And there she is, kneeling in the center of the room, covered in her mate's blood.

Maddox lurches forward, but I grab him around the waist and haul him back. "Wait!"

Ella pants, her chest heaving with each ragged breath she takes. In the distance, I hear sirens. Smoke funnels toward the sky. It's only a matter of minutes until people start descending on our property, and they can't see *this*.

"Ella," I repeat, louder this time. "Take off the mask, honey."

She whimpers as she raises her bloody hands, her sea-green eyes full of tears. She's wearing a dress that may have been white at some point. It's thin, and hanging off her body, which is covered in bruises and deep scratches. I'm not sure where she's hurt. I'm not sure what blood is hers and what blood is Ryatt's.

"Honey," I whisper, taking a few steps toward her. The mask she's wearing… I can't explain the way it seems to suck the air from the room around us. It's pulsating with power I can't begin to describe. I just know she needs to take it off. I don't know how I know, but something in the power emanating off it isn't right. My own power recoils away from it, as if it wants to curl into itself and hide.

"Isla, we need to do something," Maddox growls somewhere behind me as the sirens get closer.

"Take it off," I tell her. "Take it off and let us help you."

Her fingers brush over the crimson stones before she pulls it off with what looks like great effort. Her mouth parts as she inhales sharply, and then her eyes roll back in her head, and she slumps forward over Ryatt's chest.

"Goddess above," I hiss as I race to her, falling on my knees and pulling her into my arms.

Maddox kneels near Ryatt's head, his fingers on his pulse. He meets my eyes as I gather our unconscious daughter in my arms and slowly shakes his head.

I look down at my daughter's mate. How did this happen?

"My tears," I say to Maddox. "I have vials in the bathroom upstairs."

"He's dead, Isla."

I can't accept that. I don't know this man. I can't be a judge of his character or whether he lives or dies. He taunted Isaac for weeks before the war last summer. He was our enemy, at least we thought he was. Maybe he still is. But he's Ella's mate. There's so much we don't know. And her scream… Goddess, that scream told me everything I needed to know about the two of them.

She loves him, and if she wakes up to find that he's dead, it'll be a pain worse than whatever happened to her to put her in this state.

"*Get them*," I beg, fresh tears welling along my lower lashes. I'll need as many tears as I can get. "Please, hurry!"

Maddox rises without a word and pulls his phone from his pocket before rushing out of the living room. His footsteps thunder up the stairs to my left.

"It's all right," I whisper into Ella's hair, rocking her side to side like an infant. "You're all right now."

She's totally unconscious. Her body is a dead weight in my arms, her blood soaked hair sticking to my chest and arms. I look down at her body–at the red welts forming on her arms and legs. Burns, I realize. I choke down a sob, clutching her tight and thanking the Goddess she's not awake to feel the pain of these injuries.

Ryatt makes a breathy sound–a gasp, then goes silent again.

"Maddox!" I shout, leaning forward and reaching for Ryatt. "HUR-RY!" There's a sliver of life left in him. A single beat of his heart. That's enough. I can bring him back. I know I can. "MADDOX!"

I lower Ella to the ground beside Ryatt and crawl to his side, taking his battered face between my hands. "Come on," I plead, shaking him gently. *Don't you dare die.* Do not leave her like this!"

I shake him again, hard, ignoring the blood seeping through the gaping holes in the dark leather vest that covers his chest. "Ryatt, wake up. Open your eyes–"

Silver eyes open to slits, locking on mine. He jerks, teeth bared, but doesn't have the strength to do much else. Pain shines behind his eyes as he blinks once, then twice, as if trying to clear his vision. "You're safe," I tell him quietly. "She's safe–"

"Ella–"

"She's okay," I whisper, tears blurring my vision as I lean over him. A single tear rolls down my cheek and along my jaw before falling onto his lower lip.

Telling him Ella is all right might have been a mistake. He closes his eyes again, breathing rapidly while blood dribbles from the corners of his mouth. His mate is safe, and now he feels like he can succumb to death in peace. "Ryatt–Ryatt!"

"Isla!" Maddox lunches himself off the stairs and tosses me a vial of tears, the most precious medicine we have. I wrench the lid off with my teeth and pry open Ryatt's mouth, dumping the entire vial onto his tongue. He jerks, but I hold him down, covering his mouth and nose with my hand. I turn desperate eyes to Maddox, who has Ella's head in his lap while he begs for her to drink, to wake up, to open her eyes.

The sirens have abruptly stopped, but another noise rips through the air.

"Did you call a boat?" I ask, releasing my grip on Ryatt, who has fallen back in a state of unconsciousness and riding a fine line between life and death.

"I called Poppy," Maddox says breathlessly. He picks Ella up, cradling her limp body in his arms. "We're going to the castle directly. This was a *gas leak*." He tilts his head toward the remains of our living room.

A gas leak. Sure. Not our magical daughter and her mate falling through our ceiling out of thin air.

"Okay," I whisper over the roar of a boat engine ripping into the private cove that touches the edge of our backyard. It's too shallow for one of the big boats that take us over the sea, so it must be a skiff of some kind, or Goddess forbid, jet skis. "Maddox?"

"I'll come back for him," he says, meeting my eyes. Grim determination makes his green eyes shine in the smoke still curling toward the opening in the roof.

I don't want to leave Ryatt, so I don't. I know Ella will be okay. I feel it in my very soul that she will live. When it comes to her, I'm more worried about what she'll be like when she wakes up. They went through something awful–awful enough that she ripped the sky in two to bring her mate, a man considered an enemy to our people, back home to me.

She brought him here so I can heal him.

But he's still bleeding badly despite my tears. His pulse is weak, and his chest trembles with each unsteady breath he takes. Warriors hurry in, calling out my name, but my focus is locked on Ryatt.

Maddox's voice telling me to let Ryatt go breaks me out of what feels like a trance.

"Do not die," I demand before rising to my feet.

"They sedated him," Poppy says as we hurry down a long, open air hallway with archways that look out over the endless beach. Hot afternoon sunlight beats down on Maatua, but inside the castle, the air feels cold and suffocating. "He's going into surgery as we speak."

Poppy pants as she tries to catch back up to me.

"Isla, wait." She grabs my arm and pulls me to a stop.

"I need to check on Ella."

"She's still asleep. I swear. I have two healers tending to her. Her wounds–the burns–" Poppy's face pales as she shakes her head. "I need you to tell me what happened to them."

"I don't know what happened," I say sharply, massaging my jaw. I've been darting between the state-of-the-art infirmary where healers have been trying desperately to save Ryatt's life and the bedroom Ella is in. The entire castle is crawling with warriors and healers.

My tears healed some of Ella's wounds.

My tears did nothing for Ryatt. He's in worse shape than when he first arrived.

What I really want to do is bring them both to the falls, but Ryatt might not survive the trip at this point. We've run out of time.

"It's like he wants to die," I growl, closing my eyes and lowering into a crouch. My muscles ache from sprinting all over this Goddess damned castle for hours. My hands are raw from repeated washing. My eyes are puffy, but dry, having cried so many tears my power simply snapped and withered away.

Poppy licks her lips and kneels, her hands squeezing my shoulders in a way that makes me hum with relief. "Ella is going to be okay. Your tears healed her body. But... that wound on her thigh is... resisting all efforts. It'll need to be stitched."

"That's fine." In reality, the fact that I couldn't heal my own daughter is weighing heavily on me.

"Isaac and Maddy are on the way," she says, forcing a smile. "That's good, right?"

"I feel awful for calling them," I admit. "Maddy's in no state to travel."

"We're more than ready to deliver twins here, Isla. I think we have every healer in Maatua at the castle right now, actually."

"I think we need to get Ella and Ryatt off Maatua."

"Why?"

"Ryatt–" I suck in a breath and stand. Poppy follows, her eyes glimmering with concern as I rub my temples. "Ryatt is very powerful. That's all we really know about him."

"You're worried about his powers?"

"We don't know what we're dealing with when it comes to him, Poppy. He's weak now, but when he heals... if he's not who I think he is–"

"Who do you think he is?"

"Someone who loves my daughter."

Poppy holds my gaze, understanding blooming over her lovely features. "What can he do, exactly?"

"We have no idea." We know Ella can cause an insane amount of structural damage, if what's left of my house is any indicator of her powers.

"Well," she claps her hands, rubbing them together. "I just had the east wing of the castle renovated, so I'm in agreement that we need to move them both elsewhere... for our safety, of course."

"Of course," I repeat, but both of us know this has everything to do with the fact this matter needs to be kept secret for as long as possible. We may be in peace times now, but if the Alphas under the rule of Isaac, and even Antony, catch wind of this, rumors will spread. The people of our kingdoms need to stay under the impression they're safe.

Even if I'm not sure they are.

We won't know anything until Ella and Ryatt can explain what happened.

"On the matter of the mask," Poppy says as we start walking again. We turn a sharp corner, coming face to face with a narrow set of stairs leading down into the depths of the castle. "It's in a vault deep underground. A vault only I have a key to."

"Good, it needs to stay that way."

"Are we in danger, Isla?"

I halt on the second to the last step. "I don't know."

She nods, pursing her lips in thought. "The Teal Isles, then. The royal house there has been empty for some time. There's plenty of room for your entire family to stay, to spread out. It does have an infirmary, but I've been assured that once Ryatt is out of surgery he'll be all right, at least physically."

"Have a boat ready, please."

"I will." She reaches out and grabs my wrist. "They're going to be fine. Ella is going to be okay." Tears finally start to spring to life again. She notices, giving me a smile as she reaches up to dab one off my cheek. "I'm so happy your girl is home again, even if the situation is less than ideal."

"She's awake!"

We look to our right where a healer just ran into view, her cheeks pink with exertion.

"Princess Ella is awake and–"

A frustrated screech echoes through the corridor, followed by the clattering sound of something hitting the floor.

"Go," Poppy urges, giving me a little shove.

I don't need it. My feet barely touch the floor as I race after the healer, Poppy's beautiful seaside home passing by in a blur.

I push through the door into the large, airy bedroom. It's all white and pale blues–a calming place with large windows overlooking the turquoise water.

Ella stands in the center of the room, panting, her eyes wide and round as she whips around to face me. Three healers cower against the wall as her eyes blaze with silver white fire.

My beautiful, powerful daughter.

"Come here," I whisper, opening my arms to her. "Ella, it's all right–"

The force of her running into my arms is nearly enough to knock me off my feet, but I dig deep for the strength I need to carry whatever is weighing her down.

"Tell me everything," I whisper into her hair.

2

OUR ENEMY

Isla

IT'S A BEAUTIFUL, clear night. Waves brush against the rocky shore of the private island in the Teal Isles, a small group of islands roughly forty miles south of Maatua. The moon is full and bright, casting a long silver beam across the practically still ocean.

On a night like this, Maddox and I normally would have shifted and gone for a nice long run through the tropical forest surrounding Maatua.

But now I'm standing by a window in a snug, wood paneled bedroom in the massive vacation home of the Alpha and Luna of Maatua wondering how we got to this point.

I turn my head to look at the bed in the center of the room where Ryatt is lying on his side, his eyes pinched shut as he sleeps.

He died at least twice today, three times if we count the moment his heart stopped during the surgery to mend and close a dozen stab wounds to his chest and abdomen. My tears were the only thing keeping him alive, even when his body repeatedly tried to give up.

He's stable now, at least. His entire chest is a tangle of thick bandages. The burns on his arms and legs have healed nicely, and I believe my tears are to thank for that.

But his powers aren't compatible with mine. I truly believe they fought against my healing powers in some way.

I heave a sigh and look back out the window. I couldn't get Ella to talk today. She just kept asking me about Ryatt over, and over, and over again. I still have no idea what happened to them. I don't know how she got here, or what spurred them to make this incredible journey to save Ryatt's life.

I look at him again. He's so young, not much older than Isaac. A king, I believe. I'm not sure how it works in Eastonia.

No one here does, so no one knows what to expect when the truth inevitably comes out.

I watch the moon begin to dip below the horizon as violet, velvety morning sunlight starts to bleed across the sky.

What a day we've had. We arrived in the Teal Isles six hours ago. We'll remain here as long as we have to.

"Isla, what are you doing here?"

I turn to Maddox's voice. His eyes are narrowed on Ryatt. "Checking on him," I tell him sternly, not liking his tone.

Maddox takes up the entire doorway, but I can still see the outlines of several warriors standing in wait in the hallway just beyond the room. This entire mansion is full of warriors, both in their human and wolf forms. In fact, I had to wade through at least a dozen of them to get to Ryatt's room earlier. "What's in your hand?"

Maddox holds up a metal box, his expression unreadable. "Silver manacles."

"Absolutely not," I growl, glancing at Ryatt before swiftly crossing the room to my mate. "You're not putting those on him."

"We don't know what he can do," he says in a low whisper as he steps aside, allowing me to exit the room.

I shut the door behind me with a soft click. "He is our daughter's mate, and he nearly died yesterday, Maddox. We're not putting him in silver shackles."

"Our daughter," he grinds out, and I realize he's doing his best to keep a firm grip on several overwhelming emotions, "was *tortured*, Isla."

"What do you mean?"

He takes me by the arm and guides me further down the hallway so we're not overheard by the warriors keeping guard at Ryatt's door. "I spoke to Jane, her healer, just a few minutes ago. They have a full report now of Ella's injuries. Based on the injuries they found before your tears could heal them, and her behavior..." he sucks in a breath, looking more furious than I've ever seen him before, "she's been tortured, Isla. Physically, and mentally. The wound on her inner thigh..." He hisses out a breath and closes his eyes. "Did he do it?"

"What?"

"Ryatt. Did he do this to her?"

"He's her mate!"

"He's a stranger to us," he reminds me. "And the healers didn't pick up a shared scent between them. Ella doesn't bear his mark."

I blink. I hadn't even thought to try to pick up the scent of their mate bond. It's very hard to do, honestly, but once you spend enough time with a couple, or know one of them well enough to scent the changes once a mate bond has been established, it's glaringly obvious.

I would have noticed the scent on Ella.

"But, they have to be mates."

"They're not."

"Something must have happened to break their bond. You just said she was tortured; that could have broken their bond somehow. Maybe that's why she was tortured in the first place!"

"Isla, I need you to listen to me," Maddox demands, leading me so far down the hallway Ryatt's room and the warriors fades out of sight. "Ryatt is a prisoner here now as far as I'm concerned, at least until Isaac and I determine he didn't have anything to do with the state Ella's in right now. Has she said anything to you?"

I know Maddox is only trying to keep all of us safe, but I'm livid. "She only said his name, Maddox. Before we came to the Teal Isles, all she wanted to know is whether or not he's still alive. I can't even describe how shattered she sounded as she begged me to tell her whether or not her mate was still breathing. She loves him!"

"I have to think about our family."

"He is our family." My words echo through the corridor. "Ryatt is our family now."

Maddox rolls his lower lip between his teeth. He looks like he's about to say more, but hurried footsteps cut through the air as someone rushes around the corner.

A warrior comes to an abrupt stop, panting, holding out a phone. "Alpha Antony's Beta is trying to reach you, sir."

Maddox snatches the phone, his brow still pinched with frustration from our fight.

"What's going on?" I ask as I watch Maddox's face undergo a great transformation.

"Have them wait in Maatua until Alpha King Isaac arrives," Maddox says into the phone before hanging up, his cheeks flushed with surprise and worry.

"Maddox?"

"Cassian and Hannah just arrived in Maatua," he says slowly, calmly, but his eyes are shining with confusion. "They're uninjured."

"Hannah's back?"

Maddox nods. "Did you know Cassian was able to cross the veil into Eastonia?"

This is too much. My mind is reeling as I stammer, "N-no–"

"I have to go back to Maatua." He runs his hand over his face. We're both exhausted. Neither of us slept last night. "Isaac and Maddy should be arriving there soon. I need to speak with our son and Cassian before bringing them back here." He meets my eyes. "Do not go into Ryatt's room again. Promise me."

"I'm not going to promise that."

"Isla."

"We have a lot more to worry about right now than him, Maddox. If there's a threat coming our way, Isaac needs to be ready to deal with it. But right now, I'm going to go talk to our daughter."

Maddox exhales deeply as I turn from him and rush away. I refuse to cry. I feel awful knowing that Maddox and I are at each other's throats right now. I understand his concerns, but I know Ella wouldn't have brought him here if he was a threat to our family.

It doesn't take long to reach the room where Ella's been assigned. I open the door and find a healer helping her into a seated position. She's wearing a loose shirt from some mainland band Isaac liked as a teenager. We didn't have time to grab anything or pack to come here, and the last time our family had visited the Isles, Isaac must have been barely sixteen and Ella…

She'd been thirteen. Just a girl.

"Is he awake?" She stands, gripping the headboard on wobbly legs.

I give the healer a brief nod to dismiss her from the room and close the door behind her. "No, he's resting."

"How long will he be asleep for? I need to talk to him."

"We need to talk first, Ella."

She sinks back down on the edge of her bed, her knuckles white as she clutches the headboard. Her eyes go glassy with tears. "Mama, please, just let me see him."

"What happened to you, Ella?"

Her lips part, several tears sliding off her lashes.

"It w-was a trap," she whimpers. "Ryatt's wards failed, and the king found me before I could find Ryatt."

She was pulled, she tells me, through time and space. Summoned before King Kane, a man who stole other people's power which was then harvested into the very mask Ella wore when she arrived back home.

"I fought," she says, her cheeks wet with tears as she turns desperate eyes to me. "I need you to know that I fought back for as long as I could. I need Ryatt to know that I tried to stop him."

"What happened?" I'm fighting my own tears as I watch my daughter break apart. She hugs her stomach, rocking back and forth.

"My powers were nothing against him. He got me on my knees within minutes. Everything Westfall taught me… I tried, though. I fought back even when I felt my bones would break under the pull of his powers. I tried to kill him, but that mask…. He was a god while wearing that mask, and my powers were nothing compared to his. It was fruitless. Ryatt was right all along, and I kept pushing him to let me help. I kept pushing, and pushing, and the whole time I had no idea–" She's rambling now, hugging her stomach tighter. "He drained me, Mama. He bit my neck and sucked my powers until I couldn't move. He held me down and–" She closes her eyes. "I couldn't do anything. He cut out Ryatt's mark. He shattered our bond. He knew Ryatt would feel it when it happened. He knew Ryatt would come for me."

I edge toward her. Her thighs are bare beneath the shirt, and I can see the bandages covering the inside of her left thigh.

"Westfall is dead," she whispers absently. "He was Ryatt's dad. His real dad. Westfall never told him. He never got a chance, and now he's gone. I couldn't save him."

I don't know who she's talking about, but the pain in her eyes tells me it's someone she loved.

"I tried to get Cassian and Hannah home. I tried–I tried–Everything was going wrong and my powers–"

"They made it home."

Her head snaps in my direction.

"They made it. Your dad just got a call from the castle in Maatua. Cassian and Hannah showed up in the city a few hours ago."

"Are they all right?"

"As far as I know."

"I did it," she whispers, running her hands over her face. "Oh, my Goddess, I did it–"

"Ella," I edge closer, "Is King Kane coming after you?"

She blinks, her shocked expression relaxing.

"I killed him," she says with no emotion whatsoever, but her lips twitch into a smile. "He's dead. I made sure of it. The mask–"

The door to the room opens so fast it bounces off the opposite wall, nearly coming off its hinges.

I whirl around, stepping in front of Ella, my powers prickling to life in my fingertips.

Ryatt stumbles into the room, steadying himself on the doorframe.

Behind him, a trail of groaning warriors are left in his wake, all of them injured and rolling over the tiles trying to regain their footing.

His knuckles are busted and bleeding, and the bandages covering his chest are crimson with fresh blood.

He fought his way here.

Ella's breath quickens as she steps out from behind me. "Ryatt," she croaks.

Ryatt shakes his head, trying to catch his breath, but the corners of his mouth tick up in a smile. "What the fuck did you do, Princess?"

3

HIS TOUCH ON MY SKIN

Ella

RYATT TAKES a single step into the room before his face flushes of color, and his eyes roll back in his head.

Mom gasps and rushes forward just in time to break Ryatt's fall.

"Ryatt!" I screech, jumping in to help as he pitches forward.

"Goddess above, Ella. How much does he weigh?" Mom grunts, her cheeks puffing with effort while we try to keep him upright.

"Ryatt, come on," I urge, helping Mom lower him to the ground. Some of the warriors he tore through in the hallway are back on their feet and limping toward the door. I pull my lip back in a snarl as a trio of them stumbles into the room. "GET OUT!"

They back away, going pale.

"Shut the door, please," Mom huffs, forcing a kind smile, but her eyes are narrowed with determination and concern as she looks down at Ryatt.

The warriors reluctantly edge out of the room and shut the door slowly behind them.

"Ryatt, please." I help Mom roll him over onto his back.

"Oh, no," Mom whispers, mumbling the words under her breath as she looks down at his bandages. "His stitches came undone."

"But he's okay?"

"He's fine," she says with a hint of annoyance. "Stupid, but fine. What was he thinking fighting all of those warriors in his state? I'll call for the healer. We need to get him back to his room."

"He'll stay with me."

Mom meets my eyes. I suddenly feel like I'm sixteen again, asking for a later curfew so I can stay out with my new boyfriend, even though she knew full well I'd be finding a way to sneak out regardless of her rules.

"Mom, he's my *mate*."

"I know."

"Why are you giving me that *look*, then?"

"Your dad is... uncomfortable with this."

"With me sharing a room with my mate?"

"With Ryatt."

I should have expected this. I'm numb, to be honest. I'm still riding some kind of high brought on by the sheer reality that we survived, and King Kane is dead. But there's so much that needs to be discussed. There's so much that needs to be done. We have to go back to Eastonia as soon as possible.

But right now, I'm on the other side of the veil with what could possibly be my brother's *number one* enemy, and therefore, my dad's as well. "Oh, *shit*."

"Ella," Mom warns, clicking her tongue in distaste.

"What exactly is Dad planning to do to him?" I glance at the door. "Oh, my Goddess. All of those warriors have been standing guard outside of his door, haven't they?"

"What exactly did you expect to happen, Ella?"

"I wasn't expecting anything! I brought him here because–because I had no other options. He was going to die, Mom! You were the only person who could help!"

"I couldn't." The words settle between us heavy and thick, choking the air from the room. Her eyes darken as she checks Ryatt's pulse.

"My tears barely helped him. They might have kept him alive long enough to get into surgery, but that was it, Ella."

"Did your tears help me?"

She glances at my thigh and the exposed bandages creeping toward my knee.

My chest tightens.

"Everything healed but that."

I try to distract myself from the memory of how I ended up with a gaping wound in my leg by running my fingers through Ryatt's hair. He's beginning to stir. His brow pinches as he tries to open his eyes, but early morning sunlight is starting to stream through the floor to ceiling windows overlooking the sea and the increasingly bright sunrise.

"Ella, how exactly did you get that wound?"

"Not now," I whisper. My throat tightens around the words as the reminder of the injury brings on a wave of fresh pain. Mom's powers might have healed the bruises Kane left on my body, but I can still feel his touch on my skin. It sends a chill up my spine, my entire body suddenly racked with shivers.

"I think you should rest," Mom says quietly.

I can't even look at her right now. The act of holding myself together and burying my feelings–something I've been so damned good at before–is taking all of my strength.

A soft knock on the door releases the tension in the room, and suddenly, I can catch my breath again. I inhale deeply as Mom turns and rises on her knees, beckoning the healer into the room.

Jane, who has been hovering around me like an anxious bird since the moment we arrived in the Teal Isles, lets out a little squeak when she sees Ryatt lying on the floor. "Oh, dear. Not his stitches!"

"I'm afraid so," Mom says with a sigh. "What can we do?"

"No more," Ryatt groans, waving a hand, his eyes narrowed to slits against the glare of the sun. "Please, no more needles."

"I didn't know the word *please* was part of your vocabulary," I say lightly, giving him a teasing smile.

His eyes slide to mine with so much annoyance shining behind them that I nearly burst into tears. He's okay. Ryatt is truly alive and already back to usual self.

"It's right in between the words *shut*, and *up*—"

"My mom is standing three feet away from us," I hiss, gripping his arm and lowering my voice to a whisper. "You need to be on your best behavior. I'm dead serious, Ryatt. We're not in Eastonia. You're not the king here."

"*Yet.*"

"That's not even remotely funny!"

Ryatt thinks it is. His mouth quirks into a smug, but sleepy, smile. "I'll behave if no one touches me for at least a few hours."

"He's going to be loopy for some time." The healer's voice cuts over our murmured conversation. "The sedation from his surgery to close his wounds won't wear off until later this evening, I'm guessing."

"And what can we expect when the sedation does wear off?" Mom glances down at Ryatt with a weary expression.

"He'll be in pain, for sure." The healer tucks her hands in the pockets of her white coat, her eyes sliding from mom to Ryatt. "I'd like to suggest keeping him medicated to help with that."

"It's not necessary," I tell them, patting Ryatt on the thigh. "He's been through worse." It's not totally the truth, but in the months I've known him, I've seen him battered and bruised and incredibly worse for wear. "He'll be good as new after some rest and a glass of whiskey."

Mom raises her brows, but there's still weariness behind her eyes as she turns her attention back to the healer to discuss what to do about his torn stitches.

In the end, I don't get my way. He's going to be moved back to the room assigned to him. Whatever strength Ryatt summoned to fight his way down the hallway to my room against over a dozen royal guards fades with each passing second, and soon, he's fast asleep on the carpet while Jane and Mom discuss how to move him back to a sterile room to redo the ridiculous amount of stitches holding his chest together.

I watch as two warriors lift Ryatt to his feet and drag him away, and there's nothing I can do about it.

"Where's Dad?" I ask, hugging myself as Ryatt disappears from sight.

"He went to Maatua. I'm sure he missed all of this commotion by only a few minutes–if that."

"Why is he going back to Maatua?"

"Isaac and Maddy should have arrived there an hour ago," she breathes. She turns her gaze to me, a flash of guilt lighting behind her eyes. "I called Isaac and told him what happened."

"It would have been hard to keep this a secret, I guess."

"He's not going to hurt Ryatt."

"I'm more worried about Isaac getting hurt."

She purses her lips. "Ella, look. Ryatt is an enemy of our kingdom until proven otherwise. Your father is under the impression that he may have… that he may have done this to you."

"What? Why would he think that?"

"You were tortured, weren't you?"

I turn my expression to steel, refusing to let even a glimmer of the truth show. "He didn't do this to me."

"Your Dad couldn't scent the mate bond between you–"

"It's gone." The words hurt almost as bad as the act that severed the bond between us. I fight the urge to scream, keeping my expression painfully neutral. "It was broken. But he's my mate regardless."

"Do you love him?"

"Of course." My voice breaks despite my best efforts. "I wouldn't have flattened an entire kingdom for him otherwise."

Confusion flashes across Mom's face, but I shake my head, refusing to even think about what I've done, and what might be happening in Eastonia right as we speak. "Will Hannah and Cassian come here?"

"I don't know. Maybe, but it'll be up to Isaac."

"I'd like to at least talk to them."

"I'll try, Ella. Please get some rest." Mom reaches out and takes my hand, squeezing hard. "Everything is going to be fine."

I watch her walk away. I walk to the door and slowly close myself into the unfamiliar room. I'm exhausted, and nothing sounds better than falling into a deep, dreamless sleep, but I know once I close my eyes, I'll relive the nightmare that was my time in the fortress of King Kane.

I'll see Westfall's lifeless eyes locked on Ryatt.

I'll see Amanda and Granger in that cavern beneath the coven, not knowing if they're dead or alive.

I place a hand on my stomach and close my eyes. "We're safe," I say to myself—and to the tiny flicker of life I tried so hard to protect.

Then, I crawl into bed, and dissolve into a puddle of tears.

"PLEASE—" I shove my hands against his chest. He shouldn't be this strong. He's so small, so old, so withered beneath the mask.

Kane drags the silver blade up and down my thigh while his other hand clutches my throat. Blood trickles down my neck and shoulders from several deep, jagged bite marks.

"It was so foolish of him to mark you, to think he could claim you." His laugh cuts through my soul. "You're mine. I'll drink from you and drain you of your powers until the end of your days. You'd taste so much sweeter without the taint of his bond staining your blood."

"Don't, please! I'll do anything—"

The edge of the silver blade slices into my thigh as I scream Ryatt's name.
"No!"

I shoot straight up in bed, my hands curling around my throat. I can still feel Kane's touch there, like the imprint of his hand is now burned onto my neck. My entire body is coated in sweat, causing my shirt to cling to my damp skin. Shivers snake up and down my spine as I blink wildly into the darkness, trying to clear my vision.

Outside the window, the moon is high in the sky. It's the middle of the night. I slept the entire day.

"Oh, Goddess," I breathe, running my fingers through my hair. My hands tremble as I bring them down over my face, rubbing sleep from my eyes.

I barely register my actions until I find myself in the darkened hallway outside of my bedroom dressed in sweatpants and a crew-neck sweatshirt, my hair tied in a messy bun on the very top of my head. My bare feet pad over the cold stone tiles, and the only sound beside my footsteps is the gentle hum of the AC. Several warriors turn to look at me as I make my way further down the hallway. I ignore them. I doubt any of them have the balls to stop me. I'm still a princess here, aren't I? What authority do they have over me?

"Princess Ella," someone says, stepping into my line of sight. "You're not allowed to go in there–"

I stare up at the warrior, narrowing my eyes at him. Moonlight creeps over his face as he slowly backs away. "I'll take it up with my parents when I see them in the morning. Get out of my way."

"Princess–"

I wiggle the doorknob I believe leads into Ryatt's room based on the fact that there's a million warriors standing guard nearby. "Unlock it. *Now.*"

He reaches past me and slides a key into the doorknob, and then I'm inside Ryatt's room, locking the door from the inside.

He's asleep facing the window overlooking the endless ocean. Fresh bandages wrap around his chest and back, the sheets pulled up to his waist.

I silently walk across the room and slide into bed beside him as gently as I can. I carefully wrap an arm around his waist and find his hands, knitting my fingers between his.

I brush my lips over his bare shoulder as I close my eyes, breathing in his scent. He smells different. I can't pick up everything I used to. That leather scent is gone, replaced by the astringent the healers used to clean his wounds.

Tears sting my eyes as I cuddle closer.

"I'm so sorry, Ryatt."

He squeezes my hand just as I start to drift back to sleep.

I don't know how long I've slept, but I slowly crawl back to life to the sound of voices shouting nearby. Heavy, determined footsteps breach the quiet, peaceful climate in the room as Ryatt goes totally and wholly still. "Ryatt?"

The door opens at the same moment I roll over to face it.

I knew who it would be before the man entered the darkened room and turned on the light.

I know, without a shadow of a doubt, that Ryatt is going to do everything in his power to *not* behave right now.

"You fucking prick," Isaac sneers.

And then all hell breaks loose.

4

———

FIGHT TO THE DEATH

Ella

RYATT IS out of bed in an instant, his face dancing with shadows cast by the early morning daylight creeping through the airy curtains. He grabs me by the ankle and drags me toward him across the bed as Isaac stalks into the room.

Ryatt looks murderous. His eyes are bright, clear, and lucid as he narrows them on my brother while I swing my legs off the bed and stand at his side. He stretches his arm across me, trying to push me behind him.

I feel a flicker of something deep in my heart. It's fleeting, but Ryatt's desperation to keep me safe from this threat–my brother and his temper–awakens a single speck of the bond that was stolen from us.

"Stop," I whisper. "Ryatt, stop!"

"Get out," Ryatt sneers as Isaac comes to a stop in the center of the room. Through the doorway, I see several figures lingering in the shadows. Warriors, from what I can smell.

"What are you doing in here with him?" Isaac snarls, his eyes locking on mine.

"Do not speak to her." Ryatt's voice is sharpened to a bitter edge, such a far cry from the sleepy, teasing manner in which he spoke to me yesterday.

I wanted my mate back, didn't I?

Well, now he's back, fully lucid, the sedation having worn off sometime in the night.

Just in time for my brother to get here. The tension between them is so thick I can taste it.

Isaac's jaw flexes, his eyes matching Ryatt's vengeful gaze. "Get your hands off my sister."

"My *wife*," Ryatt says coolly, the corner of his mouth lifting in a smug grin, "is my business. I'll do as I please."

That's all it takes. I close my eyes at the very moment Isaac lunges at Ryatt. The sound of furniture crashing to pieces and their fists meeting flesh rings in my ears as I back myself against one of the windows and open my eyes to slits. I don't want to watch them try to kill each other, but it's hard not to. They haven't shifted yet, but they're beating the absolute hell out of each other with their fists.

All while the warriors in the hallway watch with bated breath.

Isaac probably told them to wait outside while he handled this on his own.

Isaac gets Ryatt in a headlock, but it's short lived. Ryatt jerks forward, sending Isaac flying over his shoulders and crashing into the side of the bed I'd just been peacefully sleeping in.

Isaac recovers a second later, lunging at Ryatt's legs. Ryatt goes down with a smack, and now they're rolling across the ground spewing the most colorful insults I've ever heard in my life.

Two Alpha males in one room is bad enough. But two Alpha Kings?

Isaac plants a fist in Ryatt's chest. Ryatt sucks in a breath, his face draining of color.

"Stop!" I shout, rushing forward.

Ryatt is trying to get out from under Isaac. His eyes meet mine, narrowed and bright with pain. "Ella, get back!" my mate insists.

Another crushing blow to his abdomen has him gasping, then snarling with rage.

"He's hurt, Isaac. Stop!"

Ryatt locks his leg with Isaac's and flips him over.

I race forward, grabbing Ryatt around the shoulders. Isaac tries to kick out, but Ryatt has him pinned. My brother grunts, wrenching one of his arms free and sends it into Ryatt's chest again.

This time, Ryatt's entire body trembles, and I can almost taste his pain as he rolls off Isaac and clutches an arm over the fresh bandages now soaking with blood, again.

"ENOUGH!" I scream, shoving Isaac, who is back on his feet and trying to make another move toward my mate.

But Isaac makes the mistake of grabbing me by the arm and yanking me toward him.

Ryatt's eyes open wide and lock on the spot where Isaac is touching me.

One of them is going to die if this doesn't stop.

Ryatt leaps onto his feet and rushes at me and Isaac. I can't do more than throw myself in Ryatt's way, my hands planting on his chest.

"Don't touch her!" Ryatt shouts, but his voice cracks, his eyes shifting from pure rage to something desperate and full of pain. "Do not touch her–don't–" He takes a ragged breath before slumping onto the edge of the bed. I hear Isaac slowly back away as I kneel between Ryatt's knees and take his face between my hands. He hangs his head, panting, his hands coming up to clutch my wrists. He doesn't push me away like I expect. He leans down, closing his eyes, and rests his forehead against mine.

"Ella," he breathes. "What did he do to you?" He's not talking about Isaac. He's talking about *Kane.*

My chest tightens. "I–I don't want to talk about this right now, Ryatt."

"Westfall? He didn't make it out, did he?"

Tears burn along my lashes. I hadn't thought about how this might feel for Ryatt when he woke up and came out of the heavy sedation he's been under for a couple of days, maybe longer. The days and hours since I cut through the veil to bring him here for help are a blur.

How much does he remember about those last seconds in the remains of King Kane's fortress, when he was dying in my arms?

I hear Isaac shift from foot to foot somewhere behind us. I ignore him for a moment and swipe my thumbs over Ryatt's cheeks. "We're okay, Ryatt. We're safe."

"We have to go back."

"I–I know–"

"Granger," he says, gritting his teeth. "Granger and Amanda, are they here?"

"They're–They should be at the Coven. They were safe when I–when I left them." I swallow hard, closing my eyes and finding comfort in his scent and close proximity.

"I thought you made it back here," he says softly, his silver eyes finally meeting mine. "I know I saw the veil part. Westfall and I were in Rifthold, and I thought you got out. I was–I walked into what I knew would be my death knowing you got out."

"I don't know what happened," I try to say, but it comes out as a strangled sob. "The wards were down around the Coven, Ryatt. He found me."

"Who found you?" Isaac's voice rips through the air. Ryatt stiffens, exhaling through his nose. "Who are you talking about, Ella?" Isaac asks, a little softer this time.

"King Kane," I tell him, turning around to face my brother.

Isaac stares at the two of us. He's developing a black eye, which he deserves, in my opinion. I know I need to start talking. I need to tell him everything, but right now all I can think about is Ryatt.

"I'm not your enemy," Ryatt rasps, his eyes locking on Isaac's battered face.

"I know," Isaac says, a little too casually. "I spoke to my Beta before I came here. He told me what he knows about you and your kingdom."

I glare at my brother. "So you had this knowledge and still barged in here to try to kill my mate?"

To my surprise, Ryatt chuckles. It's a dry sound broken by pain. He rasps, "This was a personal matter between me and the Alpha King."

"What the hell is that supposed to mean?" I ask them both.

"This was about you," Ryatt says as I lower my hands from his face.

I glare at them both and rise to my feet. "You could've killed each other."

"We were trying to," Isaac admits.

"He almost did," Ryatt says, his voice strained.

"He has around a hundred stitches in his chest right now, you jackass!" I snap at my brother, who doesn't look the least bit guilty about his actions. "Do you feel better now, Isaac?"

"We'll face off again when I'm healed," Ryatt cuts in, rising to his feet.

Isaac takes a step forward as Ryatt extends a hand in his direction. I look between them, watching as they shake on it.

"You're fucking joking," I hiss. "You're sparing over me?"

"Normally, when a man steals a woman from her family and mates her, it's a duel to the death," Ryatt says quietly, casually. "At least in Eastonia."

"It's a dated practice here but relevant all the same," Isaac agrees with a short nod.

"Give me a few days, and we'll do this in wolf form, like it's meant to be done."

"You're both insane!" I shout, wrenching their hands apart.

I'll never understand men, especially Alphas. This is ridiculous. What's even more ridiculous is that they both turn and look down at me expectantly.

"What the hell do you want now?" I sneer between my brother, and my mate. "Are you going to fight me too?"

"Dad will be here shortly. We're having a family meeting." He glances at Ryatt. "That does not include you."

Ryatt arches a brow and sits back down on the edge of the bed.

"He's my family," I snap. "Whatever this meeting is about, he'll be there, or I'm not going."

"Take it up with Dad, Ella."

I bristle a bit. I haven't talked to Dad much at all since we broke through the veil.

"Is there anything I need to know before you face the entire family?" Isaac asks. His eyes, a bright blue so like our mom's, lock on mine. One is puffy and slitted.

"You need to tell us everything, Ella," Ryatt says.

I grind my teeth. My heart aches, and my chest feels heavy. My entire body thrums with stress, nerves, and heartbreak.

I'm not ready to talk about it. I know what my powers are capable of. I nearly killed us all when I brought down the fortress. What if my powers extended beyond Rifthold and topped other cities, wiping out the packs who fight beside my mate?

"Ella," Isaac says, sensing my apprehension. "Please, I need to know if my kingdom is in danger right now."

"I don't know," I tell him, shaking my head. "We're going to go back as soon as Ryatt is able to travel."

"Why not now?" Isaac asks.

"My powers," Ryatt says, chuckling darkly. "It's going to be a few days until my body is healed enough to regenerate and…." He looks at me for a moment before his gaze returns to Isaac. "Ella used too much of her own power in the past few days. It's an especially dangerous journey in her condition."

I wait for Isaac to catch on to what Ryatt means. As far as I know, my family isn't aware of my pregnancy. Mom would have said something to me if the healers had noticed and mentioned it to her. Now is not the time to spill the beans.

"You need rest, then?" Isaac glances at each of us. "That's it?"

"I didn't come here to cause trouble," I say, biting back the edge in my voice. "We're not here because we—we want to be."

I wish, even for just a moment, that I can have this conversation with Isaac alone. There are months' worth of tension between us right now.

"I came back because I was going to lose him if I didn't. Mom was the only one who could help. I didn't think about the repercussions, Isaac. I didn't think about your kingdom, or your people. I just needed to help him."

Isaac watches me closely. I let my pain and heartache show, even if just for a moment. Maybe he sees the desperation behind my eyes, because he gives me a short nod and turns his attention back to Ryatt. "I am the Alpha King here. Your title means nothing."

I place my hand on Ryatt's shoulder, squeezing. There's been too much going on for me to even try to connect with him over the mind-link, but hopefully he takes my hint and shuts up before he says anything to piss Isaac off right now.

Isaac continues, "My Beta has told me about his time in… Veiled Valley. The only reason you're not dead right now is because he vouched for you and your treatment of my sister." He glances at me for a single second before turning back to Ryatt. "You're going to stay here, in this room, to heal, however. No wandering around. Until I decide otherwise, you are a prisoner of Crescent Falls."

"Isaac–"

"What happened in here?"

I'm on my feet in an instant, my heart threatening to leap out of my chest. I turn to the door as Maddy steps inside the room looking skeptical and upset, her dark blue eyes scanning Isaac before slowly turning in Ryatt's direction. "Isaac, I told you to be nice to him!"

I run to her but stop short. She's heavily pregnant and steadying herself on the doorframe as she smiles up at me with tears in her eyes. "Are you okay?" she asks softly. "We have a lot to talk about."

"We do," I almost sob, then wrap my arms around her and squeeze.

"Come on then. Let these two work it out. Hannah's waiting for us to meet her for breakfast."

"You're not supposed to be on your feet, Maddy."

Maddy turns and gives Isaac a look that makes not only me, but Ryatt, who is still sitting on the edge of the bed, cower slightly.

Isaac clears his throat and looks away, but Maddy's expression shifts to something bright with amusement. "*Alphas*, right? Goddess, I'm so glad you're home."

5

NO ONE TOLD HER

Ryatt

SEEING King Isaac go pink in the cheeks after his exceedingly pregnant mate gave him a look that could make the fiercest warrior cower made me feel slightly more whole.

I even felt a flicker of sympathy for the man. If the situation had been different, I would have empathized with him about the trials of being mated to a pregnant woman, but we're not friends.

I don't have friends. I prefer it that way. I guess Granger would be the closest thing I have to one, and he's on the other side of the veil right now, hopefully alive and doing his duties as my Beta.

My head still feels heavy, my senses blurred. My power is nothing but a whisper in my veins as Isaac leaves the room behind Ella and Maddy.

Ella turns back to look at me before her brother closes the door, her eyes shining with concern.

With the barrier closed, I hear a lock slip into place from the outside.

I turn to the window and watch the waves beyond this strange house built into a cliff. I want nothing more than to get Ella alone and talk about what needs to be done. I shouldn't be alive. It might have been easier for her if I'd died, honestly. She would stay here with her family if that had been the case.

I run my tongue along my bottom teeth as I watch a shockingly large boat slowly float by in the distance in the glare of the sun.

King Kane is dead. I know that without having to be told. I have fractured memories of Ella donning the mask. I remember stroking her cheek, thinking it would be the last time I ever touched her. The regret I felt was immense. Something grave had happened to her during her time with the king, and I hadn't been there to save her.

Instead, she'd saved me.

I get off the bed and stumble into the bathroom, stepping over shattered glass and broken furniture left behind from my fight with Isaac. I steady myself with my hands pressed against the counter and slowly raise my head to look at my reflection. My hair falls over my shoulders. The humid, salt-filled air causes my hair to curl more than usual.

I'm developing a black eye and sporting a split lip, but otherwise Isaac's punches only did damage to my chest and stomach. Bastard. If he wasn't my wife's brother, I would have killed him.

I'll have a chance. He wants to duel. That's fine. He only wants me back in fighting shape so it's a more satisfying fight.

I shake my head and turn on the faucet and splash water on my face, but I hear the door to my prison open and close, then soft footsteps edging toward the center of the room.

Isla's scent fills the space as I step out of the bathroom.

"Oh," she says, her cheeks going rosy as she balances a tray of food in her hands. "You're awake. I wasn't sure you would be." She looks around the room, frowning. She's probably looking for the little wooden table Isaac and I threw ourselves into. "I see that Isaac paid you a visit."

"He did." I cross my arms over my chest. It hurts, but I don't let it show. Isla's face was the first thing I saw when I came back to lucidity after Ella brought us through the veil. She's beautiful. Dainty, soft, and smells like a garden in bloom. But she's so different from Ella. I find that interesting. Isla is shorter than her daughter. Her hair is golden blonde, like the sun, and her eyes are an icy blue. She and Isaac favor each other.

Ella is her father's daughter, through and through. She has none of her mother's sweetness. Graceful, sure. Beautiful, *the most*. But Ella is all fire. She's bossy, demanding, and sometimes cold. I wouldn't have it any other way.

I thought I'd lost her. When I opened my eyes to find Isla hovering over me, pleading with me to stay awake, I'd realized where my mate had brought me. Ella had brought me home to her family. She was safe. I readily prepared to die knowing she, and our daughter, were finally out of danger and could live in peace.

Now I'm locked in a room in an unfamiliar place, alive at least, but waiting to face her father.

I'm not afraid of Isaac.

But Maddox?

I purse my lips as Isla looks for a place to set the tray. "I can take it."

"Maybe you should just come eat with the family," she suggests, but her eyes tell me that it's probably not a good idea. She's just trying to be kind.

"I'm not very hungry."

"That's just all of the medication you're on for the pain," she says, turning and setting the tray on the bed. "You haven't eaten in days, I'm sure. At least not since you've been here."

I chew my lower lip. The last time I had a meal, and a shitty one at that, had been in a camp outside of Twin Rivers before we crossed into Rifthold.

Memories of Westfall come rushing back to me. I blink, forcing myself not to dwell on him. I can't face it yet.

I clear my throat. "Thank you. I'm fine eating here."

She nods, smiling grimly. "I'm sorry about this, Ryatt. Oh, is it okay if I call you that? Or do you prefer your title?"

"I don't know what my title would be at this point."

She purses her lips. "Can you tell me why?"

I roll my lower lip into my mouth and cross the room, but I keep my distance from her. The last thing I need is for her mate to pick up my scent on her clothing. "You have an exceedingly powerful and… uncontrollable daughter."

"Hmm," she hums, a real smile brushing over her lips. "I do, don't I?"

Now I'm smiling, but I stifle it and look out the window over the ocean. "She's confident she killed the Alpha King of Eastonia. I believe her. She wouldn't have been able to take the mask from him otherwise."

"The mask is here," Isla cuts in. "It's in a vault on Maatua. It's safe."

"I don't care about the mask. It can be dismantled and dropped in the ocean," I tell her, looking at her over my shoulder. "In fact, I recommend it."

I can feel her gaze on the back of my head as I turn toward the window with a sigh. "Your mate and your son want to know if there's a threat from Eastonia. There's not. Ella and I are the only people capable of crossing the veil. Whatever is happening there is contained. As for my title… I spent my early childhood being paraded around as the king's heir. I am not his son by blood. I am not the Alpha King of Eastonia."

Isla makes a little noise in her throat. I turn to look at her, noticing her confused expression. "Then who is?"

"There won't be another."

Now, she's very confused, and I'm not sure I want to stand here and explain everything. I'm weaker than ever, and being in the presence of food makes me realize how long it's been since I've eaten. But, given the fact this woman is not only, technically, my mother-in-law but also a very kind and hospitable host, I tell her what I can.

Eastonia is an ancient place full of ancient magic. I tell her about the Firestone witches, and their queen, and the Alphas who rose up against her to enslave the people of Eastonia. I tell her about Kane's rise to power and his suspected immortality, since he held his throne for close to a hundred years. All that time he spent looking for a Firestone witch, someone capable of charging that mask to its full potential. When he wore it, he was immortal, so he never took it off.

But Ella had been able to kill him. How she did it so easily, I'm not entirely sure. I tell Isla what her daughter is, and how her mate and his ancestors are to thank for that.

"Ella is our queen," I say quietly, my eyes still searching the water for more of those massive boats I saw earlier. "Our daughter is her heir."

"What?"

Isla's voice is a whisper full of shock and confusion. I realize what I've said a moment too late. She's not confused about her daughter's title, no.

"You didn't know?"

"She's pregnant?"

"Yes–" I turn to face her, my stomach twisting with a sudden feeling of dread. "Does anyone know?"

"The healers–they didn't run those kinds of tests." Isla sucks in a breath and turns for the door. "Oh, Goddess, the baby!"

No one checked. My body goes numb as I watch the blood drain from Isla's face. She looks between me and the door, struggling with what to do. "How far along is she?"

"Three months at the most," I say hurriedly. "Do you have a way to find out if the baby's still alive? A healer or mystic?" The journey through the veil could have killed us both based on how weak we were after battling Kane. Ella had been drained of her powers by Kane. She would have tapped into the baby's powers without realizing it when she cut through the veil.

"We have ultrasounds," she breathes, "and healers, of course."

I have no idea what an ultrasound is but I nod, my heart starting to race. Surely, Ella would have told someone about the baby. She isn't showing yet. No one would suspect at first glance that she's pregnant, and with our bond severed, I've had a hard time not only picking up her scent, but being able to feel those changes through our mate bond. I can't feel either of them anymore, and it's tearing me apart.

"I need to see her," I say.

"I will go," Isla says briskly. "But you will come with me, now, to see Maddox."

"No," I shake my head. "Not until–"

"I will make sure your–your daughter… is safe." Her eyes glisten with tears, but her mouth pulls into a smile that drips with pure, unadulterated joy. It surprises me immensely to see the happiness in her expression. "Oh, a girl," she whispers. "I always knew Ella would have daughters. She'll be the best mom to girls."

My heart aches as I watch Isla nod to herself, having some internal conversation only she can hear. She says, "Ella would know if anything was wrong. There would have been signs. She would have said something."

"Yeah," I say, but I'm not sure I believe it. Ella can be secretive sometimes. At least, she used to be like that around me. She tends to bottle things up until they explode, but this is different. We've been through hell and back the past two days, neither of us fully lucid. She probably didn't even think anything could be wrong. But now the truth of what occurred is crashing down around my feet as I follow Isla to the door.

"Everything is going to be fine, I'm sure. She's with Maddy and Hannah right now."

"That's good."

"You need a shirt–"

"It doesn't matter." I detest having to see Maddox and Isaac right away. But Isla might be right. If something is wrong with the baby, Ella is in better hands with the women.

What do I know about babies? Absolutely *nothing*. Being a father was never something that crossed my mind. The idea of Ella being in pain cuts me to the core, however. The idea she could end up grieving the loss of our child makes me want to put a hole through the wall and tear a few of the guards watching Isla and I swiftly exit my room to ribbons.

Isla ends up having to keep up with me as I move as quickly as possible down the long hallway. Every step aches, but I'd be sprinting right now if I knew where I was going. An archway leads out onto a wide terrace, and I briefly stop to gawk at our surroundings.

This building is one of many, all of them connected by bridges that lead to the main house, which towers in front of us. Turquoise water surrounds us completely. A small city is visible in the distance along a white sand beach, but that's it. Isla passes me in her haste to reach the main house.

I race after her, ignoring the view all around me, and follow her through a large exterior door. Everything is all cream paint and light wood paneling with huge windows overlooking the endless ocean. "What does your mate need to see me about?"

"Oh, probably political matters," Isla groans as I follow her up a flight of marble steps. "To make sure Isaac doesn't need to deploy any armies. He's not going to kill you." She abruptly turns, and I almost run into her when she comes to a stop. "Don't touch him, please. Isaac, I mean. I love him dearly, but he probably deserved the black eye you gave him today. He's fair game, in my opinion, but he's also about to be a new father, and I'm sure his mate would be livid if you maimed him in any way."

"I'm not here to hurt your family," I grind out, losing my patience. All I want to do right now is see Ella and make sure she's all right. I've been down for far too long. I'm supposed to be the one protecting her, making sure she's healing, not the other way around. "You have my word, but–" I take a cautious step toward her. "If anyone hurts Ella. If King Isaac–"

"I understand," she says softly, meeting my gaze. "They had a rough time before she left. Their relationship was never the same after the war. She wasn't the same. You have to understand that."

I exhale through my nose. She straightens her shoulders and turns to lead me down an airy corridor with arches open to a sweeping terrace overlooking the water. She raps her knuckles against a heavy wooden door three times before opening it and shoving me inside. "I'll come back in a little while," she says, then slams the door shut behind her.

Two men rise from their chairs.

I sneer at Isaac, who sneers back, but then I shift my gaze to the man standing closest to the windows. He slowly raises his coffee mug to his lips, peering at me over the rim.

Yeah, Ella takes after her father.

And if she takes after him personality wise, I'm royally fucked.

6

IS SHE IN THERE?

Ella

SUNLIGHT FILTERS through a large window and plays over a cozy bistro table stacked high with food. Pancakes, eggs, bacon, bagels, bowls of tropical fruit, and pitchers of juice.

I smear butter and jam on my third piece of toast and bite into it, trying not to groan. How long has it been since I've eaten?

I open my eyes to find Hannah loading up another plate for Maddy, who is lounging nearby on the couch overlooking the sweeping view of the white sand beach below. Maddy's bare feet are propped on an ottoman, and she's wearing an airy cream colored dress. Her red hair is pinned away from her face, which has turned a ruddy shade of pink from the sunlight.

She looks beautiful. They both do, actually. Hannah looks fresh, new, and bright-eyed. She doesn't have a single scratch on her, and the gray pallor of her skin has shifted back to a creamy peach.

Pregnancy suits Maddy. She's glowing, her hair thick and radiating as it brushes over her cheeks while she smiles up at Hannah. She's much softer now, rounder. I remember vividly what she'd looked like when we first met. Hannah and I had been able to see every bone in her body.

But now the hollows of cheeks are rounded and bursting with color as she squints against the sun and does her best to reach for the pitcher of orange juice on the table beside her.

Hannah sits back down across from me at the table and arches a brow in my direction as she lifts a pitcher of iced coffee.

"No, thanks. I'm off coffee."

"You should try it with chocolate milk instead of creamer, Hannah," Maddy suggests.

Hannah's eyes brighten as a maid walks over and takes the pitcher of coffee for a moment, returning with an iced mocha. Hannah sips, and her mouth stretches into a beaming smile. "It's delicious!"

"I'm so happy you're home," Maddy laughs. "The chocolatier in Crescent Falls has been hurting for business with you gone."

Hannah playfully rolls her eyes.

I find this entire morning odd, honestly. Maddy had simply whisked me away to the main house and sat me down for breakfast. Hannah joined us, peppy and back to her sweet, amiable self. None of us have mentioned what happened yet. In fact, we've been talking about Maddy, and her *twins*, and the fine weather and the idea of going down to lie out on the beach or for a swim.

I meet Maddy's eyes for a moment–that dark, stormy blue that is so unique. I wonder if one or both of her sons will inherit her eyes. I hope so. I've missed seeing them.

Hannah looks between us as she shifts in her seat, her cheeks going pink. "I suppose you want to know what happened, Ella."

I meet her eyes. "Yes."

I didn't want to ruin this reunion by grabbing her and shaking her by the shoulders, asking what she remembered and how she survived the journey through the veil. I'd wondered if it had been traumatic for her, but she just gives me a soft smile, tilting her head toward the sun as she closes her eyes. A silver-white scar on her neck shimmers in the golden sunlight. Cassian's mark.

"I don't remember much about *before*. I remember some moments from the coven, and that beautiful crystal palace. They were kind to me there, especially Ravenna. But I didn't like Petra." Her face drains of color, and she grimaces like she has a bad taste in her mouth. She sips from her iced mocha to wash it away before continuing. "She came into my room one night and replaced my healers with three other people I didn't know. They gave me my usual medicine, but it tasted different, and then I just… blacked out."

I remember spiriting Amanda and myself into her room at the coven and finding three healers force feeding her an inky, black, thick substance. I find it hard to swallow, so I gently set my fork down on my plate and reach for my grapefruit juice instead.

Hannah shifts in her seat again. "Then everything just felt–well, blurry. Then I heard Cassian's voice in my ear. He told me he was so sorry, that he was sorry for everything, that he couldn't save me, that it took so long to find me. I remember a pinch on my neck." She reaches up to stroke her fingers over the scar, her eyes darkening. "Then I felt like I was being pulled apart. Everything was black, then my vision burst with light before it faded again."

She explains how she tried to take a breath, but there was no air. Water filled her lungs instead, but before she could react, she was pulled from the water by Cassian, who hauled them out of what she recognized as the falls.

"It was the middle of night, and there was pounding rain. I've never seen it storm so violently here," she says, twisting a bouncy blonde curl around her finger. She looks over at Maddy. "I've only been to Maatua a few times and had only been to the falls once. Even Cassian was struggling to make sense of where we were in the storm, and we took shelter instead of trying to find the capital. When morning came, a trio of wolves found us. Cassian's metal arm was totally fried," she says with a little laugh. "He wasn't confident he could shift with it anymore, so we followed them on foot thinking they were taking us to the capitol, but we ended up on the opposite side of Maatua in a fishing village."

"Starfall Cove is very far away," Maddy sighed, shaking her head.

"It took us a full day to get someone to put us on a boat and take us to the capital. We couldn't find a phone, either. But we made it to the castle and were taken to Poppy. That's when we found out you and Ryatt were here." Hannah's eyes meet mine. "Cassian told me what happened at the coven, Ella."

I give her a tight smile. Every time I blink, I imagine the crystal palace falling away and rolling down the mountain side toward the village–and all of the people that lived there.

"You saved us by sending us to the falls," Hannah continues, reaching for my hand. "It healed us. I feel–"

"Ella!" Mom's voice rings through the parlor we've been having breakfast in.

All three of us turn our heads as she briskly walks into view, followed by Jane, my healer.

I stand up so abruptly I nearly knock over the bistro table. "Mom–"

"We need to go to the infirmary right now," Mom says sharply.

"What happened? Is Ryatt okay?"

Hannah helps Maddy to her feet somewhere behind me.

"He's fine," she says breathlessly, searching my eyes. "Why didn't you tell anyone? Why didn't you tell me?"

My heart does a little flip. "Tell you what?"

"The baby, Ella. No one has checked on the baby."

"WHERE'S RYATT?" I ask, my heart hammering in my chest as I roughly pull up my shirt. The infirmary in the main house–nothing more than a wide room with a few hospital style beds and cabinets lining the wall–is dim and humming with a soft electric pulse as Jane swivels on a stool to face where I lie, one hand holding a doppler while the other punches a few commands into an ultrasound machine.

"He's with your dad and Isaac."

My head snaps in Mom's direction. Hannah and Maddy wait in silence beside me, Maddy's eyes locked on the screen.

"Why is he with Dad and Isaac?"

"They needed to get whatever conversation they're having right now over with so we can all move on." Mom's eyes are laser focused on Jane as she swipes the doppler over my lower belly.

I glance around at the faces in the room. All of them look stressed and concerned.

"I'm fine," I tell them for the hundredth time. "She's fine, too. I swear."

"You should have told someone," Mom says with force, her eyes shining with sudden tears.

"Mom, I–I didn't even think about it. Not with Ryatt in such rough shape–"

"How long have you known?"

"A few weeks," I tell her, swallowing hard. I have a sudden jolt of fear as I go over the last few days in my head. I'd been terribly sick during the first weeks of my pregnancy, plagued by headaches and crippling nausea. But ever since coming through the veil, I've felt... fine. Normal. No symptoms whatsoever...

My hands nearly fly to my stomach, but Jane is in the way, swiping left then right, looking for my baby.

"Where is she?" I whisper, dread sinking deep into my bones. "Jane, where is the baby?"

How could I have been so stupid? I would have known something was wrong, right? I would have bled, I would have felt myself losing the baby if...

A steady, rhythmic thump fills the room. Jane takes an audible breath, her hazel eyes meeting mine as she nods.

Mom's face flushes as she nods to herself, counting the beats. I watch her, the ultrasound screen illuminated behind her eyes. Mom used to take me to the hospital in Crescent Falls. She used to drag me from healer to healer in the small villages surrounding the castle. All of her close friends were midwives, healers, artists, and teachers. Normal people who led normal lives. She'd assisted numerous births. She would know immediately if anything was wrong.

"Is she okay?" I ask Mom.

"You're confident you're having a girl, huh?" Jane says with a smile. "Some people just know."

"It's far too early to tell for sure," Maddy cuts in. She cranes her neck to get a view of the screen I haven't brought myself to look at yet. "Looks like there's just one, lucky you." She gives me a smile while she pats her swollen belly.

I glance at Mom, whose eyes are still on the screen. Her brow furrows slightly.

"What's wrong?"

"Nothing," she says softly, reaching out to lay a hand over my shoulder.

But the look behind her eyes makes me wonder what exactly she's seen. I can tell that it's bothering her, whatever it is. "Mom?"

"Maddy, you should be resting. You've been on your feet all morning," Mom says, turning from us.

Maddy rolls her eyes and huffs, "The sooner the princes come, the better."

Mom gives her a motherly smile. "You need your strength, Maddy."

"Cassian should be back from his meeting with the warriors," Hannah says, glancing down at her watch. "I'll walk with you."

Maddy meets my eyes. The look behind her eyes tells me everything I need to know–no mind-link necessary.. We'll talk soon. She's happy I'm here. My baby is just fine, don't worry about it.

I weakly smile back. She turns to leave, Hannah guiding her away.

Jane turns from us. "I'm going to take some quick measurements. A blood test, too, I think."

Mom nods, but her eyes are still on the screen.

Neither of us say anything. Jane prints out a strip of glossy pictures from the ultrasound and hands it to me. My hands tremble as I take it and look down at the little bean nestled deep inside my belly. Little arms and legs are visible.

"She has such a big head," I say to myself.

"She'll grow into it," Mom laughs, settling down on a stool.

"I'll be right back," Jane says before leaving the room.

I sit up, smoothing my shirt back over my belly. "What's wrong, Mom?"

"Are you going to leave again?"

I look at her. She's looking down at her hands, inspecting her nails. Her blue eyes shine, but refuse to meet my gaze.

"I have to."

She nods, sniffling a bit, but her face relaxes into a mask of calm resignation. "Everything is fine with the baby. She's strong, and growing just like she should."

"Why did you look so concerned, then?"

She grits her teeth for a moment. "Childbearing for our kind is never easy, Ella. I had such a hard time. I worry about you and the baby going back to Eastonia. Are things… like here?"

"It's far less modern," I admit. "It's hard to explain." It truly is, but I take a breath, telling her how Ryatt powered his entire territory using the powers roiling through his veins. I tell her about the witches, and the magic that seems to drift in the air. Eastonia is magic, plain and simple, and for a moment I find myself *missing* it.

"I'm strong," I tell her. "I have powers, Mom. I'll be fine."

"I'll never know you as a mother, will I? Once you go, you can't come back. She can't return here–at least for a long time."

My heart lurches in my chest. The idea of taking a baby through the veil… Goddess, I can't even think about it.

"You'll need to go before you get too far along in your pregnancy," she says absently.

"Mom?"

She wipes her eyes, smiling down at me. "We'd better go find your mate. He was pretty upset earlier when he found out none of us even checked for a pregnancy."

I open my mouth, dead set on telling her to wait, to stop, but she stands and offers me her hand.

"Will Ryatt even still be alive after being thrust into a room with Isaac and Maddox?"

"We're about to find out."

7

SHE DOES WHAT SHE WANTS

Ryatt

MADDOX RISES FROM HIS CHAIR, casually sipping coffee from a mug. He sets it down, checks his watch, then fixes me with an annoyed look. "Is there a reason you're in here?"

I glance around the room. It's a wood paneled and slightly dated office with incredible views of the water. My gaze settles on Isaac, whose left eye is nearly swollen shut, and I give him a cocky smirk before looking back at his father.

I slightly bow my head before meeting Maddox's eyes again. "Your wife brought me here."

He stares at me unblinking for several seconds before blowing out his breath and sitting back down.

Isaac looks from Maddox to me. "You're a prisoner. You're not allowed in the main house."

I shrug, crossing my arms over my aching chest. "This is where I was told to go."

Isaac sits on the edge of a solid wood desk and glances behind him at the old maps scattered across it. I get a brief view of the mountains and the names of small pack territories before he roughly turns them over, glaring at me.

I step away from the door, trying my best to hide the pain I'm in. "Are those maps current?"

"That's none of your business," Isaac remarks, glowering at me.

"They're current," Maddox says, his tone laced with boredom as he sits back down. "We were just discussing possible access points of your kind into Crescent Falls and the surrounding territories."

Isaac narrows his eyes at his father before shifting his focus back to me expectantly.

"There are none," I tell him. It's the honest truth.

"How did Alpha King Kane send his troops into our kingdom last summer?" Maddox pours himself another cup of coffee. Steam rises into the air, shimmering in the midmorning sun. His sharp green eyes meet mine, but he's unusually calm and collected.

That makes me more than a little nervous compared to his hot-headed son.

I can anticipate Isaac's moves. Isaac has a short fuse and even shorter patience, but his face remains a calculated mask of steel as he looks between me and his dad.

Maddox, however, remains calm and collected, not a single emotion flaring behind his eyes.

King Kane hated Maddox. He never met the man, but his mystics and oracles constantly spied on Crescent Falls and reported back to Kane with stories of the king who almost lost his throne. By law, the Alpha King of Crescent Falls must have an heir by the time he turned thirty, otherwise the throne would be up for grabs.

Kane saw Maddox as a worthy opponent in the great game of divide and conquer, but Kane had yet to harness the power he needed to create tears through the veil. That came later, and by then, Isaac was on the throne and the kind of king Kane was weary of.

Isaac was young and bloodthirsty, and so was the army he raised to fight against Kane when the time came.

I explain this to Maddox and Isaac, telling them everything I know about Kane's spying and the army he spent decades enslaving and training, fueling them with powers stolen by the last of the Shadowsyngers, Westfall included.

Then the prophecy ignited at Ella's birth. The beasts would fly again. The queen would return, taking back her rightful throne.

"There is a river that cuts Eastonia in two," I explain, now sitting in one of the armchairs across from Maddox. "Rifthold sits to the south-east. It encompasses a vast land–forest, desert, grass covered plains. It eventually meets the ocean, but I've never traveled that far." I glance at the carafe of coffee on the table between us. Maddox watches my every move as I painfully lean forward to pour myself a cup. His eyes linger on the tattoos that snake up my forearms to my shoulders. He lingers on the pale silver scar on my shoulder–his daughter's teeth marks.

Maybe Isla was right about the shirt.

The thought of Ella creeps back into my mind. Ella, and the baby. I clear my throat, trying not to think about it right now. "Kane used my powers to open the holes in the veil. The mountain spring was large enough to send armies through."

"You helped him do it?" Isaac asks. He's leaning over the desk taking notes on a piece of paper, likely writing down everything I've said, word for word.

I turn my attention back to Maddox, who's watching me acutely.

"I had to find my mate," I say without a shred of hesitation, "before he did."

Maddox slowly sets down his coffee mug. "What did he want from her?"

"Her power," I answer. I look at Isaac. "His, too, had he known about everything the Alpha King is capable of."

Isaac narrows his eyes at me but doesn't say anything. So, the extent of his powers are a secret. I wonder how much his own mate knows.

I look back at Maddox. "My people are considered rogues. I only joined my father's–Kane's forces as a ploy to get to Ella and your family before it was too late. I taunted you, Isaac, to make you aware of the threat. I needed you at your full potential."

"What kind of game are you playing, Kane?"

"That's not my name," I say in a near whisper. Ryatt Kane, Prince of Eastonia, was never my true identity. First, I detested it. When I returned to King Kane at least, then a grown man with my own packs behind me, I allowed him to call me as such if only to gain access to his inner circle and start unraveling his army from within. I knew he sired me. At least, I thought that was the case. But now I know the truth. "Kane wasn't really my father. My mother was a breeder and a witch, a slave. My father…." I can't finish the words. "My name," I push out, "Is Ryatt Westfall, Alpha King of the Roguelands, the Shadow King of Veiled Valley." I lick my lips, finding them dry and tasteless despite the coffee I've been sipping on. "My people–my kingdom is not a threat to Crescent Falls. My packs… they'll be facing worse in the coming months, I'm afraid."

"What do you mean?" Isaac asks. He leaves his perch on the desk and edges closer.

"Kane had loyal followers. Alphas of lands in southern Eastonia. Brutal men–men willing to wage war against each other for the right of the title of Alpha King. I must return to defend the Roguelands." I look at Isaac. "I will be far too busy to deal with your precious kingdom, *Your Highness*."

He catches my mocking tone and scowls. "And you're sure only you and Ella are capable of crossing the Veil?"

"There's one other person," I say, leaning back in my chair. "But he resides here."

Isaac looks at me carefully. I slowly rake my gaze down from his face to his hands as I bring my coffee to my lips.

Maddox catches this exchange and looks at his son. "You can cross, can't you?"

"He doesn't know how," I say, my lips curving into a menacing smile. I shouldn't be baiting Isaac, but I can't help it. I know men like him. Cunning, sharply intelligent. I know he likes this game he's playing with me. Who is bigger, who is stronger, who is a more capable king?

"What reason would I have to want your kingdom?" he laughs.

"Based on what Cassian said, you lack basic amenities such as electricity. The veil keeps you trapped in a time long lost to us here in Crescent Falls."

'We have power, Isaac," I say softly. "Power your own people have let dwindle away. You may be wolves still, of course. But we don't keep our extra gifts a secret in Eastonia."

This strikes a chord with Isaac. Maddox, however, shifts the conversation before Isaac and I can start hurling the insults on the tips of our tongues.

"You'll go back to Eastonia," he says simply, calmly.

"As soon as I'm able, yes."

"And Ella will stay here."

The air in the room thickens. I let out my breath, looking down into the mug of coffee. "It would be the safest thing for her and the baby–"

"The baby?" Isaac says, shock softening his features. "She's pregnant?"

"But," I cut in, ignoring the looks on each of their faces, "Ella will not, and has not, listened to anything I have to say about her safety since the moment I met her. She will come back to Eastonia with me because it's what she wants to do, and Ella does... Ella does what Ella wants to do."

Silence settles between the three of us for several seconds before Maddox laughs. I look up at him, surprised.

"You must really be her mate, then."

Isaac rolls his eyes and walks to the window.

"I am," I say.

"I'm sorry," Isaac chuckles.

I narrow my eyes at him. "I didn't have a choice in the matter, obviously. These things are destined by powers out of our control. Had it been up to me, I would have chosen someone docile and submissive. Someone who smiles at me from time to time and doesn't–doesn't take pleasure in pushing all of my buttons."

Maddox raises his brows, chuckling to himself.

"You won't find that in this family," Isaac sighs as he sips his coffee, his eyes on the ocean.

"I love her," I say to Maddox, and Maddox alone. The only time I ever told Ella how I really felt was when I was dying in her arms. But I need her father to know more than anything. "Everything I do from this day forward is for her, and our daughter. I am allied with you, and the Alpha King, by blood."

"How far along is she?" Isaac asks, suspicion shining behind his eyes.

I don't know how I know we're having a daughter. The knowledge has just been there, lingering in my mind, tugging on the broken bond I share with Ella. I shrug because I'm not sure of the answer.

"What must be done in the meantime?" Maddox asks after a long, heavy pause.

"I–what is that?" I rise from my chair to look over the top of Maddox's head, my eyes glued to the water.

"What?" Isaac says as Maddox rises. The two men turn to face the window as I hurry over, resisting the urge to press my hands to the glass.

"That fucking *giant* boat," I hiss. I'd seen one earlier and thought it was a trick of my mind.

"The cargo ship?" Isaac glances at me.

"How is something that large powered?"

"Good Goddess," Maddox groans, turning from the window. "Here we go."

Something glimmers behind Isaac's eyes. "An engine. Have you ever seen one?"

"THEY WEIGH OVER 200,000 TONS," Isaac says. He points to the picture of a cargo ship he sketched on a piece of paper. We've been talking for an hour, mostly about boats, and planes, and cars. Things we don't have in Eastonia, at least not like the massive boat built like a city and used to trade goods all across his lands.

Maddox is asleep in one of the arm chairs.

I have successfully won them over. I think.

Well, Ella will be pleased, I'm sure.

Now we can focus on getting home, if that's what she wants.

The door to the office opens, and Ella and Isla walk in. They both look around, and Isla heaves a sigh of relief while pinching the bridge of her nose.

Ella looks at us, but her eyes narrow suspiciously as she steps into the room. "What are you doing?"

"Did you expect one of us to be maimed beyond repair?" Isaac chuckles.

"You," she says, rolling her eyes. She glances at her father, who is awake now, furrowing her brows. "What the hell is going on in here?"

Isla nears the desk and pulls one of the sketches toward her. She arches a brow, her golden hair dusting over her cheeks. "Really, Isaac, boats?"

"What else do men talk about?" Isaac grumbles, gathering the pages. He glances at me briefly before clearing his throat. "A week, then?"

"A week," I say.

"Until what?" Isla looks between us.

"Until they shift and fight to the death over me," Ella snaps, her cheeks flaring with color. She's feeling better, and seeing color stain her cheeks and that angry look in her eyes tells me everything is fine. She's fine; the baby is fine.

I meet Isla's eyes very briefly. Her expression softens as she nods to me, a silent understanding passing between us.

All is well.

I feel like I can breathe again as Ella steps to my side.

"No one is fighting to the death," Isla breathes, crossing her arms over her chest as she looks over at her mate. "This is just a... family vacation."

I have no idea what that means, but Ella knits her fingers in mine and tugs me away. No one stops us as we leave the office. Warriors aren't posted nearby, waiting to take me back to my room.

We leave the main house but stop on the bridge. She turns to me, reaching into the pocket of her pants. "Here," she says softly, placing something in my hand.

I look down, and the soft breeze unravels a strange strip of glossy paper. Black and white images stare up at me.

"That's her," she says, pointing. "That's our baby."

"She's very odd looking–"

She swats my arm, but giggles, and the sound of her laugh ignites a spark deep in my chest, the very place where our bond should be. She has tears in her eyes when she looks up at me, but she's smiling, and her eyes crease with mingled desperation and pure joy.

I caress her cheek, leaning down until our noses are touching.

"We did it," she whispers, closing her eyes. "We did it, Ryatt."

"There's so much left to do, Princess." I brush my lips over hers, and then I kiss her. I kiss her like it's the first time. Like we're back in that cottage in the Roguelands and every touch is new. I pull her close, cradling the back of her head as I swipe my tongue over her lower lip, begging her to open up to me.

But Ella pulls away, tears rolling down her cheeks. "We need to talk about this, Ryatt."

That warm feeling in my chest cracks and withers away, replaced by the dread I've been keeping tamped down.

"We need to talk about Westfall."

But a shout from the main house rings through the air. We turn, and I squint into the glare of the sun as warriors dart into the house, a few of them shifting.

"Stay here," I command.

But Isla's voice carries over the window.

"Someone find the healer! It's Maddy!"

8

———

SEVERED BOND

Ella

"Go," Ryatt says as I back out of his arms.

"I'll come find you in a little while," I tell him, my heart racing. Something's wrong with Maddy. She was fine this morning.

Ryatt gives me a tight smile, but behind his eyes is a great deal of pain I can't quite decipher. There's so much unsaid between us. Hell, before all of this madness happened, before we went our separate ways so he could fight and I could bring Cassian to the Coven, he'd essentially accused me of working for the enemy and tried to force me to come here, back to my family.

And then he'd died in my arms, the last words on his lips that he loved me. We haven't had a single moment to mend what's been broken between us.

My chest aches as I watch him turn and walk away. There's so much distance between us now without the mate bond. I can't feel that tug in my heart anymore.

Will anything ever be the same? Will we ever get past this?

Is it even possible?

57

He disappears into the small house built on the bluff. I stand on the bridge, feeling suddenly torn between going to him and going to Maddy.

Maddy. Something's wrong, I remind myself, and whirl toward the house. My sandals clack over the bridge. I'd changed into shorts and an old T-shirt before having breakfast with Maddy and Hannah, but my exposed skin does nothing to break through the heat of the day as I race toward the main house and skid to a stop inside, listening.

Voices travel down the stairs into the airy, open foyer. Footsteps sound, retreating further into the sprawling mansion. I slowly make my way upstairs, looking into each room. I open a door and run right into Isaac.

"What–"

"Just get out," Maddy pleads to everyone in the room. "I am so tired."

I edge around Isaac and notice Jane helping Maddy into bed. Maddy's legs tremble, her eyes shining with tears and her cheeks burning a vicious red.

Mom looks at Isaac, then at me. Isaac flexes his jaw as he watches his mate get tucked into a large bed made of pale wood, the sheets and duvet a fluffy white cloud now surrounding Maddy.

"What happened?" I whisper as Mom gently leads me out of the room. The door shuts behind us, but Maddy's muffled protests travel into the hallway. "Is she all right?"

"She's fine," Mom breathes, rubbing her temples. "She thought her water might have broken but it was a false alarm."

I catch my breath, sighing heavily. "I thought–" I shake my head, trying to rid my skin of the creeping fight or flight feeling creeping through my body. "I thought she was hurt or we were being attacked." Will I ever feel normal again?

"Maddy has had a really hard pregnancy, Ella. She's fine, and the twins are perfect, but her body is under a lot of pressure right now. She's supposed to be on bedrest until their birth. The past few days have been… too exciting for her, I think."

"It's my fault."

"It's my fault," she cuts in, swallowing hard. "I called Isaac and asked them to come. I wasn't thinking."

Neither was I. Not when I used my powers to totally wreck an entire kingdom to save one man. My throat nearly closes, my eyes beginning to prickle with hot, angry tears.

I'm so tired. My body aches. My heart feels like it's been patched together with tape threatening to split, spilling the fractured contents into my chest.

"That scared me," I admit, barely able to meet my mom's eyes. "I was–I thought something had happened and I…." Tears fall freely now, rolling down my cheeks and along my jaw. "Oh, Mom, I don't know what I'm supposed to do or feel right now."

Mom pulls me into her chest and holds me close. "Everyone is feeling the same way you are, honey. It's okay. We're all going to be okay." Her voice is strained, and I wonder if she's also on the verge of tears. "Your dad wants to talk when you're ready. I think you should go rest for a while, maybe take a nap. Maybe rest with Ryatt for the remainder of the day. He could use it as well, and I worry he won't lie down if you're not together."

I hold her a little tighter. "Thank you for being kind to him."

"He's not so bad," she says with a little laugh. "*Very* handsome, Ella. Good job."

I choke on a laugh. "I guess that makes up for his terrible personality," I joke.

"The two of you seem to be a good match."

"We fight well." I laugh, and memories of Ryatt come rushing back to the forefront of my mind. Every heated exchange. Every stolen kiss. Every fight that ended with me in his arms because I just couldn't imagine myself anywhere else.

"Go to him. I'll handle Maddy. I think everyone could use some space and rest. We'll try again tomorrow," she says quietly. We can hear Isaac and Maddy bickering now. Isaac is doing his best to try to explain to her that she needs to rest as well.

His voice sounds so broken by exhaustion and stress that it sends a pang of pain through my heart as I let go of Mom and turn toward the stairs. But just as my foot hits the second to the last step, I hear the door to Maddy and Isaac's room open and shut and Isaac's muffled, exasperated voice whispering tersely to Mom before he thunders down the stairs.

He brushes past me, saying in passing, "Maddy wants to see you."

I watch him go, the sun illuminating the strands of chestnut brown in his dark hair. Mom comes down the stairs next, huffing out a breath.

"Are they all right?" I whisper.

She nods, squeezing my forearm. "They're fine. Isaac is really worried about her. That's all. Your father has been trying to talk to him about it. He's nervous about the birth."

Another pang ripples through my heart.

I walk back upstairs and gently glide into Maddy's room. The lights are off, and the room is cozy and clean, drenched in natural sunlight. Maddy raises her head from the pillow before flopping back down. "Are you okay?" I ask.

"No," she groans. She tucks herself deeper into the pillows, lying on her side. "I'm tired and embarrassed."

"Why are you embarrassed?" I sit on the edge of her bed and rest my hand on her ankle, which is swollen and warm to the touch.

"I thought my water broke," she whispers, her cheeks going pinker than I've ever seen. "I was so excited. I got everyone all worked up in a panic and it turns out I just–I just…." Her cheeks turn red, and she buries her face. "I'm not in labor. False alarm."

"I'm sorry."

"Isaac wants us to go back to Crescent Falls," she cuts in. "Now, he's saying we can't because it's not safe for me to travel. He's upset about it, upset with me."

"I don't think he's upset with you, Maddy."

"He acts like it," she huffs. "He's so afraid of me going into labor, Ella. He panicked just now. He'd rather me be pregnant forever than go through childbirth. I've never seen him like this. He's so stressed out and it's my fault."

"It's my fault."

She blinks at me.

"He doesn't trust me, Maddy. He doesn't trust Ryatt. We're his enemies, and now we're sharing a house with him and his pregnant mate."

I wait for her to try to tell me that's not true, but she knows it is. I can tell by the look in her eyes that it is, in fact, the truth. It's the real problem between them.

"I don't know how to fix the rift between you two," she whispers.

"It's not your responsibility," I say, smiling at her. "Everything will be all right."

"I told him I don't want to go back to Crescent Falls," she says. "I want to stay here with you and Isla until after the twins are born."

"I don't know how long I can stay."

"Please," she whispers. "Just until they're here. I want you to see them, at least."

Because I might never meet them if I leave again, at least not for a very long time.

"I'll stay," I tell her, but the words feel hollow. "I need–I need to find a way to get in contact with Eastonia, though."

Maddy's gaze shifts to the window. "Well, that's easy."

"What?"

"That falls, of course. Didn't you call out to us using the falls?"

The blood drains from my face. "Oh, my Goddess, you're right. But...." I'd used my powers to send energy through the water during the eclipse. I hadn't known if it worked, but Maddy just confirmed it. "It might work."

For the next two hours, I sit in Maddy's room. I tell her everything, every detail, every name and face of the people I've met in Eastonia. I tell her about my powers, about the wars and the battles. Then I tell her about Ryatt and nearly dissolve in a puddle of tears when I explain his parentage–and Westfall. It feels good to just say everything–to lay it all out in the open. Maddy doesn't cut in with advice or concern. She just listens, and that feels incredible.

"What do you think is happening in Eastonia right now?" she asks.

"I don't know," I reply. The words feel heavy as I say them. "But I know nothing will be the same when we return."

———

RYATT SITS on the edge of the bed, his back to me. I close the door to the snug room he's been assigned with a soft click, but he doesn't move. An empty tray of food sits on the dresser, and someone has been in to clean up the mess left behind by his fight with my brother.

Ryatt's back is bare. I can see the stitches on his skin as his muscles flex. Several of the wounds went right through his chest and pierced through his back.

"What are you looking at?"

"The boats," he says hoarsely.

I walk to his side and sit down next to him. His scent hits me, but it's softer than before. It's probably because our bond is shattered. I look out over the water and then reluctantly turn to look at his chest.

He looks like he's been pulled apart and stitched back together again. Bruises cover his chest and stomach, blurring the dark, twisting tattoos. "Oh, Ryatt!"

He takes my chin in his hand and pulls me close, his lips finding mine in a soft, slow kiss. Ignoring his injuries, he pulls me into his lap so I'm straddling him, our noses touching as he rakes his fingers through my hair and slides his tongue over mine.

"We can't," I whimper. "You're hurt."

"It's never stopped us before."

"Ryatt–"

"Did Kane…. Did he…." He pulls back to look me in the eyes.

I know what he's asking. My entire body goes rigid as memories of those moments with the Alpha King of Eastonia come hurtling back into view.

"No." It's the truth. "He threatened to assault me but I–I didn't let him. I fought."

"I should have been there."

"You were." I grip his hands. "You warned me, Ryatt. I didn't know how powerful he really was until I came face to face with him. I'm so sorry. I'm so–"

He kisses me again, harder this time. "I failed you as a mate."

"You didn't."

"Our bond is broken, Ella. I can't help but think it's because I didn't stop this from happening."

"You couldn't do anything."

"You should stay," he tells me, and in a split second, we're back to where we were when we fought in Veiled Valley.

"No." I pull away from him. "I'm going back with you."

"Are you sure, Ella? I don't know when we could come back again, not with an infant."

"I understand what I'm giving up. I went through all of this a year ago, remember? I chose you, Ryatt. I will keep choosing you. I will choose you every day because I–"

"I love you," he says.

I swallow hard, looking deep in his eyes. "I love *you*. And I know how to reach Eastonia. I can pass along a message. But it means… taking a trip."

"Where, exactly?"

"We have to go back to Maatua."

"Your family isn't going to let me leave."

"I don't care, and I've already called for a boat. We leave in half an hour."

9

THE HEALING WATERS

Ella

IT'S odd seeing Ryatt in plain clothes. He doesn't fit here, I realize, as I watch him turn his gaze from the strangers seated nearby back to the water all around us. He's been silent since we walked onto the ferry that runs between the isles and Maatua.

I wish I could take a peek into his mind, just for a moment, just long enough to know what he's thinking.

He's dressed in navy blue athletic shorts that are a smidge too short for him, resting mid-thigh and showing off his insanely built muscular legs. His tan skin gleams in the sunlight poking through the somewhat shredded canopy above us, which is supposed to block out not only the sun, but the rain.

He's wearing a plain gray shirt–again, a little too tight–that shows off every muscle. He looks... hot. Hot as hell, honestly. But also so unfamiliar without his black leathers and belt loaded with daggers. His night-black hair curls around his ears as he slowly turns to me, expressionless, looking past me at the massive island now coming into view.

To the other passengers on the ferry, we're nobody. We're just another couple on vacation or running errands in Maatua's capital.

But looking at Ryatt, I can sense the darkness around him. His powers are returning, whispering over his skin like shadows cutting through the sun. But there's an emptiness around him as well, like he's a walking, talking shell of the man I loved–and nearly lost.

Now that the sedatives from his surgery have worn off completely, there's little light in his eyes. His mouth is straight and hard, no hint of that cocky, boyish smile. Even his tone remains steady and uninterested whenever he speaks.

Guilt and grief are eating him alive.

I swallow hard and look him over one more time as the ferry pulls into the port of Maatua. I'd found the clothes he's wearing in the main house before we left. They probably belong to a warrior, hopefully one who won't be too upset that their shorts and shirt are missing, as well as the sandals I found for him to wear.

When I'd decided we would go to Maatua today, I'd simply left the room, found the clothing he'd need, and walked to his room. I left a note for my parents, of course. Would they come after us?

The lump in my throat aches as I rise, smoothing the wrinkles in the pale cream colored sundress I'm wearing, my hair tied back in a bun at the nap of my neck. Ryatt follows me as we walk across the ferry, guided to the exit by the crowd. Some people, obviously tourists, stop to take pictures of the impressive port and private docks full of sailboats and yachts.

While I blend in with the crowd, people give Ryatt a wide berth. Tall, fit, and covered in scars and tattoos, he's a sight to behold. I don't blame them. His normally silver eyes are now a dark, stormy gray as he scans the dock.

"Come on," I urge, taking his hand. "We're safe, I promise."

He looks down at me and gives me a short, silent nod.

I grit my teeth, looking away from him as I struggle to hide the disappointment roiling through my veins. Why am I disappointed? It's not like I've brought him to meet my family and see my old home.

We're here because we're stuck, too injured and powerless to return to Eastonia.

But that could change after today, if my suspicions are correct.

"Ella!" comes a bright, feminine voice full of sunlight and stardust.

"Poppy!" I beam and drag Ryatt down the dock toward Poppy, the Luna of Maatua.

Ryatt

"GODDESS ABOVE," Poppy, a short, beautiful woman in her late forties, says as she clasps my hands and grins up at me. "You are the most handsome man I've ever seen in my life."

"Poppy," Ella grinds out, her brows raised.

"What?" Poppy laughs, letting go of my hands to throw her long brown hair over her shoulders. "Have you never noticed how handsome your mate is, Ella? I will say, you look a lot better now than when I saw you last, Your… Highness?"

"Ryatt is fine," I tell her, forcing a gracious smile. I can feel Ella watching me like a hawk.

"Is Antony home?" Ella tilts her head toward the castle that overlooks the city and the sweeping beaches surrounding us as we start walking deeper into the crowded streets.

"Not yet. He's still on KiloKilo. He's so upset that he's missing out on the action, Ella. Poor thing."

Antony is the Alpha of Maatua. Ella explained her connection to this family during our trip across the strait that connects the Isles with Maatua.

"Did you not bring any luggage?" Poppy says, stopping to turn to us.

"What luggage?" Ella asks, giving Poppy a look. "We fell from the sky, remember?"

"Oh, that." Poppy smiles at both of us, waving a hand in dismissal.

"Well, no bother. I called a car to take us back to the castle just in case, but it's a beautiful day for a walk, if that's all right."

"A walk is fine, but we're not going to the castle, Poppy. We're going to the falls."

"But you're coming to the castle afterward," she says. "For dinner, right?"

"We can't–"

"I already called your mom and explained everything, my dear. The two of you are spending the night, I insist!"

Ella looks uncomfortable. She glances up at me, her sea-green eyes shining with apprehension.

"Ella's parents and the Alpha King won't take kindly to me being out of my prison cell for very long," I say, trying to keep the bite from my voice.

Poppy hums with displeasure but shrugs. "I don't care. You're in my kingdom, darling. Isaac can take it up with me personally. Besides, it's been so long since I've seen Ella. I want to know every-thing, every detail of that mysterious kingdom of yours. I have dinner planned and ordered already, so I won't take no for an answer, and you can catch the ferry back to the isles tomorrow morning."

By now, we've reached a quiet residential area. Large houses made of pale stone rise above palm trees as I follow the two women, who are now bickering back and forth. I look over my shoulder and see three men following us but keeping a respectful distance. Royal guards, I assume.

We reach the castle in a matter of minutes, entering through a lower level surrounded by tropical gardens. While one side of the castle overlooks the sprawling city, the other has a view of a beach that shines like gold in the late afternoon sun.

"We'll stay the night," Ella says, "but only if we get a ride to the falls."

"You know where the cars are," Poppy says with a little wave of her hand. "I'll see you at… seven, then?"

"We'll be back by seven."

Poppy disappears into the castle, followed by her guards, and within a matter of minutes we're standing in a large building full of…

"Do you know how to operate one of these things?" I ask with a tinge of worry.

"A car? Please, Ryatt. I've been driving since I turned sixteen." She chooses a strange looking vehicle that's missing its top and has massive tires. "This will do."

"I don't like this."

"Maybe I can teach you how to drive," she says with a suggestive smile. "Might as well make the most of our time here."

Eastonia doesn't have cars. Or planes. Or massive boats, for that matter. The men who'd fought beside me in Crescent Falls hadn't been given the freedom to roam into the outlying territories when the war drew to a close, but we'd heard of the large cities and strange technology they possessed. We didn't have the need for these things, not when we could shift for travel.

But to think of not having to use my powers to keep the lights on, and packs protected….

Ella laid on the horn, the sound sharp and demanding enough to break me out of my stupor. "Get in!"

"Where are we going, Ella?"

"The most magical place in this kingdom."

"IT'S PRIVATE LAND NOW," Ella says as she strips out of her dress and lays it over a bench near the water's edge. It's a small pond that glitters like gems against a length of blue velvet, the water stirred by a gentle, humming waterfall in the middle at the back. Ella turns to look at me over her shoulder. Her long, thick, dark hair touches her lower back, and her ass…

She's naked save for white panties that leave little to the imagination.

Something stirs in my chest. It's not lust or longing. No, it's a sharp, brutal pain that brings forth the memory of seeing her lying on the filthy stone floor in front of King Kane's throne, blood dripping from her mouth.

Every time I look at her, I see her glassy, near lifeless eyes staring up at me.

It shatters me.

"Come for a swim."

"You haven't explained why we're here. You said you would."

She purses her lips, dipping a toe into the water. It shimmers like diamonds.

"It heals wounds. It sometimes gives people special gifts… powers."

"These are the falls that gave your mother her powers?"

She nods, turning to look at the waterfall. "The Mystic in Moonrise told me that the water between our realms is connected. It's the only thing that can pierce the veil. I can reach Eastonia. I can at least send a message. I know I can."

"You shouldn't be using your powers right now, Ella, not after what we went through."

"Our kingdom doesn't know if we're dead or alive, Ryatt," she says firmly.

She walks into the water before I can stop her, her hair fanning out around her as she reaches the deepest point. She beckons with a hand. "It feels really good. You're missing out!"

I growl as I strip off the shirt and step into the cool water. It rushes over my skin, causing it to tingle as I step deeper, and deeper, until I'm up to my neck.

The water swirls over the wounds on my chest, and I feel a sudden weightlessness as my body relaxes into the water's touch. I inhale sharply as a dull ache spreads across my chest then dissipates into… nothing.

I run a hand over my chest. The stitches are gone, and the dull pain I've felt since I finally came back to my senses is totally gone as well. Shocked, I meet Ella's gaze and find her smiling softly, her eyes shining with relief.

I want nothing more than to go to her, to wrap my arms around her and hold her against my skin. I want to kiss her and not feel like this is a dream, and she's going to fade away, falling like sand through my fingers.

I want to touch my mate without being reminded of how I failed her.

Ella swims toward me and rests her hands on my shoulders. I can touch the bottom of the pond, but the water would be at least a foot above her head if her toes brushed the smooth stone scattered below us. She wraps her legs around my waist. "You need to go under the water completely."

"Why?"

"Your face looks like it went through a meat grinder. No wonder people were staring." She chuckles lightly as I smooth my hands over her hips, then cup her ass.

I stare into her eyes, and then, without warning, I pull us both under water.

SHE SPEAKS THE TRUTH

Amanda

"YOU BETTER HAVE good news for me, Nytos," Granger growls somewhere behind me. His words whisper over a spring wind carrying ash and decay.

"The only news I have is that there's still no sign of Alpha Ryatt or his Luna."

My stomach clenches. I roll a smooth, white rock in the palm of my hand as the conversation continues without me.

"And Westfall?"

I look over my shoulder in time to catch Commander Nytos shake his head, his eyes downcast and solemn.

Granger chews the inside of his cheek, his green eyes sliding to mine.

I give my mate a tight smile, praying to the Goddess he can see the love behind my eyes—and the sorrow there.

"I've spoken to the other commanders," Nytos continues. "The Alphas need answers, Beta. Are you the King of the Roguelands now?"

My heart skips a beat as I watch fury and grief darken his eyes.

"No," he rasps. "Not until we find their bodies."

I close my eyes and turn back to the cairn situated in the center of an area of scorched earth. This is where the pack house of Granite Rise once stood.

Hundreds of rocks of varying sizes and shapes make up a great mound that is as tall as my chest.

I place the little white rock atop its peak. A memory of Gemma flutters through my mind as I blink back tears.

I need three more rocks.

I hike up my skirts and carefully step over the debris surrounding the remains of the pack house, which had been burned to the ground. I try not to think about who might have been inside when the fire happened. Granger knows the details. He offered to tell me, but I think I'd rather not know whether or not my pack members were rounded up by King Kane's warriors and locked in the pack house before they lit it on fire.

But… there's no one left. No bodies. I am the last living member of the Granite Rise Pack.

Granger's voice drifts into the background as I walk out of the village, my focus locked on the forest surrounding my homeland.

There's still a chill in the air as I walk between birch trees and thickets of alders. The entire landscape is painted a vibrant pale green. I press the toes of my thick leather boot into the ground, turning over the mud to look for rocks. This whole area outside the village is generally flat and grassy, not a single pebble to be found.

"Damn," I whisper to myself as I fold my light blue cloak tighter around my shoulders, my breath sending wisps of silver mist toward the overcast sky.

It's growing late in the day. I can't be out here for long. Granger doesn't care if I wander. He likely knows exactly where I am right now. He has a knack for that.

So, I walk further into the forest until the scent of ash and death stop staining the air and suddenly find myself in a familiar clearing.

I imagine the moment I first saw Ella in her strange black dress. I remember the glowing silver fire behind her eyes as she saw me, her expression turning from panicked confusion to protective rage.

She would have killed me. I remember that feeling vividly, and I'd run for my life before falling into...

I whirl back toward the forest and set off in a jog through the woods. The sound of running water cuts through the birdsong before I reach the creek bed, where pockets of ice still cling to the banks on either side. I kneel, panting, and rest my hands on the cool, smooth stones that cover the bank. Tears burn my eyes before sliding down my cheeks.

Just a few days ago, when Ella turned into black mist in the cave beneath the coven and disappeared, I'd been full of hope. I'd turned into Granger's arms and cried happy tears against his chest thinking our people–our child–would have a future outside of war, slavery, and secrecy.

But less than a day later, after we finally dug our way out of that cave and gazed upon the ruins of the coven, I felt like my soul was being pulled apart.

The powers Ella gifted me the night we battled the hellhounds screamed in agony, and then flickered out. She's gone.

There's been no sign of them, and Rifthold is... nothing but smoking embers.

"Where are you?" I whisper, sniffling. I swipe my hands over the rocks and find one black as the darkest, starless night. I think of Ryatt as I slip it into my pocket. I find another black stone, this one a little rough around the edges, and imagine Commander Westfall's face. He was always so kind to me. I never understood Granger's weariness when it came to him. I slip the rock in my pocket and scan the shore for the stone I don't really want to find.

The bank of the creek is a tangle of silver, black, and brown. None of which are colors I'd ever associate with Ella. She is–*was*... was so vibrant, so beautiful, so unique.

I rise and scan the creek. The other side is illuminated by pale sunlight drifting through a parting cloud.

A flicker of dark green catches my attention.

I suck in a breath and enter the creek.

The ice cold water burns my skin as my skirts billow out around my knees, my cloak dragging in front of me as the swift current threatens to pull me away. Soaked to the waist, I start scanning the water along the far bank.

It's a green rock, likely granite, and it's far larger than the small rounded pebbles surrounding it. It's just below the surface, smoothed to a buttery softness from years spent beneath rushing water. I reach down, water soaking through the sleeve of my shirt, when the water whispers all around me.

I freeze, my fingers curled around the stone.

"Hello?"

"*We're alive! We crossed the veil. I had no choice. We're alive, and well. Ryatt was injured but we're trying to find a way to come back. We're safe. We're safe–*"

I whirl around, expecting to find Ella standing across the creek and shouting the words at me, but I'm alone.

"Ella?"

"*King Kane is dead. Westfall is dead. Ryatt is alive, Amanda. I'm alive. Cassian and Hannah are alive. We made it–*"

"Ella!" I start splashing through the water, trying to find the source of her voice.

I rear back when flickers of crimson light rush against the current then explode, the whispers louder than before.

"*Go to Veiled Valley and wait. Granger is the Alpha until we return–*" Ryatt's voice cuts through the increasingly frantic murmurs rising from the water–a chorus of genderless voices blurred into one. I hear Ella laugh softly, and the sound is like the sweetest music before the moment snaps and the entire forest goes eerily silent.

Struggling to catch my breath, I whirl around at the sound of hurried steps.

A great golden wolf skids to a stop at the shore of the creek, green eyes locked on mine.

'What are you doing?' Granger growls in my mind. 'You were screaming–'

"They–they're alive. They made it out. Granger!" I pick up my shirts and rush toward him. "Granger, I heard them. They're alive. They crossed the veil somehow. Ella said Ryatt was injured and they're trying to find a way to cross."

Granger's voice is a soft whisper through my mind as he says, 'You heard them?'

"Don't you feel it?" I exclaim, climbing onto the shore. "Her power?" I look down at my chilled fingers, at the pale shimmers of crimson just below the surface of my skin. I know if I shift now, her power will burn through me, allowing me to summon the beast she turned me into the night so long ago. "She did it. She killed King Kane."

***

Ryatt

ELLA SPUTTERS WATER, gasping for breath. I cling to her, trying to find the air my lungs have been screaming for. The water all around us shines with her power–swirls of silvery fire and shimmering ribbons of crimson. It fades as quickly as it came.

"Ella," I croak, walking out of the water with her in my arms.

"Oh, my Goddess, I thought I was going to drown!"

I scan her face as I lay her down on the soft grass that surrounds the shore of the pond. Her eyes glisten in the setting sun as she catches her breath.

"Are you all right?" I ask, cupping her face.

She shoves at me, coughing sharply. "I'm f-fine, Ryatt."

"Your powers–"

"I'm fine, really. I felt Amanda. I think I got to her somehow."

I nod, kneeling beside her. She turns her head and looks up at me, grinning madly.

"What?" I ask tersely, my body still racked by nerves.

"Your chest is healed."

I run my hand over my chest. "Which god do I thank for it?"

She smiles, closing her eyes as her breathing returns to normal. "This is the Moon Goddess's domain." She opens one eye and peers at me. "Are you… doing okay?"

"I'm fine."

She knows I'm lying but says nothing further as I help her to her feet. She pulls her dress over her head and lets it fall over her nearly naked body.

It clings to her wet skin, showing off her curves.

I look away as a twisting, heavy sensation settles in my gut.

"Are you upset with me?"

"No, Ella."

"Then why won't you look at me?"

I put on my shirt, squinting into the sunset. "None of this feels real."

"How so?"

I turn to her. She looks up at me expectantly, some of that infamous temper gleaming in her eyes. "Are you sure Amanda could hear us?"

"Yes, I'm sure."

"How?"

"I just know. Amanda and I are connected by my powers. I just had to give her a little nudge." She rolls her lower lip between her teeth in thought. "I know she heard me."

My focus is on her mouth, her lips. My body begs for her–to touch her, to feel her softness and warmth, but my hands curl into fists at my sides as internal dread begins to snake through my veins again.

"I almost lost you," I say out loud before I can stop myself. My tone is harsher than intended. "I came *this* close." My fingers pinch together as I edge toward her. "I didn't protect you. I could barely protect my people, my lands. Why did you bring me here? Why didn't you leave me in Eastonia to die? Why risk your life again to bring me through the veil?"

Her eyes darken with pain, her lips parting. "You told me you'd find me again. You'd find me again in another life, another body, and we'd have time. I didn't feel like waiting."

She brushes past me, stomping off down the gnarled trail leading away from the falls.

"Ella!"

"What do you want me to say, Ryatt? That you no longer deserve me? That I'm somehow mad at you for not being able to protect me from Kane?" She stomps back up to me, fire in her eyes. "I love you, for Goddess sake. It's more than the mate bond for me. I would follow you into hell and back, and honestly, I did. I don't blame you for what happened." Tears start welling in the corners of her eyes. "I was the one that failed. I used what little power I had left to kill us all, Ryatt. I brought Kane's fortress down on top of us. You were pinned. Westfall was crushed because of me. Kane was stabbing you and I–it would have been my fault if you died. I killed Westfall, didn't I? It was my fault!"

I reach for her, running my knuckles over her arm.

"I put on the mask and it felt *good*," she sniffles. "All of that power… it sang to me, Ryatt. It wanted me to wear it, to use it, to let it *consume* me. I used it to cut through the veil. And when we landed in Maatua, for a moment I… I didn't want to take it off. I didn't want to give up that power. I probably killed so many people bringing down the fortress, Ryatt. Innocents. What did I do when I broke through the veil?"

"Stop–"

"I didn't want him to take me. I didn't want him to kill you and use me as a breeder. I was terrified and nearly killed all of us. I would have rather killed all of us—"

I crush her to my chest and hold her as she falls apart.

11

HE'S A NATURAL

Ella

WE DON'T LINGER LONG at the falls. The sunset fades to a rich, velvety purple by the time I pull the car I borrowed into the massive garage behind the castle. Ryatt didn't say a word the entire drive back. I glanced at him a few times, noticing the absent look in his eyes as he hung his arm out the window, his fingers splayed in the wind.

Now we're seated at a long table made of glass. Platters of food cover the surface. It's an informal setting in the informal dining room in Poppy's massive castle.

"Here," Poppy says, standing to lean over the table and place two huge steaks on Ryatt's plate. "Eat up."

Ryatt meets her eyes with a soft nod of thanks. She's already laden his plate twice now, and he's eaten every morsel of food she's offered. Still, watching Poppy's motherly attentiveness to his unspoken needs curls in my heart and threatens to shatter it. She doesn't really know him, and what she *does* know about him can't be good. Yet, she exudes nothing but kindness and love.

"It's delicious, Poppy," I tell her as she sits back down. "You could have ordered pizza, and not gone to so much trouble."

She gives me a smart look, rolling her eyes to Ryatt, to whom she bestows a beaming smile. "Oh, please. With Antony on KiloKilo for the rest of the week and the twins out doing Goddess-knows-what on the mainland, I've had no one to cook for."

Ryatt arches a brow. "Do you not have a cook?"

"Of course, I do," she laughs. "But I enjoy it. Plus, when it's only me and my mate, or the two of us and our children, sometimes it's just easier to cook for ourselves. Hosting parties and the like is a different story."

I look back down at my plate and smile. Mom used to cook for us, mostly breakfast. She'd make pancakes shaped like animals topped with whipped cream and berries, and if we'd been especially well behaved that morning, she'd dump copious amounts of chocolate chips into the batter.

I cut into my steak, my eyes lifting to Ryatt's face, which is drawn and closed off, the expression behind his eyes unreadable.

Poppy talks throughout dinner, telling Ryatt about our family, little memories of Winter Solstice celebrations when the entire family would gather. Memories of my parents, of my childhood, of moments, I realized, he couldn't fathom.

It's not Poppy's fault. She knows as little about him as the rest of my family does. Ryatt never gathered with his family–with parents and siblings and cousins–for holidays. He never opened presents. He never walked down to the kitchen to find his mother making pancakes shaped like birds or dinosaurs.

From birth, he lived like a slave, beaten and tormented and forced to watch his mother go through the same thing, day after day. Then, as an older child, he'd lived in a witch coven where his childhood consisted of learning how to fight, how to use those powers roiling in his blood. He was turned into a weapon, then a king.

I watch him from across the table and wonder if he'd ever been allowed to *play*. Did he have a beloved toy, a blanket, or someone he could run to when childish nightmares woke him from sleep?

As a teenager, did he test boundaries and sneak out into the night? Did he have crushes, and fall in love, and get his heart broken only to move on swiftly and passionately like most young men do?

No, he didn't.

He never had that kind of freedom.

My eyes gloss over as I look down at my now empty plate. He'd only known battle, death, sacrifice, and oppression. Not love, not safety, nor comfort. And never *fun*.

No wonder he's so… so lost right now.

"Is Maury's still open?" I ask.

Poppy raises her brows at the mention of the rickety old dive bar on the far western edge of Maatua. "Of course. That place will likely never shut down, silly! It's a Maatua staple."

"How pissed do you think my parents would be if we went out tonight?"

Ryatt looks at me, but my attention is on Poppy as she considers my question. "Out on the town? I don't see why they'd have a reason to be upset. You're young, and technically, on vacation."

Vacation, sure. If that's what we were calling it now, I definitely planned to act like it.

"You realize," I begin, leaning back in my chair, "that my brother considers Ryatt a prisoner of the crown?"

Poppy shrugs. "Last I checked, you're on Maatua, not in Isaac's territory." A cat-like smile brushes over her lips. She turns to Ryatt. "Ryatt, my dear, you're too handsome to stay in tonight. Ella's right; the two of you should go out and make a night of it. I think you both deserve a respite from everything that's going on."

Ryatt opens his mouth to protest, but I cut in. "Does Antony have any clothes that'll fit him? Jeans?"

She rises, and Ryatt follows. He towers over her as he gives her an apologetic bob of the head and says, "No, we can't. We'll stay the night like planned, Luna. I am grateful for your hospitality–"

"Antony's not that tall, but I'm sure one of our warriors has something his size." She cuts him off entirely, waving a hand. "I'll see what I can scrounge up."

Ryatt says nothing further but turns pleading eyes to me.

I ignore him. He doesn't know how badly he needs this. How badly *I* need it. To have one night–a single night–where it's just *us*. Just Ella and Ryatt, and we're normal people enjoying a normal night out. A night when we can put aside everything that happened, and everything that's coming, and just be together.

A night of fun.

An hour later, dressed in a fiery red dress that hugs every curve and falls a few inches above my knees, I walk down to the formal foyer to find Ryatt leaning against the front door talking to a trio of warriors. He's wearing jeans and a white button down shirt, the first three buttons undone and the cuffs rolled to the middle of his forearms. He's brushed his hair back from his face and shaved. His jaw is sharp enough to cut glass as he slowly turns to me, his silver eyes igniting at the sight of me in the slip of red fabric I'm wearing.

"No," he says.

The warriors disperse immediately at his tone.

I reach the bottom step, my heels clicking on the smooth marble tile. "*Yes.*"

He licks his lips with heat flaring behind his eyes. Even in Veiled Valley, where showing skin is as common as their nightly thunderstorms, my dress would be considered suggestive, maybe even immodest.

But this isn't Veiled Valley–or Eastonia.

I give him a cat-like grin as I walk toward him, running my fingers over his chest. "You're mine tonight. You're going to do everything I say."

"I don't like this," he says, his voice full of suspicion.

"You will," I urge, smiling up at him. "Come on." I take his hand and lead him out to the car.

I REV the engine of the sporty little convertible I chose from Poppy and Antony's arsenal of cars. We drive around a winding curve, the city lights dropping below us like falling stars.

Ryatt winces but keeps his eyes wide open as I tear up the hill and come to a stop at the peak. It's an overlook with sweeping views of the island below and the sea beyond, everything painted in silver moonlight.

"I used to come up here and…" I grit my teeth. "Listen to music." It's a half lie, but I doubt he really cares to hear about my years of teenage debauchery. I'll tell him at another time, I suppose. One day, we'll have a teenager of our own, and who knows what she'll get into in Eastonia of all places. I shove the thought aside as Ryatt takes in the view.

"Do you want to drive?" I ask.

He looks right at me. "Really?"

"I take it you've never driven a car before."

"I haven't. I've never seen a car before."

He looks over the dash.

"It's not hard," I continue, putting the car in park. "It's a metal death machine, though, and Antony will have your head if you scratch his paint job."

"We'll be gone by the time he figures it out, I'm sure."

I hope so. I love being here with my family, but as the days pass, I miss Eastonia. I miss Amanda, and Granger, and Westfall–

My throat closes as his memory drifts through my mind. No. *No*. I won't think about him tonight. I won't think of anything, just Ryatt. Only Ryatt.

"Sure," he says. "I'll try it."

We exit the car, and he watches me as I pass him and climb into the passenger seat. He sits down in the driver's seat and adjusts it to fit him, following my instructions.

"That's the gas. That's how you *go*. That's the brake, okay? You have to use your right foot to press on the gas and the brake, never your left." I dig deep to remember my first driving lessons with my dad. "And this is how you steer."

Ryatt clutches the steering wheel. A feral look flashes behind his silver eyes that has every fine hair on my body standing on end.

This is a horrible idea.

"Ryatt," I say slowly, carefully. *"You could kill all three of us if you crash."*

"I won't crash," he grins, and it's a smile I've never seen him use before. Before I can say another word, the car lurches forward, the engine roaring, and my seatbelt snaps into place, pinning me to the seat.

"Ryatt!"

It's too late. Ryatt whoops with boyish glee as he speeds down the mountain, testing the limits of the car to its max.

He's a natural. He handles every sharp turn with predatory precision, and the stars blur above us as he speeds off into the night.

I'm obviously terrified. My eyes have been pinched closed for most of the drive, but when we reach the end of the long, winding mountain road, his driving calms, and he slows to a crawl.

I open one eye, squinting at him, then find myself opening my eyes wide at the look on his face.

Pure, unadulterated joy.

My heart squeezes as his eyes crease with pleasure.

"I'm getting one of these."

"How?" I ask with a laugh.

"We'll bring it through the veil." The teasing tone of his voice is something I haven't heard in a very long time.

"You're crazy," I whisper, but he playfully revs the engine, and then we're speeding off again.

But when it comes time to merge onto a busy thoroughfare, both of our confidence wanes to the point that he pulls over and reluctantly relinquishes the wheel.

I pull out onto the road. "You know, Isaac really likes to drive. He has a few sports cars like this back in Crescent Falls."

"It must be nice having this kind of technology available." Ryatt's tone shifts back to something cold and dark.

A lump forms in my throat. "I think that if circumstances had been different, the two of you could've been friends."

Ryatt eyes me wearily before turning toward the window. This side of the island is much quieter, more a local presence than the touristy east side where the castle sits. "I've never had a reason to make friends."

Because of war. Because of battles and skirmishes. Because he spent his entire life training to overthrow a tyrannical nightmare who'd killed his mother and threatened to enslave his people. Because people get taken from him, and some of those people get killed.

I don't want him to be thinking about any of this right now. I want to see that joy shining behind his eyes again. *I want him back.*

"What exactly do you have planned for us tonight?" he asks.

I huff a breath, turning my slightly anxious expression into a devious smile, and turn up the music in the car until it drowns out the voice in the back of my head telling me to turn the car around and give up on filling in the gaps in Ryatt's heart.

Not too long ago, I found myself floundering. I was a walking, talking ghost. A shell of myself. I'd given up. I had no hope of ever being happy again. I tried not to care.

I didn't let anyone in. Not Isaac, not Maddy. Not my parents.

I wasn't giving Ryatt that choice.

"We're going *dancing.*"

1 2

THE SHADOW KING OF CLUBS

Ella

Music thrums through the air, sending steady vibrations over every surface in the crowded, cozy bar. For being such an old dive, it's always busy, and always full of a young crowd.

A mix of lively pop and sensual, drumming house music plays on a loop. The lights are dimmed, and all around us people dance and sway to the music.

It's unlike any tavern or pub Ryatt's ever been to, I'm sure.

He looks skeptical as I clutch his hand and wade through the crowd to the bar.

I order three drinks. A sparkling water for me, of course.

"These are my favorite," I tell him as I whirl around holding two identical mixed drinks. I thrust them into his hands. He lifts one and sniffs, then grimaces.

"What is it?"

"It's called Sex on the Beach," I purr, giving his arm a little nudge as I bring my water to my lips.

"Why am I holding *two* drinks?"

89

"Because you're drinking for two tonight, since I can't."

Another scowl. He takes a careful sip and narrows his eyes at me. "This doesn't taste like whiskey."

"I don't think the whiskey here tastes like the whiskey you're used to. The foul stuff back in Eastonia would blind most people here."

He smiles around the rim of the glass before knocking one of the drinks back in one fluid motion.

He makes a face, his jaw flexing. "This is awful."

"Too bad. Poppy made me promise I'd get you drunk tonight so you'd loosen up a little." I look around, my body already reacting to the music and livery. A new song starts to play–something dark and full of drums. An EDM beat weaves itself through the music, and a deep, rasping female voice thrums through the air. It's a siren song. It sounds both new, and ancient, and my heart begins to beat faster and harder as my hips start to sway.

Ryatt reluctantly starts sipping on the second drink. I notice him looking out over the crowd, his eyes alight as he scans the bar for threats.

"We're safe," I tell him, resting my hand on his forearm. "No one even knows us here."

He says nothing as he nurses the second cocktail.

Sighing, I sip from my water and wonder what exactly I meant to accomplish by bringing him here.

A man bumps into Ryatt. Ryatt goes rigid, his teeth bared in a snarl at the group of young, college aged guys trying to make their way toward the bar.

"Sorry, man," one of them says. "Woah, that's a gnarly tattoo on your neck. Who did it? Cashton, down at Inked Up?"

"Who–Yeah," Ryatt says slowly, his eyes flicking down to meet mine. "Sure."

"Damn! I love his work. Shit–" The guy nudges his friend, who turns from the bar and sizes up Ryatt. "Got any more? I'm thinking about having him finish my sleeve."

"If you're going to ask him to take his shirt off," I cut in, staring up at the group of men now encircling us, "you could at least buy him a drink first."

Ryatt gives me a look, but the other guys howl with laughter, and then I lose my mate to a sea of men wanting to know about his scars and tattoos.

A few minutes later, I'm watching Ryatt with interest. He's drinking whiskey now, some color staining his cheeks as he talks with guys who have no idea that Ryatt is making up stories about how he got his scars. I'm sure some of the stories are true, especially the one about him and Granger starting a full on brawl at a pub, and Ryatt getting thrown through a glass window, but he's careful not to mention Eastonia, or his powers, or the truth behind some of the silvery lines that run down his forearms, collarbones, and over his face.

I feel myself slipping away from him after a while, the music pulling me toward the swaying crowd of dancers.

The last thing I see before being swallowed by the crowd is Ryatt's lips parted in a laugh, his head thrown back and his arms crossed over his chest. His shoulders are loose, and the whiskey in his hand is empty.

He's happy.

And maybe a little drunk, but mostly happy.

Mission accomplished.

I exhale deeply, closing my eyes and losing myself to the music. Each note echoes through my mind, sending me deeper into a state of numbness that banishes the anxiety and grief that has been clouding my senses for days.

Drum beats ignite my powers. I feel the energy coming alive beneath my skin, coiling through the veins as I lift my arms over my head and sway my hips. Nameless, faceless bodies grind to the music around me.

I let it all go. The memories of war and death. The feelings of heartbreak over what we've been through. The loss, and confusion, and the uncertainty of the future. Whatever happens…Whatever we walk into when we get back to Eastonia… I'll be okay. We'll be okay.

We can build the future we want.

We have a clean slate.

I run my hands over my breasts, my hips, my skin beginning to heat. I open my eyes and spot Ryatt leaning against the bar, watching every move I make. People chatter all around him, to him, but his eyes are locked on me, on my hands, on the way I run my fingers through my hair and lock my gaze with his again.

His finger circles over the rim of his fresh whiskey glass once, twice, and then he's stalking toward me, a predatory gleam in his eyes.

My breath catches when his hands clutch my waist. He pulls me in close until our bodies are touching, and there's not a single inch of open space between us.

I wrap my arms around his neck, my fingers trailing up the back of his neck and into his hair.

His mouth finds mine in a tender kiss, and then we're dancing in each other's arms.

We finally got our dance, after all this time.

The sky is full of stars when we eventually, finally, hobble out to the car. Ryatt has a smirk on his face as he slouches in the passenger seat. I look over and see him as the man he was when I met him for the first time at my brother's ball for Isaac's twenty-first birthday. The same night he'd asked me to dance, and I'd teased him instead, baiting him for his last name.

Little did I know I'd be driving my mate, drunk on whiskey, back to the castle in Maatua to tuck him into bed.

"The whiskey here is so much better," he laughs, leaning forward to turn up the radio.

"How much did you drink?"

"I dunno," he says, waving a hand in dismissal.

I glance at him, smirking. He closes his eyes, tapping his fingers on the arm rest to the music.

"You like this music, don't you?" Who would've thought Ryatt, the Shadow King of Eastonia, would be a *club rat*.

He rolls his eyes to me and gives me a sleepy smile. "I finally got to dance with you. I hope I remember it in the morning."

I grin at him. "We'll have years to dance again. When we get back to Veiled Valley, we can throw a huge party. A ball."

His smile fades, and I immediately regret my words, but then he says, "When it's all said and done, when the packs are secure and my borders drawn, I'll throw you a ball, and I'll dance with you until daybreak."

My heart squeezes hard in my chest.

"I promise, Princess."

My eyes water. I reach over and grip his hand, squeezing. "I know."

The castle comes into view. We drive through a private gate and up a long, winding driveway. It's the middle of the night. Poppy, who is alone in the castle beside the guards and servants, likely went to bed hours ago.

I park the car and unbuckle my seat belt, but Ryatt lingers.

"Are you sure you don't want to stay?" he asks, looking up at the castle, his hair trembling in the ocean breeze.

"I'm going with you, Ryatt. I told you–"

"I can't give you this," he says, his voice dropping. "I can't give you... I can't take you out like this, Ella. We can't dance at bars and go–go driving around. You will be hunted. Your power will always be hunted. You'll be a target just by being by my side. I don't know what we're walking into when we get back. I only know that I have a fucking mess to clean up. I have–I have to be something I swore I'd never be."

"The Alpha King of Eastonia?"

Silence swells between us. In the distance, the rhythmic song of the waves is a gentle hum.

"Yes," he says, meeting my eyes.

"You're going to take the throne?"

"There's no throne left. But if my people–if the Roguelands are to remain safe–I'm going to have to build a new throne. I have to keep the allies of King Kane in check, and that means becoming what I never wanted to be. It should be you on the throne, Princess."

My stomach hollows out.

He looks at me, a ghost of a smile touching his lips. "It *will* be you on the throne, one day. I'll ensure it."

"What if that's not what I want?" I ask. My heart is beginning to race.

"I don't think either of us have a choice. That's why I'm giving you the opportunity to stay here–with your family."

I reach over to take his hand, but he gets out of the car.

I exhale deeply as I follow him into the castle. Darkness swells around us as our footsteps echo off the tiles. My mind is a flurry of noise. I can't form a rational thought or make a sound decision, not now. Not yet.

We reach the guest room Poppy set up for us. It's huge and luxurious. A sweeping view of the west side of the island with its private beaches and dense tropical forest greets us as Ryatt shuts and locks the door behind us, letting out his breath.

I wring my hands, my eyes on the tide as it pulls toward the shore, when he comes up behind me, his hands sliding over my hips as he buries his face in my neck and inhales.

Another flicker of that shattered bond between us burns to life before extinguishing like an exhausted match.

I close my eyes and lean into his touch, ignoring the throbbing ache in my heart and the tangled thoughts in my head. I understand his rationale when it comes to my staying behind. He doesn't know what we're going home to. And I'm pregnant. Our child will be born into what sounds like civil war and unrest.

But we have to start somewhere, don't we? We defeated Kane.

That should count for something.

"I need you," I whisper as his lips graze down my neck. "*Please, Ryatt.*"

He lets out his breath, his teeth lighting over my shoulder.

If he marks me again, will the bond snap back into place, or is it broken beyond repair?

His touch becomes more demanding, the whiskey in his system loosening that iron tipped restraint that has been plaguing him for days. I feel myself letting go as well, his touch thawing the numbness in my heart.

"Mark me, Ryatt," I whisper, then suck in a breath as his teeth gently bite down on my shoulder, and he herds me toward the bed in the center of the room.

13

YOU'RE STILL MINE

Ella

I CAN FEEL his hesitation as he lays me down on the bed. It's soft and cool to the touch from the gentle tropical breeze drifting through the open doors leading to a starlit balcony. A shiver snakes over my skin—whether from the chill in the air or the fact Ryatt's hands are trailing down my sides, I'm not sure.

Time is hazy. How long has it been since we've been together like this? All of the events leading up to our final, and only, stand against Kane are a blur. And here, in Maatua? I feel like the minutes and hours either crawl or flash by before my eyes, making it hard to determine just how long we've been here.

But I know it's been a while since his hands have slid down my thighs, cupping my ass as he scoots me to the very center of the large bed.

Unlike before, when the lust and tension had been a burning flame between us, this feels different. Softer. Gentler.

I realize he's worried about me, worried about touching me, and my heart threatens to crumble when I involuntarily flinch when one of his hands brushes against my inner thigh.

He rears back, his face going dark with concern–and maybe even rage. His anger isn't directed at me, of course.

"Wait," I whisper, pulling him back to me, so his body is sheltering mine. "Just–just kiss me again, please."

But he doesn't. He hovers above me, his body tight with tension, and rests his forehead against mine.

"Is it–is it because you can't feel the mate bond with me anymore?" I ask.

He opens his eyes. "You're my mate. Our bond might be severed, but it doesn't change that fact. It doesn't change how I feel about you."

"How do you feel about me?"

"You're just fishing for compliments now, Princess."

I smile despite the heaviness in my heart. I'll do anything to keep his mind off what Kane did to me, how he touched me and cut the mark from my thigh with a blade of pure silver.

"Do you remember our first kiss?" I ask.

He eases off me and lies beside me. I roll over to face him. We're practically nose to nose now.

"In that little cottage in Granite Rise," he says, smoothing his hand down my arm. "You were so mad at me."

"You were being such an asshole."

His mouth ticks into a sleepy smile. "You got under my skin."

"You still kissed me, though."

"It was all I could think about for year," he admits. I'm not sure I've heard him sound so raw. "I wanted to kiss you at your brother's ball. When I saw you for the first time, and you mouthed off at me, that's all I could think about. That's all I thought about for years."

"Did you love me then?"

His eyes are pure silver in the faint moonlight drifting through the curtains. "No."

I roll my eyes and go to swat him, but he grabs my wrist and pulls me closer.

"I loved you," he continues, his arms wrapping around me, "the night you killed those hellhounds. But I knew it wasn't just the mate bond talking the night I found you after you beat the shit out of Petra and her friends."

The heaviness in my chest lightens at the memory of Ryatt storming into the bedroom at his house at the coven. I'd been washing Petra's blood from my hands, and the look on his face….

"I knew I loved you the night I went into the water in the lake and emerged to find you kneeling on the shore. The look in your eyes… I just knew you'd have my back, that you cared. That you saw me for who I really was and didn't care."

He brushes the hair from my face and kisses me deeply, his tongue sliding along my lower lip until my lips part and he sweeps inside. I moan. I can't help it. The taste of him is like the sweetest wine and the heat coming from his body warms me to the depths of my soul, breaking through the ice there. My mate. My *mate*. Even without that silver thread woven by the Goddess to connect us.

"I love you," I whisper against his lips.

He deepens the kiss to something rougher, more demanding, and I lose all sense of time and our surroundings, and then it's just me and him, skin to skin.

The red scrap of fabric I'd worn to the club, stolen from my cousin Daphne's closet, is a shadowed heap on the floor beside the bed in a matter of seconds. Ryatt's hands graze up my sides to my breasts, which are heavy and ache more than they ever have before. When I wince, he goes rigid.

"It's not–I'm not hurt," I rush out, clutching his wrist to keep him close. "It's because I'm pregnant. They're just–heavy. And they hurt sometimes."

"They're beautiful," he rasps, dipping his head to brush the words over my neck. "I enjoy looking at them."

"I'm sure they're hard to miss now," I say, a laugh trembling through my chest. It's cut short, turning to a breathy moan as he cups my breasts and brushes his thumbs over my nipples. Then his lips are trailing kisses over my collarbone, then my chest, then dipping lower.

"Oh," I breathe, closing my eyes as his tongue sweeps over my nipple. He kneads my breast, then turns his ministrations to the other one. My eyes nearly roll back in relief as warmth spreads through my body, settling between my thighs.

His touch sets my soul on fire. Somewhere, deep down, I feel a flicker of heat that has nothing to do with the way his mouth is traveling down my belly and over my hip bones, no. Somewhere I feel a single fragment of our shattered bond come to life. A single breath of hope.

I'll do whatever it takes to bring our bond back to its full power, even if it takes a lifetime. That's a promise.

I suck in my breath and cry out his name when his tongue parts my entrance. He growls with satisfaction, his hands gripping my thighs to hold me still, and I'm totally at his mercy.

My fingers tangle in his hair, my hips arching off the bed as he laps at my core. He pulls away, panting, and meets my gaze. His eyes are heavy with desire–a dark shade of gray that sends shivers licking down my spine. I want him inside of me. I need to feel his strength and possession. I need to feel like I'm his again.

I need his mark, desperately.

He crawls to me, hovering above me with his forearms resting on either side of my head. He kisses me again–wet, sloppy kisses that stoke the fire burning deep in my soul as his cock nudges my entrance, and then he thrusts.

His name is a prayer on my tongue as he fills me, stretches me, and stills.

I find it hard to catch my breath as I look up at him, finding him gazing down at me with so much love in his eyes it threatens to bring me to tears.

"You're mine," he says, pulling out slowly before thrusting inside of me again with more force. His hips grind into mind, his cock hitting that spot that sends my head spinning. "*Mine.*"

"Always," I whisper.

He kisses me again and doesn't stop until I'm whimpering around him, begging him for more, begging him not to stop as my body tightens, and white-hot tension curls through my belly and thighs.

Blinding pleasure mounts and explodes. My entire body spasms and trembles until I'm a writhing mess beneath him.

He doesn't stop or slow. His mouth grazes my shoulders, his lips warm and rough on my skin before I feel his teeth starting to sink into the tender spot between my neck and shoulders. He bites me hard.

The metallic tang of blood fills the space around us.

My body hums as if it's finally, finally, coming back to life.

But... the bond is still broken. I can't feel it, can't sense it like I used to.

Marking me again didn't work, and that thought alone is enough to make me want to burst into tears.

Ryatt senses this. He comes undone, groaning with satisfaction, but concern lines his features as he immediately rolls off me and crushes me against his chest, holding me there as we catch our breath.

"Don't think about it now," he rasps.

I rest my cheek against his chest and will myself not to start crying.

"I love you, Ella," he says softly. "I'm so sorry. We'll figure this out."

DRESSED in shorts and a loose white shirt, I walk downstairs with Ryatt in search of breakfast early the next morning. It's a bright, sunny day. It's already stifling in Poppy's massive seaside castle–but quiet. Too quiet.

When we reach the dining room, we found out why.

Poppy is speaking to a trio of warriors, her face flushed and brow furrowed, but her expression lightens when we enter the room.

"Oh, good, you're awake."

"Is something wrong?" I ask, stepping toward her.

"No, no. Nothing bad." She takes a breath. "You need to go to the private dock immediately, though and return to the Isles. I just spoke with your mom, Ella."

"Did something happen?" Ryatt's voice is still thick with sleep and the slight hangover he's nursing this morning.

"They're angry with us," I tell him, then turn my attention back to Poppy. "We'll leave right now. I'm sorry, Poppy. I knew my parents wouldn't be happy that we stayed–"

"No, sweetheart, it has nothing to do with that." Her eyes shine with sudden excitement.

I know what she's going to say before the words leave her lips. My senses go haywire as mingled excitement and worry battle through my chest.

"Maddy went into labor a few hours ago," she smiles. "She's doing fine, of course, but it's progressing quickly–"

"We need to go, now," I say, turning from Poppy to Ryatt, who nods in agreement.

"I have a yacht waiting for you with breakfast on board," Poppy says as she ushers us through the castle. She stops us before we reach the terrace that leads down to the private royal dock. Taking me in her arms, she gives me a squeezing hug and whispers, "Everything is going to be okay, Ella. I'm proud of you. Good luck today. Give your mom my love. And Maddy and Isaac, of course."

"I will," I reply, backing out of her arms.

I look at my mate, whose face is an expressionless mask.

Twenty minutes later, we're on a boat racing back to the Isles. Neither of us touch the breakfast laid out for us.

"I told Maddy I'd stay until the twins were born," I tell Ryatt.

He breaks his gaze from the water to look at me. "She must have known we have to leave soon, then."

When we reach the Isles, a feeling of dread has settled in my stomach. It gnaws at me as we race toward the house, practically flying up the steps leading away from the private dock.

And then I hear it.

Screams.

14

THE PROPHECY

Ryatt

THE MAIN HOUSE in the isles echoes with screams. Ella runs ahead of me, her face flushed and colorless as she darts up the stairs and out of sight, leaving me standing in the foyer. All around me, archways lead out onto a wide circular terrace that surrounds the house in its entirety, the view nothing short of peaceful and serene.

But the screams... gods, Maddy's shouts of pain pierce my ears and send shivers down my spine, settling in my gut.

Two women dressed in white rush past me, murmuring to each other as they carry handfuls of towels up the stairs. They pass another woman–another healer–carrying a basket of soiled linen in her arms. Blood stains the once white fabric as she runs down another corridor.

My stomach twists at the sight, and I turn toward the terrace, unsure of what to do, where to go, or what to even think.

I step out into the sunlight and close my eyes for a moment, trying to catch my breath.

But a scraping sound catches my attention. I open my eyes and turn my head, spotting Isaac seated on a wrought iron bench on the far side of the terrace. He has his head in his hands, his shoulders tense as another scream echoes through the house behind me.

It's none of my business. I remind myself that as I glance at the foyer behind me. But then, Maddy cries out again, and I turn back to Isaac in time to see him curl into himself, dragging his hands over his face.

I graze my tongue over my lower teeth, then flex my jaw. What do I even say to a man whose mate is giving birth to his child? In his case, children? Especially when it sounds like she is in excruciating pain.

I walk back into the foyer and search through the rooms that surround the staircase. Everything is open–every room connected by arches that lead to sitting rooms, a kitchen, and eventually a small library with a bar cart resting against one stark white wall, bottles of liquor glistening in the late afternoon sunlight. I thumb through the bottles, finding an untouched bottle of scotch. It glows with amber light as I tuck it under my arm and find my way back to the foyer.

The screams have tapered off, but I can hear the gentle hum of voices lifted in encouragement. That has to be a good sign, right?

Isaac is still sitting on the bench when I walk back out onto the terrace. I know he can sense my presence, whether by my footsteps or my scent, but he doesn't look at me as I approach, nor when I sit down beside him.

I open the bottle and take a long, deep drag straight from the source, then wordlessly hand it to him.

He takes it and drinks deeply, not bothering to look at the label.

We sit in silence for what feels like a long time.

"What does it feel like?" My tone is heavy, somewhat weary, and laced with an anxiousness I haven't yet been able to voice.

He knows exactly what I'm asking. "Like I'm losing her with every second that passes," he replies so quietly I almost miss it, his voice drowned out by the waves breaking against the cliff below. "I feel everything across our bond. Her pain, her fear. Her–her strength." He toys with the bottle for a moment before taking another long pull, and then hands it back to me.

"Why aren't you with her?"

He looks at me then, his eyes a bright, glacier blue and full of desperation. "What am I supposed to do to help her? I can't–" He cuts himself off, his breath catching in his throat. "I couldn't stand there and watch her suffer. All I wanted to do was shift and shred the room around us. Her being in pain is my worst fucking nightmare."

And I did this to her.

He doesn't need to voice those words. They're written clearly on his face as he looks out at the water again.

He sucks in a breath and exhales sharply. "The other women kicked me out of the room, anyway. I was told someone would come get me when it was... time."

A smirk plays over my lips as I take another drink from the bottle and offer it to him, but he shakes his head. I put the lid on it and set it between us on the bench. "You knew about this, though. You knew she'd struggle."

He stiffens a bit, keeping his eyes on the water. It's the confirmation I need. Ella said something to me about him a while ago that's been stuck in my mind ever since. *"My brother. He can do it; he can read the stars."*

Ella and I had been walking down to the lake during the eclipse when she'd told me, likely not realizing the significance of it.

"We call people like you *mystics* in Eastonia," I continue, resting my elbows on my knees. "They read the stars, pull the prophecies from the heavens."

I'm met with more silence. I glance at him, noticing the way his jaw has gone tight.

"No one else knows, do they?"

He reaches for the bottle. "No."

"Ella assumes."

"Ella knows only what I've told her and assumes the rest. I never told her *that.*"

"Did you see our arrival here?"

"Not clearly," he admits, clearing his throat. He licks his lips before continuing, "I don't know how to decipher what I see."

"If you'd been born on my side of the veil, you would've been scooped up as a child and spent your young life in training. Consider yourself lucky."

"I don't," he says. "If I knew how to use this... faucet of myself, maybe I would have seen the outcome of the war before it began. I would have seen that my assumptions about not having a mate weren't true and found her years ago, before she went through such disgusting treatment by her stepmother."

"What else have you seen when it comes to your mate?"

He closes his eyes and exhales slowly.

"I see two kings," he says, then swallows hard. "I see my hands splayed on a desk while I choose who is to take my place." His eyes meet mine. "But I don't see her. I don't *feel* her."

All I can do is nod. Several seconds of tense silence pass between us.

"Do you want to know what I see about Ella?"

I'm not sure I do.

He doesn't give me a chance to respond. "Before the war, I saw her plunging a knife into my chest."

"Yeah, that actually did happen."

He shoots me a look. "I'm well aware. My mate can't keep a secret to save her life."

At least he's not totally bitter about it.

"Ella will raise armies, she'll topple kingdoms," he says softly, distantly. "She'll turn on all of us."

"What?" My voice strains as I turn to him.

"I see her in a mask of crimson. I see her buried alive in her own grief to the point she forgets who she is and what she's fighting for. She loses something precious, and it kills her." His brows pinch together as he stares absently at the tiles beneath us. "It changes her."

"What does she lose?"

His brows raise. "I have no idea."

I lean back against the bench and cross my arms over my chest. "I could have lived without knowing this."

"If it makes you feel any better, I don't think it's *you* she loses."

"It doesn't, but thanks."

"I'm wrong more often than not. I get strange flashes of knowledge when I'm scanning the stars–like pieces of a movie that are all out of order. I don't consider it a power or a gift, by any means. It never makes sense. Never."

I try to tear my mind from the image he just painted for me about Ella. Another scream echoes around us. Isaac stiffens, seemingly holding his breath.

"Prophecies mean nothing, Isaac. They're just warnings. Possible outcomes. Maddy... she'll be fine. She has your mother beside her. Isla's gifts of healing–"

"And if she's not fine?" he says sharply. "I nearly killed my mother during my birth. Had it not been for that fucking diamond, we'd both be dead. My mate is having *two* babies, Ryatt. What am I supposed to do without her if anything goes wrong?"

The pain in his voice cuts me deep.

"I don't know," I answer, because I don't know what he'd do. I don't know what *I* would do.

"Your Highness!" A healer comes running out onto the terrace, her cheeks flushed from tearing through the castle. "It's time."

I stand and watch Isaac go, his shoulders rigid and hands flexed. He looks at me over his shoulder, his eyes locking on mine, and he gives me a slow nod.

I nod back, a silent blessing leaving my lips to whatever gods are listening. To the Goddess that rules this realm.

Then I let my mind wrap about his vision of Ella. He hadn't told me when it had come to him, if it was recent or something he saw years ago. She'd worn the mask to bring us here. She might have toppled Rifthold in the process.

She'd destroyed a kingdom. That had already happened.

But raising armies?

Against what?

And if his vision hadn't been about the two of us coming through the veil and what should have been my death, then what does she lose that would change her so greatly?

I run my hands down my thighs, squinting into the sunlight.

Then I hear a baby cry.

I let out a deep breath, closing my eyes against the sun. Voices travel down through open windows above me–laughter, awing, murmurs of joy and relief.

But I feel the change swiftly, like it's barreling toward me on a violent tide. Shivers of power coast over my skin, my shadows flickering back to life as I sense a threat.

I rise, turning toward the house just in time for a scream to crash through the air–a sound full of such anguish I nearly lose my foot as I race into the foyer.

"Maddy, Maddy, Maddy!" Someone is begging. Other voices join in–a chorus of pain and desperation that funnels down the stairs as I rush up them, skipping three steps at a time.

I charge into the room reaching behind me for the sword that's no longer at my back, the sword I haven't seen since I knelt in Kane's fortress and watched my father–my real father–get thrown by Kane's powers.

A crowd of healers, nurses, and Ella's family members gather around the bed as Maddy writhes, her eyes open to slits as she silently begs for help.

"This baby is far too big," Jane says. "Maddy, listen, we have to move you to the infirmary, right now–"

"No–no–" Maddy cries out, shaking her head from side to side. Blood pools out beneath her.

I look wildly around the room. Isaac is standing motionless, his arms cradling his newborn son.

But then I realize everyone is motionless. The room has simply... stopped moving. Voices hang in the air. The curtains fail to drift in the now still, silent breeze.

And then I see Ella, her eyes blazing with silver fire, whispering into Maddy's ear.

"It's all right. Catch your breath. Catch your breath, Maddy. You're doing great. You just need a moment. That's all. Breathe. *Breathe.* You can do this. You *must* do this. You're strong. You're just tired. Rest now. You're almost done. It's almost over."

"Death as in the displacement of the soul. Whoever has this power would be able to move through planes of time." Arthur, the librarian in Veiled Valley… his words whisper through my head as I watch in both awe and horror as my mate stills time itself to a crawl.

Ella has done this once before. She held Isaac's life in her hands for months.

What kind of power is this?

Ella looks at me, a soft smile playing over her lips.

And then the room erupts in noise again, and Maddy opens her eyes wide, and screams with determination.

15

ENDURANCE

Ella

I STEP BACK JUST in time to catch the bundle Isaac places in my arms before he rushes to Maddy's side. He falls to his knees beside the bed, holding her face in his hands as she sobs, her mouth pulled into a delirious smile.

I look down at the baby in my arms, who looks up at me with a scowl. "H-hello there."

His mouth pinches, and he begins to whine. I bounce him gently, unsure of what to do. I look wildly around for help, but the room is a tangle of healers trying to tend to Maddy and the second, much larger baby now resting on her chest while he's rubbed down with towels.

Maddy's hands shake so violently, she's barely able to lay a hand on her son's back, and Isaac… oh, Isaac is a blubbering mess, but I've never seen him so raw. He only has eyes for his mate. Only for her. His eyes shine with tears as he says, "Thank the Goddess," over and over again, pressing the words into her gleaming brow.

Mom watches the proceedings like a hawk and then hands Isaac a vial of tears, which he helps his mate drink.

My knees wobble with relief, and shock, and... so many differing emotions all at once. My powers ripple through me, still igniting and burning over my skin. Strong... they're strong. I could bring us back through the veil...

I barely register Ryatt at my side until his arm locks around my waist. He glances down at the angry baby in my arms before looking into my eyes, his free hand brushing the hair away from my face.

I know what he's about to ask. It probably goes along the lines of, "What the *fuck* did you just do?"

"Later," I tell him, breathless. I look down at my perfect nephew. "I'll tell you later."

Ryatt's gaze leaves my face long enough to look down at the baby. "Red hair," he says with a soft chuckle. "That means good luck in Eastonia."

Tears sting my eyes as we look at the baby together.

"How is he?" Mom asks, trying to catch her breath as she appears by our side.

"He's pissed off," I laugh, bouncing him. "He knows I'm not his mom."

"Here, I'll take him." She helps guide him out of my arms, and I feel a strange emptiness as my arms go weightless.

I watch my mom's face as she looks down at the baby. Her eyes widen then crease and fill with tears before meeting mine again.

"Whatever you did," she whispers so only Ryatt and I can hear, "thank you."

I fight the creeping sensation building in my chest. How had she known I just used my powers? Did everyone feel it?

Or were some people, like Ryatt, able to break through the yoke of pure energy I'd placed over the room, pulling time to a halt?

Ryatt guides us to the wall as a flurry of maids swoops in, blocking our view of the bed and the babies now resting in their mother's arms.

"Everyone's healthy," Jane says, her voice trembling a bit as she steps back from the bed. "Let's leave Their Highnesses in peace." At the snap of her fingers, the maids, nurses, and other healers begin to funnel out of the room.

Clean sheets have been laid out over bed. Isaac and Mom help Maddy onto her feet so the old sheets can be changed.

Ryatt's fingers trace circles over my spine in an absent motion while his gaze remains locked on the twins, and on Maddy, as she's helped back into bed.

"I'll go tell your father," Isla says to Isaac, her face glistening with tears.

"Would you please call for a dinner service? I'm starving," Maddy says weakly, her face still ruddy and shimmering with sweat and tears.

"We should go," Ryatt says, but Maddy's eyes snap to where we're standing, like she's forgotten we're still in the room.

"Ella–" she says, but Mom rests a hand on her thigh.

"Rest now, Maddy. There will be time to talk about what happened later."

"Your powers are back," Maddy says to me. Her face, once bright from pure happiness, twists into sorrow. "You're leaving now, aren't you?"

Now everyone is looking at me and Ryatt.

Ryatt's hand flattens against my lower back, his touch the only thing keeping me from shaking as I look at my mom, then my brother, then Maddy.

"Yes," I say, and it takes all of my strength.

I glance at Isaac and notice him looking at Ryatt. "There's a lot we need to discuss before you go back."

"I understand," Ryatt says, his voice steady despite the sudden tension in the room. "We will return to Eastonia in two days–"

"Two days?" Maddy's voice is heartbreakingly quiet. It tears at my soul, forcing me to turn from her and into Ryatt's arms.

Tears burn my eyes. Behind me, one of the babies starts to whimper.

"We'll order the dinner service," Ryatt says before giving me a gentle tug toward the door.

My heart begins to shatter the second the door closes behind us, and I hear Maddy's murmured protests about us leaving so soon.

"We'll never see them again, will we?" she says.

"Come on," Ryatt says gently. "I have no idea who to talk to about ordering food in this place."

I wordlessly lead him through the house and stop the first maid we find. A huge dinner is ordered with instructions to have it delivered directly to Maddy and Isaac.

Hungry ourselves, we accept a few snacks and sandwiches and sit out in the sun on the terrace, wordlessly eating while watching the sun drift lower, and lower, the sky painted bright fuchsia as golden sunlight fades into velvet hues of violet and navy.

The house behind us is peaceful and quiet.

"Is there any left?"

We turn at the sound of Cassian's voice. Ryatt stands from the bench we've been perched on for the better part of an hour and bristles as Cassian edges closer, one hand outstretched in surrender. Cassian's other arm... well, his metal arm is nowhere to be found right now.

"Where have you been?" I ask, rising.

The sunset cast his fiery coppery hair aflame in streaks of crimson as he looks from Ryatt to me with a shrug. "Trying to make sense of what happened, just like you guys, I'm sure. Hannah's upstairs helping Maddy with the babies."

He edges forward again, stopping short of us by a few feet.

"I've been meaning to find you, Ella, and apologize for how things were when I arrived in Eastonia. I... I didn't know," he says with effort, his eyes shining in the sunset. "I didn't know the extent of what you'd gone through to keep my mate safe against all odds. It wasn't your fault. She told me—she told me everything. She wanted to go with you. You two basically grew up together, and she didn't want to be parted from you yet." His jaw goes tight as he looks away from me to scan the water. "I foolishly believed, for months, that you'd killed her, or enslaved her...." He tapers off, watching my face as my brow furrows with shock. "It's been a rough year. The war, then Isaac's coma, then you–you left, and we were forced to act like things were normal. I couldn't, not without Hannah. You took care of her for me, and I am indebted to you–"

"You don't owe me anything," I rush out.

He looks to Ryatt then. "Have Isaac and Maddox spoken to you about the treaty?"

My blood heats as I look between the two men.

"No," Ryatt says, "but I assumed we were headed in that direction."

"Treaty for what?" I ask, even though I already know the answer.

"Peace between our kingdoms. Isaac wants me as an ally," Ryatt answers, then turns away from us. "I'll go to Maddox in the morning, once the excitement from the birth has dimmed." He flexes his hands, then walks away, not even turning to look back at me.

I turn my attention to Cassian, however. "This isn't just some basic treaty, is it? What do they want from him?"

"I don't know much," Cassian breathes, running his fingers through his hair. "I just know your uncle Ben has conferred with Alpha Elijah in Moorn, and the two of them have written something up regarding Ryatt's... armies."

"They want Ryatt to be available to fight if there's ever a threat here in Crescent Falls, don't they? Cassian, that's not possible–"

"But it is possible, isn't it?" He steps toward me. "It's already happened once. They saw the kind of... kind of tech, the kind of powers your new people possess. We'd be stupid to let such an allegiance slip through our fingers."

"And what do we get out of it?" I snap.

"Ryatt gets *you*, Ella. Those are the terms."

"You're joking!"

"In Maddox's eyes, and in Isaac's, for that matter, Ryatt stole you away. I heard your mate and Isaac had plans to spare. This is a more... diplomatic solution."

"I'm going home with him regardless," I grind out.

"None of this is up to me."

"You men and your–your stupid fucking games of divide and conquer," I hiss, shoving past him and following Ryatt, who is already out of sight against the glare of the setting sun, back to the guest house on the bluff.

Ryatt's getting ready to shower when I walk into his room. He meets my eyes as he pulls his shirt over his head, his already tan skin an even deeper shade of bronze from the few days we've spent in the tropics so far. Even his night-black hair has softened to a bright shade of onyx flaked with rich brown.

I've barely been able to look at myself in the mirror since we arrived.

"Come here," he rasps, motioning me forward.

I lean on the door of the room to close it and walk toward him, swallowing past the painful lump in my throat. His hands rest on my shoulders for a moment before he nudges me beneath the chin, forcing me to look into his eyes. "The treaty means nothing. I would be their ally anyway."

"I don't really know why it bothers me."

"You see it as a trade," he explains, his closeness bringing me much needed comfort as he brushes his next words over my cheek. "My allegiance to Crescent Falls, in exchange for their princess."

"It shouldn't be this way. I left them. I called out to you through our bond, and you came. You didn't take me, and they know it."

"But I would have," he says. "If I'd had to wait any longer to find you again, to have you in my arms… I would have taken you. I would have waged war against your brother just to have a moment longer with you, Princess. This treaty… it's just their acceptance of *us*."

"But if there's another war they'll force you over the veil. You, and your commanders, and their generals, will be called to fight."

"Crescent Falls would have to be falling in on itself before your brother would ever lower himself enough to call upon my aid," he chuckles. "Would you rather I fight with him like we originally planned? A fight to the death as wolves, as the Goddess intended?"

I go to swat him, but he pulls me against his skin, his lips crushing mine.

I melt around him, softening into his fevered warmth and rough caress.

"How are you going to do it?" he whispers.

"Cross the veil again?"

"I have my powers but not my sword."

His sword of shadows–lost somewhere in the rubble of Rifthold, no doubt. His sword, the conduit of his Shadowsynger powers. Without it to slice through the veil… it'll take all of the power I have to break through. "The mask."

"No, Ella–"

"It's the only way. We'll say our goodbyes tomorrow night and catch the last ferry to Maatua. Then, we'll go to the falls." I close my eyes, resting my cheek against his chest. "And then we go *home*."

16

———

THE TREATY

Ryatt

MADDOX WATCHES me from across the coffee table loaded with breakfast foods. Pastries, fruit, and meat sit on delicate plates, surrounded by bottles of juice and three carafes of hot coffee.

So far, coffee is all we've touched.

He's just been… staring at me. Staring at me for twenty minutes now.

I clear my throat, pouring myself a third cup of coffee. "I believe congratulations are in order," I say. "Two healthy princes and a Luna still living is nothing to scoff at."

"It's a blessing, to be sure." Maddox glances at the door, then back at me. "I don't expect Isaac to come to this meeting today."

"We can discuss your terms without him. He might be the king, but he's Ella's *brother*." I lean forward, resting my elbows on my knees. "Your opinion on this matter means more to me, and to her, than his."

"Have you spoken to her about the idea of her staying here, at least until the baby is born?" Maddox eyes me coolly, sternly, radiating that primal aura all born Alphas possess.

"Of course."

"And?"

"What do you think her answer was?"

Maddox's mouth ticks into a brief half-smile. "Then she will go with you."

"And what exactly do I owe you in exchange for your daughter?" The words are harsher than I intended, but this conversation needs to happen, and fast. Ella is already preparing to leave. She said her formal goodbyes to her parents earlier this morning. Whatever hour-long conversation she'd had with Maddox before he called me in to speak with him is still a mystery. Now, she's upstairs doting on her nephews while I sit here, facing her father.

Maddox turns to the window, lost in thought. "I won't be giving you a dowry for her," he says.

I resist the urge to roll my eyes. "Eastonia might be far behind Crescent Falls in terms for technology, but we did away with the notion of a dowry long ago."

"What is it about her that made you risk not only your life, but the lives of your allies during your time fighting in the war last summer?"

I stiffen as he slowly turns back to meet my gaze.

"You were a double agent," he continues. "You came here fighting against us, taunting my son, making us believe you were behind the threats and eventual battles that took place in the remote villages on the outskirts of our territory."

"You're correct."

"I want to know *why*."

"Alpha King Kane would have waged war against Crescent Falls regardless of my involvement. He had the power he needed. He knew your daughter–he knew Ella was a very particular type of wolf and wanted her in his clutches to pull power from, but he also knew it wouldn't be easy to get her unless I, her mate, worked by his side." I straighten up, crossing an ankle over a knee. Then, I tell Maddox everything. I tell him about my mother and her gifts, and her tortured life within the walls of Kane's fortress. I tell him about how I was stolen out of the fortress as a child, too young to truly understand what my mother and Westfall had sacrificed to get me to safety. I tell him about the Firestone witches–how his line likely gave Ella the powers she possesses. I explain my own powers–my shadows and energy–and then how I came to know Ella was mine.

"I was sixteen," I explain. "In the coven, the men my age were preparing to head out into the Roguelands to join the ranks of warriors commanded by rogue packs. I was… not keen on being merely a follower of someone else's command." I meet his eyes. "I picked too many fights, pissed off too many Alphas. No one wanted me in their pack because of the issues I'd cause, so the man who spent nearly a decade training me, Westfall, returned from a tour of the continent and brought me to Veiled Valley to undergo a type of rite of passage."

Westfall has brought us to the mouth of a cave deep in the mountains surrounding Veiled Valley. I had one task. Return with an item, and that item would show me my destiny in the world. But inside, I found myself facing incredible danger. Magical beasts, undead, things that should have existed only in nightmares….

"There hadn't been an Alpha of Veiled Valley for over thirty years at that point. The sword had been passed down by the ruling family for centuries, going from Alpha to Alpha. I pulled the sword from its resting place and used it to fight my way back to the cave mouth. But before I could reach the exit, I had a sudden… vision of hands. Painter's hands. Long, dark hair and freckles. Eyes the color of polished sea glass. I saw Ella and felt that first flicker of a mate bond igniting."

I didn't know she was beyond the veil until years later. I saw her only through my dreams. I saw her nightmares and learned later that she saw mine.

"When I finally narrowed down her location and found out who she was, it was too late. Kane already knew about her. He'd be searching for her, for her powers, for a very long time. And he was going to take her and burn your kingdom to the ground just to have her, so I sided with him, promising to bring her back, to breed with her to ensure the full weight of her powers were available for him to harvest…. But I had no intention of ever, ever, letting him near her. My people paid dearly for my deception of the king."

Maddox hasn't said a word in over an hour, but finally says, "You met her years before our war."

"I did," I confirm. I tell him about the mirror and how my power, and her power, is connected to it. "I knew we were mates that night. I had to see her, to talk to her, selfishly just to confirm my suspicions. I didn't realize how that night would torment her."

"She looked for you for years."

"I know that now," I say, biting back the sharpness in my tone. "I know she did, and I know the bond allowed my memories, my nightmares, to haunt her."

"You said there wouldn't be another Alpha King on the throne of Eastonia," he says, crossing his legs. A maid bustles in to carry away our untouched breakfast, and we wait for her to leave before he continues, "But I need you on that throne."

"I don't have a choice, anyway," I tell him. "We're going back to unrest, I'm sure. Kane had loyal followers who will be vying for the throne."

"And Ella will be your Luna?"

I shake my head. "Whatever throne I create to rule Eastonia in whole will be hers, and hers alone. It's what was prophesied. It's what my people have been waiting for. Eastonia was ruled by the Firestone witches and only knew peace with their queens on the throne. Ella will be queen, even if I have to lay waste to my own kingdoms to ensure it."

Maddox holds my gaze for several long, drawn out seconds. I wonder what he's thinking, if he believes anything coming out of my mouth.

"You have my blessing."

"I don't need it," I say.

Maddox eyes me, but the corners of his mouth lift in a half-smile. "Neither does she, but you have it all the same." He stands and walks to a desk, picking up a folder and sliding a piece of paper from it. He hands it to me with a pen.

I don't know this Ben fellow, but he is precise. Wordy, even. The contract lays everything out. I will be an ally to the royal household of Crescent Falls. Eastonia will never wage a war against Crescent Falls, and if we are called to help Isaac's kingdom, I will accept the call to arms and fight for him.

And, to my surprise, vice versa.

I look up at Maddox as I toy with the pen. He's not looking at me. His eyes are on the ocean and the dark storm clouds rolling in, blocking out the sun.

I look back at the lengthy contract. Once a month, on the eve of the full moon, Ella and I will make contact with Maatua. Apparently, Isaac believes the connection between Maatua and Eastonia works both ways and has finally accepted that his power might be similar to Ella's when it comes to manipulating the veil separating our kingdoms.

Any harm that comes to Ella by my hand would be considered an act of war.

I fight down a pang of fury that this line was added, but I'm not in a position to press the issue.

And, finally...

"It may not be possible," I tell him as I sign the treaty.

"Isla insists."

Ella's mother insists on a month-long return trip to Crescent Falls and Maatua once a year, every year, at least when it's determined that our daughter has the power to travel safely through the veil.

I set down the pen and rise, my bones creaking from being seated all morning.

Maddox doesn't pull his gaze from the window as he says, "Ella told me about Commander Westfall this morning."

My blood freezes in my veins.

"I'm sorry for your loss. She made him sound like a great man."

"He was my best commander," I say unsteadily.

"And your father."

"I didn't know until it was too late."

Maddox nods. "And this sword... you believe it's gone for good?"

"If it's not destroyed, it's buried beneath mountains of rubble, or has been taken by someone that may not know how to use it…. I'd prefer it be gone forever than for it to fall into the wrong hands."

"Ella is confident she can take you both through the veil using that mask. Do you believe her?"

"I do," I tell him.

That's it, conversation over. He walks toward me and extends his hand in a business-like fashion.

"Welcome to the family."

Family.

He leaves, and I stand by the window in the cozy office for several minutes lost in thought before leaving the room in search of Ella.

I find her resting beside her sister-in-law in the massive bed in Maddy and Isaac's bedroom, the twins nestled between them.

I darken the doorway, and my mate looks up at me, smiling. "Come look at them."

I look at Maddy, waiting for her gentle nod of approval. Isaac is nowhere to be found, which might be a good thing, because even with the treaty signed and sealed, I highly doubt he wants me anywhere near his children.

Ella scoops up the larger twin, the second born, and shows him to me. "Unnamed baby," she says with a laugh, "this is your Uncle Ryatt."

Seeing Ella with a baby is doing weird things to my mind and body. I give the baby a tight smile, unsure what I'm supposed to be doing. "He's a fine looking baby," I tell Maddy.

Ella gives me a sharp look before laying the infant back on the bed.

"I still can't decide what to name him," Maddy says, stroking a knuckle over her second born's rounded cheek. "This, however, is Sid. Short for Sydney, which was my mother's name."

"Isaac says it's a girl's name, not a name for the future Alpha King," Ella teases.

"Well, Isaac wanted to name him Thor, so I don't really care what he thinks," Maddy laughs. "What are you going to name your daughter? Have you thought about it?"

I watch Ella carefully as her eyes cloud over. "No, I–"

Shouts lift from below, followed by the sound of Isaac's voice ripping through the air. Maddy scoops up the babies and huddles them close as Ella rises from the bed and hurries toward me.

"What's going on?" Ella asks, trying to side-step around me toward the door, but I block her and shove her back toward Maddy.

"Stay here," I growl, then edge out of the room.

The staircase landing is only a few feet from the door, and as I walk toward the railing overlooking the foyer, several wolves come into view.

"What is it–"

"Ella!" I hiss, but it's too late. Ella is rushing toward the railing but stops short. I come up beside her, noticing the way her body goes rigid with shock, the color in her cheeks flushing of all color.

I follow her gaze and find it hard to breathe as my eyes lock on the man pinned to the floor by six wolves. He thrashes against them, his black hair gleaming in the midmorning sun.

But then he stills, and slowly, ever so slowly, looks up.

17

BACK FROM THE DEAD

Ella

"Oh, my Goddess!"

I don't care that I'm screaming for the entire world to hear. My voice echoes off the walls as I barrel down the stairs, practically blind, tears springing from my lashes and rolling down my cheeks. I trip over my own feet and fall to my knees on the tile just as Ryatt reaches my side and hauls me upright.

He doesn't let me go. I squirm in his arms, panting, reaching a hand toward the bloodied man staining the ivory tiles crimson.

Westfall's glacier blue eyes meet mine, but his expression is strained as the wolves hold him down. Several of the wolves have him by their teeth, blood pooling around the wounds they've inflicted by getting him on the ground.

"Isaac, please!" I shout.

Isaac looks from me to Westfall, confusion blurring his features.

"Alpha King!" Ryatt shouts, a touch panicked as he holds me back. "Let him go."

Cassian rushes into the room, cursing audibly as he skids to a stop. Hannah is hot on his heels but he swings his arm out to stop her. She gasps.

"Isaac, what the hell is going on?" Cassian hisses.

"Who is this?" Isaac asks the room, his voice stern and lined with shock. "Do you all know him?"

Voices lift all around me. Ryatt and Isaac are arguing, Cassian cutting in and trying to explain, but my eyes are locked on Westfall as he pants under the strain of the weight still pinning him to the ground. His eyes remain on mine, and when his mouth lifts into a ghost of a smile, I feel myself coming completely undone.

The room around me spins. My vision begins to go dark at the edges.

"I'm going to pass out," I whisper, unsure if Ryatt, who is the only thing keeping me upright, can ever hear the words as I slump forward.

The voices get sharper, louder, and then I'm on the ground and my vision blurs to the darkest kind of night.

"Ella, Ella..."

"Wake up, Princess, come on..."

"What happened? Isaac, why is she..."

"Luna."

I open my eyes, blinking into blinding sunlight. Shadows pass over me, hovering above me, and then faces come into view.

I blink up at my mom, who smiles softly down at me. "Hi, there."

"What happened?"

"You fainted."

I look up at the owner of the voice, none other than my mate, who looks pale and concerned as he brushes his thumb over my tear stained cheek.

My eyes ache as Isaac and Cassian come into view.

"She's fine, really," Mom says to Ryatt, placing a hand on his back. "You didn't eat breakfast, did you?"

"What—I—" I try to sit up, but my body feels heavy and tingly. My heart begins to race again as a sudden realization strikes me, and I shoot into an upright position so quickly I nearly crack my head against Ryatt's chin.

I whirl, my palms braced on the tiles as I look at the man sitting across the room, six wolves scattered behind him.

"How?" I ask. "How are you alive? How are you here?"

"We have a lot of training to do when we get home," Westfall breathes, his shoulders uncharacteristically slumped.

IF HISTORY BOOKS are ever written about my family, this moment would be something people would read and probably not believe.

The formal dining table is full to the brim but silent save for the scraping of forks and knives. The heads of two kingdoms sit and stare at glasses of fine wine and plates full of seafood and steak.

No one says a word. No one mentions the elephant in the room. No one, in fact, has said a Goddess-damned thing all day.

Westfall had been ushered to the infirmary once Isaac deemed he hadn't stormed the isles to kill all of us, and Ryatt had promptly tucked me into bed and told me to stay there or *else*.

Hours later, I woke up to my mom shaking me by the shoulder and telling me I needed to get up and get dressed for *family dinner*.

She explained, with heartbreaking calm despite the heaviness in her voice, that she wanted one normal night with the family together before we returned to Eastonia.

This wouldn't be a normal night, however.

Two kings sit at one table. Two enemies, up until a few days ago.

I glance down to the far end of the table where Isaac is seated at the head flanked by Maddy, who is glowing and doting on Sid, the only named prince. Hannah rocks the sleeping unnamed prince in her arms, her cheeks rosy and eyes creased with happiness as she watches the baby snooze in her arms.

Cassian, seated beside her, meets my gaze as my focus sweeps down the table again. He gives me a look that says it all—what the actual fuck is going on?

Ryatt clears his throat and reaches for his glass of wine. His thigh brushes against mine under the table.

My dad, seated at the opposite end, glances at us before looking at the stranger seated beside him.

Westfall eats in silence, his face swollen and beaten to a pulp.

"We should do this more often," Mom jokes, and I choke on the iced tea I'd just taken a huge gulp of.

"I should explain," Westfall says, wincing a bit as he moves the ice pack he's been pressing to his left eye to his right cheek.

"Yes, you should," Ryatt agrees, his voice low and full of suspicion.

This is not how I thought this would go. In fact, I never once thought Westfall somehow coming back from the dead to be a possibility.

"No, this is *family dinner*," Mom says, shaking her head. "We have a strict rule in this family about not discussing business over dinner. Right, Maddox?"

Dad purses his lips. "That's correct." He doesn't sound that convinced right now.

"If you're alive, then King Kane could very well be too," Ryatt says sharply, ignoring my parents completely.

That puts a damper on things. Isaac immediately rises and throws his napkin on the table, snapping his fingers as he points to the door. "Meeting, now, in my office."

Most of the men rise, looking relieved, but Westfall winces as he tries to stand.

"King Kane is dead!" I shout, sensing the rising tension. "I killed him. I watched him turn to *dust*." I turn my gaze to Westfall. "I watched you die. *What happened?*"

Ryatt's hand curls around the back of my neck in a gentle embrace, settling me, but I'm still trembling as I hold Westfall's gaze.

"I woke up on a beach," Westfall says, his voice full of gravel. "I was taken back to what I believe was a healer of some kind, and over the past few days, I've been regaining my strength."

"What beach?" Dad asks calmly.

Westfall's eyes meet his as if for the first time. He sizes my dad up, taking in the man, the wolf, and the king he used to be. "It didn't have a name. I was on a very small island roughly sixty miles from here, to the south."

"The Andrion Archipelago?" Mom whispers, looking around the table. "How did you end up there?"

Westfall looks at me then. He really looks at me, taking in my face and the way Ryatt's hand is still resting against the back of my neck as he stands behind me.

"You used the mask, didn't you?"

"I had to."

"You shouldn't have," he scolds.

"You will watch how you speak to my daughter," Dad growls, losing that yoke he normally has on his emotions.

"Your daughter," Westfall seethes, "is the most powerful being to have ever walked not only your lands, but ours. What she can do… it rivals the powers of gods. Do you all understand that?"

Every fine hair on my body stands on end. I've never seen Westfall so raw before. He scans the room, his eyes landing on me once again. "You don't know how to spirit yet, not effectively. You could have brought an entire army through the veil by accident, Ella. You could have torn it down completely."

Ryatt goes still behind me. My parents exchange glances.

"Isaac can do that too," Maddy says from the end of the table.

"Maddy," Isaac whispers, shaking his head.

"Then he can help us get back through the veil," Westfall replies without skipping a beat. "Ella, you can't control these powers yet. Your fire, yes, but this magic is something else entirely. I should have trained you better."

"I saw you die." I don't care about the rest. I'm powerful, so what? That's been drilled into my mind over and over again. I could ruin the world, kill everyone, and will always, always, have a target on my back.

I don't care.

Westfall's eyes undergo a great change. He inhales sharply, leaning back in his seat and placing his swollen, bruised hands on the table. "I don't know what happened in that regard, but what I do know is that you left Eastonia in shambles, Ella. If Kane is truly dead, there will be war. His allies, which are plenty, will rise to try to claim his throne, especially if they believe Ryatt to be dead. We need to return. You need to return."

"Why?" I ask. My mouth is so painfully dry.

"You're the queen our people have been waiting for. There will be no peace in Eastonia until you're on the throne."

"I don't want the throne," I say for the first time. The truth rings through the room.

I know everyone is looking at me.

"You don't have a choice," Westfall says with effort. He looks at Ryatt, his son, and says, "You knew she never had a choice."

Isaac and my dad exchange looks. I can tell they're talking over the mind-link, because dad nods and spins on his heel, leaving the room. Isaac turns to us, his expression grave. "We need to leave for Maatua as soon as possible if the plan is still to breach the veil from the falls."

I swallow hard past the lump in my throat as I look down at the table at my mom, Maddy, Hannah and the twins.

"I'm so sorry," I say. For what, I'm not even sure. But it feels like the right thing to say.

"We'll be able to do this again," Mom says, but her throat strains around the words. She sets her fork down and rises.

She leaves the room without looking back at any of us.

Maddy holds my gaze for a long, long time. "I love you, Ella."

"I love you, too."

She rises, followed by Hannah, the two of them juggling the twins. Maddy starts to walk out of the room, but stops, turning to face us, to face Ryatt.

"Do you want to know the name I decided on for my son?" she asks him. She motions to the sleeping prince in Hannah's arms. "This is Ryan. I named him after you, for everything you've done to keep my sister-in-law safe, and everything you did to keep me safe during the war. Isaac refused to name him Ryatt outright, of course. But, he's your namesake. Remember him, and your family on this side of the veil, when things are dark in Eastonia. We will always be here for you."

My heart threatens to crack as I watch the Luna of Crescent Falls walk out of sight.

Behind me, Ryatt is still as stone but lets out an audible breath.

18

REMEMBER WHO YOU ARE

Ella

I CAN READILY ADMIT I've never been good at goodbyes. I left Maddy in the woods during the war, for example, running toward what I was sure was death at the hands of my own mate or to throw myself between him and my brother.

I stabbed my brother in the chest and put him into a magically induced coma rather than tell him I was thinking about leaving and crossing the veil.

And then I ruined his fancy party by having Ryatt create a Goddess-damned portal in the middle of my family's throne room.

Even faced with being separated from Ryatt by war, I chose to ignore his very valid points about how dangerous King Kane was and fought with him instead of just saying *goodbye*.

I brought Ryatt here and put my whole family through the wringer instead of letting him die because I couldn't, and never could, say goodbye for a final time.

I doubt I'll ever change.

I don't want to, honestly. I'd rather sneak off into the night than go through… this.

My family looks morose and uncomfortable in Poppy's grand dining room. We've spent the day traveling on a boat, then dancing around the memory of the tense family dinner last night. When we arrived back on Maatua, I found that Poppy had everything about our departure handled. There will be fireworks all over Maatua tonight to celebrate the birth of the new princes of Crescent Falls.

It's a distraction, obviously, to cover the light-show my powers are sure to produce when I rip through the veil.

If I'm even able to.

I glance at my mate, who is stone faced and murmuring with my dad and Isaac. At least they're getting along now at the final hour.

My mom and Poppy are talking with Maddy and Hannah while the twins sleep in one of the bedrooms upstairs, looked after by a trio of Poppy's best maids.

Maddy, Isaac, Hannah, and Cassian are headed back to Crescent Falls tomorrow with the twins. My mom will be following them to spend a few weeks helping Maddy adjust.

Just like that, their lives go back to normal.

I turn my back on the quiet conversations and rest my elbows on the railing of the balcony overlooking the quiet private beach. On the inky dark horizon, at least a dozen boats wait for the impending fireworks show. I'm sure if my viewpoint were of the east side of the island, I'd see the sprawling markets and beachside resorts alive with activity, the busy public beaches full of people milling about in anticipation of what the royal families have planned for them tonight.

All while I try to keep myself, my baby, my mate, and his father alive bringing us home.

I groan, leaning down to press my forehead against the cool stone railing.

"Poppy's going to fetch the mask." Mom's voice is soft and clear over the distant crashing of waves.

I don't bother raising my head. I don't want her to see the tears springing to life along my lashes.

I can sense her closing in on me, but she sits in a patio chair and sighs deeply. I peek at her and see that her eyes are closed, and her face is tilted toward the night sky.

"When I was pregnant with you, a priestess from KiloKilo told me you'd have great power. She also said you'd have to make an incredibly difficult choice. What I didn't understand then is that I'd be the one making the most difficult choice of all."

I raise my head. "What do you mean?"

She opens eyes clouded with tears. "Letting you go."

My heart cracks. This is exactly why I hate goodbyes.

"It's not forever," I tell her, but she shakes her head.

"Forcing your brother and father to add a stipulation in that treaty about you and Ryatt coming back here once a year is wishful thinking. It very well could be forever. I think we both know that."

"I wish things were different. I really do–"

"But you love it over there, don't you?" She meets my eyes, and a soft smile touches her lips.

I struggle to swallow past the lump in my throat, but I nod. "I miss it. I didn't realize how much I'd miss it and… Ryatt–" I look toward the dining room where Ryatt is still standing with my brother and my dad. He looks so… hollow. That spark of life, danger, and adventure is all but gone.

He doesn't belong here and never will. "He's home to me, Mom. I thought it was just Eastonia that called to me. I thought it was something about my powers and my wolf that felt at home there, but it's him. It's always been him."

She smiles wistfully, chuckling lightly as she turns to look out over the water again. "You haven't had a nightmare since you found him, have you?"

"No. Well, just one." A flash of memory of my nightmare of King Kane comes to the surface of my mind.

Mom stands and walks to my side. "This feeling will pass. Those memories of what you went through will be less painful overtime. This…." She motions to the room behind us. "Our family? We're going to be here. We have a way to communicate now. You were meant for more, Ella. From the moment I first laid eyes on you I knew, somehow, someway, you'd be a queen. It was in your blood. I thought maybe your mate was an Alpha King of some far off territory, and in fact, he is, but… the veil can't separate our family. You proved it when you came back through. Love is truly the most powerful magic of all, and that will never change."

She squeezes my hand just as Poppy's voice sounds over the conversations inside, "It's almost time! The three of you should get going if you're going to do this during the firework show."

Mom and I look at each other. "You can do this, Ella."

"But what if I can't?"

"You know what to do. You've done it twice before. You saved Hannah and Cassian. You saved Ryatt. Now it's time to go home."

Home. I'm going home.

I turn to look into the dining room. Ryatt is staring at me, his eyes heavy with an emotion I've never seen cross his face before. Resignation, I think. Maybe he's thinking I'm suddenly having second thoughts about returning to Eastonia.

I know if I went to him and told him I'd changed my mind and I want to stay with my family, he wouldn't fight me about it. In fact, he might be relieved.

But we have work to do. We have a kingdom to rebuild. We have a mate bond to mend.

And then there's the matter of his relationship with Westfall, his real father. He'll need to address that when we return to Eastonia.

I'm awarded quick hugs and tears from Maddy and Hannah, who make me promise to reach out when I can. My dad simply looks into my eyes for a long moment before leaning down to kiss me on the cheek and to tell me to behave myself, like he used to say when I was just a little girl.

It breaks my heart in two to back away from him and nod while forcing myself not to burst into tears.

I follow Ryatt, Isaac, and Westfall out of the dining room but spare one last glance at my mom. She's still on the patio, her back turned to the room and her eyes on the stars above. I know she'll stand there until the last flickers of my powers ebb across the sky and fall like stardust over the ocean.

My mate and Westfall are silent as we walk out of the castle to an awaiting car that will take us to the trailhead leading to the falls, but footsteps behind us catch my attention.

Isaac is walking briskly toward us, carrying an iron box in his hands.

"Is that the mask?" I ask.

Isaac nods and glances back at the castle with a sigh, then meets my eyes. "I'm coming with you to the falls. I need to see this for myself."

He knows the dangers. I could fail. I could hurt all of us or take him with us by accident. Without Ryatt's powers at their max, and without his sword, this is all on me.

But, like Mom said, I've done this twice before.

"Okay."

RYATT AND WESTFALL are nearly identical in their wolf forms. Tendrils of shadowy power ripples around them, cutting through the moonlight drifting through the towering palm trees overhead. In the distance, the first fireworks are just starting to crackle through the air.

I haven't shifted. Not yet, at least. While my powers are more concentrated in my wolf form, according to Ryatt, Westfall, and even Isaac, I'm not sure the mask will work if I shift.

I'm reminded repeatedly that I have no idea how any of this works as I follow behind the most powerful wolves in history.

Isaac would love Eastonia. I know that for a fact. Something about that place feeds the powers woven within us and turns them into something new.

Maybe one day this rift I've caused between us will be mended, and he can visit, one way or another.

The thought reminds me that despite all odds, I have a future. All was not lost when we defeated King Kane.

The sound of the falls cuts through the dizzying crackle of the fireworks.

It's time.

The iron box–Poppy's attempt of keeping the power of the mask leashed–is suddenly heavier than it had been during our walk to the water's edge.

'Staying in our wolf forms will be the safest manor of travel, especially with Ryatt still lacking full use of his power,' Westfall says through the mind-link.

'You sound like you've done this before,' I reply, setting the box down on the ground and kneeling before it, my fingers undoing the latch holding it closed. I meet Westfall's eyes–a sharp, glacier blue against his black fur. Ryatt is several yards behind him, silver eyes scanning the trees surrounding the water.

'Ryatt's mother did her research,' is all he says.

Pain laces his voice, and I know better than to press the subject. He's alive, which means I'll have time to force him to tell me *everything*.

Isaac, who isn't privy to the mind-link shared between myself, Ryatt, and Westfall, says, 'How are you going to do it?'

Aloud, I reply, "When I sent Hannah and Cassian home, I just imagined them landing here, in the water. I needed them both to land somewhere they could quickly get to help, and they were both in bad shape. I just… imagined the falls." I turn to my brother, whose golden fur ripples in the soft breeze coming off the falls. "I'm going to do the same thing. I'm going to imagine where we need to go."

'The lake' Ryatt says. 'The lake at the coven will be the safest option. Or, better yet, the mirror room in Veiled Valley.'

'Is that where you were trying to take me when I let go of your hand?' I ask through the mind-link.

Ryatt's cold, silver stare is all the answer I need. Yes, in fact. It was, before I went and ruined it, leading him on a wild goose chase across the Roguelands.

I pull the mask from the box. It looks like a piece of costume jewelry, like something I'd wear to a masquerade ball. Without my powers coursing through it, it looks and feels... cheap. Empty, and cold.

'Carefully, Princess,' Ryatt hisses into my mind.

I put the mask on as fireworks crash overhead, turning the sky a vibrant, electric blue. Poppy was right about the celebration being a perfect distraction from what's about to take place.

The second the mask touches my skin, I feel... everything. Every ounce of my power hurdles to the surface, thrumming over every inch of my skin.

I can't describe the feeling. It's the best, and also the worst, thing I've ever felt. It's dangerous and exhilarating.

'Ella.'

I turn to look at my brother at the same moment Westfall and Ryatt begin backing into the water. The mask begins to glow a bright crimson, the heat of it rushing over my skin.

'I don't blame you for what you did during that final battle. I understand why you did it, why you stabbed me. I forgive you. I wouldn't be here had you not done it. I wouldn't know my sons. You saved us both. You saved us all. Remember,' he says, taking a single step toward me, but my feet are already in the water, like I'm being pulled into it against my will, 'Remember who you are. Remember who used to wear that mask.'

'Goodbye, Isaac.'

My fingers curl into Ryatt's fur, and everything goes black.

19

———————

SHATTERED CASTLE

Amanda

"Lovely," I say out loud as I run my fingers over the fine lace runner covering the length of the formal dining table in the castle in Veiled Valley. "More flowers, I think. What do you think of lilies, perhaps?"

A light breeze drifts around me before crystal vases full of lilies, snapdragons, and tulips of several different shades appear out of thin air and drop onto the table. The scent of the flowers is rich and sweet, like the spring air outside. Veiled Valley is beautiful in late spring. Warm and lush and glowing with pale green as I lift my gaze from the table to the massive windows and archways leading out onto the sweeping veranda.

"I love it, thank you," I say to the house and step away to admire our work.

With Granger still traveling through the Roguelands, I've returned to Veiled Valley. It feels good to be here again. This place—this city, and this magical castle—feels like home now.

And being the Beta's wife comes with responsibilities that keep me more than busy. Like, for example, entertaining the high ranking ladies who are married to the various commanders and generals who are still off trying to restore order to the Roguelands.

"I believe the guests will be here around noon," I say to the house all around me as I walk out onto the veranda. "And after lunch, we'll have a short tea service–"

A ripple of energy courses through the house. It's not the usual flutter of air I've grown used to whenever the magical spirit of the castle is nearby. No, this is something else, something that sends a shiver of panic licking up my spine as I whirl back to the archway leading into the dining room. Multicolor specks of light dance across the obsidian floor tiles, brought to life by the stained glass windows. Nothing seems amiss.

But then the ground starts to tremble hard enough that the fine china and crystal vases on the table rattle. The shaking becomes so violent I drop to my knees, bracing my hands on the ground. "What's going on?!" I screech, praying that the house has some way to answer me. Surely, this isn't because I said we needed to add a tea service to the agenda today. The house loves to entertain.

A burst of air explodes through the door, causing every interior door to fly open and break off their hinges. Several of the windows around the room shatter, spraying multicolored glass in all directions. It sounds like the castle is coming undone, and my screams are absorbed into the echoes of showering glass.

I clutch my stomach, protecting the baby nestled there, and wait.

The trembling ceases, but I can feel the ground rocking beneath me as I slowly look up. Glass falls from my undone hair. The table I'd just spent an hour decorating is covered in shards of glass and mountains of dust. Water drips onto the ground from the now broken crystal vases, and flowers are strewn across the entire room.

Sniffling, I stand, dusting off the pale blue dress I'm wearing. The sleeves are slightly puffy but taper tightly at the wrists, and the flowing skirt hides the swell of my stomach as I slowly, carefully, step over glass toward the main door leading in and out of the dining hall.

"Are you okay?" I stupidly ask the house, but silence and still air is my only answer.

There's a ticking noise coming from the hallway. I follow it, my silken slippers silent on the stone floor as I look back and forth down the long, dark corridor. All of the heavy wooden doors are in pieces. Rooms I've never explored before are now visible–sitting rooms, offices, closets and stairwells leading who knows where.

But I'm alone in this place. Ryatt doesn't need maids or cooks when the house's magic provides that for itself.

Shuffling footsteps echo down the hallway, and I freeze.

A shadowed figure comes into view as they turn a corner, bracing their hand against the wall.

The air is stolen from my lungs as the figure sputters a rough cough, then sucks in her breath and curses audibly.

"Ella?"

"I'm sorry–oh, Goddess, what a mess–"

My heart thunders as I race forward, choking on my sobs, and throw myself at her so hard we fall to the ground with a crunch that echoes down the hallway. Tangled in each other's arms, I press a kiss to each tear stained cheek, my words a jumbled mess and broken up by sobs.

"I thought you were dead!" I cry out, practically pinning her to the ground. "It was really you talking to me in Granite Rise! I thought I'd heard a ghost!"

Ella laughs, her eyes creased and damp with tears, her hair wild and splayed out around her.

She's dressed oddly in what looks like a man's shirt with the sleeves cut off. Her legs are exposed, and her pants only hit her mid-thigh. She's also wearing the ugliest shoes I've ever seen in my life–clunky strips of leather with her toes exposed.

But she's alive.

She's alive, and she's here, in the flesh.

But...

"Where's Ryatt?" I ask, sitting up and scooting back to allow her to catch her breath.

ELLA

I REACH up and touch my cheek. It burns where the mask once touched my skin. That was the first thing Ryatt did when we appeared in the mirror room in his castle–he'd swiped the mask from my face with a massive paw.

The act felt like being dunked under water. I couldn't breathe for a moment while my power separated itself from the mask's embrace.

Where he and Westfall had gone with it is a mystery. Part of me is glad I don't know where he's going to keep it hidden and hopefully locked away, but another part of me feels a gnawing, almost desperate sensation at the sudden emptiness I feel without it.

Whatever magic was used to create such an item is of the darkest kind.

"He came back with me. Westfall, too."

"Commander Westfall?" Amanda gapes. "But I thought–"

"I thought he was dead too. Oh, Amanda–" My words are cut short as I pull her into a hug, the two of us kneeling on the floor together.

A scraping sound echoes down the hallway. All around us, a soft wind flows, carrying dust and what looks like glass in its wake. The castle groans and shivers as if annoyed by the mess I've created.

"I'm still learning how to do this. How to break through the Veil."

"You blew out every window, I'm sure," Amanda sniffs, picking a few shards of glass out of her hair.

We rise together, and I take a moment to look at my friend. I didn't think I'd ever see her again, not while being tortured by Kane.

"How are you?" I ask.

Amanda inhales sharply, blinking to clear the tears from her eyes, and then gives me a fox-like smile. "Bored out of my fucking mind. I've been hosting tea parties for the wives of the commanders since I returned to Veiled Valley. That's literally all I've done. They believe I'm about to become Luna and have been trying to weasel their way into my good graces." She arches a copper brow at me. "You still plan on being Luna, right? The last time I saw you and Ryatt together, you were about to rip his throat out."

"I can't guarantee that won't happen again, but yes. I am still the Luna."

"Well, the ladies coming to tea in an hour will be in for a surprise." She claps her hands together and looks around me. "Is Ryatt…"

"I'm sure he'll be here to inspect the damage I've done to his fancy castle shortly. I could use a shower, I think."

Amanda looks down at my arms, noticing the fine layer of soot covering almost every inch of my skin. She then looks down at her very beautiful dress with a long sigh. The pale blue fabric is now mottled with grime.

"Me too. I'll have one of the guards out front try to get word to Granger that our Alpha is back."

"Granger," I breathe. "How is he? How is… everything?"

"Don't worry about it now, Ella. Come on." She takes me by the wrist and carefully leads me over the debris littering the hallway. The house is making quick work of mending everything as we walk through a series of winding hallways and up two flights of solid stone steps. "Rest for a bit. We can have dinner together later, and I'll tell you everything. I'll take care of the commanders' wives, so don't worry about that. Honestly, telling them you and Ryatt have returned will probably be the fastest way to get word to Granger about it since they're all insufferable gossips. News will spread fast, I'm sure."

We reach the staircase leading up to the suite I share with Ryatt. Amanda squeezes my hand, then her gaze drops to my stomach. "The baby…"

"She's all right," I tell her, smiling.

"A girl?"

"Yes. At least, Ryatt says so."

Amanda places her hand on the swell of her belly. For conceiving our children on the same night, she looks far ahead of me. I haven't even begun to show yet. "I recently found out that I'm having a boy. The mystics at Moonrise held a ceremony because the Rite was successful, and I found out then." Her smile widens. "A boy and a girl, how fun! What if they're mates?"

"Over my dead body," Ryatt says dryly, and we both turn as he walks into view.

My chest tightens at the sight of him. He's dressed in all black with his black leather armor covering his chest, forearms, and thighs. Knee-high leather boots and his leather vest gleam in the raw sunlight coming through the shattered window behind us.

His hair is tied back away from his face, and his eyes shine like pure silver in the sunlight.

All he's missing is his sword.

He looks like himself again.

It's hard to describe how badly I've missed this.

I fight the urge to cower from the power emanating off him as he comes to a stop at the foot of the stairs. "Amanda," he says with a slight nod. "You look well. I'm happy to hear you're giving Granger the son he thought he'd never have."

She gapes, then quickly shuts her mouth and nods back, then meets my eyes. Her voice is a soft whisper in my mind, traveling down that faint bond between us created by my magic. 'I'll talk to you later.'

She's gone before I can say another word.

Ryatt watches me. I can feel his gaze on the side of my face as I slowly turn to look at him. "How'd you get dressed so fast?" I ask tartly, motioning to his leathers.

"I don't have time to stay here very long, Ella. Westfall and I are leaving for the Roguelands tomorrow at sundown."

I nod, knowing this was coming. "And what about me?"

"You're expected at the coven. You will travel there on your own, if you're up for it. If you want to."

"By myself? You'd allow that?" I give him a look. "Did you get knocked on the head on our way through the veil?"

His eyes darken, but he gives me a cocky smile that sends heat rushing over my skin as he replies, "I trust you not to get into any trouble on your way to the mystics."

"No, you don't," I laugh, rolling my eyes as I brush past him and start heading upstairs to our room.

He follows me, and again I feel like his power is taking up every ounce of air around us. I'd forgotten what this feels like. How powerful Eastonia is, how much it influences my own powers, and his.

We're back. We're home. And the only thing I want to do is pull him into the shower with me and wash away everything we've been through in the last week or so.

Our room is, thankfully, mostly intact, save for a few cracks in the windows. I walk to the center of the room and turn to face him before pulling my shirt over my head and tossing it on the ground.

Ryatt watches me with predatory interest, his eyes grazing over my bare skin as I step out of my sandals and shorts and kick them to the side.

"What are you doing?" he asks. "Is this little show for me?"

"I've missed how much of an asshole you are," I grin. "You were so well behaved in front of my family."

He takes a step toward me as I hook my thumbs under my panties and tug them down just a touch.

"Should I keep going? Or are you dead-set on running off to do whatever it is you do as Alpha?"

His jaw tightens as his gaze travels further down my body. "Keep going."

20

WASH IT ALL AWAY

Ella

RYATT EDGES CLOSER, slowly undoing the clasps and hooks keeping his leathers fastened to his body. There's so much hunger in his eyes right now. Gone is that distant look of resignation, of sorrow, and of disbelief that clouded his vision the entire time we were healing in Maatua and the isles. It's like coming home has brought my mate back to life.

I feel it too. My body's no longer heavy with grief and despair. My wounds have healed. My mind is no longer plagued by Kane and what he did to me and my body.

My body only reacts to the way my mate is looking at me right now. Like I'm a meal. Like he's been starving, and I'm the only thing that will satisfy him.

But it's been a while since I've seen that primal look in his eyes that makes them darken to steel. Ryatt won't go easy on me this time. He won't hold back. He's not afraid to hurt me now.

Because we made it home. Because we survived.

And because we have time he never thought we'd have together.

"Come here," he growls as his arm guards fall to the ground at his feet. I step out of my panties and walk to him slowly, my hair brushing against my lower back with each step. I stop roughly a foot away from him as he unfastens his vest. His eyes remain on mine, then drop to my chest, my breasts, and then my legs. "Turn around."

I obey, but chuckle, "Are you checking to make sure I made it through the Veil in one piece?" But then his hands clutch my waist and he pulls me against him so my back is flush with his abdomen. His mouth is on my neck, his teeth grazing my skin. His hands are rough as they slide up my belly to my breasts.

He lets out a shuddering breath.

My mind is empty. There's nothing but me, and him, and this moment. This new beginning.

I close my eyes as he presses a kiss against the new mark on my shoulder which sends an electric zing through my entire body.

"Shower with me," I breathe, unable to help the soft moan that laces through the words as his hands travel back down my body and over my thighs. "I'm covered in dust and soot, Ryatt. I'll get your clothes dirty." My words as rushed as his touch becomes more demanding. He's edging us closer to the bed. I know once we get there, there's no going back.

"I don't care. I just need to touch you," he whispers into my ear as his hand slides between my thighs.

My breath catches in my throat as his fingers glide through my core. Heat barrels through my body at his touch. He knows exactly where and how to touch me. "Gods, Ella," he rasps, roughly thrusting two fingers inside of me, his other hand pressed flat against my belly to stop me from moving.

I choke on a moan and throw my head against his chest.

"You smell like smoke," he says into my hair.

I can barely form a coherent thought as his fingers stroke me in all the right places. "That's because I'm pretty sure I was on fire at some point coming through the Veil. Oh–" My breath catches as he sinks his fingers inside of me again.

He chuckles low in his throat and removes his fingers, whirling me to face him. "You're incredible."

"I'm filthy," I tease, backing out of his arms. "I want to shower, and I want you to come with me."

"Do you know how long it takes to get into this armor?" he says, prowling toward me as I back toward the door to our bathroom.

"You poor Alpha baby," I pout, and his eyes flare with predatory lust that always has me on edge.

I used to push all of his buttons just to see that look on his face.

Nothing has to change, right?

He rips his shirt off just as I squeal and rush toward the bathroom door, but he catches me around the waist as I cross the threshold. He shoves us inside, the door slamming shut behind us, and the shower starts running as if on instinct.

I love this magic house.

His lips crush mine in a rough, heated kiss full of passion, longing, and the joy of just being alive and together. It's like everything we've done and had to endure led us to this moment.

We could do this slowly. I could run my fingers over his skin, outline each scar and tattoo. I could memorize every move he makes and every heated, possessive word he whispers against my skin, but right now, I just want him. I need him.

I pull him toward the shower. He rips off his shirt while keeping his eyes locked on mine, tossing it to the side. His pants go next, and then he's naked in all of his glory in front me, shutting the shower door.

My blood rushes through my veins and I back toward the wall. Mist curls up my bare legs as hot water slides over my skin, washing away the remnants of the journey through the veil. His hands clutch my waist, and then his mouth is on my neck, sucking the tender skin between my neck and shoulder.

I close my eyes and wrap my arms around his neck, dipping my head just as he looks up. He brushes my wet hair away from my face and kisses me, his tongue sweeping over my lower lip before plunging into my mouth and over my tongue.

Every touch reminds me that we're alive. I still can't believe it. The last time we were in this castle together, we had no idea we'd be facing death in a matter of days.

Now, we have our whole lives ahead of us.

He hooks an arm under my thigh and presses me against the wall. His cock is hard as steel and pressing against my stomach as he deepens the kiss, stealing the very breath from my lungs as I moan around him and grind against him.

"Please," I whimper, canting my hips against his. I have to stand on my tip-toes to meet him, and even then, he's lifting me a few inches off the ground as the head of his cock nudges my entrance.

"Beg," he growls, and it's my undoing.

"Please," I whimper, losing control of my body and mind. All there is is him. His touch, his cock pressing inside of me with little gentleness. He fills me completely, stretching me with each glorious inch. "Please, Ryatt."

He fucks me hard against the wall in the shower. I'll have bruises on my hip bones tomorrow from where he is holding me so tightly, claiming me as his again and again.

"Your body is fucking paradise," he rasps in my ear, groaning as he slides out fully before thrusting in again. "I can't get enough of you, Princess. You're all I think about. All I want is to be buried inside of you."

I close my eyes as white-hot tension begins to tighten through my thighs and lower belly. His praise has me coming undone as that tension gives way to blinding, soul-shaking pleasure that rips through me and tangles with the powers currently lying dormant in my veins.

"I want you to come," he whispers against my neck, biting down ever so slightly.

The climax is stronger than any I've ever felt before. It hits me like a rogue wave, tugging me under fathoms of water, drowning me in its current. I scream his name as my body ripples with energy, my muscles spasming around his cock that's still buried deep inside of me. He grunts, his teeth biting down on my shoulder hard enough to leave another mark, and fills me with his warm seed.

I open my eyes with the intention of watching my mate lose himself to the moment, but a faint opalescent glow fills my vision instead.

"Ryatt," I breathe at the same moment he notices the light as well.

The light coming from my skin, and from his.

Slowly he lowers me to my feet and steps away, looking down at his hands, then back at my body.

"What is this?" I ask, turning my hands over to look at my palms. The light fades as quickly as it came. Painless and beautiful, the light dissolves like stars being washed away by the oncoming sunrise.

Ryatt steps toward me again. His expression has softened, his eyes now lovingly locked on mine as his mouth quirks into a disbelieving smile. "I believe… that was your powers."

I make a face. "I don't know–I didn't feel anything. It was just light."

"You're… incredible," he says, his eyes so full of awe. He presses a gentle kiss to my lips, whispering, "but you're also fucking dangerous, Ella. We need to know what else you can do. I don't want to be blown to bits because I made my wife *come*."

I let out a rough laugh that's stolen by another round of his kisses.

"How do we find out? A blood test, maybe?"

"Your people are so strange," he says, shaking his head. "And they love their needles. No, not a blood test. Not like you're thinking." He moves away, edging toward the shower door. He pushes it open, giving me a full view of his muscular back and sculpted ass and thighs. I bite my lip, wondering if we have time for a second round, but he wraps a towel around his waist and leans against the counter, looking at me. "I know a guy."

"What kind of guy?" I roughly scrub my scalp with sudsy lavender scented soap.

"He's basically a mole who lives in the library here in Veiled Valley. I had him test your tears before, and he found something interesting, but we need more information."

"Is he going to poke and prod me?" I tease, and Ryatt goes rigid, his eyes darkening. Just like I thought they would.

"He will not lay a hand on you or *I will cut it off.*"

"Goddess, you need to lighten up."

He rolls his eyes and turns toward the mirror, swiping his hand over the fogged glass. "We'll go there tomorrow night, before you leave for the coven."

"You're serious about me traveling to the coven on my own?"

"I have work to do. Otherwise, I'd go with you. The coven is your domain now. You are a witch. As the last of the Firestones, as far as we're aware, you are their queen. It's your right."

"How do you know that for sure?" I ask, stepping out of the shower and reaching for one of the fluffy towels that house keeps toasty warm.

"If my mother had lived, she would have been Ravenna's heir. It's the power that determines succession, not bloodlines. Not when it comes to the witches. You are the most powerful witch this kingdom has seen in centuries. We just need to know what exactly you can do with these powers."

"I toppled the coven, Ryatt." My voice slips over the words as memories come rushing back to me.

"And the wards I placed over my lands are gone, and the packs who call the Roguelands home have been without power or safety since the moment you brought me through the veil to Maatua."

"So… we have to go our separate ways? For how long?"

"Not long," he assures me, but I can see the questioning look behind his eyes. "I hope."

"Do I at least get an escort?"

"You can take Westfall."

I cross my arms over my chest. "You don't want to catch up for lost time with your *father?*"

I realize it's the wrong thing to say a second too late. Ryatt runs his fingers through his damp hair and eyes me through the reflection in the mirror. "Nothing is going to change between me and Westfall, Ella. He might have sired me, but I grew up alone, without a family. He is far from my father."

"Ryatt, be serious–"

"I am."

"How do you think he felt? How do you think it felt having to watch you grow up and not being able to tell you who you really were? Who he really was? He loves you."

"He is my best commander." He lets out a long sigh. "I need him to be that, and nothing more, until things are settled."

"And how unsettled are things?" I ask sharply.

He grinds his teeth, his jaw tight. "Worse than I thought, Princess."

21

HER PURPOSE

Ella

I DON'T THINK I've ever been in this part of the castle before. Honestly, I feel like I haven't seen more than half of Ryatt's grand, mountainside home since the day I first landed in this onyx palace.

But this room... this room has my full attention. The walls are the same black stone that weaves throughout the castle. Towering stained glass windows scatter ribbons of purple, blue, and ivory light across faded leather furniture and ancient portraits of what I assume are past rulers. Ornate rugs lie at odd angles, their colors bleeding into one and another, worn from age.

I wonder how many people have walked across the rugs and run their fingertips over the circular table in the center of the room. I wonder how many people have looked at the incredible 3D map that covers nearly the entire table and stood in awe of it like I am now.

I run my fingers across the jagged, scaled down peaks of the mountain ranges that border the northern edge of a circular model of Eastonia. My touch dusts over the hollows and valleys where little villages have been constructed with expert skill.

My gaze catches on a long, turquoise lake made of glass surrounded by mountains and I lean down. "This is Moonrise? This is the Coven?"

Ryatt is standing on the opposite side of the table, his hands braced on the flat surface surrounding the map. He nods, but his eyes are locked on mine, and his face is shining with satisfaction. "Do you like it?"

"It's incredible." My voice is a whisper of shock and awe as I follow the nearly microscoping trails through the mountains; through the Deadlands and the forests full of beasts I still can't name, then into the mountainous, forested home of the Roguelands.

Crops of villages spring to life, nestled in a wide valley. Rivers snake throughout, and I follow the larger river all the way to…

"Rifthold," I say, meeting Ryatt's eyes.

He nods again as I walk beside the table, my gaze locking on the gray, swirling mass that was once the home of King Kane.

Beyond Rifthold is a land of… nothing. Desert and wastelands that eventually bleed into the mountains once more to the east, but to the west lies a great, endless ocean, and the edge of the map.

"Did you make this?" I ask when I reach his side.

"Gods, no. This is older than me by centuries, I'm sure."

"But it's accurate?" I look up to the far edge of the map, where Veiled Valley rests deep in the mountains, likely hundreds of miles from the nearest settlement, and the closest community to the ocean on Ryatt's side of the border between the Roguelands and Rifthold.

"It is," he says softly, almost dreamily. He takes several steps away from the table and points to the ground at his feet. "Maatua would be… somewhere around here, I'm guessing."

"We're so close to them." I look back at the map. "The Veil surrounds Eastonia completely, doesn't it? Not just the mountains between Eastonia and Crescent Falls."

"It does," he confirms.

Silence falls between us, both of us looking at the map with similar withdrawn expressions.

I heave a sigh and look around the room once more, taking in the gnarly weapons hanging on the walls. "This is a war room."

"How did you guess?" His voice is full of smoke as he chuckles darkly.

I walk to the wall and pick up some apparatus that looks like a club with razor sharp hooks on each end. I cock a brow in Ryatt's direction. "What the hell is this used for?"

"Hanging someone to a tree by their spine."

I whirl toward the door as a familiar, golden haired man walks into the room, his green eyes shining with emotion.

"Granger," I grin, then drop the insanely heavy medieval torture device to the ground and run into his arms. Granger isn't expecting it, of course. His arms don't close around me as I squeeze his chest so hard his ribs pop. He pats my head like I'm a little dog curled in his lap and clears his throat once, then twice.

"Luna. I'm happy to see you made it back in one piece."

"Barely," Ryatt growls.

I step out of Granger's arms and shoot my mate a dirty look. Ryatt just smirks and tilts his head toward the map.

"I need a status report as soon as you can give me one," he says to Granger, who nods his understanding.

"How long have you been back? Amanda said you've been in the Roguelands." I sit on one of the dusty leather couches and smooth the wrinkles from my crimson red dress. Being back in the ethereal, flowing fashions of Veiled Valley is a welcome relief. It's hot, even within the cavernous castle, and the thin fabrics that are in style are cool to the touch on my skin.

Granger walks to the map and inspects it, saying, "I arrived this morning."

Then he was able to spend time with Amanda before jumping right back into work with Ryatt. Good. I had dinner with her last night, and Granger was all she could talk about–how she worried she was about him. She'd been rather quiet about the situation in the Roguelands, and now I know why.

"Alpha Jaxon of the Southern Wastes has a small army," Granger says in a low, gravelly voice, his finger resting on a spot in the sweeping desert on the map. "He's gathered the forces of at least three packs and has another six packs on this side of the border as his allies, based on the communications I've received from our spies across the border."

"It'll take him weeks to even reach Rifthold," Ryatt murmurs as he leans his weight against the table. He didn't sleep last night. Dark circles line his eyes, and his mouth is a tight line as he mentally maps every theoretical move this mysterious Alpha Jaxon might make.

"Yes, but some of his allies were much closer to the border. They are going to march on Rifthold and take control. That's their plan. Alpha Jaxon's followers are already calling him the Alpha King of Eastonia."

"Well, they'll be sorely disappointed to hear that *I* am the Alpha King of Eastonia."

I watch the exchange with interest as they talk about the current situation in the Roguelands and beyond. Several packs in the Roguelands have combined, new Alphas have been established, and new territory lines are being drawn.

"You'll need to do your usual rounds and reestablish command," Granger says after nearly an hour of explanations to the new political climate in the wake of Kane's death.

Ryatt looks at me for a moment before sighing heavily and looking back down at the map. "I won't have time for that if Alpha Jaxon is making moves. You and Artyom will go to the Roguelands in my stead. I need a small army, only experienced warriors. Everyone is fucking tired, I understand, but I only need a few thousand men on standby and stationed at our border with Rifthold and the Wastes until I can assume control of those enemy packs."

Granger nods, but I notice the flicker of disappointment in his eyes.

"Amanda will need to stay here, in Veiled Valley. I need her acting as High Lady while Ella is away."

This surprises Granger. He looks from Ryatt to me with a furrowed brow. "Where is Ella going?"

"He's sending me to the coven," I say brightly. "I get to travel on my own–"

"Westfall will escort her," Ryatt cuts in.

I frown.

"Westfall should be traveling with you, Ryatt," I say as I rise and cross my arms under my breasts. The cool red fabric of my dress brushes over my belly, sending little prickles of electricity over my skin. This morning I'd woken up and rolled out of bed and been startled by my reflection in the mirror. A slight swell is now evident on my lower belly.

I look rather cute, I think.

I instinctively lower my arms and cradle the swell. Ryatt catches my movements and gives me an uncharacteristically soft smile, but it's fleeting. He turns back to his Beta and flexes his jaw.

I realize quite suddenly that Granger has no idea that Westfall is Ryatt's dad.

"Westfall is going to be Ella's guard for the time being."

"Why?" I ask, but neither of the men are paying any attention to me.

"I think that's wise. We've had reports of bandits and rogues along the trails leading back to the Roguelands. The coven is being overseen by the mystics right now, but they're awaiting Ella's return."

I look from Granger to Ryatt. "Because I'm their queen?"

"Yes," Ryatt says with a sigh. His eyes light on mine. "You'll likely be there for a while if I need to cross into the Wastes and take care of the threat to our crown."

Here we go. Ryatt said we'd do this together, and after only one full day back in Eastonia, he's already going back on his word.

"No."

"Ella," he rasps. "You're needed at the coven."

"I understand," I practically growl. "How long do you anticipate we're going to be separated, Ryatt?"

Granger rolls his lower lip between his teeth and lets it go with a pop. "I'm going to go see my wife."

"I think that's wise," Ryatt murmurs, his eyes darkening to a steely gray as they narrow on mine.

Granger leaves without another word, and a thick tension falls over the room in his absence.

"I'm not going to be a prisoner at the coven while you gallivant around Eastonia!"

"Gallivant?" His laugh is dark and dangerous as he takes a few steps in my direction.

"You know exactly what I mean, you asshole! We said we'd do this together."

"And we are. I have to start somewhere, Ella. I am building you a new throne–"

"I don't want a throne if it means we're separated for Goddess knows how long! I don't want a throne at all!"

Silence falls over us–thick and heavy.

"I don't know how to be a queen to your people," I continue. "They won't want me!"

"There are some who have been waiting years for someone like you to come here and save us!"

"What if I'm not what you think I am? My powers are... immense, yes, but wouldn't I have known long ago that I was meant for something as great as being the freaking queen of a mystical kingdom? Goddess, Ryatt!" I wave him away when he tries to edge closer to me. "I just want some peace. Just for a moment. I want to spend a single day with you without having to worry about the issues hanging over our heads. That's all I want."

"I'm trying, Princess."

"I don't want to be the ruler of Eastonia."

"I don't think you have a choice."

We meet each other's gaze.

"I'm sorry, Ella."

"I wasn't trained for this," I tell him. "Isaac was meant to be on the throne, not me. I probably would have married someone of rank, of course. An Alpha or Beta, or even an Alpha King, but this? I'm not..." I suck in a breath. "I just want a day, Ryatt. With you."

"We'll have that, but right now, if I don't do something, we're going to have another war on our hands."

I know. I understand where he's coming from.

I just don't like it.

"I see you in a way you don't see yourself," he says, edging closer. "Other people see you in the same light. You're a queen, Ella. These people need you. I need you."

"You speak like you're giving up your own title."

"I will be," he says. "Alpha Kings were never meant to be in power here. But you were."

I find it hard to swallow as he stands before me, tilting my chin with his knuckles so I have to look up at him. He kisses me slowly, tenderly, his lips brushing over mine. "I told you once that you're the only person I'd ever get on my knees for. I meant it. Now it's time for you to train for the role you were born for."

22

SUCKED DOWN

Ella

A FINE LAYER of mist covers the ground as I follow Commander Westfall down a steep embankment. Pockets of loose shale give way beside me, tumbling to the ground and shattering like glass. I pull my cloak tighter, grimacing as my feet slip and slide over the uneven ground.

The sun hasn't risen yet. Stars shine bright above us, the only light to be found.

"We're almost there," he says gruffly.

"Well," I say tartly, glaring at the back of his big, fat head. "Those are the first words you've said to me in a kind tone since you *died*."

He says nothing, of course. He doesn't want to be here. I don't either, but Ryatt is calling the shots, and that means I have to go to the coven to take over—or whatever.

I got one last night with Ryatt before we parted. He left Veiled Valley with Granger shortly before we left, the two of them decked out in leathers and weapons. He'd looked back over his shoulder and nodded at me.

Then he was gone.

Not having the mind-link with him anymore is weighing on me as I follow Westfall on foot toward the river at the base of the valley where Veiled Valley is nestled. High above us, the city sleeps, tucked in a cocoon of rain clouds. I can't even see the bridges and white stone houses anymore.

But before us, another settlement rises into view. It's a village—industrial, and a bit worn down, but shockingly busy for the time of day. Boats rock in the gentle current of the river, tethered to docks crawling with fishermen getting ready to start their days.

A few store fronts come to life as we approach. Women in home-spun dresses flutter behind foggy windows, pulling up shades and setting out baked goods, fabric, and fish, of course.

"What is this place?" I ask. This isn't the route I took from Veiled Valley the last time I traveled to the coven, before everything blew up in my face.

"The Docks," Westfall says without a single glance in my direction. His leather jacket is coated with moisture as we step out of the fog and onto a boardwalk. Several people look in our direction but say nothing as we pass. Wolves pull a cart laden with the tiniest fish I've ever seen toward one of the docks where a boat is preparing to set out.

"How creative," I murmur, looking over my shoulder at the towering mountains behind us.

A bell dings, and I turn to find Westfall stepping into one of the store fronts, a little market. The smell of coffee and pastries is thick as I follow him inside.

"G'mornin'," says the stout shopkeeper. Her cheeks are as round and pink as apples as she beams at Westfall, but then her dark eyes meet mine. They widen, and she drops into a low curtsy.

"Good morning," I smile. "It smells wonderful in here."

"Oh," she says, straightening up with a furious blush spreading across her neck and cheeks. "Thank you, Luna. The pastries are fresh from the oven."

"Let's buy some," I say to Westfall, who is inspecting a shelf full of sundries—bags of oats, fried fruit and vegetables, and stacks of flat-bread and salted, canned fish.

"Whatever you purchase, you need to eat now, before we shift."

My nostrils flare with impatience as I watch him gather a few items. Turning back to the shopkeeper with a graceful smile, I order a half dozen pastries and two cups of her strongest tea. I mix a copious amount of sugar and milk into mine and hand Westfall the plain cup. He looks at it skeptically before accepting it.

As the shopkeeper rings up his items, a group of grubby looking men walk into the store, bringing the scent of marshy riverbank with them.

I turn to peer at the group, who sits down at a table by the window, dirty footprints left in their wake.

"How many did he say there were?" one of them says. He flexes his bloody hands, and my heart rate flutters as I look each man up and down fully, taking in every detail.

"What the hell happened to you all?" I say, louder than I'd meant to. The men turn to me in shock and seem to have just noticed my presence. They stand abruptly, bowing low. "Luna–"

I look from man to man, and focus my attention on the youngest. He's barely old enough to shift, but judging by his clothes, and the way his eyes are shining, and his canines are still slightly elongated, that's exactly what he'd just been doing.

Their grubby, sodden clothing gives it away. Cache clothing. There's caches littered all over the Roguelands full of clothes and supplies.

"We were hunting," says the eldest man.

I feel Westfall edging closer to me as I approach the table.

"Hunting and came upon a camp around ten miles north, through Fenwyrd Pass."

"What kind of camp?" Westfall looks down at their bloodied hands, and the bruises beginning to form on their jaws.

"Rogue," says the youngest man, his voice full of gravel. "We think."

"There were at least five of 'em. Almost lost Jace here, but he ran like hell. They chased us for a while before bankin' off into the woods again. Doubt they'll follow."

The youngest man blushes and glares at what I believe might be his father and the eldest man his grandfather.

"Rogues don't run in packs," Westfall says in a bored voice. He turns from the men, but the grandfather clears his throat.

"They had a woman with them. A witch, we think. She was callin' the shots. We got outta there by the skin of our teeth, Commander."

"Through Fenwyrd Pass, you say?" Westfall sips from his tea and watches the men nod. "Thank you, gentlemen." Without another word, he grabs my elbow and forcefully yanks me out of the shop.

I clutch my box of pastries to my chest, my tea spilling over the rim of the thick paper cup. "Hey!"

"Change of plans," he murmurs, scanning the dock. His grip on my arm is like iron as he starts briskly marching forward, dragging me behind him.

Fishermen crowd the docks, loading bait and nets onto boats as the sun finally begins to rise over the tops of the mountains. Waterfalls of melted snow cascade down the mountainsides, catching the sun in ribbons of multicolored light before spilling into the wide, lazy river.

Everyone gives us a wide berth. I don't blame them. Westfall looks murderous as he drags me, their Luna, across the slippery boards of the dock, toward an inconspicuous wooden boat that is big enough to fit four people at the most.

Commander Westfall snatches my box of pastries from my arms and gives it to the owner of the boat, saying, "I'm commandeering your vessel at the behest of Alpha Ryatt." Then, without so much as a warning glance in my direction, he swoops me up and tosses me into the boat.

"What the hell!"

A shrill cry sounds in the distance. Birds are startled from the sparse trees surrounding the shore. All of the activity on the dock pauses, the only sound the flapping of frantic wings and the slow hum of the water lapping at the shore.

Then it starts. Howls rip through the air. Screams of shock, bellowed commands, and the sound of ripping clothing blur into a vacuum of noise as Westfall jumps into the boat and pushes off the dock with so much force I almost topple over..

I fumble with my tea, spilling it all over my thick pants and pale cream sweater I'm wearing beneath my cloak. "Shit!"

"Head down, Ella!" He shouts, and when I don't immediately obey, he shoves my head between my knees.

The current pulls us away from the dock, but when Westfall grabs the oars, I poke my head up and gasp.

Dozens of wolves are charging into the sleepy little fishing village. Their eyes glow with red light, their teeth a startling white against their black and brown fur. Westfall grunts with effort, trying to steer us toward the swiftly moving current at the center of the river, but a trio of enemy wolves spot us.

Spot me.

I raise a hand in their direction and send a ripple of light toward them, only for it to rebound and explode against some invisible barrier. The magic sings through my veins but burns so much I cry out in pain. That's new. It never hurt to use my fire before. A wave of dizziness crashes into me like a tidal wave. My vision goes dark and blurry at the edges and a deep, raw ache blossoms on my thigh where Ryatt's mark used to be.

"W-Westfall!" I shout, pointing to the dock.

He turns his head and curses as the three wolves leap into the water.

One of them jumps farther than the others.

I barely have time to suck in a breath before the wolf crashes into the boat and sends it tipping over, dumping all three of us into the water.

'We're being attacked!' I should through the mind-link. Amanda might be the only person who I can connect with at this point, but if enemies are this close to Veiled Valley, something has gone terribly wrong.

My head pops above water for a split second before I'm sucked under again by the current and swept further away from the dock, from the shore, and from Westfall.

"ELLA!" Westfall's voice rips over the rushing water as I break the surface against, flailing, trying to get a hold on what's up and what's down.

"Here! I'm–" I'm sucked under again, but frantically kick my legs. My heavy cloak is tangled around my feet, ballooning out behind me and acting as a sail that drags me further and further away. "Westfall!"

I reach up and unclasp the cloak, freeing myself, and fight like hell to stay afloat.

The river is deep, wide, and fast moving at the center. I can feel the way it's tugging me into that center current as I start swimming toward where Westfall is wrestling with the wolf.

I have a flash of memory of Ryatt at the shore of the lake in Moonrise when Westfall's eyes light on mine. Ryatt had been stunned, so full of concern as he'd fallen to his knees at the water's edge.

Westfall has the same look in his own eyes as the wolf turns its barrel-sized head toward me and clacks its massive jaws.

"Ella, go!"

My heart races as the wolf tries to decide between killing Westfall and following me down the current.

"ELLA, GO, NOW!" Westfall screams, and he doesn't need to tell me twice.

I suck in a breath and disappear under the water's surface just as the wolf starts to swim in my direction.

Powers. I can use my powers. I can…

I send them forward again, lighting up the water with crimson, but the ache in my thigh twists and explodes, forcing the breath I'd been holding from my lungs.

I start choking on water, my arms reaching toward the surface, but I'm sinking now, the current dragging me down, down, down until there's nothing but darkness.

Then the main current finds me and slams into my body, catapulting me into even deeper darkness.

I gasp, fighting for breath. I can't tell if the surface is getting farther away, or if my eyes are going dark, and I'm drowning, but… I slip away, my body going numb, and my panic turns into blissful, all-encompassing quiet.

Wake up, Princess.

I suck in a breath the moment my back hits something hard. I roll over, spitting out what feels like gallons of water. Sunlight burns my eyes. I blink rapidly to try to clear my vision.

Hands are pressing down on my shoulders before I have a moment to register that I'm even out of the river and back on dry land.

Where am I? How long have I been unconscious?

Someone walks toward me and crouches, their form blocking out the glare of the sun.

Long, platinum hair dusts the ground as I slowly look up.

"Look what the tide dragged in," Petra purrs, her mouth pulled into a cat-like grin.

2 3

BAD COMPROMISE

Ryatt

"WHAT THE FUCK IS HAPPENING?" My hands curl into fists as I stalk toward the group of warriors–a gaggle of dirty, exhausted men and wolves–and stop a few feet away from their general, a young man named Tanner.

His nostrils flare as he tries to stay upright in my presence, but his knees wobble. He's resisting the urge to back away. "We were attacked last night in Fenwyrd Pass. We counted six rogues."

"Rogues don't run in packs," I counter, eyeing the young general. I don't know him. He was put in his position by Artyom, who is currently speaking in low tones to Granger.

"We came upon a campsite," the young general grinds out, his teeth chattering with nerves as I lean in. He swallows hard then continues, "Two of my men were attacked from behind and hauled off into the woods. We followed and came upon a… feeding ground."

I raise my brows. "What exactly did that entail?"

The general goes a little green, but clears his throat. "It's about as bad as you could expect, my King."

175

'Rogues have been picking off travelers between Veiled Valley and the Roguelands with more frequency than usual,' Granger says in my mind. I keep my eyes on the young general for another long moment before backing up a step.

I turn to Granger and Artyom, giving the latter a nod to go tend to his unit. Artyom steps past me and starts shouting commands while Granger and I walk deeper into the woods outside the clearing where we just found them.

"Artyom says there was a witch with them," Granger says in a low voice, glancing back at the practically untrained unit of wolves who are just old enough to shift. "He didn't see her, but he could feel her power nearby."

"Did she have control of the rogues somehow?" It's not a totally outlandish notion. Rogue wolves are a lot like hellhounds. Soulless and bound by forces of magic outside of the Goddess's rule.

Granger shrugs and adjusts his leather armor, his eyes traveling through the tree line. "What are the odds of a witch going off on her own like this and building a small army of rogues? We're not even in the Deadlands, and even if we were, our forces are stationed throughout it."

"I don't like this at all," I murmur, tapping my fingers on my thigh.

The forest is quiet all around us. Even the birds have stopped their songs. Granger and I just happened upon General Tanner's unit on our way to the Roguelands. They'd just started to regroup, and Artyom, who is stationed with the unit in question at a nearby village, had come looking for them when they didn't come back to the village at sundown like expected.

The biggest concern I have is how close the campsite is to Veiled Valley.

"We're out of range from the Valley now," I grumble, turning back to the group of warriors. I watch Artyom as he speaks to a trio of them. Artyom was recently promoted to commander before the final push into Rifthold and is doing a fine job, but he's stuck with green men. Young, inexperienced warriors that aren't good for much but patrolling the villages along the borders of the Deadlands.

The fact they got away from the rogues unscathed is a miracle.

Which tells me they weren't targets.

"I'm going to go back to check out the campsite and see what I can find. I'll be able to get through to Amanda from there, I believe."

I nod, and Granger walks away, stopping to talk to Artyom for a moment as he strips back out of his leather and prepares to shift.

I cross my arms over my chest and blow out a breath. My skin is crawling with the sense that something is wrong. This was a trap, but for who?

Or for what?

"I'm sending a few of my men with Granger. The rest are going back to the Yarrow Spur Pack village," Artyom says as he walks in my direction. His pale blue eyes shine like moonstone against his dark skin, nearly the same shade as his obsidian leathers. He rolls his lower lip between his teeth and looks around to make sure we're not over-heard before adding, "Based on the description I've been given, I believe the witch in question might be Petra."

I furrow my brow. "Petra's dead." At least, Ella believes so. Word of Petra's deception of the coven has spread far and wide at this point. The commanders and generals I've spoken to in the days since we returned have said as much as well. Petra, heir of Ravenna until Ella came along, died when the crystal palace in Moonrise shattered.

But, if she's not dead, she would have been banished.

Witches aren't known to let their enemies live.

"If she's not dead, then she's controlling a small rogue army," Artyom says on a breath, shaking his head. "You know she's capable of this, too."

Artyom and I grew up together in Moonrise. He knows Petra as well as any of us men who spent their childhoods protected and nurtured by the witches there.

"She was a jealous, spiteful bitch."

"Spiteful is the key word. You said Luna Ella is headed to the coven with Westfall. How?"

"By foot. As wolves, they should be arriving at the coven within the next few hours. Westfall said he'll send a messenger when they arrive." My chest feels hollow as I say the words. Again, I have a sense that something isn't right. It's where our mate bond used to be—something deep in my chest that's begging me to act.

Sunlight peeks through a storm cloud enough to illuminate the group of weary men waiting for one of us to give the command to move out.

"Yarrow Spur has an inn, right?" I ask.

Artyom nods and snaps his fingers to his men, giving the silent command to move out.

YARROW SPUR ISN'T KNOWN for its hospitality.

Regardless of my being the Alpha King of the Roguelands, the locals cast dirty looks in my direction as I sit at a table in the inn, picking at a bowl of stew made of unnamed, and unrecognizable, meats.

Artyom returns with two mugs of ale and sits down across from me.

"Did you tuck your boys in bed and give them a little kiss goodnight?" I ask, smirking over the rim of the mug.

He matches my expression with a smirk of his own. "You realize this is the first generation in what could be considered centuries where most of the warriors have loving families at home and were raised by their parents."

"You had living parents while you were growing up and going through training."

"That's why you and Granger beat the shit out of me at any opportunity you had," he says wryly, leaning back in his chair. He looks exhausted, and I don't blame him. Artyom is a man I'd consider a friend and brother in all the ways that truly matter. While not bound by blood, we grew up together. We've been to battle together, and now we're watching a new generation of young warriors emerge who may not have to ever experience the kind of conflict we've known our whole lives.

Artyom is the man for this job. Serious and steady, he makes for an excellent commander.

Plus, he's one of the only people I can stand being with for more than a few minutes at a time.

His eyes flicker with power as he looks around. I know he's listening to every conversation, reading between every uttered, whispered word. That's his gift. He's an excellent spy. Whatever powers he inherited from his witch mother are going to be useful to me in the coming weeks.

Artyom toys with his ale for a moment, his expression unreadable, but I can see from his rigid shoulders that he also senses something is amiss.

"You feel it too," I say, then take a sip from my drink.

"There's been a shift," he says in a low murmur. "Something is coming."

I look out the grimy window. It's late afternoon. Scouts from the coven should have been trying to contact me by now, but the mind-link is clear of any and all noise. I'm starting to think Ella might not have made it to the coven.

"Why did you let her go to the coven without escorts?"

"Are you reading my mind?"

"I'd rather not be in your head," Artyom chuckles. "But seriously, what kind of game are you playing with the Luna?"

"She could flatten Eastonia with a snap of her fingers once she figures out how to do it. I'm not worried about her ability to protect herself. I'm more worried about the people she's bound to run into on the way getting on her bad side. Anyway, she has Westfall with her."

"This is part of her training, then?"

"It could be." I nod, but that feeling of unease only grows sharper.

"And if she runs into this band of rogues?"

"She's killed a hellhound, Artyom. She'll be fine." Internally, I am screaming. I had to get Ella to the coven. I didn't have much of a choice, and I knew if I acted like a possessive, brooding Alpha baby, as she likes to call me, she would have fought me at every turn.

So, I'm allowing her the freedom to do this on her own, even if it's killing me.

I trust her.

I have to trust her.

A ripple of energy flickers through the mind-link. Artyom feels it too because he straightens and looks around before settling his gaze on his drink in concentration.

But before any communications can come through, a commotion sounds somewhere in the village square.

We're out of our seats before the rest of the people dining at the inn can react.

"It's Granger," Artyom says hoarsely as we walk briskly toward the edge of the village where curious onlookers have started to gather.

He's right. Golden blond hair is the first thing I see as I shove my way through the crowd.

Granger is dragging Westfall, who is by all accounts completely unconscious.

"Alpha," Granger pants, "We have a serious problem." His face is shredded, blood pouring down his jaw and neck. His armor is in pieces, and Westfall doesn't look any better. Granger falls to his knees, but I catch him around the middle while Artyom steadies Westfall before he can fall face first in the dirt.

I look between the men, my heart rate spiking. Westfall has deep, festering bite marks on every inch of exposed skin. His fingers are gnawed down to the bone. Granger groans with pain as I flip him onto his back and rip his blood soaked shirt down the center, revealing several deep gouges made by claws.

The smell isn't right. His blood is tainted by something.

"Wolfsbane," Artyom seethes. "Someone get a healer here immediately!"

"He came out of nowhere," Granger says through gritted teeth, motioning to Westfall. "Soaking wet, saying–saying–"

"Where the fuck is Ella?" I hiss, shaking Granger's shoulders, but his emerald eyes roll back in his head.

24

THE NEW FIRESTONE QUEEN

Ella

Silver manacles burn into my wrists. The hot, slippery metal slides over my bones as I curl into myself, trying to shelter myself from the pain. Water drips onto my filthy hair. It's ice cold, which is a welcome relief from the sweltering heat radiating through the room made of sweating pale stone.

There's a single door and no windows, and I have no idea if I'm underground or high, high above in some tower. Everything from the brief moments of clarity I had after being pulled from the river to now are blurry. Flashes of being dragged by my hair through wet mud. The feeling of silver being sliced over my bruised skin. The sound of manacles being locked in place, and muffled voices lifted in snarling laughter at my expense.

I woke up some time ago thirsty and in the worst pain I think I've ever felt. The pain radiates from my wrists and writhes a snake through every vein, over every muscle, setting deep in my bones.

The worst of it lingers in my lower belly. A dull, cramping ache has started to spread there, and the confusion and panic when I first woke up here in this dull, brutally hot room is now replaced by fury and fear.

If Petra does anything to my baby, I will tear out her throat with my teeth. I will pull her apart inch by inch while she's still breathing. I will use what little power I have left to bring time to a crawl just to elongate her suffering.

I will revel in every drop of blood I spill.

A sharp, slicing pain cuts through my stomach. The pain is hot enough to make me moan as I bring my knees into my chest and lay my cheek on the hot stone floor.

But the door to the room opens with an echoing creak, and light pours into the room. I close my eyes, unaccustomed to the brightness. How long have I been left like this? Hours? Days?

Goddess forbid… weeks?

I open my eyes just in time to be splashed with frigid water. I gasp as needles of ice fan out over my skin, soaking into the battered potato sack of a dress I've been dressed in.

"Get up, you filthy whore," a deep, grumbling male voice booms.

I spit water, blinking rapidly to clear my vision. I don't recognize the man and the large cream-colored wolf standing beside him. I'll forget this man's face, just like I've forgotten all the others who have come in and out of this room to taunt me. I've been living on spoiled meat and crumbs of bread for Goddess knows how long, but they haven't broken me yet.

That's what they're trying to do. They're trying to break me. For what reason, I have no idea, because I haven't seen Petra since the day I was dragged in from the river.

"I'm chained to the floor, you fucking moron," I hiss, and he slaps me so hard my vision blurs at the edges, and my teeth puncture my lower lip.

He unlocks the chains keeping me tied to the dirty floor and hauls me up right, my wrists bound by the manacles. He shoves me, telling me to start walking, but I nearly fall back to my knees as my legs wobble and tingle from lack of use.

Goddess, how long have I been here?

My leg muscles feel like jelly as I stagger forward. The wolf eyes me with a narrowed gaze as I pass. I meet his eyes, narrowing my own, then spit in his face.

His snarl tears through my ears.

"Our Queen wants her alive!" my captor shouts at the wolf, who is currently snarling in my face with his big, white teeth. "Play later."

I tilt my head at the wolf, eyeing my own reflection in his shiny teeth, and begin to laugh. It's a hysterical sound that bounces off every wall. My eyes are wide and bloodshot, and my dry, cracked lip is split as I look up at the man and laugh in his face, too.

"She's gone insane," he murmurs. "Look at this bitch, Atticus. She's lost her fucking mind."

At first, I think he's talking to the wolf, but as he shoves me through the door, I find myself nearly face to face with a tall, white-haired man who could have been Petra had it not been for his shortly trimmed hair and scarred face.

He's blind in one eye. That's the first thing I notice. One eye is a sharp blue, while the other is a milky white with a scar running from his forehead to his cheekbone.

"She stinks," he sneers, reaching toward me to pick up a lock of my matted hair. "Bathe her. Chop off her hair if you have to." He begins to turn around, then slowly looks over his shoulder at the large man holding my chains and the wolf at my side. "Now that I think of it, the slave girls will bathe her. I don't trust either of you after what happened to that mystic we brought in a few weeks ago."

My blood runs cold. They've been bringing mystics here–to wher-ever we are? I look around, but there's no windows, no doors open to the outside world. Water runs down the stone walls in little streams that sink back into the cracked stone floors.

It's hot as hell, though. So, we're somewhere warm, or this place is kept at a brutally hot temperature on purpose.

Atticus snatches my chains from my captor with a sneer cold enough to cool the air in the room by several degrees.

Without a word, he hauls me away. With each step, the manacles cut deeper into my skin, but I refuse to let the pain show.

We reach the end of a long hallway and walk down a short flight of stairs, then I'm being shoved through a door and into another hallway lit by torches that cast more heat into the snug space.

Atticus doesn't say a word to me. A brief glance in his direction displays the disgusted look on his face as he grips my upper arm with one hand and the chains with the other.

But then he abruptly stops, his one good eye sharpening.

I resist the urge to ask what's happening when he shakes his head and looks down at me.

"Come on," he says, turning us back in the direction we came.

I dig in my heels, which surprises him. He turns toward me as I yank on the chains with all the strength left in my body. "Where are we going?"

"To see your queen, little witch."

"I have no queen."

"My sister begs to differ."

My brows raise. So, I was right. "You're Petra's brother?"

"Are we that similar?" He's terrifying to look at, but there's something in that eye of his that Petra doesn't have. It's a single shred of friendliness, maybe even humanity.

He shouldn't have let me see it.

"Is she going to kill me?"

He shrugs. "I assume so. I thought she might have wanted you… clean, at least, beforehand. But she's demanding to see you now." Clean. Not for her, but because I look like death walking and somewhere, deep down, he feels bad about it.

"She's in your head, isn't she?"

"Mind-link," he nods, and a hint of cocky smile touches his lips.

Bullseye. This dude is as good as dead now.

"What have I done wrong?" I let a tremor run through my voice. "My mate—Oh, Goddess, where is he?"

"You were alone."

"Is he dead?"

"No," he says, searching my eyes. I try to look dramatically relieved and stick out my lower lip, fake tears springing to life and rolling over my lashes.

He loosens his grip on me enough that I drop my rail-thin arms and cradle the...

Oh, my Goddess.

I cradle the hard, small swell on my lower belly that hadn't been there before. I look up at him, real panic showing behind my eyes this time. "How long have I been here?"

"Two weeks. Almost three—"

"The baby," I whisper.

"Petra won't let anything happen to that... child." He grimaces, his white teeth flashing with mingled disgust and awe.

I meet his eyes. "What exactly does she want from me? Tell me now."

He winces suddenly and grips my arm again, and then we're moving. I imagine his bitch of a sister is screaming into his skull, and that brings me a single shred of comfort as I walk down another hallway, another ill-lit corridor, and then out into a cavernous space illuminated by multiple fires that blaze to a low hanging ceiling.

But the fires are all wrong. They glow in several different shades. Battered, chained women with tear-stained cheeks toss what looks like bones into the flames. Smoke curls along the ceiling, choking the very air from the room.

Atticus shoves me along while my stomach twists. What's happening here?

The ceiling slowly rises the further we walk. Soon, the space opens up, and I follow the billowing smoke now twisting toward a hole in what I realize is a cave.

Eastonia and its *fucking* caves.

"Well, look what the cat dragged in."

I lower my gaze from the hole, what could be my only means of escape, to Petra.

She taps her fingers on... no. No, anything but this.

King Kane's iron throne with its skulls and bones is polished and gleaming like liquid metal as Petra, draped in robes of blood red, rises. Her glossy white-blonde hair is braided away from her face and woven through a crown of ivory thorns.

"Your mate has been tearing apart the Roguelands looking for you." She grins then laughs. It's a shrill sound that echoes through the cavernous space, bouncing off the ceiling.

I look up again and notice the carvings on the domed ceiling. It's not a cave like I thought, but we're definitely underground. This place… it must have been a temple of some kind, based on the gods and goddesses carved into the shadows.

"Hello?" Petra says sharply. "Did you not hear me? I just said your mate—"

"Of course he's looking for me," I say calmly, my voice thick with boredom. "Are you hoping he'd be here by now to see how far I've fallen? Were you hoping he'd find you instead, see you in all your glory, and fall madly in love?" I snort with laughter that booms over the crackling fires behind me.

"I should have killed you at the coven when I had the chance!" she screams, teeth bared.

"When? That night I mopped the crystal floors in Ravenna's castle with your pathetic ass?"

Her mouth falls open then promptly snaps shut again, her eyes flaring with primal rage. "Get those manacles off this sniffling, filthy cunt right this instant, Atticus!"

"Petra—"

She whirls on her brother, her face twisted by a type of fury I've never seen before. "Right. Now." She rolls a dainty wrist and inspects her nails. "The silver in those manacles will have caused her powers to wither to dust by now, Atticus." She looks up at us with those pale gray eyes I would love to gouge out. "And the wolfsbane in every morsel of food and sip of water she drank."

My mouth goes dry. Atticus reaches into his pocket and pulls out a key, making quick work of unlocking the manacles. They fall to my feet.

My wrists are practically worn to the bone. A quick glance shows me how terrible the wounds are.

Petra makes a pouty face. "You poor thing. You had such beautiful wrists and hands. I'm sure Ryatt won't even want to look in your direction now."

"You could peel the skin from my body and he'd still be mine, Petra."

"I am your queen now, you insolent slut! My reign was fated!"

"By the very mystics you've been hunting and enslaving?" I wave a weak arm in a wide circle toward the fires burning behind me. "They never saw you on any throne."

"It was supposed to me and Ryatt during the Rite! Not you. You had to come and ruin it all!"

"He's mine, Petra. It doesn't matter what you say. It doesn't matter how badly you beat and torture me. You can kill me, and he'll still be mine." I take a step toward her, flexing my aching hands. "He doesn't want you, and he never will."

I can tell she's seeing red. She snaps her fingers, and two women with chains trailing behind their scrawny legs come running, struggling to balance with what looks like a heavy burden carried between them.

My blood runs cold as I realize what they're handing to Petra.

She runs a delicate, milky white finger along the edge of Ryatt's sword. His sword of shadows.

"I want a rematch," she grins. "But this time, little witch, you won't have your brute strength or your powers behind you."

Petra lunges at me with hatred in her eyes.

25

ANNIHILATION

Ella

THERE'S nothing in my head but the sheer will to survive as Petra swings Ryatt's sword. She miscalculates how heavy it is, and based on the way her arms tremble and bow, she's never wielded a sword before, either.

The gem-encrusted hilt slides out of her hands, the sword whizzing through the air. A screech of pain sounds nearby, and I spare a glance in the direction of the sound.

A wolf—one of Petra's warriors—is twitching on its side while blood pools around his body.

I don't hide the smirk that stretches over my cracked lip as Petra slowly turns her gaze back to me. I step to the side, then step again, putting a few feet of distance between me and the deranged witch. All around us, warriors, guards, and even some of her slaves are starting to gather to watch the fight.

I mean to give them a show they'll never forget.

If I can muster the strength.

Each step is painful. Each breath rattles through my lungs. My blank thoughts flash with images of Ryatt. He can't find me without the bond in place, can he? He would have been here by now. What exactly has he been doing for three weeks while I rotted underground?

Petra said he'd been tearing the Roguelands apart. I don't doubt it.

"Why?" I ask. "Why are you doing this?" I wave a hand at the slave women who look little better than me. "This was your coven—your family!"

Petra shakes her head as she follows me in a wide circle. "I was supposed to be Ravenna's heir. I watched her cower and bow to Ryatt for years. That boy—that cocky, bullheaded child who grew to be King of the Roguelands by force alone—everyone bent the knee to him. He was the only thing that could stop Kane and his armies from enslaving all of us."

"Then why work against us?" I ask, my voice breaking over the words. "You broke through Ryatt's wards around the coven and brought Kane's army to Moonrise!"

"Do you realize how powerful our child might have been? Me, the queen of the witches, and him, a Shadowsygner? It was destined by fate to be so, you bitch! The mystics saw Ryatt and the heir of Ravenna being mated during the Rite. We would have been successful. We would have had a child who'd grow to take over Eastonia and rule the way it was intended. Like Kane intended."

My stomach hollows out, but Petra keeps talking.

"So much power," she hisses. "I could have had anything. I could have done anything. The coven could have been so much more than Ravenna allowed it to be. I'd been trying to convince her to join Kane's leadership for years. Together we could have—"

"He would have enslaved you all and stolen your powers!" I shout, my voice heavy and desperate.

Petra's eyes flash with greed. "Maybe them, but not me. I would have been spared. I would have been the queen he was looking for. Someone to keep the coven in line. To forget about fate and selectively breed the witches for power like he'd tried to do for so long. He knew Moonrise was still around. He knew Ryatt kept it guarded. The last of the covens, with the last witch population in all of Eastonia. He promised me I'd sit on its throne."

"In exchange for what?" Petra is starting to get closer to me as I continue to circle, but my bare feet are throbbing, and my arms feel heavy. I'm weak, so weak. If I'm going to kill her, I need to do it now.

But I need to know the whole story. Ryatt and I knew things wouldn't be easy when we returned. But this...

"I just needed to get to you, Ella. You, in exchange for the throne I wanted. With you dead, Ryatt could finally see the truth laid out in front of him. The mate by his side was always meant to be me. I just needed to get you out of the way. Ravenna had no idea I was working with Kane. When the war started, I made my move. Ryatt's powers were at their weakest. The wards of the coven would weaken. He'd warned us—warned Ravenna—and she tasked me with strengthening them instead."

"But you took them down." The words catch in my throat. "There were so many children in Moonrise, Petra. You brought Kane's armies—"

"Weak children with even weaker bloodlines!" Her scream rips through the air between us. "Most of that generation is mixed with wolf anyway. Disgusting!" She spits the last word, her teeth gleaming in the firelight dancing all around us.

"Ryatt's a shifter," I grind out. "Yet you obsess over him!"

"I am his fated mate!"

"You are *not*," I say, and it's a struggle to get the words out. I want to lie down. I want to curl into a ball and close my eyes against the pain. "The mystics never saw you on the coven's throne. They saw me. I am Ravenna's heir. I am the Witch Queen. I am Ryatt's mate."

"Not anymore."

She knows. Her cruel, cold smile tells me she knows the bond is broken between us. But how?

She clicks her tongue, edging closer, the circle between us shrinking. "Silver and wolfsbane cut through your shifter magic like butter, don't they? You're feeling so weak, aren't you? Your powers were already weakening from the curse Kane placed on you before he cut out your mark."

"A curse." It's not a question. The words ring through my head like a death knell.

"I gave Kane the spell to use. It's old magic. Something from a time long lost." She smiles wickedly. "It'll eat through your powers until they're nothing, wolf. Every day, you'll grow weaker. Haven't you felt it? Don't you feel it now that you're no longer bound in silver? Your powers should be regenerating by now, shouldn't they?"

My hands slowly close into fists.

"Nothing but divine intervention can save you now," she says, "and unfortunately all the gods are dead. They no longer listen or care about us mere mortals. Why would they care about the plight of an ugly little half-breed slut like you?"

I feel it then. My fear, pain, and anger give way to a flicker of deeper feeling in my chest. A slight tug. That shred of the bond that's left between Ryatt and I.

"He didn't cut it all away," I admit. "I can still feel it. Our bond is weak, but intact. Kane screwed something up." I shrug. "He misspoke your spell."

She sneers. "That's impossible!"

"I used to think all of this was impossible." I wave a hand around the room and the onlookers around us. "This kind of evil. You're a monster, Petra, just like Kane. You're only a queen because these people are either terrified of you or enslaved by you. You're not worthy of them. You never were, and I think Ravenna realized that, too."

Petra's face turns a fiery red.

"Ryatt knew that from the beginning."

She snaps, all teeth and pointed nails.

But she's just a woman against claws.

Like a dark storm, my ebony wolf erupts through the rough homespun dress, tearing it to pieces. Power I hadn't been able to muster in my human form flickers to life as I lunge at the witch. A bolt of her power whizzes past me, coating my back in flecks of the coldest ice.

But I'm faster than her. I leap, my claws curling her into her shoulders, and sending us both hurtling toward a wall.

With a crash that sends waves of pain through my body, I crush Petra to the gnarled stone of the hell she built as her new coven.

Behind me, shouts of protest and the keening of the enslaved witches as they realize what's happening echo in my ears. Chaos ensues. I barely have a moment to pick up a screaming Petra by her neck and slam her into the wall again before someone is trying to wrap a heavy chain around my neck.

I whirl, sending three of her men flying across the room.

Petra struggles to gain her footing and starts calling out desperately for help. Men are shifting into wolves, and the enslaved witches are watching in horror and awe.

But one of them takes advantage of the piles of shredded clothing left in the wake of the dozen wolves now bounding toward me. A single key catches the light of the fire.

My sacrifice for their freedom.

This is going to hurt.

An enemy wolf slams into my side.

I don't want to die this way. I can't die, not when Petra is still alive. I can't die because I have to protect my baby, above all else.

The thought of that baby turns my mind to fire and murderous rage, and then everything gets a little… hazy.

Howls and whimpers rise to the ceiling as my wolf begins to burn with my silver flames. Crimson light devours the room around me, and I can only pray that the other witches got out in time. All the while, the bravest of the wolves try to stop me, to get me on my back, but Westfall trained me well. They can't catch me. They can't sink their teeth into me long enough to halt my progress as I bound across the room and annihilate each and every one.

Time is a blur. My pain and fear have dissolved and left only bloodlust that I'm not sure I'll be able to shake when this is all said and done.

When the last wolf falls, I slowly turn to where Petra is cowering against the wall, surrounded by my flames. I slowly walk to her, the flames licking over my dark coat but not burning me. I stop when I reach the sword she so carelessly tossed and shift back to my human form.

My fire dies out as I pick it up and walk naked back to wear Petra is still shielding herself, chanting desperate spells and making bargains with her gods.

I swing the sword through the air to test its weight.

"The gods are dead, remember?" I smile, standing only a foot or so away. I reach through my flames and rip her crimson robe from her shoulders. "I think it's time for a new god to rise, wouldn't you say?"

"You will die from that curse before you have a chance to even glimpse the Firestone throne," she hisses, "you filthy—"

I swing the sword right through her dainty neck. Petra's head rolls to a stop just as my powers flicker out, and the fire turns to wisps of smoke.

"Goddess above," I mutter, pulling on the robe. I sniff, leaning the sword on the wall so I have free hands to try to wipe Petra's splattered blood from my face. I grab the sword again and turn, looking over the room. "Enough of that."

Dead wolves and wolf-sized piles of ash mar the floors.

But thirty shocked witches are staring at me from the entrance to this house of horrors.

"Anyone know how to get out of here? My mate is looking for me, and he's probably *really* pissed right now."

26

———

A ROGUE AND A WITCH

Ryatt

THE VILLAGE of Cerserne sits on the southernmost border between the Roguelands and Rifthold.

Quiet, scant, and nothing but rolling, grass covered hills, it's a peaceful place. The men quickly ushering their wives and children into the scattered pale stone cottages aren't at peace, however, not with a band of wolves marching into their village.

The burly man in brown leather who walks in my direction looks murderous, but his expression shifts to one of skepticism and concern as he recognizes the dark emblem of the Roguelands on the armor on the bodies of my warriors who are still in their human forms.

I walk between the dozen or so warriors, Granger walking a few paces behind me. My warriors part to allow me to edge right up to the Alpha of Cerserne–an Alpha who once allied with Kane.

"What do I owe the...pleasure?" he croons, giving me a dramatic bow. His thick black beard brushes against his chest as he rises to his full height and crosses his arms over his broad chest.

I say nothing. I let silence simmer between us while I keep my gaze fixed directly on his. I don't blink. I let my powers writhe over my skin, my shadows curling between my fingers. I am not fucking around right now.

My mate is missing. I can feel that she's alive, but that's it. Our bond is barely traceable, and I've exhausted all efforts to find her at this point. For three weeks, I've been on the verge of absolutely exploding with fury and grief, and the only reason I've been able to keep myself together and use my power to go scorched earth on anyone who even looks in my direction is because I know Ella, wherever the fuck she is, is giving her captures hell.

All we have as a clue to her whereabouts is that band of rogue wolves and the witch they follow.

The Alpha finally bristles and takes a single step backward.

With dominance asserted, Granger clears his throat and steps up to my side. "There's been reports of a band of rogues moving across the Roguelands. We've been following their movements."

The Alpha looks from Granger to me. I say with ice in my voice, "We have reason to believe they may have crossed through the north-western edge of your territory."

Several of his men begin to walk toward our group, drawing weapons from their belts. In the distance, wolves peek out from between cottages, some of them edging forward as thick, heavy tension absorbs the air between us.

But the Alpha rolls his neck and relaxes his shoulders, motioning for us to follow. "They did. Come, we were able to stop one before they left the territory."

I glance at Granger, raising a brow. Granger is stone faced beside me. He doesn't want to be here. None of us do. We should have crossed the river into Rifthold and been halfway across enemy territory by now, laying down the new laws and forcing enemy Alphas into submission.

But instead, we've been tracking my mate, and the serious threat that put her in this situation to begin with, across the Roguelands. All the while, whispers of conflicts brewing across the river into Rifthold have been flowing through each village. Another war is brewing, another enemy army posed to fight.

I'm running out of time to bring peace to my people.

But all I can think about is Ella.

The Alpha of Cerserne caught a rogue, however. This is the closest we've been to the group of soulless wolves now moving in a pack through my lands and harassing my people.

"It's a female," the Alpha says as we pass through the main section of the village. The rolling hills stretch on for miles, the grass a bright green against the stark gray sky. In the distance, a storm is rolling toward the village. Dark clouds stretch toward us like smokey hands.

The spare trees around us whisper in a warm breeze, but the birds are silent.

A sinking feeling tightens my gut as I follow the Alpha between a crop of stone cottages and a larger building rises into view.

"How do you know it's a female?" Granger asks gruffly, his voice full of disgust.

I glance behind us at the warriors we've picked up along the way. Artyom is directing them to seek shelter from the incoming storm in what looks like a barn in the distance.

Good. I have a feeling whatever we're walking into isn't going to be pretty.

"She's mostly in her human form, and our healer confirmed it." The door to the roughly built stone building is shoved open and a cold rush of air comes spilling out, followed by the sound of panting.

I blink to adjust my eyes to the darkness. The air is damp—so humid I can feel the moisture on my skin. The smell is… indescribable. Like death itself. That sweet, rotting scent of spoiled meat.

But a young woman rises from a stool nearby holding a small mortar and pestle in her hands. A witch. I can feel the power coming off her as she bows low, her flaxen blonde hair falling over her shoulders. She lifts her head but keeps her eyes down as she steps aside.

But pale fingers curl around the pestle until her knuckles turn white. I don't blame her for being nervous, and not because she's in the presence of the Alpha King. No, it's become clear over the past few weeks of searching the Roguelands for any sign of Ella that the witches who have left the coven to work as healers in the scattered packs and villages are being hunted. Many of her sisters have gone missing.

But my attention is stolen from the young witch by a scraping sound in the furthest reaches of the wide, darkened room. Something is chained to the wall. The light spilling from the open door to the village sends fractured ribbons of light stretching toward the far wall.

I pull in a breath, my chest going tight with hope, fear, and absolute despair as a filthy, battered woman in chains turns her head to look at us. Her dark brown hair is matted and falling over narrow shoulders. She's wearing a pale dress that was obviously given to her by the village, but her feet are bare, and her hands…

Pale gray paws replace her hands, her gnarled claws catching the light.

"Ella–"

She looks right into my eyes, and I feel a wave of relief sweep over me as her dark brown eyes rake over my face.

Not Ella.

For three weeks, every time we're in this situation, it's never been Ella.

The woman's lips pull back to reveal cracked, yellow fangs. I see it then–the remnants of being a rogue wolf. Her skin is peeling and coated in mange. Her body is stooped, her legs bowed and barely strong enough to hold her upright. A faint reddish gleam flashes in her eyes as a growl shudders through the building.

I whirl toward the witch. "How? How is she able to shift into a human form again?"

"I–I was asked–" The witches cheeks burn with a furious blush as she risks a glance at the Alpha of Cerserne.

"Explain it to the king, witch," he sneers, and she flinches, taking a few wobbly steps backward to put distance between her and the Alpha.

"I was asked to force her to shift. I–I make potions, Your Highness. Alchemy is my gift. She was sickly, and I had a hunch that a combination of a few of my healing potions might help...ease her back to reality."

"You were able to turn a rogue back into a regular wolf?" Granger asks with a gasp.

The witch blushes again, but her eyes are round and fixed on the toes of her boots. "Not human, no. But close. She's too far gone to ever return to the way she might have been before."

"Does she speak?" I ask.

The witch turns to look at the woman–the rogue. "No, she does not."

The Alpha of Cerserne chuckles. It's a sound that grates on my senses as I slowly turn my gaze to look at him.

"What's so funny?" I step toward him, motioning to the rogue. "This woman is essentially being tortured right now for some sick experiment, isn't she?"

"Why not? It's not like her mind is human. She's a monster."

Granger's fingers brush over his knife belt.

"I figure I can fetch a pretty penny for her. She can join a circus, or satisfy some sick individuals' fantasies."

Now, I'm growling just like the rogue woman behind us. "This kind of magic is illegal in my kingdom," I sneer. I take a step toward him, tilting my head as I stare the man down. "There are rogues running in a pack through these lands. That's never been seen before, and they're leaving casualties in their wake. You took one of their own, and I'm willing to bet they will come back for her."

This obviously hasn't crossed the Alpha's mind at all, based on the shocked look on his face.

By some divine intervention of the gods, I'm proven correct only a few seconds after the words leave my lips. Shouts of alarm echo from the village, followed by lifted screams and calls for help.

The Alpha of Cerserne immediately darts out of the building, but I steal one last look at the rogue woman chained to the wall.

"Granger," I say sharply to my Beta, "go make sure the men are ready to move. These rogues are nearby, and where they are, Ella will be."

Granger doesn't waste a second and is gone before I take a breath.

The witch, however, remains, wringing her hands. I turn my gaze to her and notice the tears in her eyes as she fumbles with her apron strings. "Go north to the village of Hannis. Several of your sisters are there and will be returning to the coven within the next month."

She nods, sniffling, but refuses to look me in the eyes. She's far too young to have been sent out on her own to set up a practice in a village. She can't be more than sixteen.

"Do you have family in Moonrise?" I ask.

She nods, wiping her nose on the back of her hand. "My mother and father."

"Why did they allow you to come here so young?"

"I'm gifted," she says over the shouts from outside this disgusting hellhole and the increasingly frantic snarling of the rogue. "The Alpha of Cerserne requested someone like me after his last healer passed away."

"Queen Ravenna never sent her coven here," I argue, my suspicions peeking as the young witch furrows her brows in confusion.

"Sister Petra brought me here. She was the one who announced my assignment. I... I was supposed to continue my studies with the mystics. They only take one alchemist every few years or so, and I was chosen..."

One of Petra's closest friends is also an alchemist.

I'm willing to bet Petra sent this young witch here, to an enemy pack, so her friend could train with the mystics instead.

I grab the witch by the arm. She yelps, her face flushing with fear. "Listen to me," I say sharply, giving her a little shake. "Calm down, and listen to every word I say. There is a barn on the outskirts of the village. My men are there. You're to go to them, and I will have you escorted back to the coven."

But her eyes fill with tears. "I can't go back."

"Why not?"

"I did–I did a bad thing. I had to. I was forced."

"What exactly did you do?"

"There's a cave system nearby, only a mile or two outside of the village. There's a creek bed, and if you follow it south, there's a water-fall, and inside the falls is a cave. I had to–" She bursts into tears. I let go of her arm. "She made me make potions out of–out of liquid silver and wolfsbane for her prisoners–"

"Who?"

In my mind, Granger shouts at me through the mind-link to say they're following a single rogue back toward the edge of the Alpha of Cerserne's territory.

"Petra," the girl whimpers. "She told me she'd kill my parents if I didn't help. The rogues–they guard the falls for her, but something happened this morning. Just a few hours ago, the rogues just... left. They came right through the village."

"And she was caught." I nod toward the rogue, who is currently trying to chew through her own wrist to free herself.

"And they came back for her," the witch says almost wistfully. "She found a family again–"

"Go to the barn, now," I say, my voice lacking even a shred of emotion. I give the witch a little shove toward the door, then send a new command through the mind-link.

I wait for the witch to leave before drawing a blade and approaching the rogue. I ignore her snarls and growls. In her eyes, past that glowing red, I see a single glimpse of the woman she was before, a woman now begging me to put her out of her misery.

So, I do.

With her blood staining my hands, I send a tug down what's left of my mate bond to tell Ella I'm coming.

I know where she is.

And if she hasn't put Petra's head on a stake yet, I will.

HEAD IN A BAG

Ella

They follow me like baby ducks.

I've counted thirty-eight of them so far, though several of the witches are barely able to walk on their own. Every time I speak, thirty-eight sets of eyes light on mine, unblinking. If I stop walking abruptly, the dozen or so strongest unsheathe blades and bows and arrows we stole from the dead warriors we left in the caves.

The caves… well, the witches and I didn't leave right away. Those strong enough to fight killed the rest of the warriors while the others went to free their sisters from the networks of cells hidden along darkened corridors. All of the strange pyres were staunched, and the walls….

I glance around at the witches setting up camp along the base of a cliff. Most of them are splattered with blood, and their hands are covered in it. They painted the walls of those caves red.

I exhale deeply and continue poking the fire in front of me. Rain rips through the camp in sheets that pass as quickly as they come. A huge storm just tore through this place, wherever we are.

"Your Highness?"

I look up from the fire as a beautiful witch who goes by the name of Giselle approaches me. She curtsies low, her tattered cloak picking up wet leaves as she rises. "Hello, Giselle."

Her cheeks go round and pink when I call her by her first name instead of just "witch" or "sister." "May I sit?"

"Of course." I scooch over and pat the ground beside me. Again, she blushes but settles next to me with her back against the dark, rocky cliff face. From this vantage point, we have a full view of the camp of witches spread out before us. Several of them are hard at work building stretchers to carry the wounded while others are tending horrific wounds and comforting their sisters.

"Some of them are very young," I say in a near whisper.

Giselle nods, exhaling through her nose. "Annalise is only twelve. She's the youngest. Her sister Hattie is fourteen, as are Yvonne, Sioban, and Rochelle."

Teenagers. Teenage girls who should be home with their mothers. Teenage girls who went through unimaginable horrors in those caves. I don't even want to think about it, especially not those disgusting warriors and what they might have done to those girls.

But I know several older witches were killed for protecting them. I'll honor that sacrifice… somehow.

"There's a village about ten miles from here called Hannis. There's several healers from Moonrise stationed there." Giselle smooths her hands over the tattered dress she's wearing that barely covers her knees. "Some of our wounded sisters won't last the night if we don't find real shelter and medicine. I'm afraid they might not last the night regardless, but I believe we should at least offer them the comfort of real beds before they pass on."

"I agree," I say with as much force as I can muster. I have no idea what I'm doing right now, I just know these women consider me their queen, and all of the training I received as a member of a royal family is being put to the ultimate test. "We've been resting here long enough, I believe. Has everyone eaten?"

"Yes."

Eaten…. I wouldn't count a stew made of a single squirrel and whatever edible plants we found during our journey from the caves, across a wide, grassy plain, and back into the woods, a full meal. But it's more than these women have eaten in days.

I've been distracted, however. Too distracted to eat. During our escape from the caves, there was one person I couldn't find. Not even his body.

Atticus, Petra's brother, somehow got away.

That leaves a sour taste in my mouth for sure.

"Tell them to prepare to set out again. We can reach Hannis by nightfall if we're quick," I tell Giselle before rising and brushing wet leaves from Petra's crimson cloak. Beneath it, I'm wearing some warrior's pants and tunic, which I swim in, but at least I'm not naked anymore. I'm barefoot, however, having given the boots I found to one of the witches whose feet had been burned over and over.

I can't think about that right now. I push the images of the wounds and absolute desperation in the eyes of the injured witches out of my mind. I remind myself that Petra is dead. In fact, her severed head is in the bag I lift over my shoulder as I watch Giselle tell my coven that we're moving again.

I am their queen. Their *queen*. But my powers only tingle through my veins now, and my body….

I place a hand over the swell of my belly, ignoring the dull ache that echoes through every bone beneath my skin.

I've been cursed. Petra made it sound like it would not only render my powers useless, but it would eventually kill me.

What am I going to do?

"We're ready, Your Highness," Giselle calls out.

I nod, forcing a smile on my face while kicking damp dirt over the fire. "Let's go to Hannis, ladies."

"I'M A HALFLING," Beth, the Luna of Hannis, says softly as we leave the large wooden pack house in the center of Hannis now acting as an infirmary. She pulls her hood over her head against the pattering rain. "Half-witch, half-wolf. But I have none of the gifts of my mother. I may as well be only a wolf shifter." Her beautiful smile lights up the pitch-black night as I walk beside her toward the scattered cabins that make up the small village tucked in the woods.

Above the trees, ancient mountains tower over us, but they're not tall enough to breach the heavy storm clouds.

The past hour has been awful. Even as we put distance between us and the infirmary, the keening cries of the witches tremble in my ears as they mourn the three who died shortly after we reached the village.

One of them, Rochelle, was only fourteen.

"This was not your fault," Beth says.

I tilt my chin up, letting the rain touch my cheeks to blur the tears now spilling over my lashes. "I'm responsible for them now. Their grief and pain is my own."

Beth's hazel eyes crease as she lays a gentle hand in the crook of my elbow. "I've heard whispers of you, Queen Ella. The firestone witch from beyond the veil…. I believed it was just a legend for a long time. The coven is lucky to have you."

I want to tell her I have no idea what I'm doing, but we reach the inn. She ushers me inside and sits me down at a table near a window while she approaches the bar. I sink into a cushioned seat and rest my chin in my hand. Exhaustion washes over me, but I keep my eyes on Beth as she orders what sounds like a feast and begins walking toward me again.

"You have a room upstairs, all right? A hot bath will be waiting for you once you've eaten. I have to return to the Alpha to fill him in on the situation, but you're safe here. Rest, please."

I nod, unable to form the words I need to thank her, but I do reach under the table and hand her the heavy bag I've been carrying all day.

"What is this?" she asks.

"It's a head."

She raises her brows but nods her understanding as she peeks inside. "I knew Petra's mother, unfortunately. She was just as terrible as her daughter."

"Did you know her brother?"

"Atticus?"

"Yes."

"He died very young, I'm afraid. I'll take this to the Alpha, we'll keep it… safe." She winces a bit but hikes the bag over her shoulder.

She says goodnight, but my mind is reeling over what she said before. Atticus died young… But he couldn't have. I saw him. He was there, in the caves, and his resemblance to Petra was uncanny.

I let my mind rake over everything that happened while I eat from a plate piled high with meat and potatoes, all while a pudgy, kind-faced inn keeper watches me take each bite, nodding her approval at my appetite. I don't taste the food. The tea the innkeeper sets in front of me, stirring in copious amounts of sugar and thick cream, tastes like stale water to me.

Eventually, my empty plate and teacup are taken away, and I'm helped upstairs by a maid. My room is sparse but clean and warm. A copper bathtub sits next to the hearth, where a fire is crackling and spreading dry, warm air over my skin as I undress and lower myself into the fragrant bath.

The maid leaves me to bathe in privacy. I scrub my skin raw with the rough rag she provided. I'm digging dirt and blood from under my nails when I hear a commotion downstairs.

Someone is shouting, and then heavy footsteps are rushing upstairs to the rooms along the second floor.

I sigh heavily, ignoring it. I really don't want to kill anyone else today. I'd really like to just go to bed.

I hear doors opening and closing, and several voices protesting whatever intruder is making a scene along the hallway.

But then the doorknob to my room rattles violently.

"Go away," I grumble, sinking down into the water until I'm submerged to my chin.

The rattling stops, and a few seconds pass before the door bursts open like someone kicked it in. The doorknob itself flies across the room and lodges itself in the wall above my bed.

I peek over the rim of the tub, see who it is, and sink back into the water.

"Hi, Ryatt."

He shuts the door more gently than he'd opened it, but I can feel the electric tension crackling through the room as he walks toward the tub. He casts me in his shadow, and I finally look up at him.

"Hi, Ryatt? Is that really all you have to say to me?" He's sopping wet, covered in mud, and looks like he's seen some shit over the past few days. But there's a flicker of amusement in his silver eyes as he starts taking off his mud covered leather vest.

"You're not getting in this bathtub. You're filthy."

"Where the fuck have you been, Ella?" His vest drops to the ground with a wet, slurping sound. He starts taking off his arm guards.

"You're not getting in, Ryatt!" I sit up and glare at him.

"I was just in a cave system, Princess." He rips off his wet shirt and tosses it in a heap across the room. "I've never seen so much blood in my life." He clasps his belt, raising his brows. "Did you have something to do with that?"

I purse my lips as he steps out of his pants, his skin glowing in the dusty amber firelight. Goddess, I missed him.

"Petra's head is in a bag. I just gave it to the Luna of Hannis."

He steps into the tub and sinks into a seated position on the opposite end from me, stretching out his legs.

We stare at each other for several minutes, not speaking.

"Are you okay?" he asks.

I blink, and I feel the tears beginning to well again. He reaches out a hand and takes mine, pulling me toward him.

I settle my back against his chest and close my eyes as his strong arms wrap around me, clutching to him. He dips his head, brushing his lips over my shoulder.

Don't cry. Don't cry. Don't cry.

"I'm sorry I couldn't find you. I tried," he whispers.

I burst into tears.

CALMING THE STORM

Ella

I'm not sure what time it is. Ryatt picked me up and carried me out of the tub hours ago, laying me in bed with so much tenderness it nearly broke my heart.

We've been lying here ever since. My cheek rests against his arm while his other one cradles me, his hand tucked under my breast.

He's asleep. His rhythmic breathing is the only sound in the room other than the rain softly padding against the foggy windows. The fire burned out long ago, and the room is cast in silver gray light as the sun finally begins to rise.

I want to stay here forever–in this room, with my mate's warmth penetrating my skin. Outside the door leading back into the main rooms of the inn, our reality awaits. War, unrest, death and despair. I killed Petra, sure, but I know we have more trials to face. More enemies to conquer.

Ryatt stirs as that silvery, stormy morning light starts to creep up the bed. His legs are tangled in the sheets, and the soft lighting makes his scars and roping, intricate tattoos all the more incredible.

"Are you awake?" he asks against my shoulder.

I blink, my eyes dry from what was probably hours spent staring at the far wall. "I am."

"You need to actually sleep, Ella."

"What happens now?"

Ryatt exhales deeply. "I have to continue south past Rifthold. There's an Alpha there who is going to try to challenge me for the title of Alpha King of Eastonia, and I need to see that matter as soon as I can."

"Are you sending me to the coven now?"

"Is that where you want to go?"

I roll over so we're nose to nose. "How is this supposed to work, Ryatt? Me, Queen of Moonrise, and you, with your... three or four titles, at this point? Alpha of Veiled Valley, Alpha King of the Rogue-lands, now Alpha King of Eastonia? Are we going to be able to... be together? Live together?"

"Of course, we will. When–"

"Don't you dare say when I am Queen of Eastonia," I say with force, but the words feel thick and sticky leaving my tongue. "I'm talking about now. Where is home?"

He runs his hand down my arm, then to my wrist, where the poultices some of the witches made for me have made quick work of healing my horrific wounds.

But the scars are atrocious and deep. I'll always carry them as a physical reminder of what could have become of the coven if I hadn't fallen into Petra's grasp.

Ryatt brushes his thumb over one of the lifted, moon-white scars. "You don't need to go to the coven right away. Giselle has been voted as your second, your heir, from what I understand."

I can't do much more than nod. I understand the coven chooses its queens and it's not a title that's passed down in a single family line, no. It's based on power alone, and if Giselle is destined as my heir, then she is powerful indeed.

Ryatt explains that once he put me to bed last night, he'd gone back into the village to speak to the Alpha of Hannis. The Alpha of Hannis then dispatched a small band of his best warriors to a nearby pack, Cerserne, and captured the Alpha and Beta. Ryatt means to make an example of that pack–to show the rest of the Roguelands what will happen if the Alphas step out of line and try to ally with the enemy that kept them all enslaved for so long.

Then, he went to the infirmary and spoke to the witches there, who gave him the whole story. They'd been picked off, one by one. Some of them were stolen from their homes before the fall of Moonrise, other's kidnapped off the roads between packs, others from their cottages and cabins in whatever pack they lived in as healers.

Every single witch in that infirmary made it clear where their loyalty lies, and that is with me. Not because I am, for whatever reason, the new queen of the coven, but because I freed them.

Giselle, a powerful healer whose gifts extend to botany and manipulating the weather, was voted in as my regent and their ruler in my stead.

She will take the witches back to Moonrise to heal.

Then, Ryatt brings up Petra's head.

"Are you saving it for something?"

"No," I reply, tracing one of the tattoos on his chest. "I just felt like I needed to keep an eye on it."

"Did you think she was somehow going to come back to life?"

I give him a sharp look. "Stranger things have happened in Eastonia, I'm sure."

"The Luna of Hannis is recommending we burn it. She offered to do the honors, and will have the skull ground into dust, then buried deep underground."

"If that's what it takes to rid this world from someone like Petra, so be it."

He swipes a knuckle over my cheek. "You're pale, Ella."

"I was in a cave for three weeks, Ryatt."

I wait for that fiery look in his eyes at my jab, but his gaze softens as he inspects my face. "This is different. You don't feel well, do you?"

"You can't feel those things anymore, remember? Our bond is broken?"

"Not entirely," he whispers, leaning his forehead against mine.

"That doesn't negate the fact that you look ill, *mate*. I'm worried that a journey past Rifthold into what we call the Wastes is going to be taxing on you in your condition."

"Because I'm pregnant?"

"Because you've been through more trauma in the last year than most people experience in a lifetime."

"I don't want to be separated from you again," I admit. The words warble off my tongue, and my throat closes around a sob. "I can't, Ryatt."

"You don't need to return to Moonrise right away," he assures me then presses a kiss to my lips. The kiss is tender, but deep, the kind of kiss that sends electricity shuddering through my soul, awakening that part of me that's only for Ryatt to see.

I bring my knee up and rest it on his hip. That's when I realize that I'm not the only naked one in bed right now.

I shouldn't even be thinking about sex at the moment. I've been in a stupor for weeks and just battled to the death with a witch who was enslaving and torturing my coven.

But my traitorous body ignores the doubts in my mind as Ryatt pulls away from the kiss, and I pull him back, sliding my tongue over his lower lip in invitation.

Ryatt runs his hand down my back but hesitates for the space of a breath before gripping my ass and exhaling with a groan. He pulls me closer so my breasts are flush with his chest.

My breasts ache—in general—but right now I'm just aching to be touched. I want to be touched in a way that won't hurt, that won't scar me or make me think of everything that happened over the past few weeks.

"Gently," I whisper before I can stop myself. Ryatt is getting ready to roll me onto my back but stops and looks down at me.

"I will only ever ask one thing of you from now on," he says, his eyes growing heavy and dark with need, "and that's honesty, Princess."

"I'm okay, really."

He shakes his head, rolling his lower lip between his teeth as he debates his next move. He's carrying so much on his shoulders right now, and the last thing I want to do is add a curse to that burden.

"Ryatt," I whisper, running my fingers through his hair and cupping the back of his head. "I love you. I'm all right. I'm going to be fine."

"Promise me."

I feel my heart beginning to crack around the lie burrowing itself deep in my chest. I kiss him again, hard, pulling him into me until there's no space left between us. The kiss is wet and hot—edging on desperate—as he nudges my legs apart and wastes no time at all sinking his cock deep into my core.

I gasp at the sudden fullness, and then let my breath out in a heady moan when he pulls out slowly. He nuzzles my neck, whispering praise against my skin as he pumps into me again, and again, one hand cupping the back of my head while the other grips my ass to keep me right where I am.

His weight on top of me is the most comforting thing I've experienced in a long time. The world around us ceases to exist, and I'm so blinded by pleasure that I don't notice the way the daylight shifts from stormy gray to a rich gold that heats the room.

I lose myself to his touch. The way his hips grind into mine sends my mind into a state of numbness, where there's nothing but the way he's making me feel and his deep voice in my ear telling me that he loves me, that I'm his.

I open my eyes to find him looking down at me, his face flushed with ecstasy as he slides his hand from my ass to grip the headboard.

"R-Ryatt!" I plead, arching my hips to meet his stroke for stroke. Tingles of pleasure burn through my belly and thighs, and then my body erupts with heat.

"Ella," he grunts, pressing his body against mine as my core begins to spasm around his dick, squeezing him tight. He growls low in his throat as he dips his head and kisses me so deeply my toes curl. "You're fucking paradise."

I can't form real words. A whimpering moan leaves my lips as he thrusts into me so hard the headboard claps against the wall. I rake my nails over his back as he comes undone, spilling himself deep inside of me.

Then he collapses, pulling me into his chest.

Slick with sweat and panting, he tenderly runs his knuckles up and down my naked spine, then over my ribs, which currently show through my skin. Several beats of silence pass before he says, "What you did in those caves... I'm sorry you had to do it. Taking a life–"

"I've killed before. It's nothing."

"It shouldn't feel like nothing. You saved countless lives. I'm proud of you. I knew... I knew wherever you were, you were giving your captors hell."

"They kept me drugged. I–" I bite down on my lip and rest my arm against my stomach. "I'm worried about the baby, Ryatt."

"I already have a healer coming to see you this morning. Luna Beth said she's the best."

"What if someone happened to our daughter?" I ask, and it's the first time I allowed myself to say the words out loud. I'm only just starting to let myself think about this baby being an actual, tangible thing. At first, when I found out, it didn't seem real. Now, especially after meeting my nephews, I imagine holding her in my arms. I imagine Ryatt looking down at her for the first time with love in his eyes as he sits in the sun with our daughter in his arms.

I love her. I'd tear the world in two in her name, whatever that will be.

"I'd go insane if anything happened to her. If they hurt her—I'd bring Petra back from the dead and kill her all over again."

Ryatt suddenly stiffens beside me. I lift my head.

"What is it?"

"Nothing," he says abruptly, but his brows are furrowed. "I just forgot I needed to do something today. That's all."

He sits up, and I follow.

"I won't be gone long. We're going to stay here in Hannis for a few days to rest. I'll have breakfast sent up."

"Do you need me to–"

"Stay here, Ella." He presses a kiss to my forehead and begins to dress.

"Where are you going?"

He pulls his shirt over his head and shrugs, giving me a cocky smirk. "I have an appointment with the Alpha King of Crescent Falls."

2 9

MOONSTONES AND WATER

Isaac

I gently lift Sydney out of Maddy's arms. He blinks, then a fleeting smile stretches over his face before he falls back asleep with milk dribbling down his cheek. Ryan is already sleeping in the double-wide crib tucked beneath the window in our bedroom, his chubby arms and legs splayed out like a starfish.

Sydney likes to be swaddled but I'm terrible at it. I mumble curses under my breath as I try to adjust his swaddle and gently lay him down beside his brother, who is in nothing but a diaper, which is just the way Ryan likes it.

Thank the Goddess it's a sweltering summer night.

I edge away from the crib with my hands out in surrender, grimacing as my foot catches that damned squeaky floorboard I keep forgetting to tell someone to fix, but the twins remain asleep.

So does my wife.

Maddy's wine-red hair falls over her shoulder and back as she rolls over on her side and curls into the blankets. She whispers something to herself in her sleep, but it's lost on me. I'm too focused on the way the faint moonlight plays over her face and neck.

217

I'd love to be in bed with her right now. In fact, that's all I've been thinking about all day.

But tonight is important.

I feel that sharp tug in the back of my head for the third time in the last ten minutes and leave the room as quickly as I can without making enough noise to wake up my family. I break into a jog heading toward the library.

It only takes me a few minutes to reach my observatory. I yank on the lever that opens up the roof to the clear, moonless sky. The metal clicks and hisses as the metal ceiling pulls apart, folding into itself, and then there's nothing but stars overhead–a clear, humid night. A new moon. The only night during the month–during the lunar cycle–when Ryatt and I can send messages through the veil.

The tug in my head–Ryatt's summons–is like someone is trying to connect with me over the mind-link, but they're incredibly out of range. I can feel it, however, which means we were right about our assumptions when it came to communicating through the veil.

I rub my palms over my navy blue athletic shorts then approach the glittering moonstone bowl I tasked the priestesses at the temple to craft for me. It rests on a simple wood table and is surprisingly heavy for its size. It cost as much as adding a new wing onto my castle. So, this better work, otherwise my efforts and money have been wasted.

Water shimmers in the bowl, reflecting the stars. The water is from the falls on Maatua and was painstakingly brought here just for this purpose. I couldn't justify a trip to Maatua every month on the new moon, but when I tried to use water from a nearby creek as a conduit, I could barely hear a word Ryatt said to me, and vice versa.

A month ago, I sat near the creek and shouted into it like a lunatic. He'd shouted back, and all I could gather from our brief conversation was that they made it back to Eastonia, to Veiled Valley, and some brief instructions about how to make this monthly ritual work better for both of us.

I'd heard the word moonstone, and it sparked an idea in my mind.

Now I have a glorified salad bowl filled with water from an island in a far off sea sitting in my observatory.

I lean over the bowl, resting my hands on either side of it, and let my mind go blank. The veil is at its thinnest during the new moon. Ryatt had told me everything he knew about the veil, and crossing it, during his time in the Isles.

The water ripples. I wait. In the space of a breath, I feel the sensation of being watched. I close my eyes, still trying to clear my thoughts, and wait for Ryatt's voice–fractured and buzzing with static–to fill my head.

But instead, I hear the quiet chirping of birds, the soft hum of gently rushing water, and the warm sun... on my face.

I open my eyes.

"You did something right," Ryatt says as he sits down on a boulder on the other side of a glistening creek. Emerald color stone litters the water, turning it a stunning green. I look around, squinting into the sun.

"How?" I reach up and pull a fresh, bright green leaf from a tree branch brushing the top of my head. I can feel the fuzzy coating on the leaf as well as smell its fresh, bright scent. "Did you bring me here?"

"You're not really here," Ryatt says with a little wave of his hand in my direction. "Whatever you did differently this time worked, apparently."

I sink down on a fallen log and continue squinting at my surroundings. We're in a dense forest, in a clearing, and it's a rich, late spring morning. In the distance, twists of dark smoke break through the canopy of the trees and stretch toward a cloudless sky.

Eastonia is beautiful, untouched, and seemingly empty.

"This is a mirage, then?"

"Exactly." Ryatt sounds bored, but one look at his face tells me he likely hasn't slept in a while. Dark circles ring his eyes, and his shoulders are slumped. But the sun catches on something beside him.

"Is that the sword?"

"Hmm? Oh–" he motions to the sword leaning on his leg, its blade resting in the water. I notice the shadows then. Inky, black tendrils that fan out from the sword into the water. "I suppose this is another reason our meeting today is so much clearer than last time. I have your sister to thank for its return."

I want to ask what happened over the last month. The last time we'd talked, much had been said, but so little was understood because of the shitty connection. I remember he mentioned Ella returning to a nearby witch coven, whatever the hell he meant by that, but this sword is the one he told my dad he didn't want falling into the wrong hands. The same sword he said would be better off destroyed or lost forever.

Now it's back, and Ryatt's withdrawn expression tells me something happened. Something big.

I bite down on the million questions buzzing through my mind and remind myself, like Maddy reminds me constantly when Ryatt and Ella are brought up in conversation, that Ella might be my sister, but Ryatt is her *mate*. Her husband, by all accounts.

I have no right to interrogate him. He'd probably look worse than he does now if Ella were dead.

"How are your sons and your mate?"

"Fine. Healthy, happy. I can't ask for more."

A beat of silence. Then Ryatt says, "I don't have much time to talk, so I'll be quick and brief. Ella was kidnapped, but she's home now. Resting. She beheaded a witch and killed at least a dozen warriors and escaped on her own accord."

I raise my brows, finding myself momentarily speechless.

My brother-in-law meets my eyes. "She's not feeling well."

"Well, obviously–"

"This goes beyond what she just went through and the pregnancy, I believe."

Another moment of silence, nothing but the trembling creek and birdsong to break it.

Ryatt rests his hands on his knees, his tattooed fingers splayed. "Have you seen anything in the stars regarding Ella?"

"I told you I don't use those gifts often–"

He raises his gaze, locking his eyes on mine. "I need you to try."

I shake my head. "What good are having powers like mine in my own realm, Ryatt? They're better kept contained."

"She said something to me less than an hour ago that reminded me of the conversation we had regarding what you saw about *my wife* in one of your visions, Isaac." His tone is ice cold. For the first time, I see Ryatt for what he truly is. Fucking powerful. The most powerful man I've ever encountered, in all honesty. His power rumbles through him, spanning past him. The trees go silent as the birds halt their songs. This man... he could topple worlds with a snap of his fingers, I'm sure.

If he is Ella's match, then my vision of her raising all types of hell isn't as unbelievable as I thought.

"What exactly did she say?"

Ryatt leans back so the sun touches his face and shuts heavy eyes. I can almost feel the exhaustion pouring off him as he tilts his chin toward the sun and exhales, "She was talking about the baby and what she would do if anything happens to that child."

I chew the inside of my cheek as I watch him lower his gaze back to mine. His expression is emotionless–a trained look I use myself during meetings and when facing Alphas who step out of line, but his eyes betray the hard planes of his face.

"I need you to try to have your mother's tears sent through the veil."

"Is something wrong?"

"Not now," he breathes, picking an invisible piece of lint from his pants. "But Ella seems off. If, gods forbid, something were to happen during the birth... or our child is born sickly...." He swallows, unable to finish the words.

While I don't know the details of what Ella just went through, I can imagine, based on Ryatt's expression right now, that he's worried. He's practically falling apart at the edges.

"I worry if Ella were to lose the child, your vision would come true."

I grind my teeth. "Don't the all-powerful creatures of Eastonia have the kind of healing magic my mom has?"

"Not at her caliber, and it's hard to find. We normally make do with herbal solutions and...potions." He waves a hand in dismissal. "Ella is being seen by a midwife from the coven as we speak."

"You're not with her for that?"

"I had to meet with you, and you were running *late*," he says with a touch of impatience.

I cross my arms over my chest, rolling the little leaf I plucked earlier between my fingers. "If the veil ever comes down, I'm buying you a fucking cellphone."

He says nothing at first but continues to stare at me. Ignoring my jab completely, he says, "Train your powers of sight, Isaac."

"I will," I reply, hoping that appeases him. "But what if I am right and my vision of Ella tearing your world apart and building an army is true? How do you know that this vision of mine shows Ella in a... bad light? What if she's waging war for good reasons, for peace?"

"She wouldn't be," he says so quickly it takes me off guard. "She was wearing the mask in your visions, wasn't she? That's dark magic, Isaac. Just like this sword and the rest of the objects made during the times before the veil, when gods walked alongside our kind. If Ella loses something precious, and that's all it takes to bring hellfire down on my people..." His eyes catch on the water, so full of emotion I find myself sitting up a little straighter. "I need your mother's tears. Find a way."

With that, he grips the hilt of his sword and pulls it out of the water, and the world around me ceases to exist. Suddenly, I'm back in my observatory, standing with my palms braced on either side of the moonstone bowl.

I curl my hands into fists before taking a step away from the table.

Something is crushed between the fingers of my left hand. I unfurl them and find a small, bright green leaf.

30

TENDRILS OF BLACK

Ella

All is well. Nothing is amiss. Our daughter is growing as she should be.

Here's a list of herbs. The alchemist in the market can make you a bundle for teas and spicing your food. You should be eating this as often as you can. It'll help with the aches and fatigue. The midwife's words echo in my mind.

All is well. No signs of distress. No inklings that a curse is eating me alive.

I watch the village of Hannis from my window at the inn as I cradle the swell of my stomach.

No one suspects a thing is wrong with me.

Maybe Petra was wrong. Maybe she lied and was only trying to scare me, but the memories of Kane's blade slicing my skin ebb through my mind and leave scars in their wake.

I need to know for sure if I'm cursed and what it means. And, more importantly, how to break it.

The midwife comes and goes with a smile on her pleasant face, but I haven't left the room. I've barely touched the cold breakfast foods laid out on a small table near the window. The tea has grown cold.

What's wrong with me? I've never been one to just… give up. Keeping secrets? Well… I'm very good at that. But I'm keeping a secret from *Ryatt*, and that feels… so wrong.

I should tell him, but then he'll make it his mission to fix me. He'll rage throughout our already broken and bleeding kingdom for a cure.

And if I'm wrong about the curse, and my fluctuating powers and aching body is only a reflection of my advancing pregnancy, then his efforts will be wasted, and I can't do that to him.

This is my burden for the time being. It's decided. I'm not telling him until it's confirmed.

I run my hands over the soft, well-crafted violet tunic and matching pants I've been provided and walk back to the bed to fetch the brown cloak laid out on the fresh sheets. I clasp it at the neck and quickly braid my hair, curling a few of the front pieces around my fingers before pinching my cheeks to bring some color back to my skin.

I eat a few large bites of food despite my lack of appetite to make it look like I at least tried to fuel myself, then I leave our snug room and head out into the village.

It's beautiful here. It's also a very old place. I can feel ancient magic thrumming through the chorus of cheerful voices wandering from shop to shop, from home to home. The worn mountains in the distance are a vivid emerald green. I slowly make my way in the direction of the apothecary shop the midwife mentioned, her list clutched tight in my hand.

"Ella."

I stop at the sound of my name and turn. Ryatt is walking steadily toward me looking like a dream in his full leather get-up. In the glimmer of early summer sunshine, I catch the rare gleam of the chestnut brown that weaves through his normally black hair. It's long enough to fall over his shoulders now, and I haven't seen it undone like this since we left Maatua.

My handsome mate in all his glory stops before me, that cocky smile on his face as he grips my elbow and leans down to kiss me.

"Whatever happened to your leather jacket?" I ask as he pulls away.

"What?"

I reach up to pull a few blades of grass from his leather vest. "The jacket you always used to wear. I haven't seen it on you in ages."

"I lost it in Rifthold," he says, a bit wistfully. He brushes my braid over my shoulder, his fingers lingering on the ribbon I used to tie it off with. "Westfall and I had to shift abruptly, and I never returned to retrieve it."

"I'll buy a new one while we're here," I offer, motioning to a nearby shop with all kinds of clothing items on display, including intricate works made of leather.

"It's not replaceable," he says softly, shrugging. "It belonged to my mother."

"I highly doubt she was your size," I tease, and his eyes crease as he smiles.

But that smile fades as a thought dons on him.

"What's wrong?"

"Now that I think about it, I believe that jacket might have once belonged to... Westfall."

"Ah," I say, nodding. Disappointment floods my mind as I watch his face undergo a great change from amusement to something like disgust. "Have you talked to him about... him being your father?"

"Of course not."

I purse my lips. Ryatt has, of course, filled me in on what happened in the aftermath of Westfall and I being attacked at the river. Westfall was terribly wounded but thankfully found by scouts dispatched by Artyom and Granger. He spent a week recovering in a rural village before Ryatt ordered him to return to Veiled Valley.

Apparently, he's on his way to catch up to us, and if only to distract myself from the knowledge of the curse gnawing at my system, I've been hatching a plan at an intervention.

"He's going to be our daughter's grandfather."

"By blood, yes."

"What's your problem with him?"

"He didn't go back for my mother."

I raise my brows and try to argue that I saw a vision of them in their final moments together. Westfall didn't have a choice. He had a chance to save Ryatt, and Ryatt's mother wouldn't take no for an answer.

But then Granger comes into view.

"Luna," he says to me with a bow.

I frown at him. "Stop calling me Luna. It creeps me out."

Granger furrows his brow at me and glances at Ryatt, whose expression is now back to its usual smugness.

"*Ella,*" Granger drawls dramatically.

"Better," I huff, and reach for Ryatt's hand, but Granger steps closer, leaning to whisper in his ear.

Ryatt looks down at me, frowning. "I have to meet with the Alpha of Hannis. It'll bore you to death. The witches are going to depart tonight for the coven if you'd like to say your goodbyes."

"Okay–"

Ryatt briskly kisses me on the top of the head and then is gone before I can take a breath. I watch him wade through the crowded market with his Beta at his side. I feel a pang of sadness for Amanda, given that she's stuck in Veiled Valley while we're here, preparing to depart for lands unknown.

At least, lands unknown to me.

I visit the alchemist like planned and leave her pungent shop with a cloth bag filled with herbs and spices. My brain spins over her brewing instructions as I walk the quarter mile or so to the infirmary.

It's busy. Witches are packing up their donated goods and clothing. Some of them are heavily bandaged, but there's a new light in their eyes, new hope.

It warms my aching heart to see it.

Two young teenagers run by laughing, the sound rich and like the sweetest music.

"Queen Ella," Giselle says as I approach. She rises from the ground where she was assisting another witch pack a canvas bag with provisions.

"Hello. Are you all heading out soon?"

"Yes. We sent a few scouts ahead of us, and one returned. It's a weeklong journey to the coven but we'll pass several villages along the way to resupply and rest."

I glance around the room. It's impossible to tell which witches are mixed with wolf, but my anxiety around their journey back to the coven is softened by the idea of their group having shifters who can scout ahead to ensure their route is safe.

"We'll be fine. The worst is over." Giselle lays a hand over my wrist, and I jump at the contact. Her touch funnels through me like a wave of pure heat. She suddenly pulls away and looks me in the eyes. Her lips part, and her brows furrow. "Qu-Queen Ella, can I speak with you privately for a moment?"

I nod as gooseflesh ripples over my skin. Had that strange heat been her powers? Ryatt did tell me Giselle was known for her healing powers…. Had she sensed something wrong with me, like I assume?

She leads me to a quiet corner of the infirmary.

"I wasn't in the temple within the cave when you battled with Petra," she says in a near whisper. "But I've heard snippets of what was said from our sisters who were in attendance. May I—may I see your scar?"

"My scar?" I ask, more to myself than to her.

She nods then motions for me to follow her through a nondescript door leading into what looks like a storage room. I walk behind her and come to a halt in the center of several crates. A musty smell hangs in the air, but my view of the space is obstructed as she closes the door, and we're cloaked in darkness.

A flash of golden light erupts and then softens. I turn to face Giselle and gasp.

She glows. Every inch of her body is glowing with golden light, and her eyes are like molten metal as she steps toward me. "Please, sit."

Too shocked to speak, I unceremoniously pull down my pants and sit on the crate, spreading my legs enough for her to inspect the scar on my inner thigh.

Her hands are hot against my skin, and at her touch, my skin begins to glow from within until every single vein is illuminated. I gasp. I've never seen anything like this before. Instinctively I pull up my shirt and look down at my belly as Giselle's light courses through me.

I can see the baby clearly, nestled deep and safe in my womb. She's bigger than I expected, but the midwife told me today that I'm almost five months along now.

"She's sucking her thumb," Giselle says with a smile, but the smile doesn't meet her eyes as she continues to inspect my scar.

I haven't looked down at it yet. I'm too shocked to pay it any mind as I examine the glowing veins and arteries visible under my skin. Even my bones glow.

But then I see it. The second I look down, my stomach twists into a knot.

Around the scar left by Kane's blade, black ripples fan out around the soft scar tissue like little fingers trying to reach deeper into my body.

But a silvery substance fights against the curse now confirmed to be lurking under my skin.

"Your powers are fighting it. That's why you feel weak." She leans back to examine the baby next. "She's fine, Your Highness. I can't see or sense the curse in your womb."

I fight the urge to vomit at the sight of the black tendrils of magic under my skin. "Can it be cut out?" I'd cut my damn leg off. I really would.

"No… but there's someone who might be able to help, I believe. And it's a good thing you're following Alpha Ryatt into the Wastes. I can't remember her name. It's been… decades, since she lived with the coven. She was one the enslaved witches in Rifthold, but before that, she was a particularly gifted healer and a scholar in curses. She's rumored to have escaped King Kane at some point and practices her craft in the Wastes, near the Alabaster Mountains."

I remember that mountain range from Ryatt's map. They're so far south, it would take months to get there, I'm sure.

"What can I do about this now?"

"Try not to get hurt or sick," Giselle says, meeting my eyes. "Any infections will weaken your powers, which will allow the curse to grow. An injury will do the same. I can smell the herbs you bought today. They will help keep you healthy for sure, but I will add some of my own to the mix before we leave tonight. You must rest, Your Highness. At any chance you can, rest. Eat well. Don't use your powers unless absolutely necessary."

"What about shifting?"

She sighs. "If I didn't think you needed to find the witch in the Wastes, I would recommend you come to the coven for healing. I think shifting is necessary for your journey, but it will cause the curse to spread. Definitely." She clicks her tongue in thought. "You'll feel worse as you go along. It's imperative you find this witch."

"How will I know it's her?"

"You will know," she says, meeting my eyes. "Intuition. Trust no others with the truth. His Highness–"

"He doesn't know." I roll my lower lip between my teeth. "I don't want him to know, not yet. Not if I want to make it to the Wastes in time to get help."

She nods, grim understanding flashing behind her golden hued eyes. Her powers slowly fade until we're cast in darkness once again. I hear her shuffle toward the door, but I ask, "How long do I have?"

She stills, and I hear her exhale deeply. "You may not survive the birth if this curse isn't broken. That kind of trauma could…. It would cause the curse to spread exponentially. Once it reaches your heart–" she cuts herself off. "You have four months, maybe five. Your power will weaken until then as it fights off the curse."

Shit. What am I going to do?

"Tell him when you're ready, and Your Highness?" She turns to me, her face and body completely shadowed by the darkness. "There is a chance this curse can't be broken."

"I understand," I whisper back. She opens the door and leaves me to sit in my thoughts.

Four months. I have four months.

But I'm not thinking about my own life as my hands rest on the swell of my belly.

Ryatt will raise our daughter alone if I can't find this witch.

I have to tell him. He should know.

But then I think of his feelings toward Westfall, and how he…how he blames him, his own father, for his mother's death.

Would Ryatt blame our child for mine?

THE TRUTH COMES OUT

Ryatt

"She's oddly quiet," Granger says as we step out of the pack house in a village called Reighnier, where the pack Silent Crest resides.

I glance at my mate who is walking back to the two-story stone cottage we've been given to sleep in for the night. Her long dark hair is neatly braided down her back, and her brown cloak is spotless as she pulls open the door and slips inside.

I exhale, my stomach tightening as I fumble with the leather armguards around my wrists. "She's tired. I spoke to her this morning. We're going to see another healer once we reach Twin Rivers."

Or what's left of Twin Rivers. The once prosperous city on the banks of the river that separates the Roguelands from Rifthold is barely more than a village of tents and refugees now. It was flattened during the war, just like Rifthold. Once we cross the river, it could be weeks until we find someone to help Ella with the pregnancy symptoms that plague her day in and day out.

"Is this wise, Ryatt?" Granger asks in a low tone that makes it clear he's growing nervous. "She's so thin. Her skin is practically gray."

"I know," I grind out. "Trust me, I've asked her to just go to the coven, or return to Veiled Valley, but she's adamant she goes with us."

She screamed at me this morning, actually. Damn near ripped my fucking head off when I gently told her she looked like walking death, and I was worried about her. But we've been on the road for two weeks already, shifting between villages, making stops at every pack.

She's seen three healers so far, and all of those meetings have been closeted. She doesn't want me there, and I'm growing suspicious.

Granger leans against a gnarled old-growth tree only a few feet from the front door to the cottage I'm sharing with Ella tonight.

"Do you want to sleep here with us? There's a couch downstairs."

"I'll take a pile of hay over having to bear witness to one of your fights," Granger replies, his green eyes lighting on mine. "You need to send her home–to Amanda."

"I'm trying." I'll never get my way with Ella. I accepted that the moment I woke up in what remained of her mother's living room to Isla shoving a vial of her tears down my throat. Ella wouldn't let me die even though it was what I wanted at that moment. Now, she won't let me help her, besides asking me to steep the foul herbs she drinks all day and occasionally letting me touch her.

She burns with a fever. She eats so much but doesn't put on a single ounce of weight. All the while, her belly grows, and it's obvious now that she's with child.

"I think *you* should return to Amanda," I tell Granger, if only to change the subject. "Ella will likely deliver the child before we return at this rate, so Amanda will too. They're due the same day, aren't they?"

"Yes," Granger sighs. "I'd love to, but I'm needed–"

"You're needed at home with your wife."

Granger gives me a look through his lashes that betrays his normally expressionless countenance. "I'll think about it."

He kicks off the tree and stalks off into the night.

I walk through the front door and close it behind me, turning the latch. Ella is in the shabby kitchen. A kettle whines as I turn the corner.

"I can make that for you."

"I got it. It's fine," she says, swallowing hard. "But thanks."

"Can we talk, Ella?"

"About what?" She turns from the wood-fired stove with the kettle and pours the boiling water into a huge mug. Wisps of steam curl around her hands. I'm shocked it doesn't burn her skin…. Gods, her skin. Those scars around her wrists make me see red every time they catch my attention.

"You're unwell."

"I'm pregnant."

"Ella," I say, trying to keep a firm grip on what little patience I have left. "This goes beyond that. What are these herbs for? I know some of them, and they're not used for pregnancy, or even during birth."

"It's to keep my strength up during our journey. Shifting has been difficult."

"Once we reach Rifthold, I'll be spiriting us where we need to go."

"I'm not sure that'll make much of a difference."

"Why are you fighting me on this?" I brace my hands on the work-table in the center of the room. She sets the kettle back on the stove, but her fingers tighten on the handle.

"Ella?"

I can almost see the gears working in her head as her eyes glaze over with some thought.

"What is wrong with you?" I ask, as gently as possible.

"If anything were to happen to me, would you still love her?"

"The baby?"

She finally meets my eyes. "Yes."

"Of course I would," I say, exasperated. "Ella, this is nonsense–"

"If I die in childbirth, would you raise her? Or would you ship her off to the coven?"

"Ella, seriously, why are we talking about this? Did something happen? Did one of those healers say–"

"Promise me, Ryatt. Promise me that you'll look after her and love her like you love me. With all of your heart. I need to hear you say it."

She has tears in her eyes now. Something's wrong. Something is terribly wrong.

"You have to talk to me, Princess."

"Promise me."

"I promise–"

"Promise me that if you have to choose between us, you will choose her."

"Enough," I rasp, holding my hand out. "Stop this. Please, Ella."

A single tear rolls down her cheek. She tears her gaze from me and gathers up her mug. She tries to step past me, but I stop her, dragging her to a stop.

"Tell me the truth right now."

"No."

I grit my teeth and look down at my hard headed mate. Be loving, be gentle. Be kind, for the love of the gods. That's incredibly difficult to manage when what I want to do is shake her until she comes back to her senses.

She tries to yank her arm out of my grasp, but I tighten my grip.

Her sea-green eyes meet mine. "Let. Me. Go."

"Tell me what's wrong, and I'll think about it," I hiss.

"I can't."

"Yes, you can."

Her nostrils flare as that famous temper flickers to life. Here we go. Our favorite thing to do–fight.

"Let go of me, you fucking brute!"

I pull her into my chest and crush my lips to hers. Her tea spills, sending a shock of boiling heat ripping over my thigh, but I ignore it, breathlessly pulling away. "Tell me!"

She shoves me back so hard I nearly crash into the doorway leading back into the main part of the cottage. "Do you really want to know? I already know what will happen if I tell you, Ryatt, which is why I haven't."

"Oh, for the love of the gods–"

"Oh, they're not listening, Ryatt. Trust me. I've been pleading for their help for weeks now!" Her voice takes on a bitter edge as her chest puffs out, her hands curling into fists. "Kane fucking cursed me, Ryatt! Goddess! He not only cut out your mark but cursed me in the process. I am *dying*. Every minute of every day I grow weaker. My powers are fighting against it but–the shifting–" She starts to crumble as my mind reels over what she just said. "Giselle said I need to find a witch who lives past Rifthold in the wastes. She can't remember her name–"

"You're going back to the coven right this instant!"

"You don't understand! This is why I didn't fucking tell you!"

"How long have you known?" Fury shreds my senses apart.

"Weeks now. Three weeks since Giselle confirmed it."

And we've been traveling for two weeks. She's been shifting for *two weeks*. "The herbs are to try to stop the curse?"

"There's only one person who might have a cure, and she's in the territories we'll be visiting soon."

"I don't believe that. The mystics–"

"They can't help me. Sending me away is as good as sealing my death, Ryatt!"

"You should have told me the second you thought–"

"My mom's tears didn't heal the wound on my thigh, Ryatt. Don't you remember?" Her voice suddenly softens. "Oh, my Goddess. Ryatt, I might never see my mom again–Oh, no–"

I catch her as she crumples to the ground. I cradle her like an infant, absently rocking her back and forth. I'm pissed the fuck off, sure. But still, a new kind of fear blurs my mind and echoes through my very soul as I feel how thin, and how weak, my mate is in my arms.

"We have work to do. I didn't tell you because I knew you'd put off dealing with your enemies and focus on this instead. Our people can't take another war–"

"I cannot lose you," I say into her hair. "For fucks sake, Ella. Why didn't you tell me sooner?"

"I couldn't. Not when all of this unrest is happening and then–and then your hatred of Westfall–"

I pull away from her and grab her by the chin. "What does Westfall have to do with anything?"

"He is your dad. He had to leave his mate to give you a chance at a better life, and you still blame him for her death. You can't see past that. How are you supposed to see past my death and still love our daughter?"

My heart caves in on itself. It's the meanest, but truest, thing anyone has ever said to me.

I'd choose Ella if I had to, and she knows it. I would choose her over and over again.

Isaac's vision comes to mind, and I get it–finally. I bury that sudden truth and lock it away, not wanting to even think about it.

"What exactly did Giselle say about the curse?"

She tells me what she knows, what she assumes. She could live a long time with the curse, but her powers would be useless, too focused on keeping the curse from ravaging her body. Any illness or injury could cause the curse to spread quickly because her powers would be even weaker at that point.

Childbirth would likely kill her in this instance. The curse would be unleashed, her powers at their most frail.

She'll die.

Fuck no.

"There has to be a way!"

"Ryatt, please–"

"We can't go to the Wastes, not now–"

"But the witch–"

"She might not be there. I'll send scouts. We'll stay here in the meantime."

"No. I have to go. I have to follow you past Rifthold. Please!"

I look down at her and realize with heartbreaking clarity that she's right. I realize that my request for Isla's tears won't matter. They'll do nothing against this curse.

We have no options.

But I do know one person who might have a temporary solution or two.

Without further conversation, I scoop Ella into my arms and carry her to bed. I tell her to stay there and then make her another cup of tea, taking stock of every single herb and spice she's been prescribed. I take it to her and then leave the cottage, traveling deep into the forest. A quick message to Granger over the mind-link is all that's needed to make my intentions known.

Keep Ella in bed. Do not let her up until I return in roughly twelve hours' time.

Using my powers like this... It's not a good idea, not when I need to be at my strongest when we cross into Rifthold within the next three days.

I draw my sword in a moonlit clearing and pull a single moonstone from my pocket. Before I can even shut my eyes, the world around me starts to spin, and then the smell of leather and parchment fills my nose, and a craggily old voice murmurs in shock, "Your Highness?"

32

LEAP OF FAITH

Ryatt

I SLIDE my sword back into its scabbard down my spine and look around the crystalline main wing of the archives in Veiled Valley. My body thrums from the enormous use of power it took to get here. Getting back to Ella is going to be painful, for sure, but if I'm right in my assumptions, Arthur is going to know how to help us.

The little man in question blinks up at me from behind cracked, circular spectacles that are so thick they make his beady eyes look like tea saucers.

"Good evening," I breathe, and it's an effort. My vision goes slightly fuzzy as I brace myself on the doorframe to the crystal atrium, the lights of Veiled Valley glimmering in the distance.

"It's three in the morning."

"Not where I just came from," I say. "Do you have whiskey by chance?"

But footsteps nearby catch my attention, and within a second, I'm face to face with Westfall.

Great.

"What are you doing here, Commander?"

Westfall looks me up and down, his dark brows arched.

Arthur, Veiled Valley's tiny historian, gets lost, sensing the tension between us. He mumbles something about finding the whiskey I asked for and is gone before I can even blink.

"We weren't anticipating your presence tonight, Your Highness."

"I'm here to speak to Arthur." I eye my father skeptically. "Again, what are you doing here so late at night?"

"Lady Amanda has tasked me with keeping her entertained, which means I spend most of my evenings after she's gone to bed looking for new books that might pique her interest." He motions to the stack of books on a table behind them. Romance, historical fiction, the works.

"I see."

We stare at each other for a moment.

He rolls his lower lip between his teeth, then adds, "I am planning on leaving Veiled Valley tomorrow with a small group of warriors as planned to intercept you in the Wastes."

"Plans have changed."

If he's surprised, he doesn't show it. His glacier blue eyes stay locked on mine as Arthur scurries back into the dusty atrium carrying a bottle of fine whiskey. "I have a glass somewhere."

"Don't bother." I snatch the bottle from his crooked fingers and wrench the cork off with my teeth, drinking deeply while still keeping my gaze locked on Westfall. "We have a serious problem."

"What is it now?" Westfall sighs, leaning his hip on the table.

I take another pull of the whiskey, loving the way it burns down my throat and reignites my senses. "Ella is cursed, and she's dying."

"What?" Westfall eyes blaze. "When—"

"When she was taken by Kane, and he cut out her mark. Petra fed him the curse, and he used the mask to bring the spell to life."

"What spell, exactly?" Arthur pipes up, adjusting his glasses like that'll do a damn thing to help enhance his vision. He moves like the wind to a towering bookshelf and begins to climb a ladder.

I explain what I can, what I know. It's something deep, something that lives under her skin and is after her heart. Her powers keep it from spreading.

"So, it's likely ancient then, from a time when the Firestone and Shadowsynger gifts were more populous," Arthur says to himself as he climbs several more rings. If he falls from this height, he will die in an instant.

Westfall looks furious as he says, "It's been months since she was in Kane's presence."

"I know."

"How long have you known?"

"Thirty fucking minutes," I sneer, letting my fury show clearly behind my eyes. "Do you think I would have wasted this much time if I'd known earlier?"

A thudding sound makes my stomach hollow out, and I turn, expecting to find Arthur's skull crushed from a fall, but it's only a massive leather bound book smeared with oily dust.

"Not that one," he says, then begins to hum to himself as he climbs toward the fucking ceiling.

"Gods above," I growl. "Listen, Westfall. Sister Giselle of Moonrise, are you familiar with her?"

"Yes, she is one of their senior healers."

"She was the one who confirmed the curse. Can she be trusted?"

"Of course. She is likely the best healer the coven has produced in the past two generations."

"She told Ella about a witch who resides in the Wastes, likely near the Alabaster Mountains. This witch is supposedly a master in ancient curses. Do you know anyone from the Moonrise coven who has a mastery in that subject."

"Your mother did."

My nostrils flare. "Well, that doesn't fucking help us at all, does it?"

Westfall narrows his eyes at me. He might be my father, but he's also my Commander and under my rule. I'll drop him in an instant if necessary.

"We'd have to check with the mystics to be sure," he growls. "To find out if there was anyone else with such mastery. Ancient curses are something that's only taught to the most gifted of the healers, a class Giselle herself didn't fall into even with her skillset."

"Why is that?"

"It's dark magic, that's why," Arthur shouts from several stories above our heads. "A mastery in curses requires practicing such curses, which has been long banned in the coven. Only a few chosen souls ever get to learn such a subject and would be under strict supervision."

"We don't have time to go to the coven and ask around," I grind out.

"Found it." Another thud makes me flinch, but I glance at Arthur to find him carefully climbing down each rung of the seemingly endless ladder. It'll take him ages to reach the ground at this rate, so I finally tear my murderous gaze from Westfall and stalk toward the heavy book now splayed open at the base of the ladder.

I pick it up and fight the urge to rip it in half. "It's written in the old tongue, Arthur!"

"Well, it's a good thing I am older than the old tongue, Your Highness. Once I'm down, I'll try to find the spell–"

"I'm looking for the cure!"

Westfall clears his throat.

"What, Westfall?"

"How is she?" His tone softens so significantly I find it hard to catch my breath. There's real concern in his eyes, and it does something unexpected to my body as I turn to fully face him.

Maybe for the first time, I find it hard to keep my true feelings hidden. Maybe he sees that fear and despair in my eyes because he shakes his head, pursing his lips, and exhales deeply as his eyes begin to shine. "I am sorry, Ryatt."

"Don't. I haven't given up hope. I need to have hope." I hate the way my voice cracks. I hate the way my body jerks around the tightening in my chest. I am a fucking *Alpha*. I am a *king*. I can find a cure for my mate before it's too late.

I have to.

I think of Ella's family who are completely in the dark about this situation. I can't contact Isaac for another two weeks at least. Does their world have access to cures for something like this?

Would she agree to go if they did?

I don't realize I have my eyes closed and I'm struggling to breathe until I feel Westfall's hand resting on my shoulder. "Keep yourself together."

I shake my head and shrug him off and stand there dumbly, waiting for Arthur to finally reach the ground.

It takes him ten minutes, but the small, gnarled man eventually takes the book from me and sets to work. I slouch in a worn out leather armchair and pinch the bottle of whiskey between my knees and wait for what seems like an eternity.

I feel sleep creeping in—making the edges of my vision blurry.

"A curse capable of severing a mate bond, yes. This is what I'm looking for."

I blink and find Arthur poring over the book with Westfall leaning over him to scan the pages. Can Westfall read the ancient tongue? I doubt it. But, I also wouldn't be surprised, given that everything I ever knew about him was wrong.

"The curse could have been any number of these, I'm afraid. It's impossible to pinpoint it without knowing exactly what Kane would have said while he cut away her mark. A witch trained in alchemy and ancient curses—"

I cut Arthur off. "We don't have that kind of time. We can't risk going back to the coven and wasting time in the event they don't have anyone there that's trained in such magic," I growl.

Arthur furrows his brows as he looks back down at the page. "This is, in its raw form, a curse of the Moon Goddess herself, wielded by the magic of a witch…. In this case, Kane and his stolen magic. Long, long ago, back when the gods and goddesses still walked among us, the mate bond was a gift meant solely for the followers of the Moon Goddess herself. It was her gift to her worshippers. Finding their soulmate. But gifts can be taken away. Hence, the only ways to break a fated mate bond are by rejection or death. Or a curse, if the Goddess so intended. It may have been used as a punishment in that case. Or if someone was deemed unworthy of the bond after the fact…"

"But if a witch casts the curse?" Westfall urges. "What does it say about that?"

Arthur purses his lips into a thin line and continues to scan the weathered page in front of him. "Nothing because I doubt it's ever been done before. Did Kane use the mask to cast this spell on her?"

"Yes," I breathe, my heart shattering.

It's Westfall who speaks next. "Cressendra used to make ointment out of diamond and moonstone to…to help ease the pain and ward off the worst of the symptoms of those slaves that fell victim to Kane's magical experiments in the prison."

I look up at him. I haven't heard my mother's name spoken in years.

He continues, "I don't know where she got the ingredients for it, but I remember how she used to make it. I could recreate the potion if I can find black diamond dust and ground moonstone."

"I'm sure the apothecary would know where to find that," Arthur murmurs.

I'm still focused on Westfall. His eyes… he looks heartbroken. Just broken in general. I wonder if he's said her name in the years that followed her death.

For a moment, I feel for him. For a single space of a breath I understand what it must have been like to watch his mate be tortured repeatedly and not be able to do anything about it. For a moment, I understand the pain he must have endured knowing he'd spend a life separated from his mate.

"Something like that would certainly buy her more time. The black diamond dust eats away at curses, you see, but it's very hard to find–"

I cut Arthur off again. "Find it. I don't care what it takes. Find it."

I toss the nearly empty bottle of whiskey across the room and snap my fingers at Westfall.

"You are not going to survive another jump, not if you came all the way from—"

"I have to get back to her. You will bring me that potion–or oint-ment, or whatever it is–"

"Stay the night at least," he urges. "I can find it here in Veiled Valley, I'm sure."

I eye him skeptically. But, the alchemist at the apothecary is known to carry obscure ingredients from far off lands and never obeyed my orders to stop smuggling in goods during the ongoing wars. His insolence may work in our favor.

"We can leave at daybreak," Westfall continues. "Amanda would love to see you. Your people here would love–"

"Fine." I move away from him and walk on unsteady feet out of the Archives and into the humid night air.

3 3

VISION OF LOVE

Ella

I WAKE to bright sunshine streaming through the window next to our bed in the cottage. I squeeze my eyes shut against the onslaught of light and reach over the sun-warmed sheets for Ryatt, but the other side of the bed is still as empty as it was when I fell asleep.

For the first time in weeks, I don't feel like death this morning.

Maybe it's the way the warm sun plays over my skin and the chipper birdsong outside, but I feel... happy. Lively. I feel like getting up and stretching my body instead of burying myself in bed again.

I can sense a shift in the air as I dress in a clean outfit of cream colored cotton and try to pull on my boots. Tying the laces is becoming a struggle because of my belly, which is now in the way. I didn't show for the longest time, and maybe I should have enjoyed that phase of this pregnancy a little longer. Now, it's over. I grunt with effort as I try to bend down over the hard swell of my stomach. I even sit down and try to pull my leg higher. Finally, red faced and starting to sweat, I kick my boots across the room and opt for the

247

incredibly ugly leather clogs Ryatt bought for me to wear because of this.

It's warm enough that I don't need a cloak as I leave the cottage in search of something to eat a short time later. I carry a giant mug of my tea in my hands and sip it slowly as I watch the sleepy little village all around me bustle with life. Everything is vivid green, all crisp morning air and freshly bloomed spring flowers.

I have a pep in my step as I stop at a bakery nearby and buy the butteriest, most chocolate filled pastry I can find. It tastes like heaven, and I'm regretting only buying one, when I notice a trail leading out of the village and into the woods.

A trio of young women around my age giggle as they walk about into the village with towels wrapped around their heads, their clothes damp from what looks like a morning spent… swimming.

I take another bite of my pastry and watch them walk past.

"It's a lovely morning for a walk," says a voice somewhere behind me.

I turn around to find a kind looking middle-aged woman carrying a basket of freshly clipped flowers. She tilts her head toward the trail, continuing, "There's a mountain spring roughly half a mile up the trail. The women in the village like to bathe there sometimes. It's said the water keeps you young."

I smile around my bite of pastry, and she smiles back, dipping her head in farewell.

I like this village–wherever we are. The names of the packs and villages we've visited have started to bleed together as the days drag on.

I doubt a walk would be bad for my condition, right?

I stuff the last bite of pastry into my mouth and dust the crumbs off my fingers, then set off toward the woods.

The trail winds through the trees and dips down several times. I walk over, and occasionally under, huge root systems and branches that belong to trees that must be several centuries old. The hustle and bustle of the village is soon replaced by lively birdsong and the sound of small critters scurrying through the brush.

Through the trees, I can see the spring in question. It glimmers in the sunshine and looks cool and welcoming against the startling humid heat beginning to creep into the air with each passing minute. But, for whatever reason, I feel a slight tug in my mind that urges me to look to my right.

A few hundred feet off the trail, down a grassy, sun drenched embankment, sits a quiet clearing full of little pink flowers. Around the clearing are rose bushes that remind me so much of my mom that I don't give my actions a second thought as I step off the trail, and walk briskly toward them.

The scent of rose and apple blossom is thick in the air as I step out of the woods and into the sunlight.

I pick a few roses, stopping to sniff deeply and run my fingers over their velvet petals. Instead of the tears I was sure would start spilling, I smile. Instead of homesickness and that all-encompassing uncertainty when it comes to what I believe is my untimely death, I feel… incredibly happy. I feel fine. Whole and well.

But then I prick my finger on one of the thorns.

"Ouch," I mumble, sucking on the wound.

"You're not supposed to touch the thorns, silly!"

I whirl toward the voice of a child.

A girl of roughly seven years stands at the far end of the clearing clutching a doll, a basket full of flowers at her feet.

She beams at me, skipping forward through the flowers between us, her dark brown hair tied back in a long braid that sails out behind her with each step. She approaches me, a total stranger, without a care in the world, and takes my injured hand to inspect.

"You'll be just fine," she says with a smile, still grasping my fingers.

"Uh, thank you."

"I'm going to be a healer one day," she continues, unprompted.

"Well, that's a wonderful profession to aspire–"

"Because I'm a witch."

"Ah, I see." I find myself at a bit of a loss about how to speak to this little girl. I don't have much experience with children.

She blinks up at me with her round, stormy gray eyes and cocks her head to the side. She lets go of my hand and holds up her doll, which has seen much better days.

"Daddy made her for me." She presses the doll into my hand.

"Oh?" I examine the toy, which is made of fabric and leather and has black hair made of yarn. It's been sewn back together several times from what I can see. "What's her name?"

"Dolly." The little girl beams.

"What a fine name," I smile back. Why is she still here? Also, where the hell is her mother? I glance around the clearing. We're alone together. No other voices drift in the soft, warm breeze.

She looks up at me expectantly, her freckled nose crinkling as she smiles. She's missing her two front teeth, and she's sporting a healing split lip. One look down at her grubby knees gives me a clear view of road rash and the same speckled bruises I used to always have as a child.

"Do you play alone in the woods often?" I ask. Again, I search for any sign of another adult.

"My grammy makes me go on a walk with her every morning so my mommy and daddy can have breakfast together in peace," she yawns.

"Where is your grammy, then?"

"I'm hiding from her!"

"Why?"

"Because it's funny!" The little girl snickers with laughter that makes me smile despite myself. "Grampa gets mad when I hide, but he was the one who taught me to run fast and climb trees, so it's his fault. I think so, at least."

She takes the doll back from my hand and I notice a smear of paint on its fabric dress.

"Do you like to paint?" I ask.

She shakes her head. "No, but Mommy does. I'm too big to sit in her lap while she paints anymore–"

A thundering begins to echo through my ears. There's something odd about this, I realize. I take a closer look at the girl as she continues to chatter like a little bird, toying with the doll's thinning yarn hair. The girl looks like… she looks like Ryatt. Those eyes are his. The way her mouth quirks into a cocky smile…

A crashing sound comes from a nearby bush, and a boy with a curly crop of golden hair comes stumbling into the clearing wearing faded overalls.

"Oooooo!" the girl taunts, whirling toward him. "Your mama is going to tan your hide!"

The little boy pants and struggles with his overalls, which are undone. "Don't tell!" he screeches, glowering at her from across the clearing. If he notices my presence, he doesn't show it.

"You're not supposed to be shifting, Evander!" the girl screeches back then dissolves into riotous, teasing laughter as she sprints away from me. "I'm telling your mom!"

"No!" he cries out, and in a puff of golden light, a fox kit appears and tears back into the woods.

My heart stops.

The girl slows at the edge at the clearing and turns to look at me over her shoulder. Her smile is soft, and her eyes turn a brilliant silver in the sunlight. "See you later." She grins, and runs into the darkening forest.

"Wait!" I burst out, but the roar of the birds singing I hadn't realized had quieted returns.

A gentle breeze brushes over me, making all of the fine, downy hair on my body stand on end.

There are no soft footprints in the flowers where the children had just been. The boy's overalls are gone.

It was like they were never here.

"What's your name?" I ask, but it's barely a whisper as it falls from my tongue.

I'm answered by the birds.

My heart hammers as tears fill my eyes. I fall to my knees and begin to laugh, tears spilling down my cheeks as I cradle my stomach.

The girl—I know her. I've been carrying her in my body for months. I would know her anywhere.

She's going to live.

So am I. I'm certain of it.

"Oh, my Goddess, thank you!" I sputter, letting go of my belly to sink my fingers into the soft grass beneath me.

The boy had to have been Amanda and Granger's son. Which means they will be raised together. They're allowed to roam the woods alone, playing, playing in peace without warriors watching their every move.

But the grandparents she mentioned… could that have been my parents? Why would they be in Eastonia, of all places? Or, is the grandfather Westfall, and the grandmother…

"Ella?"

I turn to Ryatt's voice as he slides down the embankment. He looks concerned, but his eyes soften when I turn, and he sees the delirious smile on my face.

"Ella," he rasps, falling to his knees beside me. "What the hell are you doing?"

"I just saw–I just met–" I can barely get the words out. I look back at the place where the children disappeared. I swear on the Goddess, over the whispering breeze and birds chirping in the trees, I can still hear their laughter. "I'm going to be okay, Ryatt."

I look up at my mate and for the first time in months feel *hope*.

"I'm going to be okay," I repeat, more firmly this time. I wrap my arms around his neck, letting my tears fall freely now, and kiss him. "I'm going to be just fine."

I feel the tension leave his body as he rolls me onto the grass, the two of us dissolving into desperate laughter as he presses tender kisses to my lips. He must be so confused right now. I haven't explained anything about what just happened, but the joy in his eyes is something I haven't seen in a very long time.

"I brought you medicine," he says.

I look up into his eyes. The eyes he gave our daughter.

"I… Westfall is here. He wants to see you. We all need to talk."

"That's fine," I say, my fingers brushing over his lips. All I can think of is the girl from the clearing.

I wish she'd told me her name.

"Has Granger ever mentioned the name Evander to you?"

Ryatt furrows his brows. "Why? It was his father's name."

I smile, and let the truth settle in my heart. I'm not sure what I did for the Goddess to give me this vision, this gift of hope for our future.

But I know it's the only thing I'll have to hold onto as we journey into the Wastes….

Tomorrow.

34

THE QUEEN OF EASTONIA

Ella

THE TWISTING SENSATION in my stomach is at a peak as my boots crunch over glass, then something... crackly in a thick, nauseating way that leaves me totally unsettled. I pull my foot back and look down then let out a sigh of relief. Not a bone. Not someone's mangled arm. Just someone's old cloak, I think.

I look over my shoulder at the fog rising from the river that separates Rifthold from the Roguelands. We crossed the river this morning by boat, and it had been a perilous, rocky ride, to say the least.

The way my legs tremble as I carefully pick my way through scattered debris has nothing to do with the treacherous journey across the river, however.

Ryatt is standing a few paces in front of me talking to Westfall in low tones, Granger at their side. The early morning fog is beginning to lift, showing the devastation of the once great, but evil, lair of Kane and his forces.

I truly destroyed everything. I really did. Rifthold is nothing but toppled buildings coated in ash, and at its center, roughly a mile away, begins the wide circle where nothing is left. It's where the fortress once stood, and it's all but gone.

How the hell did Petra get Kane's Iron throne back to the Roguelands? That question has been on my mind since we reached Twin Rivers, which was only a half day's walk from the village of Reighnier. I'll never know. I'm okay with that. I've come to understand there are other forces at work that I'm better off being ignorant of, at least for now.

One thing I can't ignore is the thick bandage wrapped around my thigh and the sticky, gritty salve Ryatt coated my scar with this morning. When we reached Twin Rivers yesterday, we had a night's worth of rest while Ryatt sent six scouts out into Rifthold. He's changed my bandage twice so far, and each time the white linen has been stained with a dark, almost black kind of blood that doesn't seem like my own.

It's very odd. I'm still trying to wrap my head around the strange medicine Westfall brought back with him from Veiled Valley.

On top of the salve, I've been bedecked in moonstones. Not any kind of moonstone I've ever seen, either. They're nearly black in color and depthless, and when the moonstone necklace was placed on my neck for the first time, the color seemed to bleed into me, like my body absorbed its power.

All of this is meant to keep the curse at bay and maybe suck a little of it out. I have no idea how it works. Westfall murmured that it's dark magic, a kind of magic no longer taught and rarely practiced in Eastonia anymore.

The moonstone bracelets on my wrists jingle as I edge closer to Ryatt. If this all goes to shit, I could masquerade as a gypsy, perhaps. I could read palms and tea leaves and sell fortunes. I certainly look the part.

I roll my eyes at the thought. Despite how ridiculous I feel decked out in moonstones, and the fact that Ryatt, Westfall, and Granger are constantly watching my every move, I do feel better. I can't deny that maybe, just maybe, this strange magic is working as intended.

It'll buy me some time, at least.

I reach Ryatt just as two large wolves break through the fog and trot in our direction. In a gentle flash of light, the leather armor wrapped around their dark coats transforms into armor and clothing made to fit the men that they are. The transformed warriors, now in their human forms, walk steadily to Ryatt.

They briefly bow, then one of them says, "You're clear until the Tansian Desert, Your Highness. The rest of the scouts have spread out to pass on the decrees."

"Good," Ryatt says, rolling up the map he was just poring over with Granger and Westfall.

The decrees, of course. Decrees that state to every pack in these enemy territories that Ryatt is the Alpha King of Eastonia.

During the time when Ryatt was acting as a double agent, shortly before the war with my own realm, Kane had announced that Ryatt was his heir to appease the Alphas of Eastonia who weren't keen on fighting in another war. While Kane had no intention of ever giving up his throne, publicly calling Ryatt his heir is now working in our favor.

"Several packs have already bent the knee to your rule," the second scout says. "But there's talk of unrest in Tansian, Your Highness."

I eye the scouts through the lifting fog. Blinding sunlight illuminates the destruction all around us, but no one seems to care. All I'm thinking of is the map in Ryatt's castle in Veiled Valley. Tansian is a huge territory. It's a desert, mostly. But a mountain range borders it at the furthest reaches of Eastonia… the Alabaster Mountains. The same mountains where the only witch capable of helping me is rumored to reside.

We have to go through Tansian to reach her.

"What kind of unrest?" Commander Westfall steps forward.

"An Alpha has declared himself Alpha King," the scout says.

"Let me guess," Ryatt drawls. "Alpha Jaxon of the Southern Wastes?"

The way he says this stranger's name is odd to me. There's a hint of amusement, and when I look at Granger, I notice the look he and Ryatt share.

I narrow my eyes at them. "Who is this Jaxon guy? Do you know him personally?"

Ryatt looks down at me with a shrug. "Once upon a time, we might have been friends."

"That's a very loose way to describe it," Granger says with a growl. "What are his numbers? His forces?"

"We've heard he's absorbed seven packs. That's roughly five thousand people by our estimates."

"Well, that's nothing," I pipe up, and five sets of eyes meet mine. "Compared to what, the hundred thousand or so under Ryatt's rule in the Roguelands?"

"It doesn't matter how big his pack is. It's what he plans to do with it," Ryatt says with heat pouring through the words.

I purse my lips and tuck my fingers into the pockets of my cloak. Ryatt looks me over, and I glare at him, mouthing, "I'm fine."

Satisfied, he turns to the rest of the men and starts rattling off commands.

The scouts will join their closest comrades, wherever the hell they are. Westfall and a small force of warriors will be traveling on foot, asking around about the witch we're trying to find, while me, Ryatt, and Granger are going straight to Tansian....

"We're going to have to jump," Ryatt says, straightening his leathers. He looks conflicted as he eyes me.

Granger, too, looks me up and down. "It's risky," he says to Ryatt.

"So is a full week of travel on foot through enemy territory, regardless if we shift."

Jump. He means using his powers to spirit us across what sounds like hundreds of miles.

"I'm feeling better, really. I think my body can handle it." I cross my arms under my breasts. "It would probably be easier on me than repeated shifting."

Westfall tucks his hands in the pockets of his jackets and looks down at me appraisingly. I know Ryatt went to Veiled Valley. Something happened between them there, but neither of them has said a word about it. "She should have enough of the medicine to last for weeks if the jump is too hard on her."

Ryatt nods. I frown. I hate how they've talking about me like I'm not here, but I understand their concerns. I'm concerned too.

A little nudge deep in my belly brings me back to a happier place. Ryatt's eyes are on mine as I smile and run my hands down over the swell of my belly. "She's kicking."

Ryatt's answering smile brings a rush of warmth to my heart.

Granger, on the other hand, looks slightly forlorn. He won't return to Veiled Valley. I have my suspicions about why. I'm too far away to be able to connect with Amanda over the mind-link, but I assume she's been in contact with her mate during his travels recently. My guess is that Amanda told him he's not allowed to return without me.

So, let's get on with this then.

I take Ryatt's hand then Granger's.

Westfall snaps his fingers at the scouts, and they walk away without a passing glance in our directions.

"I've never seen a desert before," I say. Ryatt gives me his cocky smile before the world spins then goes black.

THE FIRST THING I feel is dry heat. The second thing I feel is the sun burning my retinas from behind my eyelids. I blink, shielding my face with my hand as sands rushes out around my feet. A ripple of dark power skitters through the sand away from us at a high rate of speed.

Ryatt lets go of my hand and immediately starts undoing his knife belt. I notice Granger on my other side doing the same.

"We have five minutes until they reach us at the most, Ryatt," Granger says hurriedly as he starts to undress.

I feel a tug around my waist and look down to see Ryatt's hands deftly fastening his belt around my lower belly, which is a struggle. "What are you doing?" I ask, but Ryatt shakes his head and looks over the top of my head at the rippling ribbon of magic now stretching out miles away from us across sand dunes.

"Listen to me, Princess," he rasps, tightening the belt. "Granger and I are going to shift. I'm going to give you my sword–"

"Wait a minute–"

"Listen," he urges. "Alpha Jaxon won't touch you. None of his men will."

"Why?"

"Granger, are you ready?"

Granger pulls his shirt over his head and nods, but his chest heaves with a ragged breath.

"What the hell is going on?" I ask through gritted teeth.

Ryatt unsheathes his sword. Its onyx blade catches the sunlight. "It's time to be the Queen of Eastonia, Ella."

"Ryatt–"

He presses the sword into my hand, and within a second, shifts into his massive black wolf. His magic ripples through his coat as he turns from me, rushing toward Granger and the edge of the dune where we landed.

That's when I notice the cloud of sand moving in our direction. I grip the sword and edge toward my mate and his Beta, and then I spot the hundred or so wolves sprinting over dunes in our direction.

Shit. What am I supposed to do in this situation?

Ryatt is going to pay for this, one way or another.

They reach us in a startlingly quick amount of time. Golden sand billows around them as they come to a stop just below us. I straighten my shoulders as a single wolf, nearly the same color of the sand around him, walks through the crowd of wolves. They part to allow him to come forward.

This must be Alpha Jaxon.

He looks up at me. I turn my face to steel, letting a hint of my powers flare behind my eyes despite the dull ache it causes in my bones.

What would a queen say when face to face with someone threatening her crown?

"Hi, there."

Ryatt bristles beside me.

Alpha Jaxon cocks his head to the side.

I clear my throat. I can feel sand in my teeth as I tilt my chin toward the sky and say, with all the firmness I can muster, "My name is Ella, and I have heard rumors that you believe you're the King of this territory."

I swear a flutter of wolfish laughter echoes around me, but I hold steady, swallowing hard.

Alpha Jaxon shifts back to his human form, and like I saw when Ryatt's scouts did the same in Rifthold, he's suddenly covered by sand colored armor, although his chest and upper arms are bare to the elements.

He's a handsome man. Rugged, burly, and blond. Younger than I imagined.

His cornflower blue eyes narrow on mine with a look of pure amusement as I say, "I am the Queen of Eastonia. Who the fuck are *you?*"

35

CHALLENGE ACCEPTED

Ryatt

I'M NOT surprised by the warm welcome we receive. I'm also not surprised by the lush apartment Ella, Granger, and I are led into after a long walk in the unfiltered, sand-filled heat.

The luxury of this place–Oasia–doesn't shock me, nor Granger. No, we don't expect anything less from Jaxon. He's always liked the finer things, and finally, after groveling in the trenches his entire life, he has the means to make his wildest dreams come true.

The village of Oasia is a sprawling network of white stone that spreads out for over a mile, all of the buildings interconnected by tunnels built beneath the sand. At its center sits an oasis, hence the name, the only true source of water for miles.

This spring is where he gets his power. He controls the water in Tarsian, so he is king.

This is an empire I'm almost envious of. The sheer wealth of this territory–the mines, the gems, the stones–would be enough to completely rebuild the Roguelands and allow my people to live in opulence.

263

But this isn't enough for Jaxon.

The Jaxon I knew so long ago has never been satisfied a day in his life.

And now the man is seated before me, nothing but a low coffee table between us.

He swishes clear liquor in a crystal glass on his knee, his blue eyes locked on mine.

"You grew into your looks," he says in a low voice that betrays his youthful, almost god-like beauty. "You must have the Goddess to thank for that."

"I'm not here to be showered in your compliments," I say, leaning back against the turquoise cushions of a chaise lounge. A soft, dry breeze filters through creamy white curtains overlooking the oasis, palm trees dancing just outside the windows.

"Why thrust your mate at me like that?" he asks, slowly bringing his drink to his lips. His cool smile wraps around the rim of the glass. "It's not like I don't know what you look like in your wolf form." He sips from his drink.

I haven't touched mine.

"I knew you wouldn't harm her."

He raises his brows.

"Because you know I've been snooping around, don't you? I was wondering why those spies I sent into the Roguelands never came back."

"I assure you, they're happy and healthy and their inability to return to you had nothing to do with my ill treatment and everything to do with *yours*."

He finally lets that mask of cool indifference slip just enough that I can see the fiery rage behind his eyes.

"What are you doing, Jaxon? Are you really threatening *me*?"

"You of all people know how this works, Ryatt." He sets down his glass and leans forward, resting his elbows on his knees. "Our kind? They don't care about lineage. Your knuckle-dragging packs in the Roguelands might believe in titles being passed down from father to son, but we don't do that here. I am what I am because I took what I wanted, and I want the throne you were never entitled to in the first place."

"You're still the same prick I remember."

He smiles cruelly. "I've never had a reason to change."

"The packs that border Rifthold on this side of the Great River think differently. There's been reports of violence. You've killed at least two Alphas who refused to bend the knee to you and your crusade."

"Is that what you were told?" Amusement flares behind his eyes. "Do you not know what it was like here during the war with that kingdom beyond the veil? Don't think I don't know who that woman you brought here is, Ryatt. She's from that place. She was the one Kane was after, isn't she?"

"She is my mate."

"Well, she's safe here as long as you don't give me a reason to–"

"I'd be more worried about *your* safety."

"Oh? My safety? What are you going to do, rip my throat out for looking in her direction?"

I smile because I can't help it. "She would do far worse on her own. Admittedly, I'm a little afraid of her."

He arches a blond brow. "She *is* Firestone, then. The rumors are true."

I shrug. "She is of that line, yes. She is the true Queen of Eastonia, regardless of what either of us think of it."

"Well, that certainly puts a damper on my plans."

"Your plans are what, exactly? Crusade through this territory and then cross the river into my lands with your meager forces?"

"Those who control Rifthold control Eastonia."

"When Kane was king, yes. Not anymore."

"Yes, well. I have a job to do, and that requires expanding into Rifthold."

"It's not happening."

"I'm not asking your permission. I don't need it. I don't see you sending forces to claim–"

"You forget who I am–"

"The bastard born son of a witch, dumped in the coven at five, and who grew up being doted on by those witches and mystics? You had no home, just like me. You had no pack who claimed you. No one wanted you, no one but that fucking Shadowsynger–"

"Commander Westfall is my father."

Well, that changes things. Jaxon's eyes momentarily grow wide, but then narrow. "That explains a lot."

"It also should make it clear that I'm not after the throne because I believe I'm entitled to it, like you think. I am here because *my wife* will sit on that throne. You know better than to fuck with me, Jaxon. You don't know Ella yet. Her looks and her... outwardly sweet-seeming temperament can be deceiving. She is a goddess reborn, and you and your packs don't stand a fucking chance if you cross her. I am the least of your worries."

Jaxon stares at me for several silent seconds.

"You know how this must be done. You came directly here, so you're expecting what I'm about to say next, aren't you?"

Fucking Tarsians and their archaic ways. This section–these territories past the border of Rifthold and the Roguelands–don't have an official name. Kane wanted it that way. It was only Eastonia and *us*. The Roguelands held the enemies of his crown.

He kept packs like the one Jaxon belonged to under his thumb, enslaving his people, sending the young men to Rifthold to be tortured until they were docile enough to have those collars placed around their necks and forced to fight.

I can't stomach the thought of what he did to the women.

Before he can say anything else, I cut him off with a wave of my hand.

"I don't blame you," I tell him, inhaling sharply. "I'm just as angry about the treatment of my own people–"

"Your people did not have to go to war," he growls.

"My people volunteered. You could have fought Kane, raised an army like you're doing now."

"You could have come to our aid while you played house as his favorite little pet." Raw emotion shines behind his eyes for the first time.

I feel a twisting in my gut. "I am not responsible for what happened to Shahar and Esme."

"How *dare* you say their names," he says in a softer tone that pains me to hear.

I swallow hard against the lump forming in my throat. This is dangerous territory. Jaxon, who grew up in Moonrise, left the Roguelands as a spy. He never returned. Seven years older than myself with no family and no pack to call home, he ended up staying in Tarsian, finding his fated mate against all odds, and had a daughter.

Esme was three when the war between Crescent Falls and Eastonia broke out.

I only know this because word of Jaxon's rage when they were taken is now legend, and his acts that followed the rumors of their deaths are the kind of stories told in inns and around warming fires.

This man before me is no normal Alpha. Not when his heart has been ripped from his chest, and the hole left behind has been filled with nothing but hatred.

"It's not confirmed that they're dead," I say with force. "That's what this is about, isn't it? You believe your crawl into the Roguelands, your seat at the head of *my* table, will give you what you need to find them, don't you? You could have just asked me–"

"Unlike you, I've had to fight for everything I've ever had. And if you want to challenge me for the throne that neither of us are entitled to, that's exactly what we're going to do. In the ring. But–" He rolls his neck and fixes me with an icy glare. "It won't be you on the throne, will it? Your precious wife wants it."

"I want it for her."

"Then she can fight me for it. Tomorrow morning. No powers, no shifting." Each syllable is clipped. "Although I assume you have some concerns about that given her condition."

I grit my teeth and scowl at him. This fight–this is how it's traditionally done. I've been challenged before by lesser wolves who want my titles, but this is different.

Jaxon is different. He's been trained to fight from the moment he could walk. To be sly and cunning. To be lethal.

"I will fight in her stead."

He rolls his eyes. "Then it's not fair to me to fight on my own. I'll choose a proxy."

Great, knowing Jaxon he'll find the biggest, ugliest son-of-a-bitch with a taste for blood to step into the ring with me.

"Fine."

"Winner becomes king," he says dramatically, laughing.

"I have a more diplomatic solution," I tell him, but he raises a hand.

Two warriors who have been guarding the door come forward and try to grab me by the shoulders, but I yank myself out of their grasp.

"Listen to me, Jaxon. There is no reason for us to be enemies. You can keep your territory. You can be the Alpha King of Tarsian. But Ella will be Queen–"

"No reason for us to be enemies?" he laughs, ice in his voice. "The blood of my mate and my child is still wet on your filthy hands. You will always be my enemy, and I will relish watching your mate witness you getting picked apart piece by piece tomorrow morning."

My growl pierces the space between us.

I leave his tidy office, or whatever this room is, followed closely by his warriors until I reach the suite we've been housed in. I slam the door shut behind me knowing full well that the warriors are stationed outside.

Granger and Ella turn from a huge window overlooking the oasis at the same time, both of their faces bleak.

"What happened?" Ella says in a hushed voice.

I ignore the concern in her voice and look her over, sighing a breath of relief when I see the peachy color of her skin and ruddy cheeks.

I need to be sharp while we're in enemy territory, and especially tomorrow, but all I can think about is that curse lingering under her skin.

I turn to Granger and nod. "Tomorrow morning."

Granger curses under his breath. He knows what's coming.

But Ella is totally in the dark as she looks at each of us. "What's happening tomorrow morning?"

"A fight to the death," Granger growls and stalks off, closing himself into one of the bedrooms.

Ella turns to me with a concerned expression lighting behind her eyes. "Ryatt... what?"

"It won't take long, Princess." With that, I run my fingers through my hair and mentally start preparing myself to not fucking die tomorrow.

PIT OF DESPAIR

Ella

THIS IS FUCKED UP, and I am pissed off.

I readjust my position in the ridiculously comfortable, high-backed throne I've been seated in and curl my fingers around my knee. Hot sunshine beats down into a pit of shallow sand that's currently being raked while the people arriving to witness my mate's battle find seats in the stands.

Above me, a pergola protects those sitting in the "royal box" from the sun, and before me is a beautifully decorated table full of food. Fine, sparkling wine glistens in the sunlight. Platters of exotic fruit, pastries, and cold meats sit untouched.

I'm not hungry. I couldn't eat even if I wanted to. Not when my blood is boiling, and it has nothing to do with the unforgiving dry heat.

I glance around and spot Granger on the far side of the box looking grim as he watches the men raking the pit. White sand that reminds me of Maatua has been spread over the coarse, golden sand surrounding Oasia. I figure it's so everyone in attendance for today's event will have a better idea of how much blood is about to be spilled.

I can't mind-link with Granger even at this distance. At first, I thought my inability to connect with Ryatt was because of the broken mate bond, but it's gone beyond that at this point. I'm still losing my powers, despite the moonstones and special salve. I'm on borrowed time, and baking in the sun while my mate is forced to fight is the biggest waste of time we don't really have.

Granger glances in my direction and quickly nods before looking back down at the pit. He taps his fingers on his arm nervously, which is bare. He cut the sleeves off his shirt this morning, complaining about the heat.

I look down at the plain, light blue cotton dress I'm wearing, then at the ugly leather clogs I've been carrying from pack to pack. Like Granger, I'd refused the clothing offered to us by the maids who visited our suite this morning.

These people are our enemies.

This moment will determine the fate of Eastonia, and ultimately, my life.

No powers, no shifting. Those are the rules. I assume it's because Ryatt is even more powerful in his wolf form, which is saying a lot, given that he's the most powerful man I've ever met. He'll fight with fists; my stomach does a little flip at the thought.

I remember his fight with Isaac and involuntarily squeeze the fabric of my dress between my fingers. They'd been a physical match, and watching them wrestle had been brutally violent and unnerving. If whoever is fighting Ryatt today is stronger than my brother....

The stands are nearly full. People have already started shouting. Granger straightens, and I know, without being able to see the entirety of the pit below us, that someone is being led out.

I know it's not my mate because the crowd shrieks with delight as the largest man I've ever seen in my entire life walks into view with his arms raised to the sky.

I thought Ryatt and the men in my family were big.

But this man which Alpha Jaxon has chosen to represent him in the pit is built like a stone wall. He probably eats a whole cow every day to maintain his mass. Every inch of him is solid muscle, and not the lean kind. Beneath a protective layer of thick skin, every inch of this man is like iron.

I find it hard to swallow as he comes to a stop in the center of the pit. The cheers from the crowd turns to sneers and hisses, and my mate arrives.

He's beautiful. His tan skin glimmers in the sun, his dark hair undone and billowing out around his shoulders in the dry breeze. His eyes blaze a bright silver as he casually walks to the center of the pit. His chest is bare, his tattoos a dark contrast to his skin as his finely tuned muscles flex with each step.

I know he has a chance. In fact, I'm not worried that he's going to die or be mortally wounded.

I just don't want to have to watch him get hurt.

I clutch my knees again and exhale through my nose.

"You should have oiled him up this morning," comes a voice to my left. "It's a shame, really."

I turn to the owner of the voice just as Alpha Jaxon sits down at the throne beside mine. I know he told his servants to seat me here, on a throne next to him, just to taunt my mate. It's working. I look back down at Ryatt and meet his eyes. He looks murderous as he glares at Alpha Jaxon.

Rage bubbles through me as the young Alpha stretches his legs out and leans toward me, his wide mouth quirked in a sly grin.

"Do you have a little crush on my mate?" I tease, but my eyes are full of hatred.

"Luckily for you, I only have eyes for the female sex. Throwing a handsome man in the pit is always a good show, however. My people will enjoy watching all of those good looks get peeled away."

I swallow hard as a group of warriors walk out into the pit, sounding commands I can't really hear.

"This is asinine," I say to Jaxon.

"This is Eastonia," he replies, smirking. He stands and waves, then sits back down. Somewhere nearby a horn sends a sharp thrum of noise through the air, and it begins.

"My mate is an exceptional warrior."

"I know," Jaxon says, bored. "He'll be fine."

I narrow my eyes at him, ignoring the first sounds of flesh on flesh from the pit below. My stomach turns in on itself. I can't watch. Not yet. "But you want him to die, don't you? That's the whole point of this. He dies, and you get Eastonia. So why would you tell me that he'll be fine?"

His blue eyes meet mine. "I don't dislike Ryatt. That fucking brute, however?" He points toward the giant of a man circling my mate. "He's a traitor and a thief. I could have killed him outright, but I decided to give my people a little show. You just happened to show up at an opportune time."

Something about this is off. Something about Jaxon doesn't make any sense. "Do you really want to be King of Eastonia? Or is this just a dick measuring contest to you?"

He holds my gaze. Goddess, he is truly beautiful, but his eyes are sad. How strange.

"I have nothing else to do."

"That's a stupid answer."

"What would you like me to say?"

"The truth. Why are you doing this to Ryatt?"

"I'm sure he filled you in on our conversation yesterday." Jaxon reaches for a flute of sparkling wine and gulps it down before tossing the flute directly into the pit. "I used to train Ryatt when he was a kid. Training is a loose term. I was in training myself, and he was a little brat that always had a shit-eating grin on his face. I knew he'd grow up to be trouble, and I was right. But I didn't anticipate him joining Kane's forces."

"He was never on Kane's side–"

"That doesn't make a difference. I lost all that mattered to me, and Ryatt did nothing to stop it from happening. Now, Ryatt wants Eastonia to give to you as a little present. I imagine he's whispered his plans to you at night while you snuggle together in a fancy bed in

Veiled Valley, right? You on the throne like a puppet while he pulls the strings and continues being Lord of Shadows. Hmm...." He chuckles darkly.

"What are you even talking about? What do you want?"

"I want revenge," he says sharply, turning to face me. "I don't give a fuck if you're on the throne. You can raise the lost Firestone cities and bring down the veil, restoring peace to our war torn lands, and I will still paint your kingdom red like Kane painted the walls of his dungeons with my family's blood." His tone is so cold it sends a ripple of ice licking up my spine. "My daughter was three years old. My mate—gods—"

"Ryatt wouldn't have hurt them—"

"He did nothing to stop it. He sat back and watched while the people on this side of the river were enslaved and forced to fight. My people!"

I look down at Ryatt. He's bloody, a little bruised, but still on his feet.

"You blame him when you shouldn't," I say sharply, turning my gaze back to Jaxon. "Whatever is going on between the two of you sounds personal, which has nothing to do with the greater good of our lands."

"Our lands? You're not one of us."

I bristle. I mean, he's right. I wasn't born in Eastonia. But I belong here more than I ever belonged in Crescent Falls.

"My daughter will be one of you. Everything I do is to better the world for her, just like everything you do is to bring justice for your family, correct?" I barely recognize my tone. I sound like my mom, honestly. The cool, calculated voice of the Luna I remember her being. "I don't see how those two things are so different."

He's quiet for a beat, and where our conversation drops off, the sound of the crowd watching the fight begins to rise.

Ryatt lurches forward after several minutes' worth of dance with his opponent. The white sand around them is stained red with blood I'm not sure belongs to my mate.

"Do you believe your mate and child are alive?" I ask.

"It's been over a year," he says, his eyes on the fight below us. "I would have heard otherwise by now."

I realize what this is really about. Sure, Jaxon wants to expand his territory like all Alphas do. But the vendetta he has against my mate is misplaced, in my opinion. He wants access to the Roguelands to find his family, but he can't just waltz in. Not with Ryatt's forces actively watching the border. He's too proud to just *ask* for our help.

"Before I killed King Kane," I tell him, my eyes still fixed on Ryatt as he leaps onto the giant's back and locks an arm around his neck, "Ryatt and his forces in the Roguelands secretly evacuated Rifthold. Even the dungeons in the fortress were cleared out. Hundreds of slaves—women, and children—were saved before Ryatt brought down the bridge connecting the two kingdoms. He wouldn't have left anyone behind."

Ryatt rears back, taking the giant with him. They hit the ground with a crack that echoes through the pit, but Ryatt still has an arm around the man's throat.

"There are new villages cropping up all over the Roguelands," I tell Jaxon. "Villages full of refugees from Rifthold. Shahar was her name, right? Your mate?"

"It doesn't matter."

I feel the sudden urge to take his hand, so I do. The action shocks him. He tries to pull away, but I tighten my grip and lean in to whisper, "I am the queen of the witches. They are the lifeblood of the Roguelands. They are the healers, teachers, and midwives. They have connections in every pack. If your mate and your child are in the Roguelands, I will find them."

He tries to pull away once more, but I dig my nails into his skin. Meeting his eyes, I repeat, "I will find them, and they will be returned to you."

"At what cost?"

"There's only one thing I need from you."

What I'm going to say next will complicate things. I don't know if I can trust this man. I shouldn't trust him, but I've met so many

Alphas over the course of my life that I believe I'm a good judge of character, and Jaxon doesn't strike me as a truly vindictive man.

He's young, heartbroken, and doing the best he can for his people, even if that means cutting down Alphas who get in his way.

Those Alphas were our enemies, anyway.

"I was cursed by Kane. I don't have long. I believe I'll die during, or shortly after, our daughter's birth. I have three or four months if I don't find a cure."

I release my grip on his hand and turn back to the fight. Ryatt is panting and grimaces as he continues to try to choke his opponent out.

"I will task my witches with finding your family," I tell Jaxon, "if you lead me to the person I seek."

"Who do you seek?" His voice is quieter now, softer and much more gentle.

Below, Ryatt grunts with effort as the man thrashes in his arms.

And then the man's neck finally snaps, and his body goes limp.

Ryatt rises as the Alpha King of Eastonia, and I turn to Jaxon, whose eyes are on mine instead of the fight below. "I'm looking for a witch who lives in the Alabaster Mountains."

A LEAP TOO FAR

Ella

THE CROWD IS HISSING, booing, and screaming curses down at my mate.

Ryatt looks around, panting, his shoulders rigid despite the welts covering his skin.

Jaxon is still staring at me, but my attention is stolen by several people trying to climb down into the pit. A tremor of panic shudders through the entire arena.

"Alpha Jaxon, you need to get him out of there," I say hurriedly, turning back to the Alpha of Oasia, the man who just lost the crown of Eastonia to my mate.

But suddenly I feel cool metal against my neck and freeze.

"Play along," Jaxon rasps along the shell of my ear before yanking me upright so violently I shriek in alarm.

Below, Ryatt's face has turned from grim amusement to absolute rage as he spots Jaxon with his hands on me and a blade to my neck.

"If you shift, she dies," Jaxon taunts as warriors race out into the pit, shoving delirious onlookers out of the way before they can get to my mate.

"Ella!" Granger screams my name over the chaos erupting all around us. I can barely turn my head to look at him, not with a knife resting against my throat. But I slide my eyes toward Granger and see that he's being held back by four men with four blades pressed against his sides.

'What the fuck are you doing?" I hiss at Jaxon, but he yanks me backward, toward the archway that leads into his sprawling network of rooms that make up his sand covered fortress. Darkness swallows us whole, and the dry heat bleeds into the cool shadows as he guides me underground.

Only when we've turned into a room–a large, open space with windows toward the ceiling spilling bright sunlight over what looks like a library of some kind–does he loosen his grip and take the knife from my throat.

I gasp out a breath and stumble away from him, wrapping my arms around my throat. "What the hell?"

"Stay. Here." He levels me with a look that reminds me he's an Alpha. Not just by title. No, this man was born an Alpha. He radiates the kind of dominance one has to be born with, just like Ryatt. Just like my brother and my dad.

He leaves the room so swiftly I don't have time to catch my breath before the door slams shut and locks from the outside.

I stumble back another few steps until my back hits a bookshelf and then sink to my knees. Beyond the door, I hear rapid footsteps and several voices lifted in alarm. I count the seconds, then the minutes, until the lock jingles, and the door swings open.

"Gods above," Ryatt rushes out as he shoves past Jaxon and hurtles into the room. He pushes a table out of the way to get to me. "Are you all right?"

"What's happening right now?" I ask, grabbing Ryatt's fingers when he tries to caress my face to check me for harm.

"Just a distraction," Jaxon says gruffly as he closes the door.

Granger, who I didn't see enter the room behind Ryatt, is snarling at Jaxon.

"How dare you touch my Luna like that?" Granger shouts, shoving Jaxon.

Jaxon's eyes narrow. "You fucking brutes need to get what's about to happen through your thick skulls. I just gave you Eastonia on a silver fucking platter, Ryatt," he growls, turning from Granger to look at us. "Now, my people are going to riot. I can handle it, but the three of you need to get out of here, now."

"What about our deal?" I ask hotly.

Ryatt slowly rises to his feet. "What deal?"

My heart is still hammering against my ribs as I look between my mate and the man I thought was our enemy. "My witches are going to find his family if he can lead us to the witch in the Alabaster Mountains."

"Ella," Granger growls, but Ryatt raises a hand to cut him off.

He turns to Jaxon, his eyes narrowed to cat-like slits.

Jaxon raises his hands. "I wasn't the one making deals with your wife. It was her idea."

"And can you lead us to this witch, or not?" Ryatt looks like hell. His body is bruised, scratched, and still coated in bloody sand.

"There's no witches this far east," he says. "None that I know of."

My heart sinks.

Jaxon goes on. "But there's rumors, okay? The packs in the Alabaster Mountains are suspicious, untrusting people. Even King Kane couldn't get them under control. They don't take kindly to outsiders and don't, and won't ever, bend the knee to an Alpha King– or Luna Queen." He gives me a little bow. It's a mocking gesture, but he continues, "There's a witch there, according to local legend. She's a real bitch and practices a dark kind of magic."

"Is she real?" Granger asks. "Or are you sending us on a wild goose chase?"

"Their fear of her is real, and that's enough to make me believe that if this is the woman you seek, she'll be there."

"Which pack?" Ryatt says sharply.

Jaxon shakes his head. "Hell if I know."

"There's not many in that territory," Granger cuts in, his eyes on Ryatt. "We'll be able to find her, or hear word of her possible whereabouts–"

Beyond the door, I can still hear people running and occasionally shouting.

"We don't have time for this," Jaxon cuts in sharply, ending Granger's statement with a wave of his hand. "You will do your little trick and spirit yourselves to the mountains, and her witches will start hunting for my mate, is that clear?"

Ryatt looks like he wants nothing more than to snap this guy's neck, but he gives a sharp nod. "And our deal is done as well, Jaxon. I am Alpha King of Eastonia. Your forces are to remain in Tarsian. You can be the king here, I don't give a fuck, but if you so much as step a foot outside of your boundary–"

"I get it," Jaxon hisses, jabbing a finger into one of Ryatt's bruises. Ryatt doesn't so much as flinch. But then Jaxon looks down at me and sniffs deeply. "Moonstone and black diamond dust, huh? How long did you really think she'd last with only that to keep her curse at bay? I can already smell it in her blood. You're almost out of time."

To my surprise, his tone takes on a softer, more concerned edge.

"You and I," Jaxon says to Ryatt, "can finish our business at another time."

"You'll be sent a decree and a treaty to sign," Granger snarls.

Jaxon only smirks over his shoulder at Granger before looking back at Ryatt. "Keep your Beta on a leash from now on."

Ryatt shoves Jaxon away and extends a hand toward me. I take it, and allow him to help me upright. All of this is happening so fast. I can't figure out if Jaxon is screwing with us or if he's actually not the enemy I suspect him to be.

The realization clicks, however, when I notice his eyes raking over the swell of my stomach.

"You could have just asked for help," I tell him. "We would have helped you."

"Are you Ryatt's mouthpiece now, too? You know nothing of this man, little queen. You have no idea what he did in order to fool Kane into believing he was on his side."

"He did it for me and this kingdom," I tell him.

"And my family paid the price, didn't they?" He looks at Ryatt. "Enjoy your new title, Lord of Shadows. You're in my debt."

My blood grows cold as Granger steps forward and places a hand on Ryatt's shoulder, and then the world tilts, and the edges of my vision go blurry. A deep, throbbing pain rips through me, and I scream as total darkness replaces my vision. Pain I've never experienced before shreds me from the inside out.

The outside world shimmers into view. It's almost night here, wherever we are now. I can barely hold my eyes open as Granger and Ryatt's voices trickle back to my ears and grow louder with each passing second.

They're arguing about the jump Ryatt just made.

"Ella," Ryatt says, hauling me upright. Had I landed on my knees or simply slumped to the ground?

"Ryatt, I can't–it hurts, just wait–" I try to shove him away, but my arm is totally numb. I try to lift it and examine my fingertips and I… "What is that?" My fingertips are black.

Ryatt and Granger are silent for the space of a breath before Granger says, "This was too much for her, Ryatt."

"I know," Ryatt growls. "I didn't have a choice, Granger."

"We need to abandon this and get her back to the coven."

"She will not survive another jump," Ryatt grinds out.

I can taste the desperation in the air between the three of us. My vision finally clears enough that I can see that we're in a dense crop of trees. Huge, towering spruce trees that stretch three or four stories above our heads. The air is humid and thick, but cool.

I don't catch the rest of their argument. Ryatt lays me back on a pile of cool, soft leaves while Granger pulls supplies out of a large leather backpack. Then, the Beta shifts to go scout in the area while Ryatt sets to work smearing the magical, curse-eating salve on my hands, and legs, all the way up to the scar. I feel the effects immediately. It tingles over my skin, but the pain is now settled so deep I find it hard to think past it anymore.

"I'm going to call on Isaac tomorrow," he says to me, laying the back of his hand over my forehead and pulling it back with a wince.

"I'm sorry," I breathe. "I'm so sorry, Ryatt. I'm trying. I wasn't feeling well before the fight. I thought it was stress, but–"

"It was the jump to Tarsian," he rasps. "I knew–I knew it was a huge risk, Ella. This is my fault. I had to choose between weeks of traveling on foot or–or this." He sounds so broken as he massages the salve between my aching fingers.

I try to send a rush of my powers forward to warm my suddenly chilled skin, but nothing but a tearing, enormously painful sensation echoes through my body.

"I have no regrets," I tell him suddenly, my voice sounding far, far away. "This last year of my life was… well, I do have one regret."

"Ella," he whispers, "please don't talk like this now."

"I wish I'd never let go of your hand."

I look up at my mate and find his eyes closed and his face twisted with grief and guilt. I squeeze his hand as a sharp ache spreads through my back, twisting all the way to my lower belly.

"I wish I'd never let go of your hand so I would have had a few more days with you."

I imagine the girl from the clearing. I can see the freckles on the bridge of her nose as another wave of pain crushes my abdomen.

"Not yet, darling," I whisper as my vision begins to go dark. "Just a little longer."

"Ella? El–"

Ryatt's voice is suddenly very far away.

My body locks, and I fight the feeling of being shoved deep, deep underwater.

Then I simply slip away, and for the first time in weeks, feel no pain at all.

3 8

OUT OF OPTIONS

Ryatt

GRANGER RETURNS three hours after Ella slumped into a restless slumber in my arms. His golden wolf appears at the edge of the clearing I've been sitting in, unable to even blink, my mind and heart in shambles.

How could I have been so stupid? So desperately, unapologetically unaware of how hard this kind of travel would be on Ella in her state?

She whispers something in her sleep, her face buried in my shirt. For the last two hours she's been jerking awake and calling out for a little girl, of all things. She asks what her name is, over and over, each time the question leaves her lips it becomes more pleading.

She's in pain. While our bond isn't strong enough to feel those changes and emotions in my own body, I can smell it on her. I can smell the changes taking place in her body as the minutes speed by.

"Granger," I say hoarsely. My unused voice sounds like someone has taken a rake over my vocal cords.

Granger shifts back to his human form and quickly pulls on a pair of pants, forgoing a shirt. He pauses before approaching me and

285

crouching in front of us, laying the back of his head on Ella's fore-head. "She's burning up, Alpha," he says with remarkable calm, but his eyes betray his steady tone.

"I need your report." I can't talk about Ella right now. Her body goes tight in my arms again, and that scent... it's something new. Something fresh and clean. It's the baby, of course. I've never been around pregnant women for long, even during my time in the coven, but I've heard stories about how it's easy to tell when they're close to giving birth because their scents change. The baby's scent grows stronger.

But what I can smell the most right now is death lingering nearby.

"Of course," Granger whispers, his green eyes still glowing from his recent transformation. It's the only light in the dark. "There's a village nearby, roughly six miles into the mountains. Kind people but suspicious. They have a healer, but she's not a witch." I grit my teeth as he continues, "Their Alpha is gone on business, but his Beta is going to allow us entrance to their village. I was able to connect with Westfall. He's in range, just reached Tarsian, and Jaxon has made good on his promise to pull his forces out of Rifthold and the bordering packs. You're the Alpha King of Eastonia, Ryatt."

It doesn't matter. None of this matters right now as Ella whimpers and curls into herself.

"I'm wondering," Granger says in a low, skeptical tone, "if she was poisoned in Oasia. This change in her is so abrupt–"

"She's in labor."

"You're sure?"

I nod, running my tongue along my lower lip.

"It's too early," Granger insists. "Amanda isn't due for another four–no, yes... four months, give or take." Granger rarely panics, but the panic in his voice is clear as he rocks back on his heels and stands, looming over us.

I don't move. I know that when I do take that first step, everything is going to happen quickly, and I have no way to stop it.

"We're out of time." That's all I can say. I slowly pull up Ella's shirt to show Granger the black tendrils of the curse that are now creeping up her sides, weaving between each rib. Granger makes a noise deep in his throat that slices into me.

"It was the jump."

I nod. "We were wrong about how much time she had. The medicine only did so much. I don't know what to do."

"We need to move, Ryatt. Now. Westfall will be here in a few days, I'm sure. Artyom–I can contact him. He can spirit like you can, can't he?"

"It's not the same."

"It's similar. He could find the witch–"

I take Ella in my arms and rise to my feet on legs that haven't moved in hours. Defeat drips from every word as I look my Beta in the eyes and slowly, carefully, place Ella in his arms and say, "Take her to the village nearby, to the Healer. I need to get in contact with her family."

* * *

Maddy

Sunlight pours into the informal sitting room on the second floor of my home. Lively chatter and laughter fill the air, and my heart is so incredibly full. Maddox and Isla are both here now and spending the entire summer with us in Crescent Falls. A few of Isaac's closest allies–other Alphas he considers friends–are visiting as well to pepper us with congratulations on the birth of our twins.

We are the luckiest people in the world, in my opinion. Two healthy sons. A thriving kingdom currently at peace, especially since we just gave them not one, but two, heirs.

Hanna stretches out her legs on the floor below me while Ryan blinks up at her from between her knees.

"Are you all moved in yet?" I ask, giving her a little nudge with my leg. For the first time in a while, my arms are empty of babies, and instead I clutch a crisp glass of lemonade. I glance over my shoulder at my mate, who is holding Sydney, our future king, against his shoulder while he laughs with his friends.

"Yes, we are," Hanna says in a sing-song voice as she wiggles her fingers at Ryan. "Cassian doesn't have an eye for decoration, but I do want to replace that wallpaper in the living room eventually. We haven't really… well, we don't spend much time in the living room."

I raise my brows as a blush creeps over her cheeks. "Let me guess," I laugh, "you've become well acquainted with your bedroom?"

Her blush deepens, but her eyes are soft and so full of love that I'm reminded of those first few weeks with Isaac after the war, when we were finally able to just be together. We barely ever left our bedroom.

Hanna and Cassian recently moved out of the castle and into a manor on the grounds. It has a private garden and all the amenities they'd require to live comfortably, even luxuriously, but for Hanna it's been an adjustment. She's no longer a maid here. She's a Beta's mate, soon to be wife after their binding ceremony next week, and she'll be the second highest ranking female in our kingdom other than me.

Movement catches my eye, and I notice Isaac placing Sydney in Maddox's arms. Isaac runs his hand over the back of head and down to the nape of his neck, his eyes suddenly shadowed as he leans in to whisper to Maddox, then abruptly leaves the room.

I straighten a bit, peering over the back of the couch to watch my mate disappear from view. Maddox must have caught the alarm flaring behind my eyes because he approaches me, patting Sydney's back. "He said he's being summoned to his moonstone dog bowl," Maddox says with a bit of a grin.

I arch my brows. That's a new one, and a great way to describe that insanely expensive bowl sitting in the tower several stories above our heads. I call it his special salad bowl, much to his annoyance.

"But it's several days before the new moon," I argue, my initial amusement slipping. Is something wrong? I glance around the room, noticing the way the conversations continue as if nothing is amiss. I briefly catch the tail-end of a conversation between two neighboring Alphas about a skirmish taking place near their territories. Something about a new Alpha rising, having challenged his pack's previous one.

I fight to swallow as I look back at Maddox. "I'm sure it's fine. Ryatt has been making good on the terms of the treaty, I hear, and contacting Isaac regularly."

"Yes, he has," I reply, but my tone is sharper than usual. "But only during the new moon."

Maddox shrugs. I grind my teeth. Why do I feel like whatever Isaac is about to find out is the opposite of good news?

I rise from the couch and excuse myself from the room.

The library is hot, the smell of books and ink rich as I rush through the hidden door and start hiking up the steps to the observatory.

But it's silent when I reach the landing. Isaac stands with his hand on either side of the bowl, his eyes wide and unblinking as if in a trace.

"Isaac," I say, but he doesn't so much as breathe.

More than concerned, I pad over to him and lay my hand on his arm, but before I can utter a word I feel the air being pulled from my lungs, and suddenly the heat in the room is replaced by cool, damp air.

And my bare feet are no longer on weathered floorboards. I grip Isaac's arm as I gasp and take in the startling view of a mountainous forest and a sky so full of stars it's nearly blinding.

Ryatt is standing before us. His eyes slide to mine. If he's surprised I'm here, he doesn't show it. He doesn't care.

In fact, his face…

"What happened?" I rush out, seeing the tears in his eyes. Beside me, Isaac is rigid, and one glance up at him shows me that he's not looking at Ryatt in anger, but in clear, focused concern.

"My mom could come. You could bring her through the veil," Isaac says with great effort.

"I can't risk that. Isla has never traveled like this before, and if she's injured or her powers need time to recover, she'll be useless, and stuck here."

"Her tears, then–"

A shake of Ryatt's head cuts Isaac off.

"It won't work," Ryatt whispers. "I am sorry. I am doing what I can but I–" His voice breaks, and finally he turns his attention to me.

Goddess, the look behind those stunning silver eyes breaks me into pieces.

"Where is Ella?" I whisper.

Ryatt's lips part, but he says nothing for a long time. He just stares at me, slowly shaking his head.

"I'm sorry," he says again. "I am so sorry."

"Ryatt!" Isaac shouts, and the words *let us help you* are absorbed into the ether as Ryatt pulls a weathered sword from the ground between us, and Eastonia fades away.

I stumble backward away from Isaac and his dog bowl, nearly tripping over a crate, but my mate catches me around the waist and hauls me upright. "Isaac, what–"

He takes my face in his hands and leans down to press his forehead against mine. His scent is rich and thick, masking the fear and disbelief coursing through his blood. "Ella's in labor."

"No," I rasp. "It's far too soon."

"I have to go to her, to them."

"What?"

I pull away from him and look up into his blue eyes.

"No, Isaac, you can't!"

"I can get through the veil," he admits, like it's some secret power he hasn't even shared with me. "I have to go, Maddy."

I shake my head. "You could die!"

"So could Ella. Ryatt helped me once when you were in labor. He kept my head clear and focused. Ella saved you and Ryan when he got stuck. I owe them a debt, and now I have to pay it."

"This is insane!" But he pulls away from me, shaking his head.

"I love you," he says, pressing a kiss to my temple. "Tell the boys I love them. I'll be home soon."

"Don't. You. Dare." I growl, but blinding white light envelopes the room, and my mate is gone.

RYATT'S CHOICE

Ryatt

I DON'T KNOW the name of this village or the pack. I barely spoke more than three words to the Beta before being ushered out of the village and into a heavily wooded area high above the village proper. A small stone cabin sits in the center of a clearing, flanked by a few out buildings. Smoke puffs from the chimney as I approach the cottage with my hands curled into fists at my sides.

I try to tell myself that everything is going to be fine, but Granger and I are alone in this. My men–my commanders, generals, and warriors–are currently spread out between here and Veiled Valley. Everyone is on standby, waiting for whatever conflict might have come when we faced off with Jaxon.

I'm too far out of mind-link range to connect with any of my commanders to tell them the situation has changed.

I push open the door and step inside the dusty cottage. It's a single room–wide and nearly empty save for a bed in its center and a few cabinets and chairs. An elderly woman is yelling at a village girl who can't be more than fourteen.

Ella is in the bed, her eyes glassy and distant as she looks into the fire crackling in the soot-stained hearth along the far wall. She looks pale, gray, and defeated.

"Alpha," Granger says hoarsely, tapping two fingers against my elbow to get my attention.

"Is she all right?" I ask him over the sharp tongued healer's shrieking.

"Outside, I think," Granger says with a sigh, and I follow him back out into the moon drenched clearing.

It's several hours before dawn. Distant howling breaks through the rustling of branches above our heads as we take a few long strides away from the cottage.

"Ella is still feverish. The healer won't give her anything for it."

"Why not?"

"I'm not entirely sure. She started yelling at me the second I laid Ella on the bed, calling her Beta a filthy witch sympathizer and saying Ella was just 'child sick.'"

"Child sick?"

Granger shrugs, his expression helpless. "This woman is just a healer, not a witch. She believes keeping the cottage hotter than Ella's fever is the only way to banish the demons." He waves a hand in dismissal. "We need to find someone else."

"What I need–I need Westfall here as soon as possible. If he intercepts anyone along the way who has healing abilities, they need to be brought here without question. I don't care what it takes. Talk to the Beta of this gods forsaken pack and find me a new healer in the meantime."

Granger shifts his weight from foot to foot and crosses his arms over his chest. "We don't have that kind of time, Ryatt."

He's right, but I don't want to hear it.

"Go," I command. End of discussion.

I turn back to the cottage.

The air is dry and full of smoke as I walk to the edge of the bed and kneel, taking Ella's clammy hand in mine.

"I need boiling water, you foolish, insolent girl. This water is barely steaming." A wet, cracking sound fills the air, and the girl yelps in pain. I snap my gaze toward the healer who is looking smug as she clenches her meaty hand into a fist.

She just slapped the girl in the face. Tears spring along the girl's lashes as she nods and starts lugging a bucket of water toward the hearth.

The healer finally turns to me, her round, pinched face twisted in disgust. What the hell is her problem?

"What exactly do you want me to do for her?" she hisses through her teeth, wiggling a finger at Ella, who is curling into herself in pain.

"Is there not a midwife in this pack who can come here instead?" I ask hotly, not bothering to stifle the edge in my tone.

"Midwife? Bah, no. We don't believe in that kind of medicine. It's dark magic."

"You believe someone who cares for pregnant women practices dark magic?"

"I believe that a midwife couldn't help her anyway. She's a witch." She spits on the dirt floor. "Best we can do is wait and see if her labor progresses." The healer leaves the cottage, wiping her thick, dirty hands on her even filthier apron.

Ella whimpers and tries to sit up, pressing a hand against her belly.

I watch the cottage door slam shut then turn to my mate whose eyes are shimmering with pain. "Lie back, Ella. Try to rest."

I'm not sure she's entirely lucid at this point. I've only been apart from her for an hour at the most. I summoned Isaac, using an enormous amount of power to do so without a nearby water source, and told him what was happening. I'd sent Granger with Ella to the village, hoping the healer was someone actually willing to help us.

This healer, however, is suspicious and cold and is keen to let my mate suffer.

Ella murmurs incoherently then chokes on a scream of pain that sends fear and fury crawling up my spine. Her belly strains, rock hard, and she bows off the bed.

Two small hands appear beside me, placing a cool wet rag on Ella's burning forehead.

I look up at the girl, who won't meet my eyes. Her cheek is a furious red, and the outline of the healer's hand is still visible as she brushes Ella's hair away from her face and turns back to the hearth.

"Do you know anyone that could help her?" I ask.

"She's very ill," the girl says with her back turned to me. "Her fever is not going to break for some time, and Agatha is our only healer. She is… old school, in her treatments."

Apparently, by old school, the girl means just letting her patients wait it out and risk death.

"My mate is in labor and in pain. There has to be something we can do–"

Ella jerks again, crying out. She falls back panting, struggling to breathe. That's when I notice the blood beginning to seep through the sheets.

My stomach twists as I look up at the girl. She's looking over her shoulder at Ella now, her small, dark eyes wide as she wrings her hands. "There is someone–"

"Who?"

Her eyes meet mine, wide, and concerned. "I'm not supposed to say. She's not allowed in our village, but people travel to her for medicines… potions."

"She's a witch, then."

"The White Witch." She twirls a braid between two of her fingers.

I stare at the girl, narrowing my eyes. "Where can I find her?"

"She can't come here!"

"Why not?" I motion toward Ella, who is writhing in pain. "I need *her*. Does she know–does she know anything about curses?" It's a long shot, and my hope quickly dims as the girl shrugs, her expression strained and eyes watering.

"I–I don't know. I shouldn't have said anything!"

"Where is she?"

"In the mountains, a few miles from here. That's all I know. My mom–my mom gets herbs from her sometimes, but that's all I know. I swear." She chews the inside of her cheek like she wants to say more. She glances at Ella and closes her eyes, shaking her head. "The healer who just left hates witches. She's the only healer we have, though. She won't let the witch come here."

"Do you know anything about labor, then?"

She blinks at me. "Yes... a bit."

"What is wrong with my mate then? Why is going into labor so early?"

"May I... touch her?"

I nod at the girl. I can tell she's normally quiet, shy, maybe even prone to self-isolation, but she holds my gaze for a long time before taking a deep breath and laying her hands on Ella's swollen stomach. Ella jerks, crying out in pain again. It cuts through me so deeply I swear I can feel her agony as the girl begins to press on her belly.

"The baby isn't in position. It's upside down, and low... and she–" She moves to the end of the bed, gingerly lifting the bloody sheets. Her mouth drops open, then snaps shut. "Her leg?"

The curse. The black tendrils of magic that are swallowing her whole. "Don't worry about that. Why is she bleeding so badly? What can be done?"

"I don't know. A hemorrhage, perhaps. Agatha–Agatha won't stop the bleeding, though."

"Why wouldn't she?"

"She thinks all witches should die."

Thunder cracks overhead. Lightning lights up the room through the window right before sheets of rain begin to hammer the thatched roof. The girl looks stricken as she slowly looks from Ella's legs back up to her face, shaking her head. "You shouldn't have brought her here. She'll die here."

Ella is trembling now. I grip her hand, unable to let go. Her fever burns into me, through me, spreading like wildfire.

"Ryatt," she chokes, her eyes fluttering open.

At once, the girl backs away, turning around as if giving us a moment of privacy.

I brush Ella's hair away from her face, resting my hand on her temple.

"I can't bear it. It hurts so much," she whimpers. "Something's wrong, Ryatt. I need–I need help."

"I know. I'm trying," I tell her, biting back the swear words on the tip of my tongue.

"It's the curse, isn't it?" Her sea-green eyes lock on mine with so much fear behind them. "It's killing us. Me and the baby. I–" She grits her teeth, trembling through another long, painful contraction. "She's–she's too early. She won't make it if she's born now."

"I'm trying," I tell her and notice the girl is looking over her shoulder at us, her expression conflicted. I need her to go find this witch, but her fear of the healer is obvious.

As if on cue, the healer storms back into the cottage licking what looks like grease from her fingertips. She scowls at me and Ella before catching the girl's eyes and barking, "Have you been standing round twiddling your thumbs? Where is the boiling water for my tea?"

"Your tea?" I sneer, rising to my feet. 'Water for your tea? What about my mate?"

"She's going to have this baby, but there's not much to it. It's not my fault she's a foul-blooded witch who can't survive childbirth."

My eyes flare with the magic I normally keep on a tight leash. The healer stumbles back, crashing into a cabinet, and gropes until she finds a large butcher knife.

"Do you have any idea who I am?" I whisper.

"Yes–I–" The healer can't seem to catch her breath. "My–my lord, I didn't realize–my Beta didn't say the Alpha King of the Roguelands–"

"Help her," I command in a vicious tone that sends a tremor of power through the cottage.

The healer nods, wide eyed, and slowly edges away from me. I follow her with my eyes until she goes to stand next to the hearth, motioning for the girl to continue boiling the water.

I ease back to Ella's side. Ella's eyes are barely open, her breathing ragged. She's been dressed in a pale white nightgown that's now damp with sweat. I look down at my mate, at the perfect woman that I was blessed with. I never deserved her. I don't know if I'll ever deserve her. I'd put myself in her place in a heartbeat. I'd give up everything—my lands, my life, just to give her a moment's peace right now.

"I will not be responsible for this," the healer snaps at the girl. "I can't have their blood on my hands. Do you know what he is, girl? The Shadow King. The King of Nightmares."

I shake my head, trying to block out the conversation taking place near the hearth, how the healer believes I'll skin her alive and do some sort of ritual with her bones if my Luna dies.

Maybe I will, if the horrible bitch doesn't get a move on.

My heart rate spikes as my eyes catch the healer's knife—red hot, like she's been holding it in the embers.

"What are you doing?" I ask as she takes a step in our direction.

"Which one do you want me to save? The Luna or the baby?"

40

ME INSTEAD

Ryatt

"What did you just say to me?" I have to force the words out. My ears ring with Ella's whimpering. Her suffering is the only thing taking up space in my head.

I can't think straight.

"You'll lose the Luna if something isn't done immediately," the healer says sharply, waving her knife in Ella's direction. "I can stop the bleeding with herbs, but it will kill the babe. Or, I cut the child from her womb. You decide, Alpha King. Your Luna or the baby?"

"Ryatt!" Ella's voice is thick with despair. "Don't—please! Don't let her hurt the baby! I—she can't be born yet. She's not ready; it's too soon!"

I slowly tear my gaze from the healer to my mate and feel what's left of my heart shatter to pieces in my chest. Ella is bleeding out. The sheets and mattress are black with her blood. Her skin is clammy and gray as she clutches the blood-damp sheets and throws her head from side to side in agony.

"Please, Ryatt. Please—"

"Alpha!" the healer shouts. "She will die if you don't make a decision right this instant!"

I turn to my mate, the love of my *fucking* life. I can feel her slipping through my fingers with each passing second. I kneel at her bedside. "Ella, listen to me–"

She weakly curls her shaking hand around my forearm. I know it takes all of her strength to do so, and it kills me. Her fevered eyes meet mine and hold my gaze so intensely I wonder if this is it, if this is the last moment I'll ever see her alive.

"I can't lose her. I can't live knowing we lost her, Ryatt. Choose her. Please. *Choose her.*"

"*Ella.*" That's all I can say. The baby won't live. She's too early. Early by almost four months.

I'm going to lose them both.

I feel tears sliding down my cheeks–hot and furious and full of the deepest, most desperate form of despair.

"*Choose her!*" Ella begs, digging her fingernails into my arm while the healer shouts somewhere behind me, trying to get my attention, to force me to choose. "Please, Ryatt. I can't–don't take her from me, please. Don't take my baby–"

Those words are my complete undoing.

"I will cut the child from her, then. Move!" The healer bustles forward, her blade catching the light of the fire burning in the soot stained hearth in the corner of the room. The gnarled woman clutches my shoulder, and I act. My mind is blank. My body moves on instinct. I whirl, then grab the woman by the throat and look into her hateful eyes as I snap her neck.

Her lifeless body crashes to the ground in a heap of flesh and filthy, blood stained clothing.

Slowly, I turn my attention to the servant girl standing in the corner of the room holding that fucking useless bucket of water. "Go get the witch you mentioned."

The girl drops the bucket and runs outside without a word.

"Ryatt–"

"I'm right here."

I rest my knees on the weathered floorboards, ignoring the dead body at the foot of Ella's bed. I clutch her hand, weaving my fingers between hers. She feels like she's on fire. With every minute that passes, her fever gets worse. Even the sheets around her are hot to the touch.

"Do-do you remember–" she sucks in an unsteady breath. "Do you remember that night on Maatua when we went d-dancing?"

I'm falling apart. I clutch her fingers hard enough her bones scrape together, but she doesn't flinch. "We finally got our dance that night, Princess."

"You loved that music–I remember–how you smiled, and I–"

She's struggling to breathe now. Every breath she takes causes her body to jerk. More blood soaks into the mattress.

Kill me. Let me take her place. Take me instead of them. I will do anything.

I rest my forehead against our joined hands. My tears seep between our fingers as my chest begins to rattle with sobs.

"Bury me with her," Ella whispers.

"Ella, please," I rasp, lifting my head to look at my beautiful mate. "Stay with me!" Her eyes are open and locked on the ceiling. A soft smile touches the corner of her mouth as her eyelids flutter closed again. She stills. "Ella? Ella!"

The door to the cottage opens with such force it nearly comes off the hinges. Wind races inside the room, blowing out the fire, the only source of light in the room.

A flash of lightning illuminates two figures. A tall, graceful woman steps inside, followed by the shy servant girl now carrying a lantern. Her cheek is puffy and red from where that beast of a healer slapped her across the face for even mentioning the witch now walking slowly in my direction.

White witch, indeed.

Her stark white hair is tied back in a loose braid that touches her waist as she pulls her hood from her head and looks Ella over from head to toe, ignoring me completely. She's beautiful, and likely in her late forties, tall and lean and shielded by a cloak made of gray home-spun that's seen better days.

But her eyes are what's most shocking. They might have been a rich shade of blue or green at one point, but they're... clouded with gray mist that makes me wonder if she's blind or close to it. She doesn't look at me at all as she motions to the servant girl, who takes several steps into the room before turning back around to shut the door against the storm raging outside.

"Start the fire again. I need boiling water." The witch's voice is deep and smooth, which isn't what I'd expected after hearing the healer's reasoning for not allowing this woman near Ella. I imagined her gnarled and stooped with green skin and scales based on the healer's description.

Not this.

The servant girl bustles around the room with her lantern. The fire springs back to life in a matter of seconds. While the girl heats a fresh kettle of water and sets the witch's herb to steep, I watch the witch lay pale, graceful hands on Ella's stomach.

I clutch Ella's hand tighter, unsure if she's dead or alive.

The witch finally looks in my direction to ask, "How far along is she?"

"Six months."

The witch nods gravely, her eyes leaving my face to dig something out of the pocket of her cloak. "The baby is still alive. But your mate is..." She looks at me again. Her hand curls into a fist as she draws something out of her pocket and keeps it hidden in her palm. "What is your name?"

"My name?" My mouth is incredibly dry.

The witch nods, turning away from me as she opens her palm to reveal several raw crystals she's placed on Ella's belly. They glint in the firelight, swirling with colors I've never seen before, then turn an inky black.

"Ryatt."

"Ryatt... that's an old name. A god's name." She rolls my name over her tongue as she arranges supplies on the foot of the bed.

"What's your name?" I ask, trying to keep my mind off my dying mate, who is now so weak she's barely breathing.

"I don't remember," the witch says quietly. She sighs, closing her eyes. "Your mate might die."

I lick my lips and squeeze Ella's hand. "What can be done?"

The witch tilts her head to the side, her eyes still closed. She whispers something to herself in a language I'm only vaguely familiar with. It's an old tongue–the language spoken when the other Firestone cities, like Veiled Valley, were still standing. She opens one eye, squinting, and adjusts the position of one of the crystals.

I glance at the servant girl, who is back to lingering by a wall, her eyes wide and hyper focused on every move the witch makes.

"This baby will be born and soon," the witch says. "I can save the child for certain. She's strong, this baby. She's ready. But you will lose your mate."

"No–"

"Losing a mate can make a male volatile. For the safety of the baby, you'll need to leave. Just for a little while. A day, maybe two."

"No, I'm not–"

"How long has it been since you imprinted on her?"

I glare at the witch. Ella takes a shuddering breath, her body twitching. "We're fated."

The witch goes rigid. She slowly turns her head, her milky eyes meeting mine. "I can't sense that kind of bond between the two of you. You're mistaken."

"No, I'm not. Our bond was severed."

"How?"

"She was tortured. I'm not sure the specifics, but K–someone cut her mark from her."

The witch slowly turns back to Ella then snatches the crystals from her belly. "Where is the mark?" Her voice loses its earlier calmness. Suddenly, she's frantic as she repeats, "Where is the mark that was cut out? Where was it?"

"Her thigh–"

The witch stands abruptly, the stool she was sitting on clattering to the ground. She rips the sheets from Ella's legs and pulls her dress up just enough that the jagged, thick scar is visible. The swirling, whirling scar tissue looks worse than I've ever seen it before, especially covered in dark blood.

"Mom," Ella whispers. "Mama?"

"Hush now, you'll be all right," the witch says with motherly softness.

Ella takes a shallow breath, her eyelashes fluttering. She's waking up, which means the pain is going to start coming again. My heart starts to race as I watch the witch trail a finger down the scar.

"It's a curse." I let go of Ella's hand and rise. I pray to whatever gods are listening that this is the witch we've been searching for.

The witch stares at me with an unflinching gaze, her nostrils flaring. "Who did this to her? To both of you? What witch–"

"Kane," I growl.

She grinds her teeth and turns to the servant girl. "You need to leave. You weren't here. You didn't hear a single thing that was said in this cottage. Do you understand?"

The girl, petrified, nods.

"Go!" The witch shouts, and the girl darts out of the cottage, the door slamming shut behind her.

I watch with bated breath as the witch starts pulling things out of her seemingly endless pockets. Rocks and crystals and polished bones are tossed onto the bed, where Ella is starting to writhe again, her stomach tightening as more sharp contractions take hold.

More blood seeps into the sheets. The witch is mumbling again, her hands running up the length of Ella's legs.

Crimson light skitters up Ella's thighs.

I stagger backward, looking from Ella to the witch.

"You're a Firestone."

She says nothing as her powers sink into Ella's skin.

"What are you doing to her?"

"She won't survive this. This curse is ancient. He would have used an ancient blade to cut your mark from her skin, something made by the god's to cut through the Moon Goddess's powers. Cutting a mark away is never enough to sever a mate bond that's been destined. But this weapon… this blade… it was created for this purpose and this purpose alone."

"Then break the curse."

She looks at me directly, and for a moment I think I catch despair behind her clouded eyes. "There's nothing we can do, not at this point. It's far too late. It's in her heart now."

"Then she'll die?"

She nods, and I feel my legs give way. I stagger back to the bed and fall to my knees just as Ella begins to scream, pitching forward.

"She won't survive. I'm sorry," the witch says softly.

I shake my head, unable to think past Ella's cries for help, for her mother, and for me.

"Can you ease her pain?" I choke out. It's the worst thing I've ever said.

"Yes."

"Is there truly nothing you can do?" I'm begging now, my voice strained and full of desperation as I shout the words over Ella's screaming. The witch's face undergoes a great change. Her stony expression shifts to something heartbreakingly sad as she shakes her head, her eyes meeting mine.

"There's a spell, but it's…" she tapers off, looking conflicted. "I could try. It's dark magic, all right? Casting a spell like this would require some sort of sacrifice, some offer to the Goddess in exchange–"

"Do it. You have to do it!"

"If it works, there's still a chance she won't survive the birth. She's lost so much blood. She's fevered. This is enough to kill most women. She's different, but–"

"She's a Firestone witch, like you."

"Still," she says, shaking her head. "She's weak now. She's been losing strength for some time, hasn't she? Even with the spell, her body has been through too much. The birth might be…. She's lost too much blood." She gently splays Ella's legs apart and places a hand on her stomach.

"We've been traveling. I had to find you–" I choke on the words as Ella bucks off the mattress. Her face is tight with pain and so shockingly pale. "You were the one we were looking for, and we're too late. We're too late."

The witch's pale eyes are on mine as I come completely undone.

"Please, just… help her."

She nods gravely.

I can't talk about any of this anymore. Her pain cuts through me, shredding me, turning my very bones to dust as I sit next to her and pull her into my arms. I clutch her tightly, rocking back and forth as the witch begins to press on her belly.

"I'm turning the baby," she tells me.

"No, no–please, help me!" Ella cries.

"I'm so sorry," I tell her, closing my eyes and burying my face in her hair. "I am so sorry, Ella." I did this to her. I couldn't stop myself. Our bond put us in this position. The fates would have seen this end to our mateship.

And fate allowed this beautiful, loving, and brave woman to die.

"I will do anything!" I cry out. Ella screams, and the witch starts chanting softly, breaking her near silent song to whisper encouragement to my mate. I close my eyes and begin pleading with any and all of the gods, calling them out by name. "I will do anything, please! *Please!* Take me instead of them. Drag me to Hell. Punish me for what I've done. *Take my powers!*"

Something heavy and painful snaps in my chest like my ribs are breaking. "Take my powers. Take my titles. Take me instead. Spare my mate. Spare our child. Spare them. *Spare them!*"

My vision blurs, and Ella suddenly slumps against my chest. The witch stands with a bundle in her arms.

The smallest baby I've ever seen.

A flash of light nearly blinds me. That pain in my chest erupts. My shadows, my constant companions, shy away from the light and then wither away completely.

All that's left as my vision goes black is the flickering sensation of a fine silver thread weaving its way around my heart.

41

JUST A MAN

Ella

BRIGHT LIGHT. A soft, warm breeze that smells sharply of pine and cedar. Somewhere in the distance a soft, delicate voice sings a beautiful song–a lullaby. A baby whimpers and is gently shushed.

I feel hands grazing down my arms. The scent of honeysuckle and lavender fills the air, and birdsong echoes in my ears.

I snuggle deeper into the warmth penetrating my back. Ryatt's scent brushes over my senses like a loving embrace. Deep in my chest, in my soul, that thread that binds us together sings with satisfaction. His scent is sharper than before. It's everything I love. Everything that sets my soul aflame…

I jolt to awareness, and I'm blinking frantically to clear my vision. Murmuring male voices cut through the lullabies and birds singing, and suddenly I'm in an unfamiliar cottage made of dark stone, the windows open to reveal a landscape of towering pine trees and rolling mountains capped with snow.

They're people standing outside of the cabin dressed in warrior leathers. I suck in a breath as a golden haired man turns, his green eyes meeting mine and widening with shock.

Granger's mouth parts, then he pushes whoever is standing next to him out of the way before he disappears from view.

The door to the cottage opens, spilling light throughout the small space. The Beta takes up the entire doorway as he ducks his head to come inside.

I whirl to look at whoever is sharing the creaky, goose down mattress I'm lying on and find Ryatt, fast asleep, resting his head on his arm while his other arm remains draped over my waist. I wasn't dreaming. This is real. Our bond–I can feel it. What happened?

"Granger–"

"Ella–*Luna*," he says briskly, bowing his head. His eyes are wide as he meets my gaze again.

"What happened?" I try to scoot into a seated position, but Granger jumps toward me.

"Lie down, please, you should be resting–"

"I–" I reach down to push the sheets away but stop when my hands brush over my suddenly soft belly.

Dread consumes me. My stomach hollows out, and a strangled sob forces its way up my throat.

"No–no!" My scream echoes through the cottage as tears well along my lashes.

Ryatt jerks into awareness, and suddenly, I'm on my back again, Granger and Ryatt looking down at me, holding me down as I thrash and scream and cry out for the daughter I've just lost. I can't hear what they're saying to me over my cries of agony. Despair curls through me, twisting in my heart like a heated blade.

"You should have let me die!" I scream at Ryatt, and sudden hatred boils through my veins. "Fuck you! You fucking bastard! Our baby!" Each word is a sob. "*Our baby*, Ryatt! You should have let me die with her!"

"Ella," he breathes, taking my face in his hands. "She's okay."

"What?" The chaos in my mind stills. "What did you say?" I whisper, looking from Ryatt, to Granger, and back again. "Ryatt, *what did you say?*"

"She's alive,," Granger says so softly I almost miss it. "She's beautiful."

My eyes are on Ryatt though, on his tear stained cheeks and the dark circles lining his eyes.

"She has dark hair. A lot of it," Granger continues, his voice choked with emotion. "She's so small, Ella. I've never seen—never seen a smaller baby."

"She's okay," Ryatt whispers, brushing the choked words over my cheek while I lie in absolutely stunned silence. "You did so well. You both did so well."

My chest jerks with each breath. I'm not sure I'm awake. Is this still a dream? Have I cooked up this best case scenario in my mind to ease the pain of losing our daughter?

"Where—"

Footsteps ring through the air. Granger is blocking my view of the threshold, but a shadow stretches across the room. He leans away, resting on his knees beside the bed while Ryatt straightens and helps me sit up.

My back rests on a rough, lumpy pillow, but I can't feel anything as the woman comes into view. Her long, white hair is braided messily away from her face. She looks familiar somehow; it's something about the curve of her mouth and wide set of her eyes.... Her eyes. Wow, I've never seen eyes like this before. A milky white against a dark blue, or green, I can't tell.

But my gaze leaves her face on instinct as a soft, cooing sound whispers from a bundle of thick blankets in her arms.

My heart threatens to leap out of my chest.

My lips part, and the world outside ceases to exist as my daughter is placed in my trembling, weak arms. I'm so exhausted that I barely have the strength to hold her as the woman adjusts the blankets so I can see my baby's face.

She's the color of a strawberry. That's the first thing I notice. Her skin is thin and nearly translucent in the soft glow of the fire on the far side of the room. She parts her lips, her tiny brow furrowing as her eyelids flutter open. Dark, colorless eyes meet mine.

"Hi," I whisper.

Her face twists, her bottom lip jutting out before a wail of epic proportions erupts all around us. It's the most beautiful sound I've ever heard.

"She's got some lungs on her," the woman beams, resting a hand on my knee. "How are you feeling?"

"I don't know," I reply absently. My full attention is on the baby in my arms. Beside me, Ryatt slowly gets off the bed, clearing his throat.

I tear my eyes from our daughter's face and meet his, expecting to see the same kind of joy I feel singing through my heart but....

He looks away from us and says to the woman I've gathered is a witch, "I need to speak with you."

She nods, and follows him out of the cottage.

I turn my attention to Granger. "What was that about?"

"Don't worry about it."

"Ryatt seemed so angry when he looked at the baby," I push, gathering her tighter. She calms, becoming dead weight in my arms.

Granger looks down at his hands. "You almost died, Ella. He was here with you the whole time, through everything. He... he thought you were going to die. Both of you."

Granger tells me everything. From the moment I collapsed in that clearing, to the moment the baby was born. I nearly died in Ryatt's arms. Our baby, born far too early, had been on the verge of death for several days while I withered away from a fever in this very bed.

Ryatt, according to Granger, gave up hope that either of us would survive.

But then the baby turned a corner with the help of the witch, and I...

"Your fever broke yesterday," he explains, pouring a tall glass of water from a pitcher and handing it to me. "The witch has been dosing you with herbs to keep you at rest. She decided this morning that you were healed enough to skip the herbs today. We weren't confident you'd wake up."

Several women from the nearby village had come, all of them having babies of a similar age, and nursed our baby in my stead.

Ryatt sat here next to me, Granger explains, for four entire days.

"Has he held her?" I ask.

"No," he answers honestly, and it crushes me.

The baby whines, rooting against my chest. In response, my heavy breasts begin to tingle, and milk soaks through the long white night-dress I'm wearing.

How can I be so happy–and so distraught–at the same time?

"I'll leave you. Do you–do you know how to..."

"I think so," I whisper, my voice cracking over the word as I fumble with the buttons on the bodice of the dress.

Granger clears his throat and leaves the cottage.

Tears burn down my cheeks as I try, and try, and try to get the baby to latch. She's getting frustrated, and crying, her little face turning a dark purple as her wails fill the room.

"I'm sorry," I sob, over and over again. She's too small, I realize, to even breastfeed. Her little mouth and jaw can't figure out how to nurse.

I'm soaked with milk when the door opens again. I turn my head, tears streaming down my face. "Ryatt, I can't–"

It's not Ryatt. Disappointment swells in my chest as the woman–the witch–walks in and closes the door behind her. She carries a basket of supplies, setting it down gently beside the bed before sitting down near my legs.

"She's used to a bottle now. It'll take time to teach her how to nurse properly. We'll collect your milk in the meantime, don't worry."

"What did I do wrong?"

The witch looks at me, looks through me. "This wasn't your fault."

"She shouldn't have been born yet!" The words tumble out of me, falling over one another.

"This happens sometimes. The curse didn't help the matter, of course."

"It shouldn't have happened to *her*!"

"Luna, take a breath. You're alive. She's alive. Your curse is gone."

Relief floods my system but it's short lived. At what cost? What happened during those hours I spent trapped in my worst nightmares while the curse tried to pull me under and rob me of my life and child?

"He hates her, doesn't he?"

She winces, then reaches into the basket and pulls out a bottle. The milk is still warm as my fingers close around it. "Place it on her lower lip. She knows what to do." She ignores my question, and maybe that's for the best.

The baby takes to the bottle in an instant, her weight a calming comfort against my aching chest.

But I failed. I failed them both. Her, and Ryatt.

"The Alpha wouldn't let us name her, but the women from the village who have been helping have started calling her *Eadan*. It's a very old word from the ancient language. It means *little fire*. But, she doesn't seem like an Eadan to me. She loves to sit in a warm lap and listen to the birds. Little bird," she whispers, tracing a circle over the baby's forehead. A brief shimmer of light, or magic, dissolves into my daughter's skin where the woman touched her.

A blessing, I assume.

I give the witch a watery smile. "Thank you."

She grips my knee, her own smile turning wobbly. "I did what I could for you both. Your mate struggled with the situation. He still is. He doesn't hate the baby, but she might remind him of what happened to you. He believes he failed you by not finding me sooner. The curse was… advanced. It may take a long time for your powers to return."

I try to form the words to ask if she'll fetch Ryatt for me, but my body begins to ache again. She notices my grimace.

"Rest now, starling." She gently takes the baby, now sleeping, from my arms.

"Will you stay here with me?"

She pauses mid-step and turns around. My baby looks so impossibly small in her arms. The witch nods, and sits down in a rocking chair near the bed.

I roll onto my side, ignoring my damp dress. My body feels absolutely wrecked. I could sleep for days.

But my eyes stay locked on the witch. She lays a gentle hand on my baby, humming a gentle song. It's enough to lull my body into numbness as the sunlight shifts to a deep gold, then a raw violet, stars peeking through the gaps in the trees.

I don't remember closing my eyes, but at some point, I open them to find the witch is gone, and she's been replaced by Ryatt, who sits with empty arms in the rocking chair.

He's sharpening a blade.

"Where is she?"

"The baby has been staying with a local family. She's fine." His voice is level and uninterested as he slides a wet stone across the edge of the blade, the metal singing with each stroke. Finally, his eyes meet mine, the same color as the blade in his hand.

Something about him is different now. He's lacking that usual undercurrent of power I've grown so used to over the past year that I forget it's there.

Now it's silent.

But... our bond....

"We're mates again. I can feel it."

His mouth kicks up in a smile that doesn't meet his eyes.

"What did you do, Ryatt?" I ask as a realization dons on me. My stomach twists as I sit up. "How did you break the curse?"

"The witch did it."

Something is wrong, I can feel it. He goes back to sharpening his blade as new shadows form around his features.

"Why haven't you held her?"

Ryatt's throat bobs as he swallows like it's painful.

"Ryatt, what's wrong?"

"I can't protect either of you."

"From—from what? What's happening—"

His eyes lack their silver glow as they meet mine. "I begged the gods to spare your life, and they finally listened the moment I offered my powers to them. I am useless now, Ella. I am just a man. I can't protect you or her. I couldn't protect you from this curse even with my powers. I don't deserve–"

"Shut. Up," I hiss, and leap out of bed. I rush to him, ignoring the blade and sail into his arms.

I kiss him harder than ever before, tears streaming down my face.

"I don't care, Ryatt."

"I do," he says.

"Have you seen her?" I ask through tears. "Have you seen what we made together, Ryatt? Our daughter. She's beautiful, and she needs you–"

But he only shakes his head.

"Please try," I whisper. I hate the painful memories of her birth and my near death dancing behind his eyes. "Try for *me*, please."

I lean my forehead against his as the first inklings of sunlight drift through the window.

A new day dawns while I rest in my mates arms and try to sew his battered heart back together again.

The door opens like I knew it would.

"She needs a name," I tell him as our daughter is placed in my arms. I turn her so he can see her fully, maybe for the first time. "Name her, Ryatt. She's yours. She'll always be yours. No one can take that from you."

His gaze brushes over our daughter's face. Beyond the door, birds chatter in a soft breeze.

I wait for his answer.

4 2

BY ANY OTHER NAME

Ryatt

FRESH RAINDROPS GLISTEN on the trees above my head as I walk on steady feet toward the creek that runs adjacent to the village. It's quiet here. Nothing but the sound of the birds and the rippling water pierce the air as I sit on a boulder overlooking the creek and adjust the bundle in my arms.

My daughter is asleep, making little suckling motions with her lips every once in a while. Gods, she looks like Ella right now. Her hair is a dark mahogany brown, and the scrunch of her nose mimics my mate's look when she's annoyed–or teasing me or someone else.

I'm supposed to name this baby. Ella told me not to come back to the cottage until she has a name, or I'll sleep outside with the bugs and rats.

I stretch out my legs and cross my ankles. This could be a long day, and I haven't even eaten breakfast yet.

Now that Ella is recovered, we're planning on leaving tomorrow for Rifthold. Following the base of the mountains and skirting the edge of Tarsian, and Alpha Jaxon's territory, it's a three week journey give or take. I can't spirit us home anymore.

I inhale a breath and let it out slowly. I didn't tell Ella the full truth about what happened to my powers. They're gone, yes. But forever? Maybe not, based on the tingling sensation under my skin that feels like my shadows are trying to claw their way back.

All I remember from those last moments of her labor was praying in absolute desperation for their lives. I offered my powers, and once I did, I felt the mate bond snap back into place. Why? No clue. How? Hell if I know.

The witch, who I credit for saving all three of us in the hours that followed, told me yesterday that she believes I simply exhausted my powers once the mate bond was reestablished. I let them bleed into Ella, giving her the strength she needed to survive the birth once the witch broke the curse.

It nearly killed me. I've never been drained like that before, even by coming and going through the veil or being stabbed repeatedly by Kane.

This is different, and only time will tell.

Time, and the White Witch who is now a part of my court. I'm taking her home to Veiled Valley to help tend to Ella and the baby. Something about the woman—who has no idea what her name is and admitted she lost her memories over twenty-years ago during a time when Kane was on a crusade to capture and enslave the witches—is familiar to me. Maybe it's because she's a Firestone witch like Ella and our daughter. She understands Ella's magic in a way I never will. I need her in my arsenal.

She agreed to come with us, of course. The people in these parts treat her like a plague.

I sigh heavily and shake my head to clear my thoughts. What am I doing again? Oh, naming this baby. Giving her a name she'll have her entire life.

I roll my eyes to the water.

"It would be nice if you could just tell me your name," I say down to the sleeping baby in my arms. She makes a sour face then relaxes back into sleep.

During my own fitful recovery after my powers were drained dry, I had dreams. Dreams of following Ella down a marble corridor in a great castle. Dreams of lace curtains and my mate wearing nothing but her skin as I approached our bed.

And then dreams of... *her*. A little girl with brown hair and silver eyes. My eyes. Her, running on a beach, chasing two little boys and dodging waves breaking on the shore. Her, running up to me through a dense forest with tears in her eyes as she cradles a scraped elbow. Her, nestled in Ella's lap while her mother paints. But she never said her name.

I wait for her name to reach me on the slight breeze.

But instead of a name, I'm met by crunching footsteps headed in my direction. I turn my head as my body goes rigid in preparation to fight to death to protect my child, but then I see Westfall making his way down to the creek.

He pauses when he sees that I've noticed him.

"I just heard–I heard what happened," he says.

"When did you arrive?"

"Not even ten minutes ago. I haven't seen Ella yet, but Granger said I could find you here and that you've been sent away by your mate until you... name the baby."

"Yes, that's true, unfortunately." I grumble the last word.

"May I sit?"

I shrug, and Westfall sits on a boulder a few feet away from mine. I don't look at him, but out of the corner of my eye I can see him craning his neck to try to get a look at the baby in my arms.

Despite the rift between us, I feel for the man. I've accepted that I'm his son, and this... this is his granddaughter.

"Do you want to hold her?"

"Yes," he says before I can even finish the words. I stand and carefully ease over to where he's sitting stoically, his face illuminated by the shadowy sunlight peeking through the trees. I gently place her in his arms, and I swear he exhales so deeply I'm shocked he doesn't pass out.

His arms cradle her with practiced grace.

I forget he's done this before–with me.

A lump forms in my throat as I sit back down and rest my elbows on my knees. I turn my head to watch my *father* look at *my child*. His blue eyes are sharp, but watery, and the corner of his mouth tilts up in a smile I've never seen before.

I've never seen him smile, actually.

"She's beautiful." He seems to choke on the words. He clears his throat and chuckles. "Gods, I remember you being this small. It's hard to believe you were ever this tiny, now, seeing the man you've become."

I don't know what to say for a long time.

"How did you know what to do?" I finally ask. I have no idea what I mean. Maybe it's just fatherhood in general that feels daunting, damn near impossible. Maybe it's the idea of having to choose between my mate and my child, like I almost had to do. I chose Ella in those moments, but now that I've seen our daughter… I can't imagine making that decision again.

Westfall did, though.

He catches my drift. "I just let your mother tell me what to do."

I chuckle, meeting his eyes. "I imagine that's the best course of action in my situation as well."

His smile falters a bit. "It's instinctual, Ryatt. Being a father. Just like being a mate, you already know what to do. This kind of love is given. It's a blessing. It's in your blood. Whatever you do, however you fail… she'll forgive you. Maybe not *Ella*, but…" His mouth quirks into a smile again and I roll my eyes to the trees.

"Did you name me?" I ask, trying not to let my thoughts derail any further.

"Yeah, I did."

This catches me off guard. "Why did you choose Ryatt?"

He furrows his brow as if digging back through his memories to find the moment he gave me my name. "I liked the sound of it. I remember... gods, it was a long time ago. But I remember being reluctant to call you anything because we didn't know if you'd be taken from your mother immediately. Kane believed you to be his own son, as I'm sure you're aware, but you were *mine*. Your mother insisted I name you for that reason, to stake my claim. To give you something of mine while you were raised by another man. Ryatt just came to mind one day. I liked the sound of it. It's from an old legend. The name of a warrior turned god. And when you were born, your mother announced your name to Kane, and he accepted it. He didn't care, I don't think. He might have told his ailing kingdom that he had a son, but he didn't treat you as such. You were a slave, just like us. A toy for him to play with until he got bored, or you got broken." His tone shifts to something dark, but he clears his throat again and smiles down at the baby. "I wish she could have met her, Ryatt."

Damn, that rips me in half.

"I'm sorry for what happened to you, for what you had to do to keep me alive." The words warble off my tongue.

"I always would have chosen you," he says quietly. "I would have done it the same way if given a second chance. You are the only piece of your mother I have left. You are all the good things that we were, and she...." He smiles down at my daughter. "She is the same. She'll have your eyes, I can tell. She'll be tough, like you. She'll love getting in fights, I'm sure." He sighs deeply, wistfully. "She'll be beautiful like Ella. Kind, and funny, and a little clumsy with a sword but brave all the same."

Now, I'm smiling despite myself.

"Kenna," he says, matter-of-factly.

"What?"

"That's her name. Kenna. It means *'born of fire'* in the old tongue."

"Kenna," I say, letting the name roll off my tongue. "I like it. You're good at this."

"I'll tell Ella you came up with it so I don't blow your cover."

My lips twitch into a wry smile as I look at my father and really see him for the first time. Just a man. A father, grandfather. A soul who lost his mate and spent the remainder of his life in purgatory–alone, giving up his throne to raise a stone-hearted, thick-headed boy with a flair for violence into the man I am today. Into the *king* I am today.

"I want you back on the throne in Veiled Valley, as Alpha."

He shakes his head. "I'm retired. *Retiring*, you could say. Give Artyom my post as commander. I think I'd like to spend the rest of my days with this one here." He runs a knuckle over Kenna's soft, pink cheek.

I can't argue against it. He's my best commander, but this *family*... this is more important.

"You should know there's been a breach in the veil. A few days ago, we believe. I heard the news from Artyom while I traveled here, and they're looking for whoever might have crossed, if it did, indeed, happen."

I shrug. I'm not in the right frame of mind to consider any threats right now, especially this far away from Rifthold.

"I'm sure Artyom can find them–"

"Alpha King, your mate is wanting to know if you've named your child yet and would like to return for lunch or if you need more time?" The voice of the witch carries down to the creek, a hint of amusement lacing each word.

I begin to turn my head to look up at her but stop when I notice the way Westfall has gone absolutely still, his eyes locked on the creek.

"Westfall?" I ask.

He shakes his head, his eyes lowering as a wistful expression flutters over his stony features. "Sorry, I–sometimes I think I hear her."

"Hear who?"

"Alpha King–"

I rise to my feet the moment Westfall jumps up with Kenna cradled against his chest. He spins on his heel to look up the embankment at the witch standing in the glare of the sun. His eyes are wider than I've ever seen, and his lips fall open as he gapes, his brow knotting.

"Cressendra?" he rasps.

The witch looks down at him, her milky eyes whirling as if, somewhere, deep in her lost and forgotten memories, she remembers her name leaving his lips.

"No fucking way," I say aloud, and look up at *my mother*.

43

VEILED INTENTIONS

Isaac

I'M NOT sure what I was expecting to find, but it isn't this.

Instead of simply walking through a wall of mist and magic, coming out the other side and coming face to face with Ryatt and Ella, I feel like I've been dropped on my head after having every nerve in my body pulled apart and thrust back together again.

I never gave much thought to what Ryatt and Ella went through, twice now, while crossing the veil. It's nothing like spiriting myself from room to room, or from the castle to the rolling fields beyond the woods, no.

My powers are useless. Even my wolf powers are whimpering in my veins as I shift my weight on the stool I'm sitting on with my hands bound behind my back.

How many days has it been since I came through the veil? Four? Maybe five?

The man seated in front of me hasn't said a word in a long time. I can only see his jaw, the rest of his face shielded by a hood. He has dark skin, and his hands are covered in a tangle of scars and tattoos.

Other than tying me up, he hasn't laid a hand on me.

I came through the veil and found myself underground, in some kind of buried temple. Ryatt and Ella were nowhere to be found. I spent a day trying to find my way to the surface, and when I did, I realized why I'd come through the veil at that very spot, and my blood goes cold at the memory.

I climbed up a set of stone stairs toward the first hints of sunlight I'd seen and found myself at a cave mouth.

And carved into the walls on either side of the entrance were giant depictions of the two beasts of the Moon Goddess.

My skin prickles as I think about the statues that are now scarred into my memory.

My captor notices, tilting his chin so I have a better view of his face. Glacier blue eyes meet mine only briefly.

I shake my head with impatience and look down at my filthy khaki pants and what was once a light blue button down shirt. Now, it's stained with dirt and a bit of blood. A group of wolves came upon me when I tried to make my way out of the forest that surrounded the buried temple within a day, and without being able to shift, I had no choice but to surrender.

So far, no one seems to believe that I am truly the Alpha King of Crescent Falls.

So, I'm tied up in the back of some tavern.

Maddy is going to be absolutely livid when I get home... whenever that'll be.

I clear my throat and let out a soft, impatient sigh. My captor rolls his neck and stands, pulling a dagger from his belt.

I try not to flinch, but he holds the blade up in surrender before approaching me, cutting through the ropes entwining my wrists.

"Thanks," I murmur, rubbing my raw skin.

He sits back down but keeps his blade on his thigh. He reaches up with one hand and pulls his hood down, revealing coarse, black hair braided into cornrows.

Handsome, but roughened. Young, I imagine. He's probably my age, and as I sit roughly three feet away from him, I can tell he's powerful as well. His energy thrums around him like a current of electricity.

I flex my jaw. He motions to my smartwatch, which died several days ago.

"What, do you want my watch or something?"

His mouth ticks into a smile. "What good is it to me if it doesn't even tell time?"

"Are you letting me go or not?" When I was first captured, I explained who I was and why I came here, who I was searching for.

I even, at one point, begged on my knees to be let go, telling this man and his band of leather-clad roughens that my sister was dying.

"You're no longer our prisoner."

"Well, thank fuck for that," I sneer. I rise, and he follows, blocking my path to the flimsy wooden door on the far side of the room. "Move."

"You have no idea where you're going."

"I came here to find my sister and her mate–your king. She's in danger, and you've already hampered my progress–"

"Luna Ella survived the birth of the princess," he cuts in quickly.

I feel the writhing pressure in my chest ease a touch. "And the baby?"

He nods, and a ghost of a smile touches his lips.

I need to sit down, so I do, the tension I've held in my bones since the moment Ryatt told me what was happening finally snapping and leaving me at ease. Kind of.

"Where are they now?"

"Not nearby."

I roll my lip between my teeth and fix this stranger with a glare. What am I supposed to do now?

"How far away are they?"

"It'll be at least a week before they reach Rifthold. I've been asked to bring you to Veiled Valley."

I have no idea what Rifthold is, but Veiled Valley is familiar. Ella must have mentioned it at some point when we were all in Maatua.

Actually, it was Cassian. He'd been in Veiled Valley–and that magic castle…."Then you've talked to them?"

"Granger, my Alpha's Beta, has been keeping me in the loop."

"And what are you to your Alpha?"

His eyes fill with amusement as he sits down across from me again. "My name is Artyom. Commander Artyom. You're safe. No harm shall come to you as long as you remain in my care. I will see you to Veiled Valley myself, and once there, you'll be treated as an esteemed guest."

I don't have much choice. My mangled powers aren't strong enough to break back through the veil yet, and I obviously underestimated the strength of the magic keeping our kingdoms apart.

"How far is it to Veiled Valley from… here?" *Wherever the hell we are.*

"Two days on foot," he says. "Can you shift?"

"Possibly," I tell him, then pause, looking down at my hands as guilt starts to creep through my veins. "I need to contact someone beyond the veil. Is that possible from here?"

"Not until we reach Veiled Valley," he says.

I'm sorry, Maddy, I think, picturing my sons, whom I miss terribly, and wringing my hands before rising and stuffing them in my pants pockets.

"Fine. Let's go, then."

Artyom inhales deeply and nods, and I follow him through the door. The tavern below is nearly empty save for a few dust-covered drifters dressed in leather and plain, likely homespun, fabric. The smell of roasting meat and sour, bitter beer is thick as we pass through the dining area and out into a cool, crisp summer night.

Men dressed in leather armor are milling around a fire pit. No one even looks in my direction.

This place feels like it was lost to time.

And Ella was right about how magical this place feels. Even my own recovering powers feel different…. Stronger. More precise.

I look up at the stars like I'll be able to see the veil. I think about the conversation I had several months ago with my Uncle Ben. Had he been right about the veil's purpose? Was it meant to keep the people of Eastonia out of Crescent Falls or to keep their powers contained?

Does this mean that in Crescent Falls, our powers–our wolves and special gifts–are… restrained?

I lick my lips and follow Artyom toward the forest surrounding the sleepy village, itching to shift to test my theory.

MADDY

IT'S BEEN FOUR DAYS.

I stare at the moonstone dog bowl for the thousandth time. Isaac is alive. He'd better be, at least. I've never been more angry at him than I am now.

I shouldn't be. I have everything handled here, and after hearing that Ella's life was in danger and she was in early labor, I… I simply don't know how to feel.

I just miss him, and I'm worried. Worried about him, and Ella, and the baby. I'm even worried about Ryatt who looked so broken when I interrupted his conversation with Isaac from beyond the veil.

It's been four days. Did Ella survive? Did her baby?

I leave the observatory feeling worse than when I climbed up here to begin with.

The library is quiet and empty. It's the middle of the night, my only true downtime from the hustle and bustle of my life as Luna, and as a new mother.

But as I walk to our room, I hear a door gently close, then brisk footsteps.

I turn toward the sound, expecting to find a maid working late for some reason, but Isla turns the corner.

"Oh, I didn't know you were still awake." She tries to give me a smile but it falls flat. "You were in the observatory, weren't you?"

I let out my breath. "Yes. I can't sleep."

Isla sighs and runs her fingers through her hair. It's loose and falling over her shoulders in a sheet of golden, softly curling at the ends. "Any news?"

I shake my head. I told my in-laws everything, of course. They're supposed to travel back to Maatua at the end of the week to see to the reconstruction of their new house, since Ella wrecked their old one, but now there's no telling when they'll be able to leave.

Because none of us have any idea when Isaac will return.

I try to not think about the what ifs, especially... What if he doesn't come back?

"He will come back," Isla says like she's reading my mind. "Once he knows Ella is safe, he'll return."

I nod. It's all I can do.

"You should try to sleep, Maddy. You've been up for days."

"I know," I whisper, nodding. She's right, but every time I close my eyes, I envision the moment Isaac dissolved into streams of light and simply vanished.

My world has been cold without him. It's like I'm back in the freezing chateau in Celestoria again, alone. So desperately alone.

I hear a distant whimper. One of the babies must have just woken up.

"Goodnight," I tell Isla and turn, but she stops me with a hand on my forearm.

She squeezes my arm with a soft, knowing smile on her face. "Everyone is okay, Maddy. I can feel it."

"I hope you're right," I whisper back, then walk to my room and shut myself inside.

Ryan is fussing. Sydney remains warm and cozy in his swaddle, fast asleep. I gently pick Ryan up and cradle him against my shoulder, walking to look out the windows at the moon drenched back garden.

Ryan settles in my arms. I look down at him. He looks like Isaac, at least I think so. He has the same chin and nose as his dad, but his hair is red like mine.

And his eyes... They favor my coloring. That dark, stormy blue Isaac says he loves most of all.

I swallow hard and force my mouth into a smile before kissing Ryan's forehead, breathing in his baby scent.

"Daddy will come back," I whisper. It's a prayer. The same prayer I say on my knees several times a day.

Come back, Isaac. Please, come back.

4 4

THE BOND IS BACK

Ella

THERE'S a commotion outside of the cottage. It's just after noon, from what I can tell, and the little village girl who follows the witch around everywhere has just dropped off a basket full of cold sliced meat, bread, cheese, and an assortment of fruits and vegetables for a quick lunch when the door to the single room cottage bursts open.

I rise from the pile of clothing and gifts we've been given from the nearby village, in the process of packing up for our journey home, when Ryatt strides in and shuts the door with a snap. He locks it and stares down at me absently.

"Uh, are you okay?" I straighten as he turns to the single window and pulls the curtains closed. "Ryatt, where's the baby?"

"She's with Westfall."

"He's here?"

"He just arrived."

Something in Ryatt's tone puts me on edge. It's been several days since the baby's birth, and he's finally coming around. Dark circles no longer cloud his eyes and his shoulders have been relaxed, but now?

"Are we under attack?" I ask, rounding the bed.

"No."

"Then what?"

"The witch," he says slowly, turning to face me. He tucks his hands in the casual brown pants he's wearing with a homespun gray sweater that makes his eyes look like the color of steel.

"What about her?"

"What have the two of you talked about?"

I furrow my brow. "The baby, mostly. She's a talented midwife. *Obviously….* What is this about?"

He heaves a sigh, leaning against the wall between the window and the door. "Have you asked her about her past?"

"She doesn't remember, Ryatt." All I know is something happened to her twenty to twenty-five years ago, by my estimation. Knowing the history of events in Rifthold, witches were often captured and enslaved by Kane and subjected to all kinds of abuse and sick experiments. But she doesn't know if she was ever kept in Rifthold. The brief conversation we had regarding our shared Firestone gifts was surface level–forgettable.

She did tell me her memories of her childhood are fuzzy at best. Her young adult life is missing from her memory almost entirely. In our few moments together, while tending to the baby and my own recovery, she told me she remembers stone walls that drip with water and grime, lanterns that glow red, and screaming.

"I believe she was held in Rifthold, possibly a slave," I tell him, taking a deep breath. "The witches who were in the cave with me were tortured, too. A lot of them were traumatized, even during such a short time there. If the witch was held by Kane in any way and was able to escape, I imagine that trauma would have been… far greater than anything we've seen so far. She has amnesia."

"Amnesia," he repeats softly. It's a whisper full of an emotion that borders on vengeful. That's enough to send a shiver up my spine.

"Ryatt, are we safe?"

"Yes."

"Then what's wrong?"

His eyes meet mine for the first time since he stormed in here and wrecked my peace. "Westfall... we were talking. He was holding our baby, and the witch approached us and called down to me to let me know that you wanted me to join your for lunch if I'd named the baby... Kenna–"

"Kenna? Is that her name?" My heart squeezes around the word. "I love it. It's beautiful."

"Thank you," he says briskly, the corners of his mouth twitching, but he doesn't quite smile. "Anyway."

"Anyway...." I move a little closer to him, not liking the way he looks down at his boots as his body goes rigid.

"She might be my mother."

I choke on a laugh. "Ryatt, you can't be serious. I saw a vision of your mother, remember? She looks nothing like–"

The look on Ryatt's face cuts me to the core. He's serious about this. The look in his eyes tells me there's no doubt in his mind that the witch, who doesn't even remember her name, is his mom.

"How do you know?" I ask, my voice laced with a tremor I can't hide.

"Westfall. He looked up at her and said her name, and now he's.... Kenna might be the only reason he's still in one piece right now, which is why I left them together. She's asleep, and he will take care of her."

"I know that," I cut in, edging closer to my mate. I lay a hand on his forearm and squeeze. "I know he wouldn't hurt her, but what happened exactly?"

"He said her name. She... looked down at us for a moment, like she remembered, but...." He tapers off, shaking his head. "She walked away."

"She just walked away?"

He nods. "Westfall was paler than I've ever seen him. He asked me if I saw that, if she'd really been there. I told him that yes, the witch had come to talk to me, but Westfall sat down, turned his back to me, and started murmuring some song or story down to Kenna, and I figured I was better off coming here."

"You just left him down there?"

"Well, what was I supposed to do?"

"Maybe talk to him about it? Is she really your mother, Ryatt?"

Ryatt pauses, tilting his head in consideration. I step into him, manually wrapping his arms around my waist. I feel a jolt of warmth when his hands settle against the small of my back, and I lean into him, resting my chin on his chest.

I realize with a start that we haven't touched like this in a long time. There's always been something between us—the baby, and the curse—but now it's just us. And our bond…. Wow. The mate bond is really a pull a person can't ignore. His scent overwhelms my senses.

He must feel it too because he smooths a hand up my back and settles me closer.

"I think this is between her and Westfall," he says, his voice gravelly and full of smoke. He brings his hands down and cups my ass.

I let out a breathy moan.

I used to tell myself that this feeling inside of me—this roiling, liquid heat whenever he so much as looked in my direction—was just the mate bond talking. But now, it's so much more than that. His touch sets my soul on fire.

"What were we talking about?" he rasps, leaning down to brush the words over my temple. He inhales deeply, taking in my scent, and groans.

"I can't remember," I murmur, tilting my head to the side to give him access to my neck. His lips brush over my skin in a featherlight touch, sending ripples of electricity skittering over me, through me, and a warm heat settles low in my belly.

Maybe we shouldn't be doing this. I just had a baby! But the witch, who is possibly my mate's long lost and presumed dead mother, has been feeding me potions and tonics that have definitely sped up my recovery ten-fold.

I feel better than I ever have and more than ready to be laid down in that creaky bed by my mate so that he can ravage me.

But now, Ryatt is thinking the same thing. He pulls away slightly, looking down at me with eyes glassy with desire. "I don't want to hurt you, Princess."

"What if I want you to?"

A muscle in his neck ticks, and his jaw tightens. "Don't do that. I can't—our bond is back in place, and that's making it hard to even be around you without wanting to rip off your clothes and do unspeakable things…." He takes a shuddering breath and dips his mouth back to my neck. His teeth graze my skin before he sucks that tender spot between my neck and shoulder.

I draw in my breath, my mind laser focused on the way he's touching me.

"I don't think I'd be able to stop, even if you said so," he says against my skin, biting down.

My eyes flutter closed. I clutch his waist, trying to get closer to him. I need him closer.

"Ryatt," I breathe, my hands gliding up and under his sweater. His skin is so warm, his muscles flexed beneath my touch.

He nudges my neck, trailing kisses up to the base of my jaw. "You smell so good," he groans. "Like everything—everything warm, and comfortable. You smell like home."

He whirls us around so my back is to the wall. I'm wearing a dress that brushes my ankles, the fabric made from what feels like thin cotton. He slowly inches the fabric up my leg, his hand smoothing over my skin.

"Ella," he says, his lips hovering against mine. "I love you."

I find it momentarily hard to breathe as his warm, calloused hand slides up my thigh.

"Tell me to stop," he whispers, bracing the wall with his free hand.

"I don't want you to stop," I whisper back. My tongue darts out to swipe over his lower lip, and then his mouth is on mine—hot, wet, and demanding.

He presses me to the wall, and my whimpering moans echo around us as I wrap my arms around his neck, and he carries me to the bed.

We might only have a few minutes alone. We both know it, too.

Someone will come to the door looking for us. Kenna might wake up wanting milk. Granger might stop by to ask if we're still planning on leaving at nightfall.

So, we waste no time.

He drops me on the bed, making quick work of taking off his pants and sweater. His chest heaves with every breath he takes as I pull the fabric of my dress over my hips and let my legs fall open, his name a prayer on my tongue when he settles between my knees and clutches the back of my neck to guide me into another desperate, all-consuming kiss.

His cock nudges my entrance, and it's enough to send a spark of heat rushing to my core. "Please," I beg. I don't care if it hurts or if I'm not ready. I have no idea when we'll be alone again, and I can't take it. I need him. My wolf is in agony, pleading for her mate. And his wolf?

Ryatt's pupils are so large that only a hint of his silver irises show when he slowly guides his cock inside of me. I know it's taking all of his strength to hold himself back. I can see the hint of transformation in his eyes, like he's on the verge of shifting, like this is almost too much for him.

I've forgotten how feral things used to be between us. I have a brief flash of memory from that night, during the Rite in Moonrise, when he'd almost fucked me publicly against a tree after we had sex for the first time.

I arch off the bed as he fills me, the stretch of it almost too much, but I take it.

"That's so good," he says. "You're such a good girl."

My breath catches in my throat as he presses in another inch, then another, each slow thrust done in a testing fashion that tells me he's doing everything he can not to lose control and hurt me by accident.

"I'm okay," I say, and it's an effort to get the words out.

Ryatt nods, his lips parting as he lowers his face to mine.

I reach up and cup his cheeks, deepening the kiss.

He grinds his hips while buried inside me. An involuntary whimper of the deepest kind of pleasure works its way up my throat.

"Please," I whisper against his lips, arching my hips against his to find more friction. "Please, Ryatt." I want him unleashed. I want him to know that I'm his, forever, any way he wants me. I need to know that we're okay after everything we've been through the past few months.

I need this more than he realizes.

He nods, but there's still hesitation glimmering behind his heavy, hooded eyes.

So I sink my nails into his back and bare my teeth, letting some of my wolf show behind my eyes.

That's his undoing, and before I can blink, he flips me onto my stomach.

45

WHAT DID YOU DO TO ME?

Ella

I CRY out Ryatt's name as he thrust in from behind. He grips my hips, adjusting me so I'm where he wants me, and begins to absolutely lay waste to my body.

It's like every piece of me—every cell, every nerve—is honing in on his movements. He lowers himself over my back after a moment, pressing me into the mattress with one of his hands pinning my wrists above my head.

He kisses the base of my neck, then bites down, holding me there.

For whatever reason that bite ignites something in me I've never felt before. It's something ancient. Maybe something tied to my powers? I don't know. But whatever he does awakens that spark of light deep in my soul, and soon my skin is glowing a pale gold.

Each stroke of his cock has me edging toward a climax I already know is going to be stronger than anything I've ever experienced. I lose sense of place and time. The bed is threatening to fall to pieces beneath us. His free hand smooths over my side, clutching the slope of my hip, and he thrusts into me as deep as he can go.

"Ella," he groans, holding himself there as I slip over the edge and fall headfirst into a wave of ecstasy. I spasm around his cock, and he grunts, his grip on my hip tightening. Another thrust and he's coming undone as well, spilling himself deep inside of me.

It takes several minutes for us to calm down, and even then my skin continues to glow like a fucking lantern.

He flips me over so I'm facing him again and rests beside me, his fingers tracing lines down my heaving breasts as I try to catch my breath.

"Was that—I think I blacked out for a moment there, I..." Ryatt uncharacteristically fumbles over his words. I roll onto my side so we're chest to chest. He continues apologetically, "Did I hurt you?"

"No, the opposite." I place a glowing hand on his chest.

Ryatt jerks, then inhales sharply, drawing away from me.

"Oh, my Goddess! Did I just burn you?" I frantically sit up to inspect the glowing handprint on my mates chest.

He sits up as well, and we watch my power soak into his skin, then disappear.

Seconds pass. Neither of us breathes. Then he chokes on a breath and looks me in the eyes. "What did you just do?"

"I don't know. Does it hurt?"

He shakes his head and extends an arm toward the end of the bed. In the dim sunlight passing through the moth holes in the curtains, I can just see the outline of his roping tattoos, but there's something else.

Shadows curl between his fingertips—faint at first. I feel it then, those powers of his, the powers he sacrificed to save me and Kenna but....

His eyes meet mine, and they glow.

"How is this possible?" he asks in a whisper.

I open my mouth to reply something along the lines of, "I have no fucking idea!" when a sharp knock on the door cuts me off.

The knock is followed by a wail, and we both let out a sigh of relief that it's just someone bringing us our daughter.

"Hurry," I urge, and smile at Ryatt. He smiles back, and for a few seconds, we hold each other's gaze, unable to break away.

Whatever just happened between us… we'll have to talk about it later. I did something to him, but I don't know what it means or why it happened.

I pull on my dress and quickly walk to the door while Ryatt dresses as swiftly as he can.

I throw open the door and come face to face with Granger who's holding a squirming and very unhappy Kenna in his arms.

He takes a single step into the cottage and stops, glancing between me and Ryatt.

"Sorry to interrupt," he says dryly as I take Kenna in my arms. He gives Ryatt a look, and Ryatt just smirks as he adjusts his belt.

"Poor thing," I coo to my daughter. "Was Granger mean to you?"

Granger glares at me. "She didn't want me anymore than she wanted Commander Westfall. I wasn't mean to her."

"I'm just teasing," I tell him before settling into the rocking chair next to the window. Ryatt strides over and opens the curtains, which highlight the crumpled sheets and the pillows that have been tossed from the bed.

Granger chews his lip looking more than uncomfortable, but I find it amusing.

"Jealous?" I whisper as Ryatt sits down on the edge of the bed to tie his boots.

Granger scowls, rolling his eyes to the ceiling in what I imagine is a prayer for the gods to strike him dead rather than continue with this line of conversation.

The Beta closes his eyes and exhales. "Actually, yeah, I'm jealous. I want nothing more than to be heading home to my wife. But instead, I just spent the last half hour talking Westfall off a ledge." He turns to Ryatt, who is still lacing up his boots. "He told me his mate has returned to him. I was sure he was having a stroke because that would mean your mother is alive."

"She might be," Ryatt says, entirely too casually.

I watch the exchange with interest. Ryatt and Granger have

known each other since they were kids, and Granger is a lot more shocked about this than Ryatt.

"The witch who's been helping Ella is your mother?" he presses, jabbing his thumb in my direction for emphasis.

Ryatt shrugs, standing. "I don't know."

"Wouldn't you recognize her? Wouldn't you have known–"

"I don't have many tangible memories of her. I don't remember her voice or the way she smelled. I don't have a clear picture of what she looked like," he says coolly. "I don't know, Granger. Either Westfall has lost his mind, or that witch is really his mate, and my mother."

Granger turns pleading eyes to me like I can do anything about this. I'm just as stumped as the two of them. "I think," I say, gently rocking Kenna back to sleep, "that we should do whatever Westfall thinks is best."

"He was debating throwing himself off a cliff, Ella," Granger says hotly. He turns to Ryatt. "Seriously, Ryatt. We've seen this before, remember?"

Ryatt smooths his tongue along his lower teeth and crosses his arms over his chest. His eyes darken a shade as he looks down at his boots, nodding.

"What do you mean?" I ask, pulling down the straps on my dress as Kenna continues to fidget. She finally got the hang of nursing this morning, but I still fumble with it. It hurts, too. Ryatt watches me closely as I help her latch and then lean my head back against the rocking chair, grimacing.

"He's talking about something our kind calls Mate Fever. It's rare, but in Westfall's case, we can't rule it out." He walks over to me and rests a hand on the top of the rocking chair, tilting his head to get a better view of Kenna. "It usually happens when someone's mate dies. You can slowly go insane."

"Westfall isn't insane," I persist, scoffing at the notion. "He's the most level headed person I know."

"We have to consider it," Granger says, nodding at Ryatt.

"He recognized her voice, and before he turned around and spotted her, he told me that he sometimes hears her voice. It was like he saw a ghost." Ryatt smooths his hand over Kenna's fuzzy head, and she momentarily stops suckling, then starts again with a vengeance.

I take a deep breath and glare up at him. "Do you mind?"

He only smiles at me then looks back at Granger with a sigh. "Westfall wasn't going to leap over the cliff, Granger. I've already decided that the witch is coming back to Veiled Valley with us, so she'll be traveling in our company. I'm guessing Westfall might have gotten his hopes up that she was, in fact, my mother, and is now just going through the motions when it comes to broken hope and grief." I narrow my eyes at Ryatt as he claps Granger on the shoulder and continues, "I'll talk to him."

"You're being incredibly casual about this," I snap.

Both men turn to me.

"You are," I say with more emphasis. "You act like the mate bond is just something you can ignore, which we all know isn't the case. If Westfall believes she's his mate, then she is. Maybe she's not actually your mother, but he's feeling a new bond, and that's why he's acting this way."

"Having two mates is impossible," Granger cuts in.

"It happened to my dad," I argue, shrugging.

They exchange glances, then Granger sighs and shakes his head. "I don't know what to think, but I'm not going to babysit him, Ryatt."

"I'm not asking you to do that," he says hotly. He turns to look at me again, his expression softening. So much so, actually, that I feel a blush begin to prickle across my cheeks.

"I'd recognize Ella's voice anywhere. I'm sure you feel the same about Amanda."

Granger nods. "Then we're going to believe him. This witch is your mother, and she somehow survived Kane?"

"She has no memory of Westfall, or me, for that matter. Right now, she's just a witch with no name and–" Ryatt cuts himself off abruptly and furrows his brow. Granger, too, turns toward the door, hanging his head.

"What's wrong?"

"Mind-link," Granger murmurs, and a few seconds later his head snaps in Ryatt's direction.

Ryatt meets his eyes and raises his brows.

Then they both slowly turn to me.

I slouch in the chair. "Great, what's happening now? Another war?"

"Your brother is here, in Eastonia," Ryatt says. "He fucking did it. I knew he would."

"What are you even talking about? There's no way–" I bite down on my reply. Actually, yes. Isaac is extremely powerful and stubborn enough to come here despite the dangers. "Why is he here?"

"I talked to him before everything happened with you and the baby." Ryatt clears his throat, looking peeved, to say the least. He looks at Granger. "This is likely why I wasn't about to get through to him these past few days."

"Where the hell is he now?" I growl. I try not to shout, especially since Kenna is on the verge of sleep.

"He's being escorted to Veiled Valley," Granger says. "From what the scouts we have in Rifthold just told us, Artyom's band of warriors found him, and he's in good health. He's safe."

"I'm going to kill him," I say, then laugh sharply. "Is he seriously here?"

Ryatt nods.

Oh, great. And none of us are powerful enough to get him back to the other side after everything we've just been through. "Oh, Maddy," I groan. "She's just as livid as I am, I'm sure. How long is it going to take to reach Veiled Valley from here? A week? Two?"

"Three, since you'll be on foot with the baby, and Ryatt can't shift–"

"I can," Ryatt cuts in. We both look at him. "We can jump, I think."

I lean forward a bit. "Your powers–"

"Whatever you did to me, Ella," he says, motioning to his chest. "I think it changed something. The witch did say she wasn't sure if my powers were gone or just completely depleted."

"What about Kenna? Can she handle a jump like that?"

"We can't go straight to Veiled Valley, no. But to Rifthold? Possibly. She's a Firestone witch. She can handle it."

He looks at me and the baby with nothing but certainty in his eyes.

I gather her a little closer. She's so small. Not even a week old.

But Ryatt is sure, so I'm sure.

"Let's go home, then," I tell him.

46

LET HER REMEMBER

Ryatt

THE BARTENDER at the quaint inn we're staying at for the night pours me another glass of whiskey neat. I nod my thanks as little jolts of pain run up my spine, skittering like mice. It took three jumps to get from that hell-hole where my daughter was born back to Rifthold. I was barely standing by the end of it, and after two full days traveling on foot, we've finally made it to a familiar pack, a familiar village, and are back in the Roguelands.

We'll be close enough to Veiled Valley that I can spirit us the rest of the way there after another day of travel.

I turn back to the table where I've just left the Alpha and Beta of this pack to finish their platters of roast beef, bread, and stew. Granger already retired to bed an hour ago, and the witch, still unnamed, is visiting with the local healer.

Westfall has made himself scarce during our journey here and is fine acting as a scout while we navigate the Roguelands. Something has to be done, however. He's on edge and flighty. I can tell he wants to talk to the witch but won't.

It's like he can't bring himself to believe it. I understand his hesitation.

The witch doesn't remember anything about her life up until twenty years ago.

I sip my whiskey and let it bloom through my veins. It numbs the ache in my bones but does nothing to clear my head. After tasting the whiskey in Maatua, I've lost my taste for the bitter, young whiskey found in the Roguelands.

I set the unfinished glass down and throw a few coins on the bar before walking toward the stairwell to the rooms above the tavern.

I pause at the door to our room. Ella is singing softly, some song about a clock and a mouse running up it. I've never heard her sing before. She's not very good, but I still fight a smile as I slowly, quietly, enter the room and shut the door behind me.

Ella glowers at me from across the room when the floorboards creak under my weight. She's sitting up in bed with Kenna resting against her shoulder. Ella is also completely undressed from the waist up, and her breasts are....

Tantalizing. To say the least.

I grind my teeth as I start taking off my leathers, trying not to stare too long at my beautiful mate, but it's hard not to.

"Let me take her," I whisper. "You haven't touched the food they brought up." I ease onto the bed dressed in undershorts and a loose top. The mattress is softer than I expected, uncomfortably so. Just a few more days and we'll be home, in our own bed, and I don't plan to leave it until it's absolutely necessary.

Kenna squirms a bit in my arms before resettling with a long, dramatic sigh. She opens her eyes with a scowl, giving me a glimpse of those gray irises that are starting to fade from view. She'll have something of mine, at least. Her little scowl and clenched fists remind me of my wife, however.

"I'm not very hungry. I went to the bakery with the witch before coming up here for bed," Ella sighs as she reaches for her shirt.

"How is she?"

She shrugs. "She has no inclination that Westfall is losing his mind over her. She's rather oblivious, actually. I wonder if there's something wrong with her, you know? It's almost like she's been stripped raw and was left that way."

"What do you mean?"

"Like… you know how we feel when our powers run dry? That emptiness?"

I nod. It's how I feel right now, honestly. I wonder if I'll ever have them back, at least like they were before.

Ella lies back against the thin pillows and curls into herself, wrapping one of her legs around mine. "She's like that all the time. Those clouds in her eyes… it's magic, I think. Something is trapping her in her own head, her own body. I think she should go to the coven, Ryatt. Giselle and the Mystics will be able to help her."

My head rocks back and forth in agreement. That's actually the plan.

I haven't told Westfall, though.

"Have you talked to your dad?"

"Westfall?"

Ella gives me a look. "Who else, Ryatt?"

"No, I haven't."

"I think you should demand an audience with him tonight. Once we're in Veiled Valley, I'm sure he'll find excuses to ignore this situation completely."

"He's already doing that," I counter.

"You're his Alpha, remember?"

I look down at my daughter and sigh. She's asleep and looks very cute in a soft, red knit onesie one of the women in this village made for her. News of her birth has spread like wildfire through the Roguelands. Our bags are full of gifts for our princess.

"I'll see what I can do."

"Tonight," Ella says, giving me a little nudge. "I need to start calling this woman a name, anyway. Calling her *the witch* is getting old, and it will be entirely too confusing when we bring her to the coven."

I gently lay Kenna down on the bed between us. She stretches her tiny arms over her head and slumps back into sleep.

Rain patters softly against the window as I redress, a little vexed that Ella is forcing me back out in the rain to try to track down my father and ask about his love life, but if our hunch is correct, this witch is my mother, and that means Westfall's mate–the woman who sacrificed herself so he and I could live–has been alive all these years.

I haven't given it much thought because when I do, it's painful. I don't remember her well. I feel guilty about that, especially when the memories I do have stem from nightmares of our time in Kane's clutches.

The forest surrounding the village is dark and damp as I walk along, no light to guide my path. I pick up Westfall's scent eventually and decide against shifting to track him down. He's around. He's been staying close under the guise of scouting, but if I want to sleep in bed with my mate tonight, I need to talk to him.

Otherwise, Ella will likely force me to sleep outside in my wolf form–in the rain.

"Have you been following me?" Westfall comes into view as I hike up a sharp embankment. He's standing between two large, jagged rocks, redressing. He pulls a shirt over his head before I can glimpse the spidery network of scars on his back and chest, similar to mine, but deeper. Scars forged by years of being tied up and whipped by Kane's warriors.

"It's not healthy for someone of your age to be in their wolf forms for long at a time."

His eyes meet mine through the darkness, a soft blue glow. "I'm barely fifty."

I shrug.

He clears his throat and sits down on a boulder to put on his boots. "What is it, Ryatt? Or is this a conversation that requires I call you *Alpha*?"

"I think you know what conversation we're about to have."

He exhales, resting his elbows on his knees. I lean against a rock face opposite of where he's sitting and cross my arms over my chest, ignoring the rain.

"She is your mother," he says, knitting his fingers together. "I have no doubt about it."

"Then why avoid her?"

He meets my gaze. "She has no idea who we are to her, and I believe it's best we keep it that way."

"Why? She's been alone–"

"Whatever happened to her for her to lose her memories is a blessing, Ryatt. I'd rather live like this, knowing my mate is alive but doesn't recognize me at all, then have her remember everything that she went through and have to relive it in her nightmares like I do." His voice is cool, collected, but sharply edged.

"What about *you*?"

"What about me?"

"Can you handle this? Knowing that she's here? Alive? She is your mate, yet you've decided to ignore that bond."

"The bond is severed, Ryatt. I felt it snap that night I stole you out of Rifthold. You were the only reason I didn't turn back and fall on someone's sword so I could go with her. I thought she died."

"So she can't even feel that your mates?"

"No, she can't."

"Can you?"

He's quiet for a long moment. "I thought what I felt all these years was just... a piece of it that lingered after she died. A memory. But hearing her voice, seeing her... I feel it. It's driving me mad. It's why I've been out in the woods."

"I need you around."

"I can't," he says with so much raw emotion I can taste the despair. "I can't. She can't remember, okay? I don't want her to remember."

"But you could have decades with her now. You could have the life you both deserve!"

"At what cost? She's... she's fine now. She doesn't remember, so it doesn't hurt. I can't hurt her, Ryatt. I can't–I won't allow it."

"She doesn't deserve this."

"She is my mate. It's my decision."

"She is also *my* mother, and Kenna's grandmother, and you'd deny her of that? Really?"

He shakes his head. "Even if I wanted to, I don't know if there's a way to unlock those memories."

"She's going to the coven, not the valley. Giselle and the mystics can help her."

He looks at me, conflicted.

"She might have done this to herself, Ryatt."

My stomach twists. I hadn't thought of that.

He nods to himself. "I believe she actually did. She wiped the slate clean."

"How is that even possible?"

"Who knows? But I understand why she did it. She knew she would die, and if she didn't, she faced a life of torture under Kane's rule. He wouldn't have killed her. No, he would have done far worse for as long as possible. How she escaped, I don't know. We never will know because we're not going to force her to remember. She chose this." He believes it, too. That certainty is laced through every word he says. "Meanwhile, I will be fine."

"You don't seem fine."

He chuckles darkly. "It's my duty to protect her, even if that means staying away from her and not risking her memories coming back. I must ask you, as your subject, to leave the coven out of this, for now."

"And if we find that she didn't do this on purpose, and she was somehow… cursed, and lost her memories, what then?"

He sucks his lower lip between his teeth, letting go with a pop. "I don't know."

"We'll bring her home to Veiled Valley then. I'll tell Ella."

I straighten, preparing to walk back down to the village, but then stop and turn back to him. "I look at my mate and my daughter and I finally understand why you did this. Why you hid who you were from me for so long. I get it now. I'm… I'm thankful for it. Grateful, even."

His eyes shine in the dark.

I continue, "Your actions gave me the greatest shot of actually surviving this place. You built me to be a king, sacrificed your own title. You were supposed to be the Alpha of Veiled Valley, weren't you?"

He shakes his head. "My older brother. He was next in line. He died, alongside my father and my mother, shortly after I was captured and taken to Rifthold."

I nod.

He continues, "I couldn't claim the throne while you were young because Kane knew I had you. He would have found us, and you had to be able to fight and take care of yourself."

So he waited until I was a teenager to take me to that cave to find the sword his father must have stashed before his death at the hands of Kane's forces. I ascended the throne Westfall was entitled to, that he gave up, to keep me hidden until I was ready.

"I think you've sacrificed enough for one lifetime, Dad."

Westfall looks at me like I just struck him. His surprise is written clearly, even in the dark. I've never acknowledged him as my father.

Until now.

I turn and walk away.

47

WHERE THE HEART IS

Ella

EVERYBODY LOVES KENNA.

We have been endlessly showered in praise and gifts over the last few days. Word spread about her birth, and every village we've passed through on our way home has been the same—lit up like a bonfire with music and revelry in her honor.

Granger grunts under the weight of the heavy leather sack he's lugging behind us as we walk out of the village proper. I don't even know the name of this place, but everyone knew us, that's for sure.

"This is going to be you in a few weeks," I tell him over my shoulder as I follow Ryatt into a moonlit clearing. He meets my gaze with a smile and looks lighter than he has in weeks.

One more jump and we're *home*.

"Is everyone ready?" Ryatt says, a little breathlessly.

I adjust the sling across my chest that someone fashioned for me and Kenna. She's sleeping right now, gathered against my breasts with a little fist clutching my sweater. It's chilly for a midsummer night and currently sprinkling a misty kind of rain that sticks to everything it touches.

"I'm ready," I tell him. My chest is tight for a number of reasons. One, the idea of returning home doesn't feel real yet, and I doubt it will until I feel the embrace of our magical house all around me. Two, seeing Amanda again and spending the next few days telling her about everything that happened is something I've been greatly looking forward to. And three, my idiot brother is waiting for us in Veiled Valley, and I need to send him home to his wife–immediately.

I glance over my shoulder where the witch is waiting patiently for Ryatt's instruction. She looks regal and drop dead gorgeous in a pale silver cloak nearly the same color as her hair, which is loose and pin straight, falling all the way to her hips.

Cressendra is her name, but she doesn't know it. She doesn't know that the man standing beside her is her mate. She has no idea that the baby in my arms is her granddaughter.

And, apparently, Westfall wants to keep it that way.

I huff out a breath as I meet his eyes. He's looking forward, refusing to make eye contact with me. One day we'll all be one big, happy family.

I hope.

Sighing, I turn back to Ryatt, who looks like he's been through hell and back. He's exhausted and depleted, but this is it. One more jump, one more excessive use of his strained powers, and we'll be home.

I edge toward him, roping my arm through his. "Let's go home. I want to sleep in our own bed tonight, and I think Granger will kill us all in our sleep if we wait any longer to reunite him with Amanda."

Granger makes a noise in his throat that borders on confirmation of that idea, and I chuckle. Ryatt cracks a smile and exhales deeply, motioning for Granger to come forward.

Westfall and Cressendra walk up next, our group forming an odd semi-circle. Above us, the full moon casts the clearing in silver light that thrums with power. Ryatt planned this last jump perfectly. We're both at our most powerful right now.

"Do not try to help me," he says to me gruffly. "You almost wrecked the entire castle last time."

"Fine," I grumble, adjusting Kenna once more.

I watch as Westfall offers his hand to Cressendra. She smiles up at him—a kind, oblivious smile—and it cuts through my soul when I notice Westfall goes rigid when she knits her fingers between his.

The grief in his eyes is the last thing I see before the world goes black.

The metallic taste of magic fills my mouth. My ears ring. I'm pulled apart and gently put back together again as space and time collide. But just as suddenly as it began, the jump ends, and my feet land on solid, stone ground.

An excitable whoosh of warm air rushes around me like a comforting hug, and I open my eyes, my cheeks straining from how big I'm smiling.

Home. We're home.

Ryatt stumbles forward, his hands braced on his knees as he fights to catch his breath.

I barely have a moment to react before a flash of coppery blonde hair zooms past. A squeal follows in its wake, and then Granger is on the ground, and Amanda is on top of him, peppering his cheeks in kisses.

"I thought you'd never come home!" Amanda cries, then kisses Granger firmly on the lips.

Westfall clears his throat and steps away from Cressendra, running his fingers through his hair as he murmurs something about checking in with the guards. I watch him walk away while Cressendra gazes up at the domed onyx ceilings, her profile shimmering with the multicolored light spilling through the stained glass windows that surround us. "What a beautiful home," she whispers, and a flurry of air ruffles her cloak in answer.

Then the magic of the house is honed on me and the baby snoozing against my chest. The air stills, then erupts in flower petals that fall from the ceiling like confetti.

"Thanks," I smile. "We missed you, too."

My heart couldn't be more full, but Ryatt is obviously struggling to get his bearings. I lay a hand on his back as I gaze around the room.

It feels impossible that we're really here.

"Are you going to survive?" I ask my mate while giving him a little pat on the shoulder.

He grunts, then straightens, waving a hand toward the corridor that leads to our suite. "I'm going to go lay down for a while."

I don't blame him. What I really want is a long, hot shower and a fresh pair of pajamas, then a big dinner and a long, long nap.

Later, though. Right now....

"Let me see that baby," Amanda says as she launches herself at me. She's still spry for being so pregnant.

I catch her in a tight embrace, both of us on the verge of tears. I pull back and loosen the sling, and Amanda hoists Kenna out of my arms. Her eyes are glassy with tears as she cradles my daughter like she's the most precious thing in the world.

"How are you?" I ask, roping my arm over Amanda's shoulder. I glance over at Granger who's leading Cressendra out of the great room and down a narrow hallway, probably toward whatever room she'll be staying in.

"I'm done being pregnant, that's for sure," Amanda sniffles as she strokes Kenna's perfectly round cheek. "Gods, Ella. She's perfect. I heard what happened and I–I can't–I am so happy you are both okay."

"Me too," I say, trying not to burst into tears out of sheer happiness. "I'm just happy to be home."

"You can't leave again for a long time, okay? Promise me."

"I promise."

She nods, blinking back tears. "Okay, great. No leaving, no more battles, no more getting kidnapped. I'm serious, Ella."

"So am I. I've had enough of that for a lifetime!"

The house around us groans as a draft of air laced with what feels like impatience, if that's possible, ripples around us.

"We've been working on something. Come on," Amanda whispers, giving me a playful smile. She trots off with Kenna in her arms, resting over the enormous swell of her belly. Amanda is perfectly round and glowing in a way I'm sure I never glowed while pregnant with Kenna. I've never seen her more beautiful.

I follow my friend through the network of hallways and stairwells toward our suites, which are thankfully close enough together that it doesn't take more than a minute or two to reach our respective wings of the castle.

A set of doors along one hallway open, two rooms on either side. She steps into the one on the left, and a crystal chandelier glimmers to life.

The walls are a creamy white. The ceiling height windows offer a sweeping view of the mountainous city scape below. Built-in book-shelves are full of children's books and fluffy stuffed animals. A crib along the wall is shielded by a pale pink canopy.

Fresh flowers sit in vases sit on every surface. The air smells like lilacs and fresh linen.

"Do you like it?" Amanda asks. She shifts her weight, her cheeks turning pink. "I–I maybe overstepped. I didn't have much else to do while you were gone–"

"This is Kenna's room?" My heart is about to explode out of my chest as I turn in a circle to drink it all in. "Amanda, it's perfect."

"You think so?" Amanda bites back as smile. "It's not too much pink?"

"No," I laugh, tears rolling down my cheeks. "No, it's perfect. I didn't even think–I didn't think about a nursery. I–" I'm at a loss for words, truly.

"Do you want to see Evander's room?"

I turn to her, momentarily in shock. "Is that his name?"

She nods, her lips curving into a smile. "It was Granger's father's name."

"I know," I say, my mind drifting back to that vision I had of the little boy in that clearing. My lips part in preparation to tell Amanda everything I saw when someone clears their throat in the doorway.

Amanda and I turn at the same time.

"Is this my niece?" Isaac says. His eyes are locked on mine, eyes so

like our mom's it almost brings me to my knees. He looks...
conflicted. Excited, relieved, yes. But also very unsure.

I nod, unable to form a single word to say to him as he takes
another step into the room.

Amanda looks at me, her expression shifting to one lined with
uncertainty and concern as Isaac edges closer to get a better look at
Kenna.

"Would you like to hold her?" I say, but my voice trembles over the
words.

Isaac looks at me again, and the raw emotion behind his eyes
makes a sob work its way up my throat as he nods.

Amanda carefully sets Kenna into my brother's arms, and quietly
leaves the room, shutting the door behind her.

Silence swells. Even the magic presence in the house is leaving us
alone, giving us the privacy we need right now.

Kenna wraps her tiny hand around Isaac's pointer finger, and my
brother's chest heaves with a silent sob.

"You came," I say. It's the only words that come to mind.

He nods, his eyes still on Kenna as he replies, "I had to. You were
in—you were in trouble."

I take a few steps toward him.

Isaac and I used to be close. Thick as thieves. But nothing has been
the same since the war between Crescent Falls and Eastonia.

The rift between us is my fault. I lied. I kept my powers from him.
I stabbed him.

Also, my mate was his enemy.

I reach his side. Together, we watch Kenna slowly start to wake
up, blinking into the soft daylight drifting through the lace curtains.

"She has Ryatt's eyes," Isaac whispers, a smile touching his lips.

"I know," I smile. "My hair, I think."

"Time will tell," Isaac says. "Ryan and Syd—" He sniffs like he's
holding back tears. "They still have red hair like Maddy."

Tears blur my vision. "How are they?"

"They miss you. We all do. I'm so glad—Goddess, Ella, I am so glad
you're okay—"

The tension between us snaps, and then I'm in his arms, Kenna tucked between us as my brother and I hug it out like we used to do when we were kids.

"You shouldn't be here, Isaac! Maddy is going to kill you."

"I know," he laughs, pulling away and laying Kenna in my arms. "I know. I didn't really think before I did it; I just did. It was easier than I thought it would be."

"Then why haven't you gone home?"

"I needed to see you first. I needed to make sure everything was fine. And…"

"And you wanted to see Eastonia?"

"Yeah," he admits, looking more than guilty about it.

"What do you think?"

He cuts me off abruptly, his expression turning serious. "We need to talk about the veil."

"What? Why?"

"I think there's more to it. I think–I think it's doing something to our powers in Crescent Falls."

"I know, I feel that way about it too."

"I think we need to take it down. We need to destroy it."

4 8

BALANCE OF POWER

Ella

WE'VE SPENT several days in the castle... doing *nothing*, and it's been the best three days of my life. Every morning I wake to Ryatt laying Kenna down between us and crawling back into bed for a few moments of peace as a family. Tender kisses and soft laughs fill those blissful minutes before we drag ourselves out of bed to dress for the day.

Amanda and Granger haven't been seen since we came home, but that was expected. Today is different, however. Today, we all gather in Ryatt's office as heavy rain glides down the windows, and a storm brews outside, cloaking Veiled Valley in sheets of heavy gray mist.

While the rest of us recovered from months of travel and torment, Isaac has been... well, my brother is the most annoying kind of tourist. He's been out with Westfall every hour of the day for three days buying gifts to try to butter Maddy up when he returns home. He's seen every inch of Veiled Valley, talked to just about everyone, and has been trying to figure out how he can mimic the magic that brings our home to life.

Right now, however, he's sitting stone faced in an armchair facing Ryatt's desk.

I lean my hip against the desk, crossing my arms under my chest as I scan the paperwork on his desk. Moves have been made recently, big ones. I'm not even going to try to understand the politics of this country, not yet. I have a lot of studying to do, but Ryatt is making good on putting me on the throne of this kingdom as queen.

"Do you think Maddy is planning on having you bound and tortured the second you waltz back through the veil?" Ryatt asks, giving Isaac a wry smile.

Isaac taps his fingers on his knee and shrugs, giving him a sly grin in return. "The jewels in Veiled Valley are exquisite. I'm sure once she sees her gifts, she'll change her mind."

Ryatt chuckles, but I'm not laughing. There's a reason Isaac is still here. Sure, Ryatt taught him how to use our magic mirror so he can check in with Maddy and my nephews, but he could have broken through the veil easily on his own.

He's still here because I agree with him…. I agree that the veil must come down.

And there's only one person who can do it.

Me.

Westfall and Granger arrive together for this meeting. Amanda is with Kenna, like usual. Cressendra, too, has been spending most of her time bouncing between Kenna's nursery and the archives in the city. What she's looking for there, I don't know, but I hope for Westfall's sake it's a way to unlock her memories.

"My wife is spoiling the princess rotten, I'm afraid," Granger says as he comes to a stop at one of the windows.

"I wouldn't have it any other way," Ryatt says to his Beta.

Goddess, they both look so well rested and peaceful right now.

I hate that I'm about to wreck their day.

At least Westfall is being his usual gruff self.

"So…" I kick off the desk and stride to the center of the room, my deep red silken gown shimmering in the gray daylight filtering through the storm clouds. It feels good to be back in Veiled Valley fashions instead of wearing leather and coarse homespun.

"What is this about, Princess?" Ryatt says smoothly, leaning back in his chair. "You called such a formal meeting for a Sunday morning."

"This *is* a formal meeting. A business meeting. Consider this–" I wave a hand around the office with its onyx walls and dark furnishings, "the war room."

Granger, Ryatt, and Westfall stiffen, but Isaac looks mildly amused as I walk in a slow circle around the men, my hands tucked behind my back. I've started wearing that ring I threw at Ryatt's head months ago, when he *barely* asked me to marry him. He deserves it now, I guess.

I catch him watching my hands as I come to a stop to face them again.

"I'm bringing down the veil."

Everything I expected to happen, happens. Ryatt stands up abruptly, posed to shout. Granger and Westfall look like they're about to pull their blades.

And Isaac clears his throat and rises, picking invisible pieces of lint from his shirt.

"Have you hit your head this morning, *darling*?" Ryatt croons in a mocking tone.

I bat my eyelashes at him before narrowing my gaze into a glare that I let sweep over every face in the room. "I've conferred with my brother, the *Alpha King* of Crescent Falls, and we are in agreement that this needs to happen."

Ryatt sighs heavily, glancing between Isaac and me, then sits back down. He waves a hand, motioning for me to continue.

Westfall and Granger are looking at me like I've indeed hit my head and lost my marbles.

"Isaac, take it away." I lean against the windowsill.

Isaac clears his throat, fixing his gaze on Ryatt. "I believe the veil does something to my people. It dampens their powers, including those who only have the ability to shift. I've always wondered why Maatua and KiloKilo have the highest concentration of people with gifts. I used to believe it was simply because of the falls, but we know better now."

"We know the water in Maatua is directly connected to Eastonia. It's the only thing that is able to breach the veil, and is thus concentrated with Eastonia's natural magic," I add.

"My people aren't like yours, Ryatt. My commanders don't have hereditary gifts. My kingdom doesn't have that electric pulse that hangs in the air like in Eastonia."

"And you want it?" Ryatt asks with lethal calm.

"Speaking plainly, I believe Eastonia is a ticking time bomb, Ryatt. There's too much power here. You've seen it yourself." He turns to Westfall and Granger. "Every conflict you have in this kingdom turns into an all-out war. There has never been peace, even now."

I look down at the toes of my red silken slippers. "He's right, Ryatt."

My husband chews his lower lip as he holds Isaac's gaze.

Isaac continues, "Based on what we know about the war of the gods, Eastonia was, for whatever reason, closed off and buried under the veil. For a long time, I believed it was to keep something here *contained*, but now I'm not so sure." Isaac looks at me then, his eyes darkening. "Ella came here because she believed the balance between our kingdoms was off. She thought she belonged here, and she's right. She does, because her powers are at their strongest here. She was never able to live peacefully in Crescent Falls. And now that I'm here and feel what my powers are like under this veil I... Ella and I were never meant to carry such a burden. These powers shouldn't be consuming us, eating away at us. You and your father's gifts are enormous. That power is..." he trails off. "How many times have you almost died by simply using them?"

Ryatt's throat works as he swallows, eyeing Westfall, who is listening to Isaac intently.

"Something is off, Ryatt. *Brother*. I believe the legends about the war are untrue. A false narrative. I don't believe the Moon Goddess crafted the veil and wove it in place. She was cut off from this magic, which means our kind has suffered the consequences. The veil has to come down."

Ryatt licks his lip and looks down at the papers strewn across his desk. "Do you realize what kind of political upheaval this would cause? There are hundreds of packs in Eastonia. Our population is more concentrated than yours, Isaac. Your kingdom would be at the mercy of the packs that border the mountains between us. It would only be a matter of time before my people see the opportunity to spread out–and take it."

"We are allies," Isaac says firmly. "We will handle it."

"We're family," I tell them both. "We have the opportunity to connect our lands." I turn to my mate with pleading eyes. "Eastonia is lost to time, Ryatt. You've seen Maatua. We have the chance to usher in a new era for our people by connecting our kingdoms."

"The benefits go both ways," Isaac says. "Our kingdoms are unbalanced. My people have been losing touch with their magical abilities for decades–centuries. Your people grow stronger to the point that some powers can't be controlled. The balance is off, and eventually this will lead to war that we can't avoid, even being allies."

I watch Ryatt go through several different emotions while his face remains a mask of steel. His eyes show me everything–the unease, the distrust, and eventually the understanding.

"I can bring down the veil with the mask," I tell him.

"You're never using the mask again," Ryatt says firmly, his tone so sharp it could cut through stone.

"I figured it out, Ryatt. It's not dark magic. It's just stolen magic. It's my duty to use it as intended–for good. Not for the kinds of evil Kane was known for." I edge toward him. "You want to make me Queen of Eastonia because you think it's my rightful throne as a Firestone witch. If that's true, then this is it, Ryatt. This is what I've been meant to do all along. This is what Isaac and I were meant to do with our gifts."

We explain everything to him then, everything Isaac and I have discussed over the past three days. Isaac came through the veil and found himself in an old temple dedicated to the beasts of the

Goddess. It was a clear sign that Isaac was supposed to come here. We were supposed to reunite in Eastonia for one purpose, and one purpose only.

"We have to take down the veil so the Goddess can once again shine her light on Eastonia. Otherwise, there will never be peace here." I know it in my heart. I feel deep in my soul that this is what I'm meant to do.

So, I'm doing it, whether Ryatt likes it or not.

"She's right, Ryatt," Westfall says. I turn to my father-in-law and give him a grateful smile, but his eyes are heavy and dark with emotion I can't describe. "They're right about the unbalanced power between the two kingdoms. We've already received word about another coven rising deep in Tarsian, in Jaxon's territory. Their leader is… enormously powerful."

Ryatt nods, but this is news to me.

"Who is it this time?"

"Someone we thought was dead a long time ago," Westfall says.

"Atticus, right?" I ask the room. "Petra's brother?"

Ryatt nods. "Jaxon has it under control–for now."

"If you brought down the veil," Isaac cuts in, "it would be easier for me to send you the backup you needed in war times."

"And vice versa," Granger says with a nod.

I feel the tension in the room begin to lift as everyone starts to agree.

"We're doing this then?" I ask the men. I meet my mate's gaze and hold it for what feels like an entirety.

Before he can nod, the doors to the office open, and Cressendra walks in holding Kenna. "Sorry to interrupt, but–"

"You," Isaac rasps.

Oh, *shit.* I hadn't realized Isaac hadn't met the witch yet. He was three or four when she burst into our parents' throne room and seemed to die on the marble tiles. I have no recollection of it happening, but Isaac remembers.

And he recognizes her.

"Isaac, wait," I snap, but he's turning to face her fully, his brow furrowed in confusion.

"You're alive?"

Cressendra looks confused. She glances around the room, her gaze lingering on Westfall the longest. "Who are you?"

Isaac takes several steps in her direction. I watch Westfall closely. He makes no moves to stop my brother from advancing on her until he's within touching range, and then Westfall grabs Isaac's arm. "Don't," Westfall growls, much to Isaac's confusion.

Isaac looks over his shoulder at Ryatt, his eyes narrowed. "What's going on here?"

Ryatt silently shakes his head. "Isaac–"

Isaac shoves Westfall hard enough the commander is forced to let go of his arm, and then he reaches for Cressendra. He brushes a lock of hair from her face, his fingertips coasting over her cheekbone. He's looking into her milky eyes, his jaw tight and brow furrowed.

"Isaac, whatever you're about to do–" I say hurriedly.

My brother can unlock anything with his powers. *Anything.*

"How long have you been stuck like this?" he asks her, and then a pale shimmer of light erupts on her cheek where he touched her, and her eyes go wide.

4 9

———

FATE KNOWS

Ryatt

My mother blinks, then blinks again, that milky, whirling magic clearing from her eyes. Eyes the color of emeralds lock on mine, then slowly graze toward Westfall.

Her skin goes pale.

"No," she says, so softly we all almost miss it. "Where–" She backs away from Isaac and Westfall, shaking her head.

"Cressie," Westfall says, his voice trembling with emotion. "It's okay."

Her eyes dart to his, and her face crumbles. "Adrian?"

I watch my parents find each other after over two decades apart, and it breaks me.

She looks at me again, then at Ella, then down at the baby still in her arms. "Who is this? Whose baby is this?"

"She's ours," I say, loud enough that my voice echoes around the room. Her eyes meet mine, and she shakes her head.

I wait for her to ask me who I am. How do I explain that I'm her son? It's been twenty years since she last saw me. I was just a child, and I was too young to hold onto the memory of her face, and now....

"Ryatt?" Her voice cracks as she looks back at Westfall for confirmation.

He nods, reaching for her with a shaking hand, but he can't bring himself to touch her.

Ella shifts her weight nervously beside me, her eyes locked on Kenna, like she's worried my mother will drop her.

Isaac grits his teeth and mumbles a brief apology while taking Kenna from my mother's arms and backing away.

Silence settles–sharp and heavy.

Granger says in my mind, 'She needs to see a healer immediately.'

'I know,' I reply. 'Go call for one, please. Be discreet.'

Granger walks away without a passing glance in anyone's direction while the silent room threatens to cave in on us all.

I watch him go then notice my mother is staring at Ella with an intensity that makes my stomach turn in on itself.

Ella holds her gaze, her chin slightly lifted. Isaac backs himself to the far wall and gently bounces Kenna, his eyes darting between me and Ella and my parents.

"I remember you," my mother says, and then tears begin to stream down her cheeks.

Ella nods. I rest my hand on her lower back, noticing how rigid she is.

The touch is caught by my mother, and her eyes grow wide. "It's true, then. She was meant to be your mate. I was right."

"We shouldn't be talking about this right now," Westfall says, taking a step in her direction.

She looks at him and inhales sharply, like she just came to after years of being stuck in some in-between world. She brings her hands to her face, cupping her cheeks, then runs her fingers through her hair. She looks at my dad again, tears shining in her eyes. "You're so old," she chokes on what might be a laugh.

Westfall smiles through tears. "So are you."

Ella takes a deep breath beside me as the tension eases itself from the room.

But then my mother's laugh tapers off. She turns her attention back to us, back to me.

"I'm so sorry."

I fight to swallow, finding it impossible. "There's nothing to be sorry about."

"I wasn't-" she sucks in a breath as her face twists with the deepest kind of despair. "How old are you? How much have I missed?"

I know we can't have this conversation. Not right now.

"Ryatt, I think-" Isaac tries to speak up, likely feeling the same way, but my mother suddenly falls to her knees, caught by Westfall before she hits the ground.

He swoops her into his arms. "A healer-"

"Granger is on it," I cut in. He nods, and leaves the room, carrying my mother, without another word.

Ella lets out her breath and turns her sharp gaze to Isaac. "What were you thinking?"

"Did you all do that to her?" he snaps, walking toward us.

"Of course not, Isaac." Ella takes a wriggling Kenna from his arms and settles her against her shoulder, gently patting her back. "But you just overstepped Westfall. He didn't want her memories unlocked."

"Why not? I could feel some kind of magic on her the second she walked into the room!"

"What kind of magic?" I ask hurriedly. I might have left out several parts of my conversation with Westfall, especially about how he believes she did this to herself.

"Some kind of binding magic," Isaac says, waving a hand. "Ella, you know how the old chef used to try to lock us out of the cabinets to keep us from eating all the cakes and cookies he'd make for events? He thought a key would be enough to keep us out. I don't need keys."

"I know," she says gruffly. "Get to the point!"

"It was similar. She was simply locked in her head like those cakes we used to steal from the cabinets. It wasn't hard to break through whatever magic kept her stuck there."

"So it was a curse or a spell?" I eye him skeptically.

"Yes," Isaac confirms. "Definitely. You really couldn't sense it? I can still taste it, Ryatt. That's how strong it was."

"Could she have done something like this to herself?" I ask, and Ella's head whips in my direction.

"I highly doubt it," Isaac says, looking confused. "Is that why Westfall didn't want her to remember? Because he thought she willingly locked herself in her own mind?"

"Ryatt, is that true?"

I nod at them both.

Ella lets out her breath, but then her mouth quirks into a disbelieving smile. "So, she's back?"

"She's back," Isaac says, but his voice is strained. He licks his lips, looking suddenly apologetic. "I'm sure this is going to be a shock. It could take some time for her to… get a grip on reality."

"I understand."

"I'm going to go make myself scarce, then, to avoid the wrath of your father," my brother-in-law says.

"That's probably for the best," I tell him with a flat smile.

Isaac looks at Ella for a moment before turning on his heel and walking briskly out of the room.

Alone together in my office, I turn to my mate and motion for her to give me my daughter.

"Are you all right?" she asks as I take Kenna in my arms.

"I suddenly have both of my parents back after a lifetime of believing I was alone in the world, but I'm fine."

"I'm serious Ryatt. Are you okay?"

"I'm okay." I press a kiss to her forehead. "I'm just going to take a walk."

"I could come with you."

I shake my head. "Go hangout with Amanda. We're going to the coven tomorrow morning at the latest, if not tonight. She's going to be heartbroken."

Ella nods, her beautiful eyes holding my gaze. "We're bringing down the veil, then?"

"Yes."

"So, that's where the mask is, huh? At the coven?"

"They have a vault that's more powerful than mine."

She gives me a soft smile, but her eyes flash with guilt.

"I understand if you don't agree–"

"I do agree. If anything, this will be better for our daughter. She'll have more opportunities, more access to her family. Your parents, your brother, her cousins…"

Ella nods but looks conflicted. "Am I making the right choice?"

"You've always made the right choices, Princess. I trust you."

Ella takes a breath and nods.

"I'll be back," I tell her and leave the room with Kenna. I think we could both use some fresh air.

***

KENNA WHIMPERS as I pick her up out of the cot next to our bed. She grips my fingers as I quietly carry her out of our bedroom suite and into the quiet hallways of our mountainside home.

"I couldn't sleep either," I tell my daughter, resting her against my shoulder. She's been inconsolable tonight, and Ella went to bed with tears in her eyes after I practically begged her to let me take over. For the past five hours, Kenna and I have been up and down, and up and down, walking here and there and trying to get a few minutes of sleep.

I don't know much about babies, but I know that they're complicated. Kenna seems happy to be out of our dark room and in the softly lit hallways, probably because the house makes the lanterns flicker in a way that makes the light they cast dance along the dark walls.

She tries to lift her head to look over my shoulder, but she's not quite strong enough yet.

"Where should we go?" I stop near one of the balconies overlooking the great hall. Moonlight cloaks us in silver light, and I feel a pull toward the far end of the castle.

For whatever reason, I follow it, knowing exactly where it will lead.

I quietly open a door and step inside a small sitting room. Westfall is resting in a chair by a fireplace. The fire has burned down to embers, and his eyes flutter open to squint into the dark.

"Sorry to wake you," I say, shutting the door behind me.

"I wasn't asleep."

"That seems to be the theme tonight."

"Is Kenna not sleeping well?"

I shake my head and walk toward him. He opens his arms to Kenna, and I lay her in his lap. She gives him a sleepy smile before her eyes close.

"Hmm… maybe you should be our night nurse from now on," I tease, but my dad only gives me a soft smile in reply as he adjusts her weight in his arms.

"You didn't sleep for the first two years of your life."

"Don't tell Ella that," I warn. "She was in tears tonight. Kenna has been crying nonstop."

"We're all going through an adjustment period." He sighs, pulling a blanket over them both. "Kenna more than any of us, I assume. She's only been alive for two weeks, I imagine that's jarring."

I chuckle, crossing my arms over my chest. I never would have thought Commander Westfall would have such a soft spot for infants. He's amazing with Kenna. He has the touch, so to speak, which is insane, given the fact I've seen him kill full grown men and wolves with his bare hands.

"Your mother is through those doors." He tilts his head to the far side of the room. "I doubt she's asleep either."

It's an invitation I wasn't sure I'd get tonight. I take it, leaving Dad and Kenna to rest, and softly knock before entering.

This bedroom is less luxurious than my suite upstairs but comfortable all the same. My mother is sitting on the edge of her bed, her back turned to me, her long silver-white hair twisted into a braid.

She turns her head slightly as I close the door behind me.

I'm not sure what to say.

"Your father tells me that you plan to bring down the veil."

"Tomorrow."

She nods and pats the bed.

I grind my teeth as I approach, but I don't sit. "How are you?"

"I'll be fine."

"I'm sure this is… an adjustment."

She nods, her eyes briefly meeting mine before looking away. "I can't believe how big you are. I'm not sure I believe any of this is real."

"It's real." Questions whirl through my head. "Did you do this to yourself?"

"Not entirely," she admits. "I didn't do the jump correctly when I tried to go to Crescent Falls to warn the royal family that Kane planned on invading. But I saw Ella and knew she was the witch from my vision. I lost my grip on my powers and was pulled back and… survived." She swallows. "Your father got you out, but Kane knew he'd escaped. I caused a distraction that nearly cost me my life, and I wanted it to. I was ready to die knowing the two of you would be safe, but somehow I got out of Rifthold. I left with several other witches, but I wanted to die. I knew I could never go near either of you again without risking Kane finding you. He would have searched everywhere for me. So… I asked one of the witches to curse me, to force me to lose my memories, and she did. It was the greatest mercy anyone could have given me other than killing me outright."

She turns to look up at me. "I'm sorry I wasn't able to do more for your mate right away, during your daughter's birth."

"You saved their lives."

"You did, Ryatt. The Goddess heard your pleas, heard you begging to be taken in their place. I did nothing but break the curse Kane put on her."

I sit down next to her, my hand shaking as I slowly, carefully, take her hand in mine. We sit in silence for a long, long time.

"I'm happy you're back," I tell her. "Westfall–Dad, he… he wanted to keep your memories locked. He didn't want you to suffer through them."

"I know; he told me." She smiles, squeezing my hand. "We have a second chance now, all of us. And… Ella is right about the veil. But what will come after… Ryatt, you need to be prepared."

"For what?"

She turns to me, looking me in the eyes. Her smile is soft, full of some ancient knowledge I can't begin to process. "The world your daughter will grow up in will be very different from ours."

"Will it be better?"

"Only fate knows, and fate has brought us this far, so all we can do is trust in her. In Ella."

5 0

LADY IN THE LAKE

Ella

GISELLE WATCHES me as I dip my toes in the lake. The little stone dock is probably older than the coven itself and so narrow only one person at a time can fit at the end.

It's not a full moon, but I can feel power all around me as I shed my cloak.

I look over my shoulder at where Isaac and Ryatt are standing on the shore, their faces shielded by shadows. Ryatt's sword glimmers in the moonlight, and Isaac looks odd standing next to him dressed in khaki pants and a blue button up shirt. He was wearing them when he breached the veil, apparently, and had them mended in the meantime.

I exhale deeply, humming to myself as I look past them toward the twinkling lights of the coven. Somewhere in the depths of the glimmering village, Amanda, Granger, Westfall, and Cressendra are waiting, watching over Kenna for us.

None of us knows what's going to happen. I'm not even sure how to do this.

379

But as I sweep my gaze back toward my mate and my brother, I see the mystics appearing in their white robes and crystal masks, and then one of them appears behind me.

She places the Firestone mask in my hands then brushes her thumb over my forehead in a silent blessing.

Chills skitter up and down my spine, but I hold firm. I will not be afraid. I will not yield.

I will not *drown*.

Because I feel, deep in the marrow of my soul, that this lake is where it all began–and where it will end.

I put on the mask. It only takes a few seconds for my power to merge with its own. Ancient voices whisper, falling over one another to be heard.

I take one last look at my mate. I drink him in, every line, every curve, every angle–and then I step off the dock.

The only light comes from my mask. The moonstone glistens a deep crimson in the lake water, melding with the inky blackness as I let myself drift deeper, and deeper, until the pressure is enough to pull the air from my lungs.

It's empty here. Quiet and still. I have a moment of reflection as memories of this morning flood through me. Kissing my daughter's cheek before passing her off to Amanda. Falling into bed with Ryatt. My mate's mouth on my neck, and my breasts, as we tangle in the sheets. Cressendra and I talking in hushed tones on the balcony overlooking the city.

Then memories from long ago rush in. Me as a child playing in my father's office. My mother brushing my hair while I play with her makeup. Hannah and I arm in arm, drunk out of our minds on cheap wine and warm beer, while walking back to our dormitory at Wellington.

But memories that aren't my own filter in, fragmented and blurry.

Cressendra holding Ryatt for the first time. Westfall meeting his son, holding him, while wondering how he's going to get his family out of this situation, their slavery.

The memories stretch further, deeper. I see my mother walking up a set of steps in the rain, fighting to swallow as she looks up at a set of double doors. *"Can I really do this?"* she thinks, before the memory slips away, replaced by one of my father pacing outside her bedroom door wondering why this *breeder* has such a hold on him.

Then I'm thrust into the gloom, and a city lost to time sprawls out in front of me.

I open my eyes.

And I'm standing in a throne room.

"You found my mask," she says, turning toward me. Her black hair is tightly curled and fixed atop her head, woven through a crown of pure gold and dripping with gems. She's beautiful in a way I didn't think was possible. Young, likely my age. Her sea green eyes crease as she smiles. "I've been waiting so long for you, Ella."

I know this is just a vision. I'm underwater, but here, I feel like I can breathe. The sun is shining on my skin as I walk toward her. Through archways built of pale stone, the lake is much smaller. It glistens in the distance beyond a city of marble where music hugs the air and flowers bloom, sending the soft scent of spring in my direction.

The mountains are familiar. This is where the coven stands now.

This is the city beneath the lake.

The Firestone kingdom.

"You cannot take this back," the Firestone Queen says, her eyes still locked on mine. In my vision, I see her clearly, the woman who ruled here before me. "Once you bring down the veil, it cannot be undone. Everything will change."

"I have to. It's what I was born for, wasn't it?"

"Yes." Her smile is radiant. "Do you want to know a secret?"

I nod. Why not?

"Your mate loves you deeply."

"That's not a secret," I laugh.

She tilts her head. "You are so blessed, Ella, to have been given such a mate."

"What do you mean?"

"Not all bonds are gifts."

I feel a shattering kind of unease settle in my stomach.

She sighs, turning to look through the archways of her grand castle. "You will live a long life, Ella. A grand one. Your people will love you, cherish you. Your name will be written in the books children read centuries from now."

Still, I feel like something bad is about to happen.

"Why are you telling me this?"

"Because you need to know that despite what trials come your way, everything you will do will be for the good of your people."

"Is something going to happen?" I ask.

"Many things. You will love deeply. Your bond with the Shadow King is the purest kind. Your daughter will rule one day, but…"

"But?"

She meets my eyes again. "Your family will be tested. Two kings will rise, and two queens, but without a veil to keep them apart."

I open my mouth to ask what the hell she's going on about, but suddenly she's before me, holding the crown that was once on top of her head.

"It's time to rise to your full potential, Queen Ella of the Firestones."

"Wait–"

She places the crown on my head, and the world spins out of control.

I'm going to die. I feel it in my bones. I can't breathe. The veil–I'm in the veil, and it's pressing down on me with all of its magic.

I scream in agony as the mask burns into my skin until we are one. My last thoughts are of Ryatt, and Kenna, and how I'm doing this for her. For them. For my family.

I made my decision. The veil must come down, despite what I just saw, just heard.

And so I do it. I don't know how, but I feel like I'm shifting into my wolf form–no, just that power. That lupine strength. I hang onto it, and then everything around me shatters.

The ancient voices stop. The crimson light all around me dims until I'm looking up at the stars again, and water is lapping at my legs.

"Ella! Gods above," Ryatt grunts as he drags me from the water.

A blast of energy ripples over the lake. The sky seems to part, shimmering with bands of violet and the brightest blue, and then the world is still and quiet for a few seconds before *it* begins.

Ryatt gathers me in his arms and runs. I hear Isaac call out then shout over the sound of the waves suddenly racing our way.

From the depths, the ancient city rises, sending water bursting into the coven.

"High ground!" someone shouts.

I must have blacked out because one minute I'm in Ryatt's arms, and the next, I'm opening my eyes to daylight, to trees and birds whispering overhead.

I blink as I sit up. Ryatt is sitting next to me, hugging his knees.

"Where are we?" I whisper, my body thrumming with power, but it's… different. I reach up as a tingling sensation along my hairline catches my attention. Little scares pepper my skin–symbols and lines and whirls I don't recognize.

I look over at my mate. He's holding something in his hands.

It's the crown. I wasn't imagining that.

"Ryatt."

"Look at it, Ella," he whispers and points.

In the distance, a great city is nestled between the mountains where the lake used to be. It's soaking wet, covered in waterfalls that stream down from a massive castle and into the city proper. Weeds coat the city as well as a thick layer of sediment.

"It's happening all over," Ryatt says softly, in obvious disbelief. "Cities are rising all over Eastonia. From the rivers and the sand." He goes on to explain that in Tarsian, Jaxon's people awoke to Oasia giving way, and rushed to safety in time to witness an ancient kingdom emerge from the sand. In the Roguelands, temples and old villages broke through the very ground they stood on.

Rifthold collapsed in full, and the river separating the once towering fortress from Ryatt's lands filled the space left behind, burying it under water.

"Where's Isaac? Crescent Falls…"

"We can mind-link with Maatua from here," he says wistfully. "He's already spoken to Poppy."

I feel like I'm going to pass out. He looks over at me, scoots closer, and gathers me into his arms. He kisses the burning scars on my forehead.

"How did I do it?"

"I don't know," he whispers. "But you came back with this." He hands me the Firestone crown.

I reach up to touch my face where the mask should be. Ryatt traces a finger over the network of scars on my hairline.

"The mask is gone, isn't it?"

"I think this is the mask now," he says, and he sighs. "There's a lot we don't know, Ella. But the veil is gone."

I rest my cheek against his chest as we look over the kingdom I freed.

"What now?" I ask.

THREE YEARS LATER…

"I DON'T GET IT," Kenna grumbles, clutching my nightgown. "You need to tell it again."

"Again? I've been talking for two hours, Kenna. I know you're tired."

"But what happened after, Mama?"

"After what?"

"After you flooded the coven!"

"Oh, that." I roll my eyes. "Daddy and I went home, sweetie. We went back to Veiled Valley and slept for like, a week. Your uncle Isaac took a boat home to Maatua, and your aunt Maddy didn't kill him like I thought she would. Meanwhile, you hung out with Gramma and Grandpa for a while."

"So Gramma got her memories back?"

"She did, and she was so happy about it." I kiss the tip of my three-year-old chatterbox's nose. "Seriously though, Ken, this is textbook manipulation. I know your dad told you this same story last night."

Kenna growls at me. Little demon. I kiss her on the forehead and tuck her blankets around her body until she giggles. "That tickles!"

"Then stay still!" I laugh. "Goodnight, for real this time."

"But I'm thirsty."

"No, you're not," I reply in a sing-song voice. "Goodnight."

Another growl as I shut the door. I sigh, running my fingers through my hair as I lean on her door for a moment then set off to find my husband.

Ryatt is in his office like usual. Crates of books are stacked everywhere, and I have to pick my way across the room.

He looks up from a stack of paperwork. "Is she asleep?"

"Of course not." I slide onto the edge of his desk. "What are you doing?"

"Going over the checklist again."

I purposefully slide the paper away and scoot across his desk, then straddle his lap, wrapping my arms around his neck. He leans back with a sigh. "This is nice."

"You know we can't move to Moonrise for another year or so. There's so much construction going on in the city."

"This is our checklist for our trip to Maatua."

"Mmm… I see." I lean in and kiss him, smiling as I say, "We won't have a moment alone while we're there."

"We don't get any time alone anyway," he says into my neck.

I close my eyes. "But we're alone right now."

"What should we do?" he rasps, then nibbles my neck.

"Whatever we want," I smile.

"I hope you left out some of the more… inappropriate bits about our love story," he whispers against my skin.

"Of course," I laugh, my fingers tangling in his hair.

"I think what I want to do right now is... relive them."

So we do. And when I wake the next morning cozy in my bed, I let the sun warm my face and count every blessing.

Kenna crawls into bed between us like usual, snuggling deep, while beyond our bedroom windows, the city of Veiled Valley wakes to peace.

Finally.

THE STORY CONTINUES *in Shadow of the Alpha.*

EPILOGUE

Isla

"Do you think we have enough?" I ask my mate as I brace my hands on the kitchen island in our sprawling, but cozy, beachside home. We rebuilt the one Ella destroyed and added four extra bedrooms, which are needed at a time like this.

The whole family is here for the Winter Solstice next week.

Maddox turns from the stove wearing an apron with little flowers all over it—a gift from our grandchildren. Four messy little names are scrawled on its pale blue fabric. Sydney, Ryan, Kenna, and Misty.

Had anyone told me that one day I'd witness Maddox with a spatula in hand, wearing an apron while making pancakes shaped like animals, I wouldn't have believed them.

But look at us now.

Maddox opens his mouth to answer my question but is interrupted by a shriek coming from beyond the double doors leading off the kitchen, which are open to the perfect day outside.

I glance over my shoulder at the three children chasing each other in the backyard.

"They're going to wake up Misty," Maddox sighs, shaking his head, but his lips curve in a smile he couldn't hide if he tried. "Poor thing hasn't had a real nap since she arrived."

"Well, I'm sure she's used to it, Maddox. Do you think the twins give her any peace back home?"

Another smile that melts my heart. Poor Misty indeed. She's the newest addition to our family. A year old, big blue eyes like me, and her father, Isaac. Unlike her brothers, she has blonde hair instead of Maddy's wine-red tresses. She's beautiful, and Maddy and Isaac dote on her.

Everyone does, in fact. She was the best kind of surprise.

Well, that's what Maddy and Isaac told us, anyway. Maddy had no intentions of ever getting pregnant again, but I doubt they were taking many precautions to prevent it.

I smirk to myself, and Maddox chuckles before turning back to the stove. "To answer your question, yes. We have enough food to feed a small army."

I look down at the platters of scrambled eggs, bacon, sausage, biscuits, muffins, fruit, and several jars of jam and honey. Since he's retired, he enjoys cooking for our family, something else I never thought I'd see. "I should get the juice out."

"Will anyone want more coffee, do you think?" he asks.

"Ryatt, for sure. But he likes your fancy espresso machine. I heard him talking to Isaac about having one shipped to Eastonia."

Maddox grunts with laughter. "I won't make a new pot then. He needs to figure out how to use it if he's going to buy one for himself. I've been his personal barista for the past week."

"Gramma!" Kenna's voice drifts through the double doors, followed by rapid footsteps. I turn and smile down at my grand-daughter, at her silver eyes flaked with blue and her messy brown hair. She likes to wear it in braids, but currently her hair is damp and covered in sand. "What did they do to you this time?" I say as I crouch to catch her in my arms.

Five-year-old Kenna sniffles dramatically as she turns on the water works and makes herself cry. She's so much like Ella was at this age.

"Syd dumped a bucket of sand on my head."

"I'm sorry, darling–"

"And then Ryan told me I looked like a sand crab and pinched me!"

"Your parent's told me you've been training with your grandpa," Maddox says. "Go whoop them both. You have my permission."

Kenna looks up at Maddox, who the kids lovingly call *Papa*, and wipes her nose on the back of her hand. "Really? Can I use a stick?"

"Yes–"

"*No*," I say firmly over Maddox's voice.

"My pinchers?" Kenna makes little crab claw motions with her hands. I sigh and nod. "And I won't get in trouble?"

Maddox looks at me then, maybe coming to the realization that he's about to start a war between our grandchildren, but shrugs. "No, you won't."

Her tears immediately dry, and she beams up at her papa, then races back outside to terrorize her cousins.

"Why do you rile them up so early in the morning?" I ask my mate as I rise and begin gathering platters to take outside.

Maddox shrugs, his expression dripping with feline amusement. "I love watching Kenna give Ryan and Syd what they've been asking for. They taunt her constantly."

"Well, one day she might actually snap. You shouldn't forget what she... *is*."

His eyes meet mine in understanding, but there's no concern in his expression. "Who knows, maybe the twins will start showing some hints of power like Isaac and Ella did at this age?"

I roll my lower lip between my teeth and turn back to the food, making quick work of taking the enormous breakfast spread to the outdoor table on the patio. In the distance, along the white-sand beach, two female figures are making their way into view. Maddy and Ella have been taking morning walks every day since they arrived. I'm sure it's the only quiet time they get together all day.

Ryatt and Isaac must still be asleep upstairs.

I smile to myself at the thought. The two of them tend to stay up late talking about politics and such.

It is so good to have this month with my children and their families. I look forward to it every year.

But a week has already passed, and soon, I'll start feeling that creeping ache that comes with telling them goodbye, especially Ella, Ryatt, and Kenna. While the veil is a thing of the past, Eastonia is still so, so far away. Veiled Valley is a week's journey from Maatua by boat, and planes and cars are not allowed to pass the mountains between Crescent Falls and Eastonia because it's still too dangerous. At least, for now.

Maybe one day it'll be easier, but for the time being, Ella and Ryatt have a lot to deal with in their strange kingdom.

I set a few platters of juice on the table as Ella and Maddy come into view. Maddy's cheeks glow a pretty pink, and her eyes are shielded from the sun by huge sunglasses. "Is Misty awake yet?"

"Not yet," I smile.

She pushes her sunglasses to the edge of her nose. "Really?"

"She's gotta be totally worn out," Ella laughs, eyeing the table. "Wow, Mom. You really went all out."

"This is your dad's doing, not mine." I laugh, but my eyes settle on the strange band of symbols etched along Ella's hairline. Right now, the markings are pale silver lines and whirls, almost like scars.

It's easy to forget that Ella, who is dressed in cut off jean shorts and an oversized T-shirt with her mass of dark hair piled on top of her head, is one of the most powerful beings in our universe, and that her mate, whose voice is now drifting outside from the kitchen behind us as he asks Maddox to make him a latte, also wields enormous powers.

I look over at Kenna, who is straddling Ryan and taunting him with her pinchers. My heart tightens as my mind wanders to a place I try to avoid. Who will she be one day with such powerful parents?

"You okay, Mom?" Ella asks, snapping me back to reality.

"Yes," I tell her with a smile.

"Oh, I hear her now," Maddy says, plucking a piece of bacon from a plate before walking inside to get Misty from one of the bedrooms upstairs.

Ella sits down at the table and tilts her face to the sun. A shimmer of golden light is now visible in those markings as I pour glasses of juice for the kids.

"Ryatt and I decided something," she says, leveling me with a look. "Kenna is going to start school at the coven next fall."

"School?" I have no idea what that entails in Eastonia. I can't imagine Kenna skipping to a bus stop wearing a sparkly backpack and sneakers that light up.

Ella's mouth quirks into a smile. "I know what you're thinking. She's not going to learn how to use a wand and turn people into frogs. It's a real school. She'll be in kindergarten, learning how to write her name in an intelligible way." She sighs wistfully, her eyes going momentarily glassy. "And it's nearby, just a few blocks away from the castle."

"You got moved in, then?"

She nods, toying with the empty plate in front of her. "Yeah, we did. We miss Veiled Valley, though. Ryatt, especially, but... Moonrise does feel like where we're supposed to be. Kenna likes it there. The city is starting to fill up now that everything has been repaired and modernized. She's made friends." She pauses, sighing. "She misses her Grandpa and Grammy."

I sit down next to her and begin putting food on her plate. "How are Westfall and Cressendra?"

"They're fine. Westfall is still a little miffed Ryatt forced him to take over his rightful throne, though."

"Next year, you should bring them." I pour Ella some orange juice and motion to her plate. "I'd like to see Cressendra again. We really hit it off last time I visited Eastonia." That was last year. It was the first time Maddox and I ever visited, and it was overwhelming. I hadn't been prepared for the history, the culture, and to see the place where Ella went through so many trials.

But what she and Ryatt built together is amazing.

Over the past year, the ancient city that rose out of the lake when

Ella brought down the veil five years ago finally opened up to the public, and it's now where Ella and Ryatt rule over Eastonia. It's incredible. We saw it during its reconstruction, and I still have a hard time believing it's real.

"I'll bring them for sure!" Ella's eyes brighten. "Kenna would love it. Maybe we'll get Granger and Amanda to finally come, too."

"Will Kenna be going to school with Evander, then?"

Her eyes darken a shade, and she shakes her head. "Evander is being privately educated and trained…." She tapers off, toying with her food. "He recently showed signs of being able to shift. Not fully, yet, but… he's a fox, like Amanda, and even though things are different in Eastonia now, it's not safe for either of them yet. They're the only foxes, Mom. He's just a kid. He wants to go to school with Kenna and is heartbroken about it, but if he were to shift during class–" She shakes her head. "Granger says that until Evander can control his powers, he'll be at home."

"I'm sorry to hear that."

She shrugs, looking over the grassy backyard to where it meets the beach down a small, rocky slope. "Hey! Ryan, you know you're not supposed to go down to the beach by yourself!"

Ryan's head pops up over the edge of the embankment. He looks defeated.

"We'll go play at the beach after breakfast, honey," I add.

"Okay, Gramma," he grumbles and crawls back up onto the grass.

"Mama!" Kenna launches herself into Ella's arms.

"Come eat, kiddo," Ella says, pressing a wet kiss to Kenna's sand covered head. Ella grimaces and tells Kenna to go shake off in the yard, and she does, which causes another ruckus between the three kids.

Maddy walks out to the table with a bright eyed Misty on her hip, who is giving us a gummy smile. She only has two teeth, which is the cutest thing I think I've ever seen. "Gramma," Maddy says sweetly, lowering Misty into my lap. "I believe this is yours." For the next three weeks, at least.

I snuggle Misty as the rest of the family joins us at the table. Ryatt ruffles Ella's hair before taking a seat next to her, leaning in for a kiss. Isaac carries Ryan and Sydney under each arm and deposits them next to Maddy before sitting down. Kenna sits next to Maddox and begins whispering to him, likely buttering him up so he'll give her the pancake that looks the most like the elephant she requested.

I look around the table at my family. At this beautiful thing Maddox and I created. Everything I've ever gone through, every trial, every tribulation, every bad and uncertain day led to *this*.

The most beautiful, most powerful, thing in the world.

"Will you build a sandcastle with us after breakfast, Gramma?" Sydney asks.

I nod, smoothing my fingers through Misty's soft golden hair.

"Always," I tell him and smile.

THE END

Thank you for reading! Book 8 is coming soon! Don't miss Kenna's story!

SHADOW OF THE ALPHA
CHAPTER 1: CAME UP SHORT

Kenna

IT'S QUIET HERE. The golden walls and spiraling columns soak up the sun as I walk steadily toward my dad's office. Beyond giant ceiling-height windows, the sparkling city of Moonrise, the capital of Eastonia, spreads out in a sea of cream and gold until it touches the banks of a lake the color of polished turquoise.

On the opposite shore, at the base of a towering network of mountains, sits Old Moonrise—the original witch coven native to the Roguelands. Once, twenty or so years ago, there used to be a palace built of crystal sitting on a ridge overlooking the old village and the lake.

Until, well, my mother destroyed it.

I smile softly at the thought of my mom and pick up my pace, my sandals clacking against the white marble tiles.

I turn a sharp corner, nodding hello to a trio of maids who pass me, and slip into my dad's office like a shadow.

He looks up from the massive mahogany desk in the center of the room, his dark brow lifting as I gently close the door behind me.

Behind him, bookshelves stretch toward the domed, muraled ceiling.

A map lies on his desk beneath untidy papers and a scattering of old paperweights. He sighs heavily, checks his watch–a rather expensive and gaudy gift from my uncle Isaac, the Alpha King of Crescent Falls–and leans back in his leather office chair.

"You're supposed to be packing," he says, crossing an ankle over a knee as I edge toward his desk and lean my hip against the side of it.

"I'm packed."

"That didn't take long."

I roll my eyes to the ceiling, to the sweeping depictions of some battle that took place during the Great War when the Moon Goddess rebelled against the gods who wanted to tether her, to leave her powerless, and her people in shackles. I click my tongue and look down at my manicured nails. "Aunt Maddy is my size. She said I could borrow whatever gowns I need while I'm there. I didn't see a point in bringing any of my own. They take up so much room!"

"The fashions in Crescent Falls are different from here, Ken. Are you sure?"

I run my hands down the vibrant violet pants I'm wearing–made of silk with swirling embroidery–that cuff around my ankles. My top, with its long, loose sleeves that gather at the wrists and shows off my midriff, is made of the same fine fabric. I shrug.

"I want to fit in."

Dad stares at me for a long, long time saying nothing.

I run my tongue along my lower teeth and give him another little shrug. "I packed two gowns of my own."

"Good," he finally says softly, and looks back down at the paper he's reading.

I can tell by his gruff demeanor that he's as wound up about this upcoming trip to visit my cousins in Crescent Falls as I am but for completely different reasons.

To him, this is an opportunity to stress about my safety for two months. I imagine he'll pace back and forth in front of his desk, or the magic mirror he uses to call my uncle, until the floor turns black from scuff marks. Mom, too, will worry. They always do.

It's because I'm not like them.

I watch my dad, Alpha King Ryatt of Eastonia, mark a few lines on the paper before signing the bottom of it. He's all sharp lines and rigid muscles. He has a spine of steel, and a heart just as strong.

He met his match in my mom, Ella. The Queen of Eastonia. The Luna of Moonrise. The Firestone Witch.

While my parents would cut someone down just for looking at them the wrong way, I've always been more of a pacifist. I lean toward kindness, and I'm far too trusting, too soft, too willing to please.

My soft heart isn't interested in conquering kingdoms or squashing my foes. No, there's only one thing I want, and I have two months to find it in Crescent Falls before it's too late.

I roll my lower lip between my teeth and smile as my dad meets my eyes again, his gaze softer than before. "Say what you want to say, Dad."

"I don't like this at all."

Sighing heavily, I hop onto his desk. "Why not?"

"You're practically putting yourself out to auction–"

"It's a Moon Festival, Dad. There's going to be balls every night to help people like me find their mates."

"There will be more balls held here, in Eastonia."

"I went to every mating ball and festival held this spring, Dad. I even went to Tarsian, remember? I didn't find anyone."

Dad narrows his eyes and blows out his breath at the mention of Tarsian, the desert kingdom across the river boundary that used to be the marker between the Roguelands and Rifthold. Now, Alpha King Jaxon rules over Tarsian and maintains a strained relationship with my parents, although deep down, I think he and my dad might actually be good friends, but would *never* admit to it.

"You only turned twenty-one this spring. You're so young–"

"But I'm old enough to take over Veiled Valley this fall when Grandpa Westfall steps down."

A hush falls over the room.

When Dad doesn't say anything, I continue, "I did everything you wanted me to do, Dad. I graduated from college. I trained with you and Grandpa. I trained with Mom...." I taper off. "I need one summer of freedom before I take over as Luna of Veiled Valley, one summer to try to find my mate, and then..." And then my real training begins. Training that includes preparing myself to be queen of this entire kingdom one day.

My stomach curls in my belly at the thought.

I couldn't be farther from my mother in temperament and poise. During my childhood, I was wild, practically uncontrollable, but that changed as I matured. I excelled in school. I learned to keep my enormous and varied powers under lock and key until I needed to harness them, and I can harness those powers *well*.

I attended the exclusive Moonrise Academy of Mystical Arts–a school for witches and shifters with special gifts–and graduated this spring as valedictorian of my class with a specialty in healing and midwifery.

I'm a skilled healer. I have knowledge of, and can harness the use of, dark magic, including curses. I can create and control magic fires that burn cold and silver and turn my body into a mere shadow of mist.

But I'm nothing like them. I haven't ever used my powers in battle. I've never needed to.

I've never wanted to.

"I don't want to rule alone," I say, and my voice breaks around the words.

Dad looks at me with so much love in his eyes that it makes me consider not stifling the tears now brimming on my lashes.

"I don't want you to go and come home disappointed, Kenna."

His words ring through his office.

I chew my lip, unable to meet his eyes. As a family, we've skirted around this subject for a long, long time. While I am, most definitely, a witch, my wolf abilities are minimal in comparison. Shifting is fine and dandy, but I'm clumsy, tiny, and comparatively weak in my wolf form, and there's question about my ability to feel any kind of mate bond whatsoever because of it. My witch side is just too strong and overwhelms my wolf gifts.

That hasn't stopped me from obsessing over finding my mate, though.

"And you won't be ruling alone," Dad says, rising and organizing the papers. "Evander will be your Beta, like Granger is mine."

It's like a knife to the chest.

I stifle my emotions, turning my expression to a mask of steel, but he catches the single flicker of uncertainty behind my eyes.

"He'll come around, Kenna."

"I haven't spoken to him in five years."

"He's been busy."

"Mhm…" I nod. Busy, sure. If that's what they want to call it. Busy roaming whatever kingdom he's called to serve as a *Ghost*, the greatest and most lethal kind of spy the Allied Kingdoms have.

Right now, I think he's in Celestoria. I honestly don't know. I haven't seen him since the day after my sixteenth birthday. I haven't talked to him, either. I doubt he wants to give up a life of danger and adventure to stand beside me in Veiled Valley, just like I doubt he ever thinks about me at all.

I slide off Dad's desk and cross my arms under my chest, my mind reeling over the past twenty-one years of my life all at once, picking through every memory of Evander despite my internal desperate pleas not to.

He was my best friend. We grew up together. We played in the woods and at the lake shore. We had sleepovers and trained together until we started school and went our separate ways for the first time.

It was my fault we grew apart. One day, I didn't want to play in the woods anymore. My interests shifted from climbing trees to playing with dolls, then shifted further to my piano and the romance novels that cover every surface of my room. Evander fell to the wayside, and it was natural. He is a boy, and I'm a girl. I'm a witch, and he's a shifter. I'm a princess, and he's… *a lethal machine trained to inflict quiet, swift death.*

I find it hard to swallow as I turn from Dad and pretend to be invested in his bookshelves. My mind races to our last encounter. Evander, having been gone for years while training in Tarsian, returned to Moonrise shortly after my sixteenth birthday.

I'd been sitting outside reading a book on the terrace overlooking the private garden in the back of the castle. I didn't realize he was there until he said my name, and I turned.

It's hard to describe it. I didn't recognize him at first. The goofy little boy with freckles, copper blond hair, and startling emerald eyes had turned into… something *beautiful*, but also dark and empty.

The rest of the encounter is buried deep, deep down in my memory. I refuse to think about it, or how much it hurt when he tore through the friendship we'd built and left ashes in his wake, with no remorse for my sensitive feelings. For my *heart*.

"Kenna?"

"Did you say something?" I ask Dad. He's staring at me right now, his brow furrowed.

"Are you all right?"

"Where's Mom?" I clear my throat, giving him my best smile.

He arches a brow and sighs. "She had a meeting in Old Moonrise with the mystics. She'll be home in time for dinner she said."

I nod, trying again to swallow past the lump in my throat.

"Are you sure you're okay? You look pale. Are you sick? Maybe we should postpone your trip–"

"I'm fine," I say hurriedly, shaking my head.

Dad walks over to me and lays a hand on my shoulder, squeezing. I have to look up at him to gaze him directly in the eyes. I'm several inches shorter than my mother, which means I'm over a head and a half shorter than my dad. I don't know how I lost the genetic lottery in terms of height and emotional composition, *but here I am*, short and trying not to burst into tears.

"Don't rush into anything. You'll find your mate one day. It shouldn't be your priority right now."

He's right. I hate that he's right but… I've looked all over Eastonia for any flicker of a mate bond. I've attended countless balls, visited almost every village here, and nothing.

In two months, I'll move to Veiled Valley and rule as their Luna, alone. My opportunities to find my mate will be significantly diminished.

I know I sound pathetic. I know that I have everything I could ever want. I've never needed for anything, never gone hungry, never been brutalized or scared.

But I want what my parents have.

I want love, more than anything. Even if I can't feel the mate bond, I at least want something close to it.

Dad kisses my forehead. "Don't let Ryan get you into trouble, either."

"I can't make any promises about that," I laugh.

Desired by the Devil series

Whispers of the Devil

Banter of the Devil (coming soon)

The Mafia Kings series

Indebted to the Mafia King

Loved by the Mafia King (releases 9/15/2024)

Sign up for Bella's newsletter here.

Follow Bella on Facebook here.

9 781964 125244